Love in
and a Half Shapes

A novel by Judith S Glover

© 2024 by Judith S Glover

All characters and events in this publication, other than those in the public domain, are fictitious and any resemblance to real persons, living or deceased, is purely coincidental.

Cover design by Judith S Glover

1

West Ham Park on a mild afternoon in May might not seem a particularly promising place to start my story, but there was a chewed-off finger lying under the park bench in front of me – and I wanted it.

Back then, England was still smarting from yet another thrashing in the World Cup, the previous summer, and everyone at school had gone Bay City Rollers mad. Me – I preferred the Goodies' Funky Gibbon. They hadn't quite hit number one in the charts but they'd come close and had, at least, made it onto Top of The Pops.

A young nine going on ten, I was the youngest in my school year and still believed in Santa Claus and the tooth fairy. It would be many years before I learned anything of the unique circumstances concerning my entry into the world and that afternoon, I was just a lonely kid doing my best to pass the time.

Anyway, back to the park in May and that finger.

"You, boy. What are you doing, there? Speak up..." The woman on the bench seemed unduly cross but seemed to instantly regret the harshness in her tone. Or maybe she simply noticed the look of terror on my face. At any rate, she coughed and then reached down to soothe the little Dachshund that lay all sausaged-out in the cool shade of her not inconsiderable bulk.

"You'll have to forgive me," she added glancing up again. "My heart is still fluttering against my ribs like an agitated budgerigar."

I held my tongue and hovered a little closer. I didn't know her personally but recognised her type. Headscarf and tweed skirt, marcasite broach. A likely stalwart of the WI. Probably made a lot of jam. The sort of busybody my mum took care to avoid, though she would never be so impolite as to make it obvious.

The old battle-axe sniffed and peered at me more closely, her eyes alighting first, as everybody's inevitably did, upon my hair. Blonde and curly. I always put them in mind of... But *she* didn't say it. Perhaps she was not a fan of football. Her eyes shifted to my school shirt and grey flannel shorts and then rested thoughtfully on my fair-isle sleeveless pullover.

I shuffled my feet. So it was a bit old-fashioned. I didn't care. I'd never fitted in with other kids and had long ago given up trying. Then again, I suppose she might have liked it. Taken it for evidence of a caring mother somewhere in the background. I swapped the football I had been kicking around the park only moments ago to beneath the crook of my other elbow. Her face softened. She straightened the handles of her handbag and adopted a more conciliatory tone.

"Come now, I don't bite. What is it you want?"

I felt my eyes stray to the space beneath the bench. It had to be there somewhere. I had seen it fly off and drop to the ground but then if the dog had seen it, he would almost certainly have been gnawing on it by now. I diverted my gaze and tried to look nonchalant, a word I'd learnt only that week and it was already a favourite. I repeated the word in my mind enjoying the feel of it. I liked words, though not as much as I liked numbers. Numbers were simply terrific. But I was getting distracted. In any case, it was getting dangerously close to tea time. I wondered why she couldn't just get the hint and clear off.

"Sorry. Missus. I was just waiting to sit down."

My nemesis, (another great one, I'd got from Marvel comics,) knitted her brows then tucked her skirts beneath her and shifted sideways.

"Well, I didn't think I was taking up that much space but I'm sure I was brought up well enough to understand that this bench is not my private domain. Please, be my guest. There's plenty of room for a littl'un."

I gawped at her in frustration. I could tell from the studied informality of this last remark that she was trying to be friendly. I, however, was in no mood to reward her efforts. I scowled and shook my head.

"I was waiting until you'd gone..." it was the truth, simple and unapologetic.

"Well, there are plenty of other benches, you know..."

"I like this one."

At these words, she pursed her lips, placed one hand on her chest and then tugged inquiringly on the leash with the other. Doubtless, the answering vibration told her that the little dog was still trembling as I could certainly see from where I stood. She stared at me and sighed - more to herself than to anyone else;

"Since when did I become a magnet for all the world's unfortunates?"

"Sorry, Missus?"

"Your name, Boy. You must have a name?"

My reply came late - late enough to pronounce itself a lie, yet she had no reason to doubt its truthfulness.

"Billy," I said, in a flat voice.

"And to whom do you belong, Billy?"

I blinked at this. It hardly seemed a proper kind of question. My interrogator heaved another sigh.

"Your parents, child. Who are they? Would I know them?"

I went to reply then hesitated. A memory of my mum, dressed for a dinner dance, a vision in aquamarine satin with her hair piled upon her head and a fur stole draped around her shoulders glimmered before my eyes. It was the happiest I had ever seen her.

"Please Missus, my mum is a princess…"

"Doubtless, she is. And your father, who is he? The King of England, I suppose."

I could have kicked myself for saying something so foolish, yet the hurt that clouded my little face must have been enough to put an end to both the sarcasm and the inquisition. The woman frowned and regathered her handbag straps. Rising to her feet, she tugged once more on the leash to signal their imminent departure but faltered a moment.

"Well, never mind, my boy. I shall leave you in possession of this bench if it is that important to you. But I think I should warn you that there are some very strange characters hanging around this little park this afternoon. Did you perhaps witness the incident a few minutes ago?"

I shook my head.

"I was playing football, missus."

The old bat blinked rapidly and shook her head. *She had observed that much, herself. Nevertheless, I must surely have heard the shriek. The barking even?*

I fixed my gaze on her no-nonsense lace-up shoes. She rolled her eyes.

"But you must have seen the man," she intoned in an exaggerated whisper, perhaps fearing that the provocateur might still be around. "He was walking past us and Colin suddenly went for him. Snapping and growling and I don't know what. I've never seen anything like it. Colin is such a gentle soul by nature. I simply cannot understand what the villain could have done to upset him so. I pulled him back, of course, and the odious fellow rushed away. But the language. Shocking. I simply couldn't repeat it. Gave me palpitations, it did. And Colin, well, you can see how traumatized the poor creature is. And I ask you - what sort of person uses such language? I tell you, it doesn't bear thinking about. And look you, he may still be around. So rather than sit here, I rather think you would do better to go home…"

I nodded gravely and then forced a wide yawn.

"I will, but right now I feel so awfully tired. I'll just have a little sit-down and then go straight home, I promise."

"Well, mind you do. One cannot be too careful these days." And, so saying, she rose from the bench, smoothed down her voluminous skirts and sailed off with the little Dachshund in tow.

Thanking The Lord Above that she had finally gone, I plopped myself down on the bench. The sun felt good on my face. It would not be long until Summer and the school holidays. I placed my football next to me and watched the matronly dreadnought and her sausage-shaped companion until they disappeared around the bend of the path that led out through the park gates.

Yawning for real this time, I squinted at my Spiderman watch. The webbed hands announced that it was a quarter to tea time. Dawdling now would almost certainly make me late. Never a good idea. I drummed my fingers and chewed my lip. It was a risk I had to take. I looked all around me. The little park seemed quite empty. It was now or never. Taking a final glance around, I leaned forward and felt beneath the bench with my fingertips. Nothing.

I would have to get down on my hands and knees. I sidled off the bench and onto the ground and then poked my head beneath the bench. Bingo! There, in the far back corner lay an object that had no rightful business being there. But I couldn't reach it. Standing up, I wandered casually around the bench. The coast was still clear. And now came the big moment. With my heart in my throat, I took out the clean handkerchief, my mother had issued me with that morning, dropped to my knees and quickly scooped up my treasure. Panting with relief, I hastily wrapped it and then thrust the little bundle into my pocket. There was no time to examine it more closely, it would have to wait for later. Then, grabbing my football, I set off for home at a canter before catching myself and tempering my pace. The last thing I needed was an asthma attack or to alert suspicion with an unusually red face.

Back at home, all seemed exactly as it always was as I let myself into the hallway.

"Just in time..." called my mum from behind the open fridge door. "Tea will be ready in a tick..."

I poked my head around the kitchen door and held a hand up in greeting. She set the butter dish down on the side and turned on that smile of hers, the one that drove the darkest clouds away.

"Get up to much at the park, Jumbo darling?" she enquired airily. She had long since given up asking if I had met with any friends.

"Nah - just had a bit of a kick around." It was the second lie I'd told, that afternoon. It seemed unlikely to be the last. And I was not a practised liar. Not back then, at least. I removed my shoes and headed off to my bedroom before she could ask any more questions.

"Well, don't forget to wash your hands, Darling," she sighed and set to scraping the butter with a knife. It was hard. I could have told her that it would soften on its own if she would only give it enough time but I think she enjoyed the challenge. I heard her muttering softly behind me as I bounded up the stairs, something she had done quite a bit since my father had left. I never really minded. It made him feel more real in a way. "Darn it, Julian," was the gist of it. "The boy needs a father. Now more than ever. It wasn't meant to be like this..."

Upstairs, I closed the door of my bedroom and tossed the ball into a corner. I looked around and then plumped myself down against the door to bar any unwanted intrusion. Not that I expected any. Mum was the last person to enter my room without the courtesy of a warning knock. She had, after all, and as she never tired of informing me, grown up with two elder brothers and was therefore no stranger to the clandestine activities of pre-pubescent boys. But I was taking no chances.

Drawing the handkerchief out of my pocket, I placed it gingerly on my lap and stared down at it in awe. A dark, crimson fluid had seeped through the fabric and blossomed amaryllis-like across the surface of the bundle. I chewed my lip.

Slugs and snails being equal, I was generally no more squeamish than most boys of my age but there was something ominous about that patch of red that made me shudder. I swallowed and then, exhaling sharply, picked at the edges of the handkerchief, folding back its bloodstained edges. There it lay, a solitary human finger. Not your everyday find, I'll grant you. But that was not the half of it. Something was happening. Something entirely unexpected. If my jaw did not hit the ground literally, then it must have come pretty close.

Right before my eyes, the dark stains began to stir into life. Individual droplets of blood appeared to start to attention and then almost to crawl forward in the same direction, as though shepherded by some invisible force. Their destination soon became apparent. The ragged edge of the finger. On they crept, pooling into little shining red globs as they converged and oozed back into the vessels out of which they had leaked.

I don't know how long I sat and watched in unblinking disbelief. It seemed like forever though it could only have been minutes, at most. But for a while there, I'm not sure I could have torn my eyes away if the house had been on fire.

"Jonathon Cooper? I don't hear the taps running, young man. What about those sticky fingers?"

I snapped back into awareness. What indeed? The familiarity of my mother's voice floating up from the downstairs hallway had broken the spell. I shuddered in horror and I dropped the finger and its wrapping into my lap. My first impulse had been to brush the thing off me and away into the further recess of the room. Anywhere away from me. That had been the impulse, yet as powerful as it had been, something stronger trumped it. Curiosity.

Puffing out my cheeks I peered downwards. The severed digit lay entirely clean and waxy pink in its wrapping. Furthermore, not so much as a solitary splatter of blood now marred the pristine cotton of the handkerchief. I shook my head and reached down.

"Don't make me come up there, young man."

I scrabbled to my feet and looked around in panic. Whatever was going on, it would have to wait until after tea. I scanned the shelves of my room. My eyes settled upon the screw-top glass jar I kept for collecting butterflies and stick insects. It was empty now and would do perfectly.

"Coming, Mum," I called, unscrewing the lid. Then, carefully placing the finger inside, I breathlessly resealed it and stowed it under the bed. That done, I made a dash for the bathroom where I had never been happier to wash my hands.

Back downstairs, I sat at the tea table, knife and fork in hand, and tried to behave as normally as possible. It may have looked as though I was staring at the baked beans on my plate, but images of amputated digits, moribund squirrels and animated droplets of blood jostled madly for attention in my mind's eye. I clenched my jaw and willed my thoughts into an orderly line. For the moment the finger under my bed pushed its way to the fore and gained the upper hand.

Perhaps it was plastic, after all. Some kind of elaborate prank or hoax. I had found enough snails at the bottom of my school milk to know what it was like to be the butt of the prevailing prankster's joke, but I could not believe that anyone would go to all the trouble of staging so bizarre a tableau just for my benefit? No, that explanation seemed utterly ridiculous. Besides, I had seen the little Dachshund lunge at the man's hand with my own eyes. Like a thing possessed, it had been. I replayed the scene in my mind one more time. The frenzied canine shaking the severed pinky from its mouth, the little finger flying off into the grass beneath the bench. The wounded man springing away in shock, the look of terror on his face and most baffling of all, his complete silence as he skulked away, acting for all the world as though *he* had been the guilty party. And then that woman, the dog's owner, pulling at the leash in injured indignation, oblivious to the assault her precious pet had just perpetrated.

Why, the man did not even seem to have done anything to provoke the animal; the nasty little brute had just gone for him.

Perhaps he just smelled odd? I thought, wrinkling my nose. It would make sense.

I shovelled up a forkful of baked beans and tipped them into my mouth. I paused and closed my eyes. There was something comforting about the familiarity of the tomatoey taste.

"Jumbo, Sweetheart. You're very slow this afternoon. Not looking for patterns in the baked beans again, I trust?"

"No Mum. Just thinking. That's all. Maths homework – you know."

"Very well. But tea time is for eating, not solving mathematical problems."

I nodded and shovelled in another mouthful. I didn't see why you couldn't eat and solve equations at the same time but Mum was funny about these things. I chewed on a bit of toast and gathered my thoughts. The finger was not plastic, of that I was all too certain. I had been positively loath to touch the object at all. But touch it I had, just as Mum had called. Even the recall was enough to send my stomach into a sickly gambol and it was all I could do, not to gag. I bowed my head and pursued an errant bean around the edge of my plate, grateful for the smallest distraction. Yet face it I must. There was a mystery here and every detail counted.

I looked up. Mum seemed preoccupied with something in the kitchen sink. I put down my fork and took a slow breath, forcing myself to focus.

The sensation of living flesh had been unmistakable. Yet, surely, it should have turned cold to the touch by now. *Just like the squirrel. Yes, of course – the squirrel.* The injured little squirrel I had found over in the park the previous spring. I had tried to nurse it but had ended up watching in helpless fascination as it heaved its last gasps. Its warm and furry little corpse had grown cold with within an hour and quite stiff by the time I had eaten my tea. Mum had told me that it was something called *rigor mortis*.

"Will that happen to me, one day?" I had asked solemnly.

"Not if I can help it, Darling," she had replied ruffling my hair. She had smiled but it didn't make sense because she sounded sad. The whole thing had stayed in my mind for weeks afterwards, though I couldn't have told you why.

But the finger had felt soft and warm. Not a bit like the dead squirrel. I stared down into my tea. And suddenly my Mum was standing over me, her palm against my forehead.

"Seriously Jumbo, are you sickening for something? Beans on toast is always your favourite and it's not like you to toy with your food."

"Mum..." I whined, shrugging her hand away.

My forehead was precisely as cool and dry as it always was. I shook my head in annoyance. I was a big boy now and had begun to resent her fussing. She raised her hands and backed off but then switched to a more direct tactic.

"Look here, Jumbo, you'll be ten years old next month. I know you're growing up fast, but it can be a difficult age. You do know that you can always tell me if there is anything wrong, don't you, Luv? At school, I mean or well – you know, anything at all. You do know that, don't you? I know your Dad isn't around but I did have two brothers and ..."

"Yes, Mum, I know," I groaned, "But there isn't anything wrong, so perhaps you save your over-solicitousness for someone who requires it."

"Alright, Jumbo. If you say so. But I'll tell you this much, young man, the possession of a precociously extensive vocabulary does not make you any the more mature. And I'll thank you not to take that tone with me again..."

With that, she turned to the sink. After a moment, I heard a little sniff and saw her raise her wrist to wipe her cheek. Telling me off always seemed to upset her more than it did me. I sighed.

"Sorry, Mum. I'm fine. Honest. But you know I don't like it when you worry about me for no reason."

It was enough to make her turn back.

"Well, how about some ice cream?" she enquired brightly. "I got that chocolate one you like and some of that new chocolate sauce, they've been advertising on the TV. I know that Saturday night is ice cream night, but well, I reckon you deserve a treat and perhaps we could have a game of chess after you have done your homework?"

I weighed the options in my mind. The ice cream and chocolate topping were tempting, but not as tempting as the strange curio I had left upstairs in the little glass jar. Still, I couldn't afford to raise any suspicions and it wasn't as though the jar was going anywhere. Another ten minutes couldn't hurt. As for chess, normally the offer of a game would be enough to make me rush my homework, but this evening, not even my mother with her best game was about to compete with what waited for me upstairs. But again, the last thing I needed was to alert her to the idea that anything out of the ordinary was going on with me.

"That would be great, Mum. Thanks."

Mum went to the fridge and removed a block of ice cream from the freezer box. She peeled back the cardboard container and cut two neat slices, placing each in a glass bowl, then replaced the remaining block. I watched as she reached into the cupboard, my interest piqued by the promise of the new chocolate sauce. A glint of the deepest magenta caught my eye. My mother's home-pickled cabbage. There was no mistaking it. She had a penchant for all things pickled, but this was her speciality. She was tremendously proud of the way it crunched between the teeth. Better than anything shop-bought, she would say – and Mum was not one to boast. And she was right. The purple cabbage really did remain fresh and crispy for months.

Suddenly an idea hit me. "Eureka…" I hissed under my breath and very nearly spilt a fork full of baked beans down my front in my excitement. But honestly, old Archimedes could not have been more pleased with himself when that famous bath of his overflowed.

"Everything alright, Jumbo?"

"Yes, sorry, Mum. Just thinking."

"Well, eat up, then. Ice cream and choc sauce to follow. We don't want it to melt, now, do we?"

Back up in the safety of my room again, I closed the door and panted with relief. The chocolate sauce had been jolly good but was no competition for what lay in wait for me beneath my bed.

Wriggling my arms, I removed the bottle of vinegar from under my jumper and placed it on the bed. Next, I returned to the door and pressed my ear against it. I was pretty sure that I had managed to sneak into the pantry under the stairs unseen but my heart was still hammering and I needed 100% certainty. I held my breath. All I could hear was Mum moving around the kitchen and the clink of plates and cutlery in the washing-up bowl. I squeezed my fist in a gesture of silent self-congratulation. The walls of our little house might be annoyingly thin at times but at least I would hear the tread of her feet on the stair should she venture up after me.

I scooped up the bottle of vinegar and peered into it. Mum used it for pickling all kinds of vegetables and had even been adventurous enough to try pickled eggs one Christmas. But the less said about that the better. Devoid of the magical purple tint the cabbage had lent it, the fluid looked more like weak tea than anything else. Still, it was function, not appearance that interested me and the dull-looking fluid looked reassuringly similar to the stuff someone had used to preserve the rather repulsive assortment of specimens that occupied the top shelf in the school biology lab.

Besides, it wasn't as though I had anything to lose. The finger could not remain unspoiled for long. I recalled the squirrel and that sickly-sweet smell of decay and heaved. I certainly couldn't be doing with that again. And Mum would almost certainly be onto me the moment any odour so vile reached her nostrils. No, the vinegar had to be worth a try and there was no time to lose. And then the finger would be mine for keeps. After all, *finders keepers* – everyone knew that. All the same, I would have to keep it well out of sight. A pickled finger was not the kind of thing you wanted your mother to stumble over. Not if you could help it anyway.

2

Goodness only knows how I managed to sleep at all, that night. I had placed the little jar on the nightstand next and lay wide awake for the best part of an hour staring at the finger lying at the bottom. Submerged in the vinegar, it appeared oddly pale and inert. Even so, once or twice I could have sworn that it twitched ever so slightly. I had sat up to inspect it more closely a couple of times, only to conclude that it had just been my imagination playing tricks on me. In the end, it was all too distracting and I decided to shove it back under the bed.

Much good did that do. My head was still buzzing with fingers, pickled cabbage and small brown Dachshunds when I heard Mum peep around my door with a "Sleep tight, Jumbo" and a soft sigh before padding off to her room for the night. I had lain as still as I could and kept my eyelids firmly closed, panicking that she was somehow on to me but, a moment later, it suddenly occurred to me that she probably looked in at about the same time every night.

I rolled onto my side and peered at the little clock next to my bed. 11 pm. Four hours past my bedtime. That meant that she probably spent four long hours on her own every night reading or watching TV. I'd never stopped to wonder whether she ever felt lonely before, but now that I thought of it, I rather wished I hadn't. I knew what that was like and it sucked. I thumped my pillow and flopped back onto my other side.

When I *did* finally get off to sleep, I had the oddest and most vivid dream. I was back in the park. A small man in a raincoat and flat cap was pacing furiously around the bench where I had been sitting only hours earlier. He seemed familiar to me, yet I couldn't place him. I looked more closely.

The raincoat had seen decidedly better days, as had his shoes which were badly scuffed and worn down at the heel. With lank greasy hair and a face that was somehow wholly nondescript, there was nothing to distinguish his appearance except a vague impression that he fitted the bill of exactly the type of cove, parents all over the country advise their kids to avoid. After a moment he sat on the bench and seemed to look directly at me.

I remember experiencing that awful sensation you sometimes experience in a dream when you want to scream or run but find yourself completely mute and rooted to the spot. He raised a hand and pointed an accusing finger at me. I thought that I must be in danger but when I looked more closely at his face, saw nothing to fear. His mouth and eyes sagged in an expression I had seen just once before on the TV news when I wasn't supposed to be watching. It had been the previous summer.

Somewhere up north, a lift carrying a group of thirty miners had plunged to the bottom of the shaft killing almost twenty of them. Later that morning, the news cameraman had captured the looks on the faces of their wives and children as they waited for news. Pure anguish – my Mum had called it, before promptly turning the channel back to the reassuring images of Florence, Dougal and *The Magic Roundabout*.

And suddenly I recognized him. Not because I knew him - I didn't. But I had seen him before. He was the man I had seen the Dachshund bite. He was the man who belonged to my finger.

I didn't recall much after that until seven the next morning when the ringing of my alarm clock jangled rudely in my sleeping ears. I reached out and pressed the snooze button then turned onto my side without fully waking. Ten minutes passed. The alarm sounded again and this time I was fully awake. I sat up and tried to recall the dream in more detail but the images that had filled my sleeping mind were already dissipating like vapour on the breeze. And then I remembered the jar under my bed. I flung back the duvet and leapt to my feet.

"Jumbo!" it was my mum calling from the foot of the stairs.

"Get a move on, Sweetheart. You don't want to be late for school."

Didn't I though? I had something even more interesting than algebra right here at home. I ducked down and peered under the mattress to make sure that the jar was still there, though the notion that somebody could have stolen in and taken it during the night seemed patently ridiculous. I caught a glimpse of the glass and screw top lid and breathed a sigh of relief.

I glanced around for my school clothes but my mind refused to bother itself with such mundane details. I began to feel panicky. I needed to focus. I was already running late and there was no time to spare. Breakfast would be on the table and the last thing I needed was for Mum to come upstairs to find out what might be keeping me.

I'll confess that the idea of skiving a day's sickness crept into my mind but then I thought of all the stress it would cause my mother. Another day off work to look after me would not go down at all well.

Not that my health was the problem. I don't think I'd ever taken a day off sick in my life, but school holidays were long and frequent compared to the holiday entitlement my mum received. Her employers were understanding but only to a point. The summer holidays were around the corner and they would use up all the goodwill she could expect.

She had lost her own parents years ago and her brothers and their families lived up north so there was no one to call upon and she hated to ask the neighbours, even though I had heard Mrs Worth offer a dozen times. I guess she was a little proud that way. She always took it personally when someone on TV or in the papers would refer to children like me as "Latchkey Kids", though one-parent families like ours were common enough in the East End. Be that as it may, it was not the ideal model of childrearing she had envisaged. Divorce, she told me, and particularly mothers who worked full-time were still a novelty in the northern middle-class market town where she had been raised.

Still, it was what it was. Employers did not keep to school hours so there was nothing to be done but make the best of the situation. Fortunately, Mrs Worth who lived next door to us was happy to take on regular afterschool child-minding duties for the first couple of years following our arrival in the neighbourhood.

Small and fluttery with arms and legs as thin as twigs, she might have been a little bird, dressed up in a floral housecoat and carpet slippers. I always thought of her as completely ancient, though she was probably only in her early sixties. She certainly complained about something called lumbago a lot, especially when the weather turned damp, which was often.

Every day there seemed the same as the one before. The woman lived to clean and when she wasn't cleaning, she was cooking or washing up. She seemed terribly set in her ways and I had the distinct impression that the last thing she needed was a kid under her feet, even one as easily occupied with a book or jigsaw puzzle as me. Nevertheless, she was only ever kind to me and even told me that I could call her Aunty Glad. I never did though. And I never saw her as anything more than a fussy old biddy whose house smelled of peppermint and bleach.

Her tenure as my childminder ended abruptly when she had a bad fall, one frosty morning two winters ago. After that, my mother had presented me with a house key and allowed me to shift for myself for a couple of hours after school, so long as I checked in with her on the way home; a little ritual that had since become a part of my daily routine.

The solicitors' office where she worked as something called a *paralegal* and general dogsbody was only around the corner and almost on my way home. Besides that, she had drilled me in fire safety and how to dial 999 in an emergency. And then there was always Mrs Worth next door, in case of absolute necessity.

Once I had proved myself responsible, my mother even came around to the idea of me spending a half hour or so in the park during the spring and summer months. Ours was generally a very safe neighbourhood though I had first to endure long and repeated lectures on the perils of talking to strangers, especially those with puppies or the promise of them, at least. I don't know what made puppies quite so dangerous but I was certainly never going to go down that road.

Thus far, the arrangement had worked out well. The idea of a whole day was however quite a different kettle of fish.

"Jumbo," she had said to me, "you may be very grown-up for your age but I could not leave you for a whole day alone unsupervised. I am your mother and my most important job is to look after you."

Fortunately for us both, perhaps, I never got ill. Not ever. Not even a sniffle. I had a bit of trouble catching my breath sometimes, a condition Dr Driver, our GP, had diagnosed as childhood asthma, but so long as I had my inhaler, I never even thought of it as a problem. "Young man," he had said scratching his head, "you're a bit of mystery. Respiratory problems apart, you're as fit as a butcher's dog." I didn't know any butchers or their dogs but it seemed to please my mum.

But none of this was getting me washed and dressed. And, as much as I would love to have stayed home with my new treasure, it would have to remain undisturbed under the bed until I returned from school.

Down in the kitchen, Mum had already warmed some milk on the stove and placed my Ready Brek on the table. She handed me a spoon and made her usual joke about me glowing all over as I scraped the bowl. She never seemed to tire of it but then, neither did I.

"Oh, I have to work a little late this afternoon," she suddenly remembered, reaching for her purse. "Here, buy yourself a treat from the corner shop. I'll be back in time to make tea, but I expect you'll be starving by then. Oh, and if you want to stay a little longer in the park, that'll be okay. Just let me know when you drop by. You know I like to know what you're up to."

I felt my face turn pink and it wasn't from the Ready Brek.

"That's all right, mum. I'll probably just watch TV," I volunteered, cringing at the clumsiness of the lie as it tumbled out of my mouth, but my mother was too busy tucking her purse back into her handbag to notice.

"Just as you like, Jumbo. Now, come along, Luv. There's never a reason for tardiness - only excuses."

The school day crawled by like a snail on a union *go-slow*. Usually, one of the more interested and motivated students, I stared out of the window and then at the large clock above the blackboard, willing the hands to move a little faster. At lunchtime, I spent the break sitting on the grassy bank of the school playing fields pretending to pore over my latest Spiderman comic, but that afternoon, not even Peter Parker's sticky web was enough to ensnare my wandering thoughts.

I looked around. Everyone else had formed into little huddles or organised themselves into ball teams, tumbling onto the playing field with whoops of laughter without giving me a second glance. It was not that they bullied me, or even actively consigned me to Coventry or any of its outer-lying districts, it was more that they seemed to overlook me entirely. The way you overlook a daddy-longlegs that has made itself at home in the corner of the bathroom.

I can't say it bothered me generally. I had grown used to it. That day, however, I would have welcomed a little distraction, even the unpleasant variety.

Needless to say, the end-of-day bell could not have been more effective had it been a starting pistol. Off I raced, as swiftly as my legs would carry me and was reaching inside my blazer pocket for my inhaler by the time I reached home. Then, fumbling in my pocket again I pushed the key into the lock, still panting for breath.

"Everything all right, Dearie?" twittered a voice close to my ear.

It was Mrs Worth, in her house coat and slippers. She'd stepped out to place her empty milk bottles on the doorstep, something she often did just as I arrived home. I'd always thought of her as a sparrow but she was beginning to remind me of a cuckoo popping out a cuckoo clock. I held my chest and gasped.

"I'm sorry...?"

She gazed at me with her birdy eyes.

"Are you all right Jonathon? You seem to be struggling for breath. Would you like me to fetch your mum? The hooligans aren't terrorizing you again, are they?"

The hooligans to whom she referred did little more than play French cricket in the middle of the road when there wasn't much traffic about. Doubtless, they occasionally took sly pleasure in deliberately aiming the ball at me as I passed by, but it rarely inflicted more than a tender blue bruise to the calf or back. Certainly, none of them were ever likely to be called upon to bowl for England. They had, however, provided Mrs Worth with an axe of her own to grind. Earlier that year, an over-enthusiastic square drive had punched through a pane of glass in one of her upstairs windows. I can still see her limping after them, waving her walking stick and threatening to call the Old Bill. The cocky sparrow chasing off a pack of crows. The lads who were generally an inoffensive bunch, (my personal persecution notwithstanding), had scarpered immediately without so much as an "old bag." But boys will be boys and it was not long before they appeared again, though they took pains to move the wicket further towards the end of the street. Still, the damage was done and from that day onwards they remained, for Mrs Worth, the very embodiment of what she termed the anti-social element.

"No, no. I'm fine, thank you." I panted. "Just ran a bit too hard. I'll be right as rain in a sec. Honest. I have my inhaler. Thanks for asking."

"Come again, Dear?" chirped Mrs Worth cupping a twiggy hand to her ear as a delivery truck thundered past.

"I AM FINE! THANK YOU."

With that I stuck my thumb up and disappeared indoors, leaving Mrs Worth shaking her head and squinting down the street on the lookout lest the hooligans dared to make an appearance.

Safe in my own hallway, I slung down my satchel and blazer and bolted up the stairs. Halfway up, however, I froze, gripped by the momentary idea that my mother might somehow have returned home early from work. I strained my ears to check for any tell-tale sounds but the house was silent. I got to my bedroom and closed the door. Just in case.

Then, launching myself forward onto my tummy, I tried to wriggle under the bed but became jammed halfway in. I had grown too big to fit. I cursed myself for pushing the jar quite so far to the back. I could make out a small glint in the gloom, but that was all. I stretched out my arm, straining every muscle to reach it. At last, feeling the cool glass against my fingers, I tickled it towards me rather as though I had been fishing for trout. And there it was at last. The finger. Except that it wasn't. A finger that is. In its place, squatted an eye of all things. A blinking, rolling, sore and somehow very angry-looking eye, complete with a pink lid. *The vinegar*, I thought as my own eyes smarted in sympathy. But an eye? *How on earth could the finger I had left there in a jar of pickling vinegar that very morning suddenly have become an eye?*

3

Once the shock had worn off my overriding impulse was to drop the jar and make a run for it. It wasn't just surprise I felt, it was full-on spine-crawling horror. But, somehow, I resisted. I forced myself to look more closely. I could have been wrong but that eye really did not strike me as happy. Not happy at all. In fact, I was pretty certain that it was glaring at me. Glaring at me in red and irritated accusation. Maybe it was the vinegar. Or maybe it was just the fact that it had spent a day under my bed, trapped in a jar.

"I-I'm sorry," I stammered, unhelpfully, although it was probably a bit late for that. Then, realising that my hands were shaking, I set the jar down on the floor for safety and stared at it a bit more.

I was just thinking that I had never seen anything so strange in my life when something even more astonishing occurred. Right there in front of my very eyes, as the saying goes, the eyeball in the jar melted back into a finger. It happened so quickly and with such fluidity that I couldn't begin to describe what I saw. But, see it I had. Then, as though that were not enough, the finger began to move of its own volition, wagging and jabbing violently towards me. And this time the meaning was entirely unambiguous.

"I didn't mean to steal anything," I wailed, though it seemed unlikely that it could hear me. But the next second the eye had reappeared again. It seemed to expect something. I scratched my head, wondering if it could lip read.

Slowly and carefully, I repeated myself, taking care to form the words clearly with my lips. I did not have a clue what I was dealing with, but that it possessed some kind of consciousness seemed undeniable. If only there was a way to communicate. But perhaps there was. Every problem had a solution. All I had to do was think it through. The eye blinked and then blinked again. Not reflex blinking. Slow deliberate movements.

An idea suddenly struck me.

"Can you follow what I am saying? Blink three times for yes."

The eye blinked. Once. Twice – and a third time. Yes. It could not be a coincidence. But yes/no answers could take forever to achieve anything. I scratched my head and racked my brains.

"I know," I said suddenly, "just give me a second. It's something I saw on Tomorrow's World…" and signalling the eye in the jar to wait a moment, I leapt up and moved to my desk.

Gathering together some pens, I ripped a blank piece of paper out of my A4 pad and set to drawing out a rough chart. Back in the jar, I could see the eye as it followed my movements. I felt a shiver run down my spine but I was committed now.

When the chart was complete, I settled myself down in front of the jar once more and moved my face in closer.

"This will help us communicate." I mouthed pointing to the chart. "I will ask a question and you are going to spell out the answer."
I checked the legibility of my diagram and held it up.

"See - there are five circles and each has a number. Now each circle contains five letters, and each letter is also paired with a number from 1-5. (I know I've left Z out but I'm hoping we can do without it.) In any case, say you want to spell something out. You find the letter you want, note which circle it is in and then blink the number for that circle. You know – once for one, twice for two and son on. Then, I'll ask you to blink out the number that is paired with the letter itself."
I paused, not at all sure that I was making sense. The eye blinked once.

"Okay - look. Say your first letter is N, right? You blink 3 times to let me
know it is in circle number 3. Then you blink 4 times – which is its number, right?"
The eye stared back at me. It wasn't giving much away. I sighed and moved my lips as close to the jar as I dared.

"Do you understand? One blink for yes, two blinks for no."
The pause that followed was long and excruciating. Perhaps this was just going to be a long and tedious exercise in futility. Still, what other choice did we have? I held my breath. And then the eye blinked. Just the once. I cheered and stuck my thumb up. But then again, perhaps it was just blinking anyway. I sagged wearily. I needed an answer with a negative – or better still something a little more substantial.

"Okay. Just to be sure. Can you blink the number for the letter D, please?"
The eye blinked four times. I punched the air and almost leapt to my feet in delight. Then, collecting myself, I placed my lips close to the jar and mouthed the words –

"Now, where are you? Right now, I mean. As simply as you can, please. Just spell it out, d'you see?"
I held the chart up again and watched intently. The eye blinked four times. I counted carefully.

"Circle 4, yes?"
One blink.
"Right we are. Now the number of the letter, if you please."
One slow solitary blink.
"P, right?"
One blink. I bit my lip and laughed out loud. This was going to work. Three more letters and the answer to my question proved blissfully quick and easy to spell out.
"The park..." I whispered. "You're in the park, right now? Is that right?"
One very emphatic wink.
"And I'll bet you're sitting on the bench, right?"
Another equally emphatic wink.

I seized the jar in my hands and scrambled to my feet and then bounded out of my bedroom and down the stairs into the hall. The contents of the jar, meanwhile, must have been swilling around wildly. All at once, I remembered my manners and pulled myself up. Setting the container down at the bottom of the stairs, I moved my face close to it.

"I'm so sorry - I forgot. I'll try to be more careful. Stay right where you are and I will be with you, in a tick."

I did my best to continue as calmly as I could but nothing could take the edge off my exuberance. *How easy was that?* I thought as I closed the front door behind me, *I rather thought that it would take us hours to get anywhere at all. Good old Tomorrow's World.* If I felt any apprehension, the excitement of the moment really did seem to have swept it all away.

It did not take long to get to the park gates, and when I glanced down to check how the eye was doing, I was only marginally surprised to discover that it had changed back into the finger once more. I cradled the jar securely in the nook of my arm, swallowed hard and marched onwards.

I halted as I rounded the path. In his shabby raincoat and flat cap, the figure sitting on the bench appeared as unpromising and drab as the drizzle-filled afternoon. I faked a hesitant cough. He looked up and we recognized one another immediately, though I think it would be fair to say that neither was quite what the other was expecting. He nodded and beckoned me forward with one hand. I shuffled towards him and stopped in my tracks just a few feet in front of him, quite forgetting the jar under my arm. He seemed to be staring at me in some confusion. I guessed that the glass and vinegar might have distorted my features somewhat but it seemed more than that. He narrowed his eyes, (one of which, I observed, was strangely red and sore-looking), and stared some more as though struggling to place me

"Deja Vue," he said at last. "Deja Vue. I get it a lot, recently."

I, meanwhile, had taken the opportunity to study his features. I was not entirely sure what I had expected but was pretty sure it involved penetrating eyes, furrowed brows and a hint of cruelty about the thin or even scornful lips. I'd already dismissed any hopes of long black robes, swirling silk turbans and ornate rings one might ordinarily associate with magicians or necromancers. But nothing had prepared me for this - a face so bland that finding a distinctive feature was like searching for a hook on which to hang a coat and then just having to drop it on the floor. *Why it's completely symmetrical,* I thought to myself in surprise. And the funny thing is, for months after, I would struggle to call that face to mind and would come up with a blank every time.

The disappointment must have shown on my face.

"Not what you were expecting, huh, kid?"

I lowered my eyes in shame unable to find a response.

"It's okay. I get it. But believe me, if life has taught me anything, it is the desirability of blending in. Especially when it comes to dogs. Bleedin' dogs..." he half spat. "I hate them. I hate them all, but the little ratty ones, they're the worst. Creep up on you, they do. Shouldn't be allowed. Just go ballistic every time. Cats now, they'll just stare and stalk off. Mind their own business, see? Discreet like. But dogs, oh no. Have to announce it to the world, don't they? Have to show off. So eager to please their owners. Pathetic. Now, where's me bleedin' finger?"

I felt the blood rush to my cheeks. I was not used to being addressed so bluntly or in such colourful language. Not by an adult in any case. I'd never heard a swear word pass my mother's lips and you certainly never heard a four-letter word on the BBC – not in those days. Still, I had made off with a part of the guy's body so perhaps I was in no position to feel hard done by. Checking around to ensure that the coast was clear I held out the jar.

"I don't like dogs either, Sir. I don't like the way they sniff you. They make me very nervous."

"Is that so? Well, perhaps that's something we have in common, then."

He leaned towards me and I stepped back involuntarily. He knitted his brows. It did not seem to have struck him that I might be afraid.

"If you would be so kind," he added quietly.

I took a step closer. His eyes lit on the contents of the jar. He blinked a couple of times and then something marvellous happened. A smile spread across his features, transforming his face completely. Then, just as though someone had turned out the light, it vanished again. He reached out his hands. As they made contact with the glass, the finger inside jolted into life as though waking from a troubled slumber. I shuddered involuntarily and let go of the jar. I felt my legs tremble beneath me. The man in the shabby raincoat might look ordinary yet he was anything but.

"Now sit there, boy, and I'll show you something you'll not forget in a hurry," he whispered, his eyes never leaving his prize.

I hovered uncertainly, aware that my insides had begun to feel as though they were turning to water. Inside the jar, the finger shuddered and pressed itself against the glass like an anxious lover.

"I said, sit."

I wanted to take my place on the bench next to him, I really did. But a million years of evolution is not so easily silenced. The fight or flight reflex had kicked in again and was urging me in no uncertain terms to get the Hell out of Dodge. At the same time, I was a boy and used to doing what adults told me. I hopped from one foot to the other for a moment and finally elected to sit despite my knocking knees and the sudden lurch in my belly, warning me that I might need the toilet at any moment.

The little man next to me unscrewed the lid from the jar and then held it to his nose. He wrinkled his nostrils and then, tipping the jar, carefully drained off the vinegar. I watched as he laid his right hand on his lap and splayed his fingers. I immediately noticed a space where his pinky should have been although I could see no sign of either a wound or a scar. Next, he closed his eyes in concentration or perhaps some kind of silent prayer. That done, he tipped the digit out onto his lap, picked it up and then offered it to the flesh where the pinky finger used to be. I stared in paralysed anticipation, hardly daring to breathe. The finger and hand jumped together with the kind of strange force you feel when you place a magnet close to a lump of iron. And before I knew it, it was as though the finger had never been missing. My strange companion wetted his lips, made a fist and then flexed his fingers. He tipped his head in a satisfied nod.

By this point, I think that I may actually have stopped breathing. My head was swimming and the blood throbbing through my ears was almost deafening me. My heart meanwhile, seemed to have decided that if I was not going to escape, it at least would make the effort and was trying to batter its way out through my rib cage. And then, just as suddenly, it all stopped. The little man turned to me with the warmest and most wonderful laugh I had ever heard. He clasped my hand in a vigorous if formal handshake and thanked me from the bottom of his heart, exclaiming:

"Pleased to meet you - er?"

"Jonathon. Jonathon Cooper."

"Excessively pleased to meet you, Jonathon Cooper. I am Sherton Myam."

"What kind of name is that?" I did not mean to be abrupt but was still feeling very shaken.

"Why, it is *my* name. And didn't your mother tell you it's rude to stare?"

"I'm so sorry, Sir. But, well, the finger, the eye - you're not human, are you?"

"Oh my, a smart lad. I thought as much. Not a lot gets past you, now does it? And that stuff with the chart. Quick thinking. First-class logic."

"Thank you - well, humans, they can't do what you just did…"

"Is that right? So, what's your theory, Einstein?"

I wasn't sure if he was being sarcastic, I find it difficult to tell, sometimes. But even if he was, I ploughed on undeterred. My head was clearing now and the ideas were flooding in like water from a burst pipe.

"Well, in my superhero comics people have special powers, though I never heard of a superhero who could change his finger into an eye. Now, Peter Parker, *he* was human, but then he got bitten by a spider and became *superhuman*. And then Thor, well he is a God, though most superheroes I suppose are not – although you might argue that Superman…"

I was probably getting a bit over-excitable now. My words were tumbling out fast and increasingly loud.

"Okay, kid. Let's keep the volume down. No need to broadcast it to the entire neighbourhood, is there, now? Have you ever heard of a shapeshifter?"

I thought hard and then shook my head.

"Well, I'm a shapeshifter. A *skinwalker*, if you prefer. It's all the same. I can pretty much change into any living form I choose, so long as it is roughly the same size."

"Same size as what?"

"As me, you plonker. I mean there's a lot of latitude – but basically within the same ballpark."

"Cool." I breathed. "Can you do it, here?"

"For Chrissake. No, I cannot. I'm not a bleedin' performing flea and besides, I think you've seen quite enough already."

I pouted thoughtfully and kicked my legs. *Adults could be such spoilsports sometimes.* Then, I looked up and met the shapeshifter's eyes. They were an unusually pale shade of grey, like the ocean on a rainy day. Strange in their way, yet I couldn't help thinking that there was something oddly comforting about them.

"Are there others like you?"

"Didn't that mother of yours also tell you that it's rude to ask so many questions?"

I kissed my teeth and shrugged. She most certainly had. Like most children my age, I fairly brimmed with questions at the best of times. In fact, Mum had bought me a copy of Every Child's Answer Book before I was even out of reception class. The book contained all sorts of fascinating facts about snowflakes, atoms, rockets and the history of the solar system, but I was pretty sure that I'd never seen any reference to shapeshifters. I wanted to burst from frustration but remembered my manners.

"I'm sorry, Sir. I didn't mean to pry."

The shapeshifter softened. He turned away and gazed into the distance, his face falling into shadow.

"To tell the bleedin' truth, I'm not entirely sure. In answer to your question, that is. I seem to be having problems with my memory, just recently. Sometimes I think I remember something clearly and then, poof, it just goes. Now and then, I think I see another of my kind – but I can't be sure. Truthfully. Between you and me, I'm beginning to think that it's all just wishful thinking…"

"And what about the lip reading? How did you get to be so good at it?"

He shrugged.

"You don't want to know much, do you? But if you must know, it helps to have certain skills when you're an outsider. Means you can learn stuff without getting too close, if you know what I mean. Get the lay of the land, like."

I nodded. I had never thought of it like that but it made sense to me.

Sherton Myam continued on in the same vein, talking in a low voice, almost as though to himself. I think that I must have made an attentive and sympathetic listener for it was some time before he realised that the conversation had become rather one-sided. I, for my part, had no complaints and had been completely enthralled. But he insisted that I tell him something of myself. Perhaps he too was unusually good at listening, as I soon found myself confiding in him about my life and how my father had left us when I was very young. Not something I generally chose to share.

The shapeshifter studied me intently all the while and then re-visited his sentiments about Deja Vue. He was sure that he knew me from somewhere or that I reminded him of someone he had once known, but the memory remained obstinately elusive. I empathised with him. I might have looked a little young to complain of memory problems, but the truth was, I could barely recall my own father's face.

By and by, the air turned cooler and a wind began to blow the petals of fallen blossom around our ankles in little eddies. I glanced down at my watch. Spiderman was pointing directly above his head. It was well past a quarter to teatime. The afternoon had slipped away without either of us noticing.

Crumbs, I thought, Mum would be home by now and I had forgotten to tell her that I was going to the park. I would have to move, pronto and make up some excuse on the way. I looked up at my new friend.

"Mr Myam."

"Yes, lad?"

"I have to be going now and I'm glad I met you but – well …"

"Spit it out…."

"Well, I think you seem rather sad…"

"S'that right? And what would a shrimp like you know about it, I'd like to know?"

"Well, 'cos I think maybe you're lonely. Like me. And I feel sad most of the time."

The shapeshifter cocked his head and thought for a moment.

"Suddenly everyone's a bleedin' expert in psychology, eh? I'm alone *ergo* I'm lonely, is it? Watch yourselves lads, we've got a sharp'un here."

I had no idea who these lads might be, I certainly couldn't see any, but persisted regardless.

"Well, maybe you don't have to be. Alone I mean. Maybe we could be alone together, as it were?"
I tried to look into his eyes but he looked away.
"Yeah, well, I wouldn't get your hopes up, if I were you."
Refusing to accept defeat so easily, I consulted Spiderman again, rose to my feet and held out my hand.
"Same time tomorrow, then?"
"Don't count on it, Sonny. Some of us have lives to live."

4

The following morning, I awoke with a pleasant little tickle of anticipation in my tummy that was generally reserved for Christmas and birthdays. I thought about my meeting with Sherton Myam and smiled. I told myself that this was going to be a good day - and I believed it. Picking up on hints had never been a strong point and people would sometimes have to spell things out before I finally grasped their meaning.

Not surprisingly, therefore, as soon as school was over, I found myself heading straight for the park. Well, perhaps not straight. I was mindful to stop by and inform Mum first. She had not been happy the previous afternoon when I had arrived back late, without having informed her of my whereabouts, though even I could see that she was more relieved than angry.

By the time I got home, she had been out on the doorstep having a loud conversation with Mrs Worth and I could hardly have avoided catching an earful, if I'd wanted to.

"I don't know, Gladys. I still wonder if he needs a man in his life. I've thought about moving back up north to be closer to my two brothers. But then there's my job and the house, and Jumbo would have to start at a new school. And he doesn't cope that well with change. I know it's silly, but I feel like I'm short-changing him, somehow."

"Margot Cooper, I don't know a more devoted mother than you. It's not your fault his father buggered off. He's just growing up – tugging free from the apron strings. He's a good kid..."

However true her words might have been, the "good kid" felt pretty lousy right at that moment. My mum was fab at being a mother and I hated to see her upset by my thoughtlessness. Still, the misdemeanour did not go unpunished. Indeed, it took every last ounce of my powers of persuasion to avert being grounded. Instead, I earned myself a list of extra chores by way of penance - but that was cool as Mum would almost always forget what they were after a day or two. As for self-recrimination, my head remained so full of the shapeshifter all that evening that I scarcely had time for anything else.

At any rate, it was with a racing heart that I found myself back in the park yet the excitement was short-lived. I returned to the bench where we had met but it stood resolutely unoccupied. I waited awhile and then hunted all around but the shapeshifter was nowhere to be seen.

Nor could I find any sign of him the following day or the one after that. Day after day, week after week, I made my little pilgrimage to that same park bench where we had met, but it was always the same disappointing story. Soon the weeks became months and still, I did not give up. The long summer holiday came and went without so much as a sniff of him. The leaves on the trees that lined the little path turned yellow, then red, and then fell off altogether, leaving the branches to shiver through the chill of the lengthening nights, clothed in nothing but their birthday suits.

Bonfire night came and went. The air turned bitter-cold and the ducks in the park took to huddling together for warmth. And still, I kept an eye out.

Most times, I would take my football with me, bouncing it from my knee to my head and back to my foot in an unrelenting rhythm that soothed the excesses of my over-excitable brain. Never missing a beat. Willing myself to whatever surpass whatever personal record, I had currently set.

At other times, when the wind blew in from the north, promising snow but failing to deliver it, I would simply trudge the circuit around the park until my fingers began to sting and then return home, my cheeks burning from the cold. When, finally, the snow fell, I would leap about and build a snowman. Once or twice, I might almost forget my reason for being there. It was then that I would catch myself and look around, my eyes desperate for a glimpse of shabby gaberdine.

In the week or so before Christmas, I had walked around the park with a Christmas card in my pocket, just in case. By New Year's Eve, I had pinned my hopes on the spring. By the middle of spring, I convinced myself that summer would be the time.

The logic which drove me on was, to my young mind, unassailable. The shapeshifter might merely have changed his form and could have been close-at-hand, all along. Perhaps it was a test or a game. For months, I would pause and stare at complete strangers until they grew uncomfortable under my gaze and moved away or told me to sod off.

Whatever way I looked at it, that one brief meeting with Sherton Myam had left a profound mark. Mum aside, it was the first time in my short life that I had not felt out of place or superfluous to requirements. And that is a feeling that no one would give up lightly.

As it was, nearly a year had passed before I finally hit the bottom of the deep well of optimism that had fuelled my tenacity. There was nothing particular to mark the day from any other. Just a few undeniable hints that time was moving on.

In the park, the brightly coloured petunias in the carefully tended flowerbeds were drooping their bell-like heads and beginning to fade. Green shoots were beginning to punctuate the yellow patches of scorched grass that still bore testament to the power of the blazing August sun. Another Summer was reaching its end and with it my optimism. I slumped onto *our* bench and mentally threw in the towel. If it was a test, I had failed. If the shapeshifter *was* around, he didn't wish to be seen. *But why would he hide from me?* I wondered sadly. *He must have felt the same connection that I did. I know he must have.*

Meanwhile, despite the disappointment, or perhaps because of it, the mystery of the shapeshifter's existence and disappearance came to feature as the defining factor in my young life. Post Sherton Myam, I ceased to see the world as simply as others did and the feeling that I was a fish out of water among my peers only increased. They had seen my lone wanderings in the park and had long since taken to giving me an even wider berth.

Not that it should have bothered me. Loneliness of this sort surely had its compensations. I thought about my heroes - Peter Parker and Clark Kent. Condemned to a life of secrecy and subterfuge, but all for a greater purpose.

Still, I was no superhero and longed for someone in whom to confide. Someone, anyone, with whom to share my extraordinary experience. Yet I never once mentioned it to a living soul, not even my mum, for she could not possibly have believed me and would only have worried. So instead, we played chess, chatted about school and watched Mastermind and our favourite shows on TV until even I could almost believe that life was perfectly ordinary after all. But I never stopped hoping and, in all that time, it was as though I was waiting for my life to begin again.

Yet, life had not stood still. Not by a long stick of chalk. Over three years passed, dragging me from the seemingly stagnant shallows of childhood slap-bang into the turbulent depths of early adolescence. In its wake came the move to "big school" - the high school, a bus ride away in Stratford. (Not the one on Avon, of course, the one that is next stop to Mile End on the Central Line.) The transition wasn't such a big deal in the end. I didn't like change but I did enjoy having new puzzles to solve, like where to find the classroom for my next lesson and how to remember all the new and different teachers' names and even working out how long to hang around the shopping centre before the crowds of rowdy kids jostling to get onto the buses finally thinned out.

It wasn't only the changes in the outside world with which I had to contend. Nothing about me seemed to fit together properly anymore. Mum swore that I grew taller by the week and joked that I was beginning to eat her out of house and home. I was forever tripping over my own feet and it wasn't only my extremities that were growing. My body seemed intent on all sorts of mischief and puberty seemed to delight in playing a new trick upon me with every passing day. It was no picnic. Some mornings, I found myself staring at the scowling youth in the bathroom mirror and wondering who he was.

At least my chess was improving. I routinely thrashed everyone in the school chess club, even those lads a couple of forms above me, and was becoming a bit of a mentor to the younger members. Occasionally I would even get the better of Mum, although those matches remained few and far between. My talent for the game earned me a degree of grudging notoriety and even respect at school but only among the nerds. And then, no matter how amicable the match, the friendship never seemed to extend beyond the perimeter of the chessboard. Maybe it was because socially, we were all as hopelessly inept as one another. Then again, I was not playing for popularity. Whatever the case, once Chess Club was over, I remained firmly in the outer orbit of our little social system.

And as for girls, well, that was a complete non-starter. Without a friend to let it slip to the girl that I fancied that I fancied her, I had zero means of communication. Not that I fancied many of them in any case. They all seemed preoccupied with their hair and make-up or giggling over who had appeared on Top of The Pops that week. It didn't help that Chess Club had effectively become a girl-free zone. Females made us uncomfortable and even if one turned up, the welcome was less than encouraging. And then they would have to face the inevitable ribbing from their friends to whom they suddenly appeared a three-headed oddity. No wonder they preferred polishing their nails.

I tried my best not to let it all get to me and, most of all, I did my utmost to hide my isolation from my mum. There was nothing she could do about it and the last thing I wanted was to worry her. I was used to my own company and it could have been a lot worse. After all, even if the other kids could be unkind, no one ever tried to stuff my head down the school lavatories or steal my lunch money. Things could *certainly* have been a lot worse.

Nevertheless, as I watched the other kids at school take the first tentative steps towards pairing off, I began to wonder whether I was truly fated to go through life alone. Until at last, the afternoon arrived, when it would all change.

It was early May which was, as it happened, around about the same time of year I first met Sherton Myer, all those years earlier. A damp Monday morning had turned into a pleasantly warm afternoon and the sun was shining as though someone had just given it some good news. I don't normally notice my surroundings that much, but it suddenly struck me how utterly blue the sky could be. A bit like seeing it for the first time.

Late spring had always been my favourite time of year and an afternoon cooped up in a stuffy lab for triple biology had left me looking forward to a breath of fresh air and a kickaround. It should have been an interesting afternoon. The scheduled practical had been to dissect bulls' eyes but Mr Would-you-believe-it Hardy, a beloved and inspiring biology teacher, had unexpectedly taken sick leave. Dissection prac. postponed, the class had been left to read up on the anatomy of the human eye under the supervision of Chemistry Jones who was no fun at all.

Everything else had seemed ordinary enough. I'd even managed to bag the front seat on the top deck of the bus before a gaggle of giggling third-form girls could get to it. They had complained loudly and then retreated to the back seat, where they continued to whisper and snigger all the way to The Romford Road Swimming baths.

Once home, I'd thrown my bag into the corner of the hallway and grabbed my football. It was only as I was pulling the front door closed behind me that I remembered my mum. I was thirteen now, soon to turn fourteen, and she had long since given up on insisting that I inform her of my whereabouts in the hours or so before she made it home, but I liked to surprise her sometimes, all the same. My communication with her seemed to have deteriorated into monosyllabic grunts recently. It wasn't her fault and, in a way, it wasn't mine either. We just seemed to have lost the knack of being able to have a civil and protracted conversation. Indeed, had it not been for chess, I'm not sure we would have spent much time together at all. I just seemed to need my space. But, even if I was an only child, she hadn't bought me up to be selfish. There was no mistaking the expression of pain in her eyes when I headed straight for my room the moment tea was finished. As it went, a small gesture like dropping by to say 'Hi' went a long way and it certainly made me feel better about myself.

I headed along Ham Park Road, past the Spotted Dog and across to Upton Lane to the office of Skynner, Sykes and Skynner, where my mum still worked. It was located above a shopfront that had once been a wool shop but had recently been converted into one of the ubiquitous self-tanning salons that had popped up throughout the east end. Cheaper than a week in the Costa del Sol, getting your tan topped up weekly had become the new obsession amongst sun-starved Brits.

A young man exited as I drew near. Naturally fair, his face appeared a kind of deep bronze save for two white patches around his eyes, tell-tale signs that he had at least had the sense to wear protective goggles. The guy smirked and puffed himself out as he passed, though what he had to be proud of, I really couldn't say. Never, *ever* use tanning beds, Mr Hardy had warned us all. Over-exposure to ultraviolet light can give you skin cancer. Fact. And he had been gravely serious. I shook my head. Let him enjoy his smugness. Ignorance, it seemed, really was bliss.

The door to the stairway that led to the solicitor's offices stood ajar. A powerful whiff of disinfectant assaulted my nostrils. I wrinkled my nose. It was strong, but not strong enough to entirely mask a heady top-note of stale tobacco and urine. I was never sure what it said about the tenor of Skynner, Sykes and Skynner's clientele, but this was after all the heart of the East End.

I held my breath and made my way up the flight of dingy stairs to the half-glazed inner door on the little landing. I could see Mum talking to Joan, one of the receptionists and hesitated before sticking my head around to say Hi. Mum looked up with the familiar smile of welcome she always reserved for me, no matter how busy she seemed.

I returned her smile with a thumbs up and then grinned and nodded to Joan, whom I had known since I was knee-high to a grasshopper. She was the gatekeeper for the firm and something of a well-groomed bull terrier. No one got past her without an appointment and the explicit declaration that "Mr S... will see you now."

That being said, her no-nonsense face always seemed to melt into the softest of welcomes whenever she saw me and today was no different. I grinned again and then gestured that I would be off then. Mum nodded back, her eyes crinkling with happiness. She never needed the big conversations. Just those little gestures that reminded her how much she meant to me.

"Getting to be quite the handsome lad, isn't he, your Jonathon...?" commented Joan as I was ducking back out. "Takes after his father..."

"Joan!" exclaimed my mother, catching her breath.

I couldn't recall her sounding so rattled. Stopping in my tracks, I turned back. There was Joan, burning bright crimson and staring at my mum in horror.

"Not that you - I mean. Him being so blond and athletic-looking and all, while you - oh, Lord, me and my big mouth."

But Mum seemed to have found her sense of humour and was already laughing. She rolled her eyes at me and shook her head. I think, she still found it difficult to believe that I was her son herself, sometimes. With her tiny frame and beautiful brunette hair, few people automatically took her for my mother. Especially now that I had begun to tower over her.

I didn't stay around to hear anything else. It didn't take much to mortify me and if there was one thing worse than going unnoticed - it was attracting unsolicited attention.

My timely escape did not stop my ears burning though. Doubtless Mum would be unable to resist some gentle teasing, later. Another good reason to withdraw to the safety of my bedroom. Still, it had probably made her day and I could not begrudge her that much.

The park, when I finally got there, seemed unusually empty given the welcome sunshine. A teenage mother wheeled a pushchair towards me, fag in mouth. I don't think she could have been more than a couple of years older than me, though I didn't recognise her. I stepped off the path to make way for her as she drew near though received no acknowledgement for my trouble. I thumbed my nose to her back once she had passed and then continued along the path, past the tennis courts to my usual corner hang-out, close to where the bench stood. I slipped off my blazer and began to bounce the ball, counting off a new number with each contact. First on the side of my foot, then onto my knee and up onto my chest and head. *One-thrum, three-thrum, five-thrum.* On and on it beat until my whole being seemed nothing more than the echo of the numbers and an infinite rhythm.

Then suddenly, something new caught my attention. I let the ball drop and cradled it between my palms. There it was again, something unexpected in the extreme periphery of my vision. I turned to look. The sun shone in my eyes, half-blinding me. I shaded my face with my hand and squinted.

There on the park bench slouched a figure in a crumpled raincoat and flat cap. He neither moved nor spoke, yet his eyes were fixed on mine. I felt the hairs stand to attention on the back of my neck. Tucking the football in the crook of my arm, I approached the bench.

Sherton Myam did not look happy

"I hate the bleedin' sun," he grumbled.

"Because it makes you seem more visible," I offered, though it was more a statement than a question.

"How would you know?"

"I know. I feel the same."

"Hmph. Maybe. Maybe not."

"I see you are still alone."

"As, I observe, are you…"

"How's the finger?"

Sherton raised his hand and waggled his pinky finger.

"Good as ever. Though, sometimes, I reckon it's developed a mind of its own."

I laughed and shook my head although it occurred to me that he may not have been joking.

"You don't look a day older."

"Whereas *you* most certainly do. All grown up now. Quite the young…wots-is-name? You know. I thought how much you reminded me of him last time. But I'm still having a bit of trouble with my bleedin' memory. That bloke – blonde curly hair. You know. Oh, never mind. Leave it. I've been down this mental cul-de-sac so many times I've named it Frustration Close."

I stared at him, not quite following his meaning. We both looked at the ground. It was the shapeshifter who spoke first.

"I see you're pretty handy with a ball. A bit of talent for it, I'd say…" He nodded at the soccer ball.

"Oh, that? Yeah, I don't play though, or anything like that. I don't even like football. It's just a thing I do. You know, to pass the time."

"Why not?"

"Why not, what?"

"Why don't you like football?" I sighed.

"I thought it was rude to ask questions."

"Touché. ..."

"Nah, you're all right." I grinned. "It's just a bit of a long story. It's Mum, if you must know. She hates it. I mean, *seriously* hates it. She generally changes the channel when it comes on the TV but she let me watch the last World Cup Final back when Germany won, you remember? Well, before the match even began they showed the replay of The England Team collecting the cup back in 1966, you know. I'm too young to remember that but, of course, it's all anyone ever talks about every time the World Cup comes around. It's the same this year with our team off to Argentina. Anyway, there was The Queen handing Bobby Moore the trophy and she just burst into tears. My mum, I mean, not The Queen. Went out and started doing stuff in the kitchen - said she just hated the whole thing. It was obvious that I wasn't going to get any sense out of her so I just switched the TV off. It's no loss, really. I prefer chess.

"Bobby Moore?"

"Well yes - and Geoff Hurst, Trevor Francis, Bobby Charlton – the whole squad."

Sherton Myam shook his head and stared at me as though I had just fallen out of the sky. I could see him struggling with some idea but then he just fell silent again. And then, just as unexpectedly he spoke.

"Still interested in puzzles?

"Oh, yes. And chess, as I said. And numbers and maths. Sometimes when I bounce the ball, I try to count off the prime numbers, as I go. The school is saying I should think of maths at university, but I don't know. Don't think I could leave Mum. I'm all she has, really."

"You could stay local."

I nodded. It was a good point, though Mum insisted that it would somewhat defeat the purpose of going away to university.

"How is she? Your mother, I mean."

I shrugged.

"I think she still misses Dad, though she would never say as much. She is still at Skynner and Sykes. They think the world of her but..."

The thought of Mum made me look down at my watch. Spiderman had been replaced by a Cassio digital chronometer last Christmas.

"Look, I have to get going, she'll have tea ready by now and I'll be for the high jump if I'm late. But, promise me you'll be here again tomorrow. I had so much I wanted to talk to you about. You must promise."

Sherton Myam paused and tilted his head.

"Well, you know me, kid. Not exactly the reliable type. But I'll see what I can do..."

I knew better than to place too much hope on such a lukewarm guarantee, but the next day he was there, and the next, and the day after that. And it turned out that we did, indeed, have more in common than met the eye. Sherton Myam shared my fascination for numbers and we ended up discussing pi, irrational numbers and the problem of infinity for hours. It wasn't as though I needed any encouragement to pursue my interest in mathematics, of course, but finding someone with whom I could finally share my passion was a joy that was entirely novel to me.

And soon I found myself confiding in him about things of a more personal nature. My feelings of isolation; how all that the boys at school seemed to want to talk about was sex and prog-rock bands; how I had come to dread the reek of testosterone that washed around the changing rooms before and after P.E. when my classmates would flaunt their genitals or boast about some porn they had watched; and finally, how recently my only refuge, the lunchtime Chess Club had become a new source of misery since my unrivalled winning-streak had earned me the nickname *Spassky* after Boris Spassky, who had been much featured in the world news since the much-heralded Match of The Century with Bobby Fischer. It hadn't taken long for *Spassky* to become *Spastic* which, like most unkind names, had stuck. *For someone who disliked attention,* I moaned, *I had managed to become my own worst enemy. The other kids saw me as some kind of freak and I knew it. Which, by the way, was the reason I kept my natural soccer abilities closely under wraps.*

Once I got started, it was as though a damn had burst somewhere inside. Yet, through it all, Sherton Myer never so much as raised an eyebrow. Listening patiently, he merely nodded from time to time and said little. It was enough for me. We were both square pegs in round holes.

On the fourth afternoon, I decided to take the plunge. Call a spade a spade. Perhaps it was too soon, but if Sherton Myam was going to disappear on me again, better sooner than later.

"Mr Myam," I ventured tentatively as I got up to make my way home. "Do you think we could become friends?"

"Maybe, but don't expect me to kick any footballs around," he warned. "I reckon I had enough of that with bleedin' Bobby Moore and co."

I shot him a quizzical glance but let it pass. Instead, I smiled and nodded my farewell.

"See you later then, Mr Myam."

"Right, you are. Oh, and the name's Sherton," he winked, "and you might want to bring your chess board next time. I reckon I might be in the mood for a game."

I ran home, my head buzzing with excitement. Sherton Myam was going to be my friend and that was all I could have asked for.

5

The following day was the first time in a week that I had made my way to the park without having to keep my fingers tightly crossed. I hugged my schoolbag to my chest and grinned. I had been right. The connection I'd begun to think I had imagined all those years ago had been real, after all. For the first time in my life, I knew what it was to have a friend and it was much like the feeling you have after eating a truly satisfying meal – contentment. Pure and simple contentment.

And chess? Boy, could *he* play chess. Sherton Myam's curiously flat grey eyes had lit up when I pulled my little travel chess set from my satchel. He joked that he would be rusty but I could detect no fault or hesitation in his strategy. I hadn't even minded when he subtly and casually manoeuvred me into Check Mate. Well, not too much, at least. I was tired of winning and needed an opponent to stretch me. I seldom bested Mum but was used to her game and could often see my defeat coming. I could sometimes avoid it by forcing a stalemate or conceding but that was hardly the same as winning. Mum said that you learn from every defeat and that was true, but defeat at the hands of an unfamiliar player, now *that* was truly stimulating. What's more, Sherton Myam seemed to enjoy the match as much as I had. He shook my hand and confessed that he had been relieved to discover that he could play at all.

"It's the memory, you see. It all seems to be hidden behind this bleedin' veil of clouds - if you'll pardon my French. Sometimes the clouds seem to clear away for a few precious minutes and I get a glimpse of my past but it's never long enough to make any meaningful sense of it. Then, at other times, I find myself swept up by a storm of memories so dense, they completely drown me. It's all just a sorry jumble."

I felt sad for him and nodded in quiet sympathy. There was so much that I wanted to know about him but I held my tongue. It was, I reasoned to myself, a bit like befriending a wild animal. I was winning his trust but any sudden or intrusive move could still frighten him away. And that was the last thing I wanted.

My instincts proved to be spot-on. Not only did Sherton Myam enjoy my company, but it soon became clear that he needed a friend as badly as I did. After that, everything else seemed unimportant. And, over the next few weeks, the uniqueness of my new friend's physiology did indeed become increasingly incidental. It had been over three years since I had witnessed the bizarre incident with the eye in the jar and I guess you could say that the novelty had simply worn off. It's amazing how quickly something can lose its shock value. There used to be a boy in my class who somehow learned the trick of turning his eyelids inside out and began to do so in an attempt to win friends. At first, everyone had been blown away but by the fourth demonstration, the little crowd of admirers had quickly dispersed and the boy had been designated a one-hit-wonder. I don't know what became of him. I think his parents moved away and he went to another school. Perhaps he had more success with it there, but the thought of him getting grit trapped under the lid still made me wince.

Our afterschool meetings settled into a comfortable routine though I took care not to make any mention of them to Mum or anyone else. The relationship, I told myself, was not so much secret as unspoken. If Mum asked, I had been in the park, which was true. The fact that I made no mention of any friends was as it always had been.

Most days we played a game of chess or watched the cheeky squirrels cavort among the flowerbeds, digging up the bulbs and scattering the primroses in all directions. When a shower of rain swept in, we took shelter beneath the veranda of the sports pavilion until it cleared. Sometimes Sherton Myam would help me with my maths homework. He loved a good algebra equation or a complex bit of calculus, though was surprisingly useless at geometry.

In quieter moments, I would voice my anxieties about my life and the future. How I would do in my exams; which subjects I should choose for 'A' Levels. Sherton Myam seldom offered any advice or asked any questions but I could tell he was listening because, every so often he would refer to some minor detail I had mentioned in previous conversations. Sometimes I had the impression he was about to say something about himself but something seemed to hold him back. Then, one afternoon it all changed.

It started with an idle question. May was coming to its close and I would turn fourteen on the first of June. It seemed terribly old to me and I was not sure that I was ready for the responsibilities. I looked at my friend and twisted my lip.

"How old are you, Sherton? I can't really tell."
Sherton closed his eyes and groaned quietly.
"Honestly? Centuries probably. Millennia even. I can't be entirely sure."
"You're kidding, right?"

"No. No, I'm not." His voice was deadly serious. "We've always been here, as far as I can make out…"

"We? Hang on a minute. Who are we?"

He sighed heavily.

"I'm not sure about that either. Not bleedin' sure about anything, to tell the truth. I guess I just kind of *know* it, if you get my drift."

I wasn't sure that I did.

"But, if that is the case, where are the – the others, then?"

A shrug.

"Search me. I've looked all over, these last few years. Never found one, though sometimes I get this sense - I dunno. Maybe they've all gone. Maybe, it is just me, now. I could be the last of my kind for all I know."

I fell silent. My brain seemed to whirr but find no gear. I hadn't thought of Sherton as anything *but* a one-off. I hadn't so much as entertained the idea that there might be an entire species. Though that seemed very shortsighted, now that I thought about it. Suddenly, all sorts of questions filled my mind.

"Can I ask you something, something a bit personal, maybe?"

"What the Hell? I reckon we're already heading down that street. Take your best shot."

"Do you look like me inside?"

"I beg your pardon?"

"Do you have, you know, bones, organs etc?"

"Well, I'd be a bit floppy without a skeleton, wouldn't I now? Yeah, I think an Xray would show that I have bones etc. But, hey, - you must NEVER let them Xray me, you understand? Seriously, now. Even if I get mown down by a double-decker bus. Never under any circumstances call an ambulance. Just drag my body up an alley, if you have to. But no X-rays - and do not for God's sake let them take any blood, taking blood would be a bad idea, a very bad idea…"

He was getting agitated now. I felt his fingers digging into my arm and he had started to shake me. I tried to calm him, promising that I understood and would never let it happen.

"But why? What's the problem if you have all the internal organs, etc?"

"You remember when my finger shifted into an eye?"

I snorted. I couldn't help myself. *That* had hardly been something I was likely to forget.

"Well, this body is made up of individual cells, much as your body is, only the cells in mine are many times smaller than even the tiniest of yours and each exists and functions as an entirely autonomous entity. They can unite together to create larger structures, say a blood cell or an organ, but never lose that autonomy, which is why they can re-organize into an entirely different form, at will. Putting it like this is, of course, a gross oversimplification, because although each cell retains its autonomy, it always remains part of the whole, even when physically separated."

I knitted my brows and chewed this over for a few seconds.

"You mean the way you were able to control the finger - and the way the blood crept back into it?"

"Yes. Sort of. Only it wasn't so much me controlling my finger – the finger *was* me, if you get my drift."

I wasn't sure I did. I stared at my own finger and wiggled it a bit. I certainly thought of my brain as being *me* but I wasn't sure about my finger. Then again, I couldn't work out why that should be. It was an interesting conundrum. Sherton watched me for a moment and then sighed.

"The point is, when I take human form, for example, my cells work together to mimic the building blocks of the human body and replicate its structure. But it's not an exact reproduction – more a simulacrum."

I looked at him and frowned. I liked the sound of this new word but had no idea what it meant.

"Sorry, kid. I forget how young you are sometimes. How can I put this? In many ways, it's more like a 3D illustration than a working model. Parts can function as they are meant to and can, for that matter, function independently when required, especially on a mechanical level, but other processes, well not so much."

I shook my head. He was beginning to lose me now.

"What do you mean, other processes?"

"Well, my digestive system for example. I don't derive energy from food as you do. So, I could swallow something and it would eventually pass through my digestive tract, but there would be no digestive process – if you get my meaning."

He pulled a face in obvious distaste.

"You mean the food would just come out much as it went it?"

"Well, yes, I suppose – but could we just move on, if you don't mind? The point is, I could pass any superficial medical examination but it wouldn't take much to reveal something very different going on underneath."

"You don't need to tell me. I saw the blood creep back into the finger. It was awesome."

"Yeah, well. That little trick means that I could survive and recover from just about any injury. So, no matter how bad you thought it was – you could just scrape me up off the ground and take me home in a bleedin' carrier bag and I would be okay. You get it? But X-rays, of course, well they could be catastrophic – in more ways than I care to go into."

He fell quiet, as though even contemplating the idea was more than he could bear. I patted his hand, desperate to reassure him.

"I get it, no X-rays, ever. Not on my watch. Just take care crossing the road, eh Mate? Green Cross Code and everything, all right?"

I swallowed hard. The whole-scraping-him-up-in-a-bag business had got to me a bit. I reached into my pocket to check for my inhaler but managed to calm my breathing. I decided a change in direction would be a good idea.

"But you seem to be one whole person. How does that work if every single cell is doing its own thing?"

"Well, it's not so very different for you when you think about it. Your gut gets on and does its stuff, without you telling it to. You breathe and walk without a debate with the cells in your muscles about how and when they should do it. We – my cells, can simply operate independently as well."

"Okay, I get the physical bit but that wasn't really what I meant. Put it this way, right now, for instance, I don't feel as though I'm talking to a group of you. I mean, you seem to be all one individual, just like me."

"Well, maybe. But what you call the ego or consciousness arises from millions of interactions in the brain. It's just as much an illusion of unity if you think about it."

I tugged at my lip. I sort of got what he meant but it still all seemed so impossible. Except that I had of course witnessed it with my own eyes. I had so many more questions, I felt like my head was going to burst. Fortunately, Sherton seemed to be enjoying the limelight.

"But you said you couldn't remember anything. How do you know all this then?"

"Well, I just do. It must be a different kind of memory, I guess. Like I still remember how to play chess. But it's a good point. I've been trying to work out what has gone wrong with my memory because it can't always have been like this. I wonder if it is just my human memory, yeah? Because that relies on my brain, which is where humans store their memories, right?"

"I guess so…" I was not especially big on neurology and psychology, but it sounded about right. On the other hand, it struck me as vaguely inconsistent that his brain would function when his digestive system did not. But then I was no expert. I closed my eyes, aware that my head was beginning to ache.

"Hey, are you paying attention? Well, what if every time I change, my brain structure changes and the memories from that form are lost? Or maybe not lost altogether but severely disrupted, you know? Perhaps they do get transferred but get corrupted in the process, like a damaged tape recording. To be honest, I've been avoiding shifting just in case. I think it might just be too risky. But I don't really know. And then, seriously, what is the point of a shapeshifter that never shifts their bleedin' shape?"

With this, Sherton Myam lapsed into a dejected silence. I stared down at my hands, floundering to restore the conversation. I found it painful to see my friend so low. I examined the possibility that a nudge in another, more positive direction might help so I said the first thing that popped into my head.

"So, what exactly makes you think that you've lived so long then?"

"Do you really want to know?"

"You bet I do." I nodded enthusiastically.

Sherton Myam's face brightened

"Meet me here tomorrow and I'll show you. Oh, and make sure you bring your bus pass. I'm not exactly what you'd call a fan of walking."

6

I couldn't imagine where Sherton Myam was planning to take me and knew better than to ask when we met up the next afternoon. Nevertheless, I was more than a little surprised when the shapeshifter shepherded me out of the park and up to The Princess Alice on The Romford Road, where we rounded the corner just in time to hop onto a northbound bus. And he obviously wasn't kidding when he'd said that he didn't like walking because only minutes later, we alighted again at Wanstead Park station.

From there, Sherton Myam guided me across Woodgrange Road and along a back street which opened into Capel Road on the southern edge of Wanstead Flats. I gazed around in surprise. A line of houses ran down the right-hand side of the road, while the other gave directly onto the common, providing an unimpeded view of the vast open and ancient grazing land. The double line of trees which bordered the common gave the quiet road more the feel of a leafy country lane than a suburban thoroughfare. I smiled. I knew both the road and the common well. When I was little, my mum would often take us there to fly kites or have a picnic, but I had quite forgotten how peaceful the area could seem once you were away from the sounds of the traffic.

"Nearly there…" chimed Sherton Myer trying to chivvy me along. He had remained fairly quiet throughout the journey and I had the distinct impression that it was in his nature to avoid any actions that might draw unwanted attention.

I tramped on a little further and then paused for breath, scanning the broad span of grassland in the hope of spotting the cattle that still grazed on the common at certain times of the year. I had been just a little bit scared of them as a young child, but the way they wandered around, unfenced and unsupervised, had never ceased to fascinate me. My mum told me that they had been known to stray onto the road and to stop the traffic from time to time, but that otherwise, they were never any trouble to anyone. They had, she said, grazed on that same common since the twelfth century. Imagine that. They were nowhere to be seen that afternoon, however, so I kicked a clump of grass.

Sherton, meanwhile, seemed unconcerned as to the doing of his bovine neighbours and was starting to fizzle with impatience.

"Come along now." He chided. "No time to stand beneath the boughs and stare as long as sheep and cows..."

I shook my head. Surely, he was missing the point. The poem was bemoaning the fact that people never seemed to take the time to just stand and admire the natural world around us. I was about to say as much when I realised that he was already heading off down the road with a briskness that surprised me. I closed my mouth and trotted behind to catch up.

"So where are we going?" I panted when I finally caught up.

"Shhhh..,"he hissed, in reply. "You'll see soon enough."

I raised my eyebrows. As far as I could tell, there was no one around to hear us yet he seemed in complete earnest. Just then, we heard the sound of a car engine start up a little further down the road. The shapeshifter froze in his tracks and then suddenly dodged behind a tree. He did not peer around until the car had passed and disappeared into the distance. I stood and casually swung my arms, not knowing quite what to do with myself. I'd suspected that my friend was a little eccentric but this seemed to be taking it a bit far.

"It doesn't do to let too many people know where you live," he whispered hoarsely when he at last stepped back onto the pavement. And that is when the penny finally dropped. I don't know why it had not dawned on me earlier that he was taking me to see his home, but now it came to it, I felt a dozen or so butterflies flutter into frenzied activity in my tummy. I thought of Mum and suddenly wondered if this feeling was fear. She had drilled it into me so often. *Never trust strangers.* Well, Sherton Myam *was* strange. No doubt about it. But he was no stranger and had never so much as mentioned puppies or kittens, for that matter. And I knew how much he hated dogs. Besides, I felt no more sense of danger than I would have done, had he been Mrs Worth. No, it was something quite different. It was excitement. The shapeshifter was inviting me into his private world and I couldn't even begin to describe how privileged I felt.

Sorry Mum, I whispered under my breath as we continued down the road. But what she didn't know couldn't hurt her.

The traffic noise had almost completely died now, leaving only the cheeping of the sparrows and the raucous cackling of the great crows that hunkered in the tops of the trees, like jet-black cut-outs against the sky.

I had walked along this edge of the common many times but gazed with renewed interest at the houses as we passed. These were not the bog-standard Victorian terraces that populated the surrounding streets. Instead, there rose up a variety of stand-alone homes and semi-detached villas which suggested an air of bygone prosperity – gentility even, more in keeping with the character of Wanstead, the once prosperous village on the far side of the common. These days, all the suburbs to the east of The City of London ran into one another, but I guessed that it must all have looked very different back in the previous century. I found myself wondering how long Sherton Myam had called this part of the world home or whether he could, indeed, remember.

By and by, Sherton Myam came to an abrupt halt. He placed a finger on his lips and nodded towards an impressive-looking pair of gates, set in a high brick wall. On closer inspection, the gates seemed to have been fashioned from seriously barbed iron railings. I pulled a face and peered through. Behind them, though screened by a handful of overgrown trees, towered a three-story property of considerable proportions. I glanced at my friend and breathed - "cool."

Maintaining his cautiousness, the shapeshifter took a step back into the road to check that we were unobserved. But the only creatures who could see us were the crows who turned their beaks to watch with tilted heads. Sherton Myam glowered back at them then opened one of the gates and waved me through. The clang from the gate closing behind us sent the crows flapping and complaining vociferously behind them. *So much for keeping a low profile*, I thought.

The house loomed into clear view as we passed along the tree-lined path. I hung back, struck by how imposing it suddenly appeared.

"Wait - you live here?"
Sherton Myam shrugged.
"Someone has to."
"But - but it's enormous."
Sherton shrugged again.
"The whole house? By yourself?" I asked.
"What were you expecting? A dingy bedsit in a forgotten corner of a rundown council tenement? Credit me with a bit of bleedin' class, would you."

I stuck out my bottom lip, hardly knowing how to reply. I went to say something about the shabbiness of his clothes but thought better of it. He seemed prickly enough already.

While Sherton began to fumble around inside his raincoat for a key, I took the opportunity to step back and examine the place more closely. To the right, I immediately noticed a double garage that stood just a little around the corner. It had a tiled roof and a rusting tilt-up door that had seen better days. The tiles were covered with thick moss and I spotted at least half a dozen that appeared to have been broken for quite some time. Home maintenance, it seemed, was not the shapeshifter's strong point. I turned my gaze back to the front of the house. Perhaps it was not so very different from his clothing, after all. Straggly weeds spilt out of cracked and broken gutters while paintwork peeled to reveal rotting wood. Every window, save one on the second storey, appeared to be shuttered from the inside and the front step was littered with dry leaves and all manner of debris.

Just then, Sherton let out a grunt of relief and I watched with a growing sense of apprehension as the shapeshifter inserted an ancient-looking key into the great brass lock on the front door and deftly turned it. The butterflies had started up again, but this time it felt distinctly different. The collywobbles, my mum would have called it. That little internal warning light blinking on to alert us that something is not right.

I shot an anxious glance at my friend but I was in no danger from him, of that, I was sure. He was odd, I'll grant you, and grumpy at times, but completely harmless. Something deep down inside me just knew it. No, it was the house. And it wasn't fear exactly. It was a visceral response to a sense of loneliness and neglect so powerful that a part of me simply wanted to turn and run. I rubbed my arms against a chill that had nothing to do with the weather.

Suddenly the lock gave with a loud click. Sherton grinned.

"It's okay..." He said, with a wink. "I know I've let things go a bit, but it's perfectly safe. And I rather believe that it used to be quite splendid."

With that, he pushed the door which swung open with a small groan of protest. Sherton Myam held out an arm in welcome. I took a deep breath and stepped forward. Inside, I could see that we were entering a long gloomy hallway, yet the thoroughfare seemed blocked with all manner of junk, from rolled-up rugs that lolled against one another to great ornate picture frames, propped empty and gaping along the walls. Clutter of some description filled every spare corner and we were obliged to pick our way around discarded side tables and tea chests, stuffed full of ornaments and broken candelabras.

"It's a bit of mess…" confessed the shapeshifter somewhat shamefacedly, "but I promise there are no rats or, at least, none worth mentioning. Captain sees to that."

I suppose I felt some relief to hear this, though I had no idea who Captain might be and Sherton Myam remained characteristically unforthcoming on the subject. I was just plucking up the courage to ask when he removed his flat cap, hung it on a hook on the wall and then took down a pair of plain cotton gloves and pulled them on. I might have been more curious about the gloves had I not been entirely thrown by the business with the hat. Not that there was anything amiss with his head or hair, per se, it was just that I had never seen it before. Now that I thought about it, he had always kept his cap on, no matter what the weather. In any case, both the colour (an unremarkable light brown) and thickness of the mop of curls, he revealed, seemed to transform his face. I had always supposed him to be a middle-aged man. He certainly dressed that way and at my age, anyone over twenty-three pretty well falls into that category. But, right then, I couldn't have told you how old he was if my life had depended on it. Still, if the shapeshifter truly was as ancient as he claimed, it was all a bit immaterial.

I chuckled to myself, relieved to feel my collywobbles start to abate. Sherton, meanwhile, beckoned me on with a wiggle of a gloved finger. I was just trying to form an enquiry about the need for the gloves that would not sound rude when we arrived at a door that opened into a poorly-lit reception room. Sherton nodded eagerly. I peered hopefully around the lintel yet, through the gloom, the room seemed even more tightly jammed with junk than the hallway. The shapeshifter nudged me with his elbow and indicated a narrow passage between the piles of boxes and assorted items of furniture on all sides.

"We can squeeze in…" he said, by way of encouragement.

"Really?"

"Oh, yeah. Bob's your uncle. Just watch your head, though…" he said, ducking his head as he led the way. I followed suit, narrowly missing the base of a large moose head that hung down below the frame of the doorway. I moved further into the space and hovered patiently between several tottering pillars of enormous old books. The next moment, Sherton Myam pulled a cord, flooding the room with glittering light. I blinked, dazzled by both the light and the spectacle before my eyes whilst the shapeshifter shunted me blindly onwards.

At last, my vision cleared. We were standing in a small oasis that had been cleared in the centre of what seemed to be a very large and once grand room. The windows were partially blacked out by those folding wooden shutters you sometimes see in London's old houses and were framed in ornate heavy velvet curtains. Above us, an enormous, cobweb-covered crystal chandelier hung from the high and ornate stucco ceiling. I blinked up at it in awe. It might have been dulled by dust but must have been quite splendid once.

In every corner lay heaped-up bundles of richly coloured Turkish rugs, rolled-up oil paintings and an assortment of silver candle sticks and decorative ornaments. And there, watching over it all like two eternal guardians, towered a man and a woman of exquisitely sculpted marble.

I felt completely lost for words. I may have been a little young to consider myself an expert in antiquities, but if me and Mum had a favourite TV show, it was The Antiques Roadshow on a Sunday afternoon and before that, it had been Going for a Song. I don't think we'd ever missed an episode. And I assure you, I did not need Arthus Negus to tell me that this was no rubbish heap - this was a hoard of treasure that would have shamed Ali Baba himself.

Sherton Myam rewarded my astonishment with a sly smile.

"I suppose I'm a bit of a collector."

"Hoarder, more like…" I joked.

Sherton winced and I immediately wished that I had bitten my tongue.

"You don't understand. I don't think that this is just random stuff. I believe that these are all the things I have kept with me over the years. Souvenirs, if you like."

"But how do you know, if you can't remember?"

"But that's the point. They are *true* souvenirs. They *hold* memories. Listen, I'll try to explain. The house is stuffed full of such artefacts and some of them are very old. And, by old, I mean extremely old. Ancient even. There may be too many to count but I feel a strong emotional connection to each and every item. These are things, I have loved and amongst which I have lived for many, many long years. I feel it. Most of the time I can't recall it *in my mind*, but when I touch something, it is as though the cells in my body *do* and I am momentarily flooded with the sensations and thoughts from that time. I can never hold onto it and sometimes if I should happen to come into contact with some object accidentally, it quite overpowers me and can be pretty disorientating – hence the gloves."

He held up his hands. At least those made sense to me now. I looked at the chaos around us and wondered how he could bear to live among such chaos. I must have shaken my head because he seemed to read my thoughts.

"You might think me foolish, but until I somehow get my memory back, I'm not sure I could bear to part with a single stick of it."

"But some of this stuff must be worth a fortune."

"Maybe. But money only buys more things."

I shrugged. He had a point. What did the value matter? And I couldn't get the idea of a mere touch eliciting such memories out of my mind. I was bursting to ask him to give me a demonstration but it felt like prying somehow. I gazed around and bit my lip.

"C'mon," he said." I'll show you the rest."

We made our way back into the hallway and Sherton flicked on some more lights. We passed a couple more doorways and the foot of a rather grand-looking stairway. The upper stories of the house lay in darkness and the stairs themselves were as crammed-full with objects as everywhere else. I placed my hand on the finely carved finial and peered up into the blackness, longing to explore but Sherton shook his head and indicated that we should keep on moving to the back of the house.

The feel of the house began to change as we moved further down the passage and it seemed more modern somehow. We arrived at a cluster of framed black and white photographs out of which smiled an assortment of glamourous women and handsome men in dinner jackets. Some were studio portraits while others appeared to have been taken at parties of some sort. Many of the portraits bore scribbled signatures and messages and I wondered if they must be film stars, though I didn't recognise any of the faces. By and by, however, I stopped in front of one of them and exclaimed,

"Why, Sherton, that's Bobby Moore. It can't be all that old at all. Surely you must remember how you came by this."

The shapeshift peered at the spidery writing and read it out aloud.

"With thanks for all your encouragement and belief. Your friend Bobby. 1966."

"Why, that was the year he captained England to win the World Cup. Just a year after I was born."

Sherton looked at the photograph and stared at my face.

"Bleedin' 'eck, I knew you reminded me of someone…"

"Yeah, I get that a lot. It's the blonde hair - But did you *really* know him?"

Sherton shook his head.

"Can't say. It's all so vague. I must have been before I lost my memory…"

"Touch the photo." I suggested. "Go on. Maybe something will come back."

I could hear my mum's voice in my head telling me not to be so cheeky but I couldn't help myself. I needed to know what Bobby Moore was doing on his wall.

Sherton squinted sideways at me and then kissed his teeth. Pulling off a glove, he reached out a hand and placed it gingerly over the smiling face. His body responded with a dramatic flinch. Yet that was not all. I stared at his face in astonishment. It had changed somehow. Different features flickered across it– almost as though some unseen projectionist was projecting the image of somebody entirely different over it. Someone young and female and undeniably pretty or so it seemed. I tried to make sense of what I was seeing yet the illusion vanished as quickly as it had appeared. Sherton began speaking and if he was aware of the strange transformation then he did not refer to it.

"We used to all hang out, together. I don't know why. There was a lot of laughing and drinking. And cards. I get the impression that there was a lot of playing cards."

"We?"

"What now?"

"You said, *we* used to *all* hang out…."

"Did I?"

Sherton pulled his glove back on and shuffled on, seeming done with the conversation.

"You okay?" I asked, wondering if I should mention the strange face thing. But he merely scratched his head and ignored me. I wondered if it had upset him somehow and felt cross with myself for making him touch the photograph. But there was still so much I longed to ask him.

The next photograph we came to was of a group of about eight extremely stylish-looking men and women, seated around a round table in formal evening dress. Taken in a fancy club or restaurant, by the look of it. They were all raising glasses of champagne in a toast. There was something so familiar about the men that I felt as though I knew them, though that was crazy. After all, it wasn't as though I mixed with any adults at all. A man and woman on the photographer's side of the table had their faces turned away, as though unaware of the camera. Yet even the backs of their head and shoulders seemed to ring a bell. What could be going on? For a moment, I wondered if I had somehow been infected with the same affliction as Sherton.

"Look familiar, do they?" he asked

"Yes. How do you know?"

"Well, you see their ugly mugs in the newspapers often enough. Those two stiffs there, they're the bleedin' Kray Twins, aren't they? You don't need a very long memory to recognise Ronnie and Reggie."

"But what are The Kray Twins doing on your wall."

"Search me. And to tell the truth, there are some things I'd rather not know."

I looked at him and started to wonder just how many more surprises lay in store for me. Seeming almost anxious to move on, Sherton ushered me down a small flight of stairs that led down through an old-fashioned scullery and into the kitchen. The room could not have been more different from our kitchen at home. Chilly and unwelcoming, the room, though large seemed tight for space.

A workbench, camp bed and a battered old armchair took up the middle of the room, whilst crates of bottles leaned against the banks of kitchen cupboards obstructing any hope of access to them.

"Crikey, Sherton. Are you living in this one room? And how on earth do you manage to cook and eat?"

"Eat? I told you. I don't bleedin' eat."

"Oh, yeah sorry. How could I have forgotten? But you must get nutrition from somewhere. Even plants make energy from sunlight. We did it in biology."

"I've got all the nutrition, I need, right here, mate, haven't I?" He patted a cardboard box and then lifted the flap. It was full of bottles of what looked like-

"Vodka," he beamed. "You can't beat it."

"You've got to be kidding me."

He stared at me and shook his head. I glanced around. My eyes alighted on a rack of empty bottles and a bin that overflowed with them. He was telling the truth. I had hardly got my head around this piece of information when something else caught my attention. Something metallic and grey.

"Christ-on-a-bike, Sherton. Is that a gun?"

"Don't touch it..." he warned, his voice shrill with panic. "There may be bullets in it." And with that, he picked it up, span the barrel and then placed the muzzle against his temple.

For a moment I thought that my legs were going to give way beneath me. I watched in rigid horror as he squeezed the trigger, his gloves still on. There was a click – and nothing. I dropped to my knees feeling like I was going to burst into tears.

"Your face," he said with a laugh. "Priceless."

"That wasn't funny, Sherton," I spluttered, scrambling to my feet.

"Relax. I never keep it loaded. Couldn't even tell you where the bullets are."

"Can I hold it?"

"If you like."

I took the gun in my hand. It was unexpectedly heavy. I turned it over in my hand, enthralled. I'd only ever seen one in films before, but this was no prop.

"What are you doing with a revolver, anyway?"

"Search me? I have some flintlocks upstairs, properly old they are, I reckon and – well. I suppose I shouldn't really, but what the hell, eh? In for a penny, in for a pound, I always say."

He took the gun from my hand and laid it back where I had found it. Then, opening a drawer in one of the kitchen cupboards, he fished about until he found a key which was attached to a piece of string. I looked down at my watch, mindful that I would have to think about getting home soon. He had sharp eyes.

"Never mind that. This won't take a tick."

He steered me to a door at the back end of the kitchen and unlocked it. A rough flight of cement steps led down into the underbelly of the house. I peered down into the darkness and wrinkled my nose. Dank, stale air. The unmistakable smell of a cellar. We had a small one at home though something told me this one would be quite another story. The butterflies in my tummy were starting up again. The word dungeon sprang, uninvited, into my mind. Normally, it was a word I rather liked, yet now I rather wished that I had never heard it. I glanced at Sherton's face. It appeared as bland as usual. I was just being silly. He tugged on a light pull, flooding the small space with electric light. I took a deep breath and placed my foot on the first step.

I'd deduced the nature of the cellar before I reached the bottom step and it wasn't anything so very sinister. It was a vault. Not that it required much mental effort. Nestled in the corner were a couple of stacks of sturdy strongboxes and an impressively large and sturdy-looking safe. I let out a low whistle. Given the valuables I'd seen just lying around the rest of the house, whatever was locked away in this room must be of significant value.

Sherton Myam winked at me and lifted the lid of a particularly large strongbox that had been left unsecured.

"Go on, take a gander."

I leaned forward. Shotguns. A whole case full of them. With ammunition. I gaped at him and he licked his lips. He seemed to be enjoying himself immensely. He bent down and twisted the dial on the safe. The tumbles clicked into place and he swung open the door.

"Strewth..." I breathed. I had never seen so much money in my life. That wasn't saying much, I suppose, but not even in films or on The Sweeny. Bundles and bundles of notes.

"That's nothing," whispered Sherton Myam with a wink. He reached into the back of the safe and drew out an ornately carved wooden box. Blowing the dust off the top, he handed it to me. I opened the lid and let out a small gasp. I didn't know much about jewellery but this looked like the real deal. There were necklaces and earrings and rings boasting gemstones so big, they made my eyes bulge. I peered questioningly at Sherton, who gave one of his shrugs.

"Is this all yours?"

"I don't know. But if it ain't, how come I know the combination and how come no one else has come forward to claim it in all the years I've been here."

"Which is how many?"

Another shrug.

"Well, it's got to be seven or eight. Earliest real date, I can recall is Christmas 1970."

"Look at this, I'm pretty sure this is very old indeed. I mean - really, really old." I had picked up a large and remarkably beautiful gold cross that had been inlaid with pearls and richly coloured precious stones.

Sherton looked at me with an expression, I could not read. He wetted his lips then removed a glove and reached out to touch the cross. His face seemed veiled for a moment and then, suddenly, I saw a transformation, similar to the one I had witnessed earlier, only this time I made out dark features with a goatee beard and moustache.

Then, all at once, he was gasping and staring at me.

"I was there, Jonathon, my lad," he grinned. "Elizabeth Regina, the Virgin Queen. I was in her court. She gave me this with her own two hands. She – she…" He buried his face in his hands and shook his head.

"No-no. It's no good. It's already gone."

I could sense the grief in his voice. I held out the cross, once more, but Sherton shook his head sadly.

"No, kid. It doesn't work like that."

I reclosed the box and knelt to replace it in the safe. Something about the bundles of notes caught my eye. I picked one up and took a closer look.

"Crumbs, Sherton - this is old money. These notes pre-date decimalisation, which means…"

"They are effectively worthless? I know"

"Then, why have you kept them?"

"Didn't know what else to do with 'em, to tell you the truth. I don't think you can just swing by the local bank and deposit this kind of cash without raising a few eyebrows. And now, slinging them in the bin doesn't seem the brightest idea. Even having a bonfire might attract unwanted attention. Besides, I've got a feeling my people do things on a cash-only basis…"

I replaced the wad of notes and shifted uncomfortably.

"But, Sherton, your people, as you call them. The guns and the cash. Doesn't the idea of them coming back worry you just a tiny bit?"

"Not really. Look, I know how it looks and what you're probably thinking and I wish I could remember. I really do. The trouble is, the only clues I get are when I touch some of this stuff and then, well, it dissolves like a dream. But it's never anything really bad. And I think I would just know if it was. Believe me, I really don't think there is anything to worry about. And I don't want you to worry about it either. That's the last thing in the world I meant to do by showing you all this."

His face fell with these words so I patted his arm. I had no doubts on that score. The fact was, I longed to explore the rest of the house but knew that I needed to be heading home and said as much.

We were just making our way back up the cement stairs when I gave a sharp shriek and jumped, nearly leaving my skin behind me. Something had brushed against my calf. I had felt it.

"Blimey, what a fuss," chortled Sherton Myam. "It's only Captain. I'd wondered when he'd put in an appearance. After some tasty mice, eh, boy?" He clicked his tongue and bent down. An enormous orange cat wound around his legs and leapt into his arms. The shapeshifter carried it into the kitchen and set it down on one of his boxes.

"Captain – this is Jonathon. Jonathon – meet Captain. As fine a ratter as you'll ever have the pleasure to meet."

I nodded to Captain who stared back at me with eyes the colour of green marbles and then seemed to wink.

"Is he – you know?" I tapped the side of my nose,

"You're kiddin' me, right? I just said. He's a bleedin' cat."

I changed the subject feeling rather foolish.

"Well, he is certainly very fine-looking. Where did you get him?"

I reached out a hand to stroke the cat's head but he leapt down and sauntered off towards the hallway.

"Epping Forest."

"Really?"

"Really. There's a whole bunch of them wot lives out there. A good crew. Salt of the earth. No airs and graces."

I was puzzled.

"But how did you get there? Get him back here? Not exactly on the bus route, is it?"

"I have my means."

I stared at him in blank disbelief.

"What? You don't think I can ride a motorbike?"

"A motorbike?" I don't think I had ever been more taken aback in my life.

"Yeah. You must have noticed the bleedin' garage, as we came in. I've got a Royal Enfield. Don't ask me what model. She's got a few miles on the old clock but still goes like a bomb. I'll take you to see her, if you like."

There was almost nothing I'd have liked more but I was already going to be late getting home and I wasn't sure how I was going to explain myself, already. I shook my head ruefully.

"Well, maybe next time then, eh?"

"Oh, yes, please. I can't wait."

The shapeshifter nodded with obvious satisfaction and began to guide me back towards the front door. As we passed through the kitchen doorway, I suddenly noticed a very old-fashioned phone set mounted on the wall - the type with a dial and a receiver with a curved mouthpiece. I looked up at him in astonishment.

"What now? It's a telephone. Everyone has one these days, don't they?"

"Sorry. Yes, of course. It is connected, though, is it?"

At this, Sherton rolled his eyes. I decided to let it go. I was sure that he would give me his number when he was ready. After all, it wasn't as if I had given him ours.

As we reached the front door he stopped and turned to me.

"Thank you for having me," I said, remembering my manners.

He seemed to search my face for a moment and then clasped my hand between his gloved hands with unusual warmness.

"No. Thank *you* for coming, Jonathon. I mean it. I can't tell you how much this has meant. It must be years since anyone except me has set foot in this place and it's been like a breath of fresh air."

7

By the time I got home, the back of my throat felt raw and my hair was sticking to my forehead. I doubled over on the doorstep and panted. My lungs wheezed in protest so I took a puff on my inhaler. Then, wiping my face with my hanky, I slipped my key into the yale lock and peered around our front door. Mum's jacket hung from the pegs on the coat rack.

"Sorry, I'm late, Mum..." I called, strolling as nonchalantly as I could down the hall. I caught a glimpse of her standing in the front room. Her arms were folded and her face looked unusually grave. I gave her a passing wave and began to head up the stairs but she was already calling me back. I detected a definite stiffness in her tone. It was the voice she kept for those rare occasions when she was severely displeased with me. Surely, this could not be one of them. *I wasn't that late for Pete's sake*. I turned back, bit my lip and sloped into the sitting room.

"Sit down, Jumbo," said Mum in her I'm-not-joking-with-you-now tone. "I'm not angry, Jonathon, but I *am* concerned. *Very* concerned. Where have you been?"

I shuffled my feet and hunched my shoulders. She had called me Jonathon. This was going to be bad.

"Just out and about, you know. I'm sorry - I just lost track of time..."

Mum frowned. An odd look crossed her face. I looked away.

"The fact that you are concealing it from me makes this all sound a lot worse. I just had Mrs Worth around. She tells me that she saw you boarding a bus with a middle-aged man. So, I will ask you again, young man. Where have you been? And you had better tell me the truth."

This time, I felt the sting of blood rushing to my cheeks. I had lied to my mum and been caught in that lie. She was not stupid. I would have to tell the truth. Well, some of it, at least.

"He's just a mate, Mum. Really, he just wanted to - wanted me to see where he lived..."

I have never seen my mum's face turn so white. For a horrible moment, she seemed to sway a little and I thought that she was going to collapse or something. I moved towards her but she held out her hand to stay me. I wanted to hug her – beg her forgiveness, but she had already turned her back and buried her face in her hands. I couldn't hear her crying yet my stomach turned over. Even so, I couldn't quite grasp why she should be so upset by this information. She was about to enlighten me. She turned back to face me, her mouth and eyes taut with a mixture of emotions I could not decipher.

"Jumbo. Did this man – has he, I mean, did he touch you in any way? Because I won't be angry with you, Luv, I promise – I just…"

"No. God. No. Nothing like that. Honestly, Mum. He's just a mate, I told you…"

Mum seemed to sag with relief.

"Jonathon. Listen to me carefully. I realise that you may like this person but you cannot be friends – I know you turn fourteen in a couple of days' time, but a fourteen-year-old boy cannot be friends with a middle-aged man. It is simply not appropriate. Do you understand me?"

I nodded.

"Now, I'm going to regard this as an isolated error of judgment on your part, so I'm not going to ask for this person's details and speak to them myself, even though I would have thought that they should know better themselves…"

"But, Mum…"

"Don't *but Mum* me, young man. I don't want to hear another word about it. I mean it. You are too young to understand - but let me make it clear. If you see this man, or talk to him, or attempt to have any contact with him, for that matter, I will not hesitate to report him to the police. Do you understand me?"

I stared at her in horror. A mental picture of the boys in blue hammering on Sherton Myam's front door danced before my eyes. That seemed like a very bad idea indeed. Too bad to even imagine. Mum, meanwhile, was awaiting my reply.

"Do you understand me?"

I sniffed an affirmative, trying desperately not to cry.

"Good. Now, I have no wish to punish you as such, but I'm going to have to insist that you come straight home from school for the next couple of weeks. Just to put my mind at ease. And I trust you to do as I say. I can do that, can't I?"

I nodded and wiped my cheeks with the back of my hand.

"Now go to your room. Tea will be ready in half an hour".

"Sorry, Mum," I whispered, though I could not look her in the eye as I said it.

Mum glanced away and made no further reply. Bowing her head, she turned her back and then stared silently out through the net curtains. I ran up to my room and threw myself on my bed. That last look stayed with me. Her lips had been quivering and I could tell that it was all she could do to hold it together. I buried my face in my pillow and sobbed. I hated it when I did something wrong. It felt a bit like feeling sick inside, only worse.

Yet, as I lay there and contemplated the idea of never seeing Sherton Myam again, it was something else I began to feel. So, what, if I had only really known him for four weeks? He had become the best friend I'd ever had – the only friend if I was being honest. And Mum of all people, should have realised that but, instead, she had coldheartedly chosen to destroy my life.

I think I came as close to hating her in that moment, as I ever had in my short life. But, even as my head cooled, I could see that I was being unfair. As kids, the chilling shadow of the notorious Moors Murderers hung over us all. We may not have understood why, but the world outside our front doors was far from safe. Even the school regularly drummed the perils of stranger danger into us, so we all knew the drill. Over-friendly adults were immediately suspect particularly those who so much as mentioned the puppy thing. I knew that well enough. Mum was responding as any parent would.

Still, this had been so different. Sherton Myam had not approached me. We had found each other; drawn within each other's orbits by chance or fate, like characters in a film or comic book. Spiderman would have understood.

I wanted so badly to protest, to stand up for my friend and explain that he was no ordinary man, but how could I? I couldn't even begin to imagine how my mum would react. I knew she had an open mind - but a shapeshifting organism with amnesia, a cat, and a dodgy collection of souvenirs was a bit of a tall order for anyone. At best, she might assume that I had lost the plot. Or that I was on drugs, though that seemed a bit unlikely. At worst, she actually might believe me and panic. I'd watched enough sci-fi films to know that adults were notoriously prone to such overreaction. Sherton Myam might not be an alien, like Michael Rennie in The Day the Earth Stood Still, but he wasn't human either. There was no way that it would end well.

And then something occurred to me for the first time. I sat up and rubbed my eyes. Sherton Myam was not an alien *now*, not in the true sense of the word. After all, he seemed to believe that he, if not his race had inhabited the Earth for many centuries. But what if his race had originally arrived here from another planet? Lots of cultures had myths about shapeshifters, I'd looked it up in the school library's encyclopaedia, but all of them were regarded as supernatural. Sherton had offered a perfectly logical explanation for his unique ability and had never once mentioned magical powers. Come to think of it, I'd never met anyone so down to earth. But his unique biology did not fit into any evolutionary theory I'd read about. The shapeshifters must have come from another planet. It all made sense.

I sat up and rubbed my eyes. I longed to see him and ask him what he thought about my theory but, given the way things stood, that would be out of the question. And besides, he probably wouldn't remember anyway. The main thing was that I had a mission now - and that was to keep my friend and his secret safe - and if that meant staying away, then so be it.

Two whole days had passed and I was already missing the company of my friend. What's more, I knew that he would be expecting me and would be wondering why I had not returned. For all I knew, he would just assume that seeing his home had put me off him. If only I could have explained. Still, taking the risk of going to the park was not an option. I knew full well that Mrs Worth would be keeping an eye out to make sure I came straight home from school and would report to his mother should I fail. I'd always looked upon her as a kind of aunt, but now I felt as though she had become the enemy.

It was my birthday the following day. Mum always made a point of ordering a special cake from Percy Ingles for me, even though I never had a party. For years it had been decorated as a pink elephant for her "Jumbo", though by the time I reached eleven, she had decided I was too grown up for that sort of thing and the elephant had been replaced by a train and, the following year, a cheerful looking brachiosaurus. Last birthday, she had presented me with a perfect fondant-covered replica of the Tardis. I'd been so excited that I'd literally yelped in delight as she took it from the box.

That afternoon, when she came home, she called me into the kitchen and presented me with large cake box, tied with a shiny blue ribbon.

"Happy Birthday, Jumbo."
I stared at the box glumly.
"Go on. Open it, then."

Sighing, I pulled off the ribbon and lifted the lid. Inside sat an icing-covered sponge in the shape of a rocket ship, complete with a fiery tale.

"Look," said Mum pointing to the carefully piped icing letters, "it's Apollo 11 and you can even see Neil Armstrong peering out of the porthole there, see.."

It was true. It was probably the coolest cake I'd ever seen but it wouldn't bring my friend back and I hated myself for even thinking it was so great. I mustered enough grace to thank her and then went upstairs to wash my hands for tea.

"But Jumbo," she called after me. "You haven't even opened your presents yet."

Later that evening, when it was clear no amount of cake or even the awesome pocket calculator, she had bought me, (complete with logarithmic, trigonometric and square root functions), was going to cheer me up she sat me down for a "peace talk."

She had not meant to be severe or to destroy my friendship, she claimed, *but I would have to trust her on this. Lads my age simply did not hang out with adult males. Not unless they were related, at any rate. And even then, it should be confined to prescribed activities like football matches and fishing. She knew that it seemed harsh, but I would understand better when I was older.* I could tell that she was hinting about sex stuff because her hands tended to flutter about when she felt embarrassed. Not that I had seen her embarrassed very often. Normally it was the other way around. Indeed, if anything, she tended to be cringingly open about that sort of thing. She'd given me a full and frank talk on the facts of life while I was still in primary school, complete with diagrams and would have no truck with using euphemisms for penises and vaginas. I'm pretty sure I was better informed than most sixth-form biology students before I had even taken the eleven-plus.

In any case, she assured me that I would find a friend more my own age in time, and perhaps there would be a special girl - or boy - one day. And that would be fine. But this was not the way.

I must admit that her words only confused me. I got that she didn't want me to end up dismembered in a shallow grave in Epping Forest but she seemed to be doing a lot of beating around the bush. It certainly didn't make me feel any better and it was all I could do not to slam my bedroom door, afterwards. Whatever she *was* trying to get at, she had it all wrong. Sherton Myam was the only person I wanted as a friend and so what if he was a few centuries older than me? Life was just so unfair.

Nevertheless, I stuck to my word. I continued to go straight home after school and avoided the park completely, though I confess that my eyes lingered over the end of the road that led to the entrance as I passed.

On the fourth afternoon, I was passing through the school gates when a familiar voice made me jump.

"Oy, Mate. I thought you'd fallen off the edge of the world. Where have you been for the last couple of days?"

The shapeshifter was smiling. There was no reproach or disappointment in his voice – just pleasure in seeing me again. I grinned involuntarily then caught myself and looked around in terror.

"Sherton, Mate. Listen - I can't talk to you and I can't see you anymore. I'm sorry, truly I am, but it's my mum. She says that I'm too young to be your friend and she threatened to get the plod onto you if I speak to you again. Look, I've got to go. I'll see you around."

With that, I took off. I didn't even dare look back over my shoulder, but there was no need. The look on the shapeshifter's face remained seared on my retinas all the way home. I felt like such a heel for brushing him off so abruptly but was worried sick that someone might have seen us. After all, for all I knew, Mum could easily have thought to alert the school as to her concerns. She was used to thinking like a solicitor and could be very thorough about such things. I couldn't afford to take the risk of talking to him, not even for a couple of minutes.

I barely closed my eyes all that night. I kept picturing the pain and puzzlement in Sherton's eyes and trying to imagine how I would have felt, had the shoe been on the other foot. I thought about writing a letter of apology, explaining myself, but although I'd been to the shapeshifter's house, I could not for the life of me recall seeing the house number. And any attempt to hand-deliver anything right now was completely out of the question.

The next morning, I tried my best to hide my yawns and grumpiness but made rather a poor job of it. I mumbled incoherently into my cornflakes in response to Mum's questions about what the day held for me and shied away from the touch of her hand on my shoulders. She stared at the dark circles under my eyes and knitted her brows.

"I'm so sorry, Jumbo. I hate to see you like this, but growing up can be very difficult sometimes."

I focused on my cornflakes and ignored her. I didn't care. She was responsible for everything that was wrong in my life and I would never forgive her. *Never.*

8

Four long weeks passed. I hadn't expected being fourteen to feel so very different from thirteen, but that was before losing Sherton and the falling out with Mum. Now, however, I struggled to concentrate in class and couldn't be asked to raise my hand to answer a question, let alone pose the kind of query that would normally have had my classmates rolling their eyes. My homework grades plummeted and Mr Would-you-believe-it-Hardy observed that *a new off-handedness seemed to have seeped into my personality, replacing my perennial passion for learning.*

My enthusiasm for Chess Club flagged as had my patient coaching of those less gifted. I played purely to crush my opponents, no matter how inexperienced, and crush my opponents I did. Not that it made me feel any better.

The climate at home, though less combative, had remained distinctly chilly. I tried my hardest but found it hard to feign a forgiveness I could not feel. Then, one evening I overheard my Mum chatting to Mrs Worth on the doorstep. I froze and listened intently. But, like many eavesdroppers, I soon wished that I had not.

She only hoped my anger would pass soon. Until then, she would just have to ride it out. I didn't have to like her. She was my mother, not my friend. She got it. But she would have chosen severe toothache over the torture of this polite yet devastating estrangement.

Her words strung as sharply as the nettles in the neglected corner of our little garden yet even that was not enough to break through the wall of resentment, I had built around me. Trapped there behind it, I could neither imagine a way out nor see how anything could change. Puzzles had always been my thing, yet this one had defeated me.

Nevertheless, a solution was on its way –and that solution, when it did arrive, took me completely by surprise.

It was a Friday afternoon, much like any other except that you could practically hear a silent cheer as the end-of-day bell sounded. The weather had been gorgeous all week and anyone with any sense would be heading for the coast or the nearest swimming pool. *Lucky them,* I thought. All I had to look forward to was another lonely weekend trying to keep out of Mum's way.

I was slouching out through the school gates when I heard a piercing whistle. I looked up, though it could not be meant for me. A group of my classmates were milling around the pavement outside of the wrought iron fence like words in search of a sentence. The whistle came again.

Directly ahead, a lanky teenaged lad with slicked back hair, dark glasses and an unzipped parka sat straddling a Vespa scooter, one foot on the kerb. I stared at him in awe. This guy oozed coolness despite the heat of the afternoon.

"Oy, Cooper! You comin', or wot?"

I looked around. The other kids were gawping at me, their eyes shining with the admiration of the well-impressed. *Could he really mean me?*

"Sherton..." I breathed. Then, needing no explanation, I heaved my satchel onto my shoulders, ran forward and slung my leg over the seat behind my mate. My driver revved the throttle noisily.

"Be seein' you, losers," he yelled after us as we sped away leaving a sea of
astonished faces in our wake.

Ten minutes later we screeched to a stop at the park. I half fell off the scooter, panting and feeling about in my pocket for my inhaler.

"I can't believe it's you. This is amazing...."

I wheezed and grinned so wide I thought my face would break in half. The lanky scooter driver shrugged.

"No seriously, Sherton. I mean it. I thought you couldn't change again, not without, you know, losing your memories..."

The lanky kid said nothing. He just surveyed me with an expression so deadpan that it made the skin on the back of my neck begin to prickle. I sucked hard on my inhaler and stared at the unfamiliar face. It *was* my friend and it *was not*. The sharp, keen youthful face looked nothing like the bland mug of the middle-aged man in the dishevelled raincoat, I had known, yet somehow, there he was. Something unmistakably Sherton lurked in the unsettling regularity of those features and in the flatness of the grey eyes, didn't it? Or could it just be my imagination? He spoke at last.

"I don't know what you mean, Dude. I've never seen you before..."

Whatever the look was that passed over my face, I wished I'd been able to see it myself. It certainly amused my abductor who doubled over in a spasm of laughter and waved his hands in amused apology.

"Nah, just kiddin' you. Listen. Truth is, I wasn't sure I could do this – this shifting thing again. In fact, just between you and me, I was even beginning to wonder whether it was just a story I had made up. Sometimes I told myself that I should do it just to prove to myself that it was real, but I was so fearful of losing what little memory I had that I just bottled out when it came to it.

But turns out, I had it all wrong. Straight up. It knocked the stuffing plain out of me when you told me what your mother had said, I won't deny it. But you know what? She was right. And I should have thought of it myself. I guess I still have trouble getting my head around the whole being a normal human being thing, but I got it, truly I did. But we had become mates, right, no matter what age I appeared. And losing your friendship mattered to me. More than I wanted to admit, at first. The idea of shifting into another form struck me as a massive risk, but I reckoned I had nothing to lose. If I forgot everything, at least I'd forget how much I missed you and it turns out, my theory about the brain and memories was all wrong. I still can't remember anything from before, but there has been no further memory loss so whatever caused it to happen originally – well, I guess there must be another explanation and perhaps I'll never know. And, pardon my French, but I don't much bleedin' care right now. We've got the old team back. How cool is that?"

Suddenly I seemed to be laughing and crying all at the same time. I went to hug him then pulled back and punched him in the upper arm instead. The shapeshifter grinned in delight, revealing a dazzling set of perfect teeth. I punched him again. *He certainly was one cool dude. And the scooter, where had he got the scooter? It was brilliant.*

"Let's just say I sold a few things," he replied with a wink and tap to the side of his nose.

"Tell me you didn't sell the Enfield, Sherton."

"Relax. Nothing important – I promise. Oh, and none of your Sherton, if you don't mind - you're going to have to get used to calling me by a new name."

The idea that Mum would be thrilled by her son taking up with a would-be Mod was always going to be a bit of a long shot. But a sixteen-year-old youth with attitude had to be more welcome than a middle-aged man with questionable intentions.

"He's just moved into the area, Mum. He doesn't know anyone, but we both love maths and he's a real ace at chess. I may be a couple of years below him but I'm the only one who can give him a proper game…"

"Hmm, well, he's not in a gang, is he?"

The film Quadrophenia had recently been released and The Mods and their run-ins with The Rockers had become a hot topic in the media. Mum said she did not need any celluloid portrayal of antisocial behaviour to remind her of the history as she recalled it well enough from the time. Not that it had been her scene, of course.

"No mum. He's not in a gang. Quite the opposite. He's a loner, just like me. He just happens to be super cool."

And, once she had seen him, she had been obliged to admit as much herself. She may have been on the wrong side of thirty, but she had been young once. And then, Shalto Meyers just seemed to exude this natural charm. I could have sworn she'd blushed when he flashed that smile of his at her.

"Well, I'm not overly happy about you tearing around on a scooter but I guess it's no worse than a pushbike, really, and it's all the rage on The Continent – but make sure you wear a helmet. It's good to see a smile back on your face, Jumbo. But I warn you, young man - if I see your grades drop by one iota…"

"Won't happen. He's a whizz at maths. I mean it. Think about it. With Shalto as a mentor, it can only help my chances of getting into a top university."

I wasn't blagging. What my new mate Shalto did not understand about my maths was probably not worth knowing. By the end of term, he had become a regular and welcome visitor to our house. We would spend our evenings poring over my maths homework before playing chess and listening to music. Needless to say, my grades shot back up. Everything was good again. Better than good. At school, I suddenly acquired something that I had never enjoyed before. Recognition and respect. The lads in my form would greet me with a nod in the corridors and I was no longer the last to be picked for soccer teams in PE. Best of all, nobody ever referred to me as Spastic again – at least, not within earshot. It was like a small miracle.

I even got myself a paper round so that I could afford to go to the cinema or for a burger at the local Wimpy Bar. As it happens, Shalto always offered to sub me – there was, he reminded me, plenty more stuff he could sell back in his house. But I guess that I took after Mum. I prized my independence and preferred to pay my way. Not that Shalto was a fan of hamburgers, of course, subsisting as he did on neat vodka. But he seemed to derive a perverse enjoyment from watching me scoff one down with a plate of chips whilst he sipped on a coke. Strange, but you get used to anything, after a while.

Besides, he said that he wanted to do all the normal things that mates our age would do.

If Mum continued to foster any reservations about the age difference between us, they seemed to melt away as our relationship finally thawed. *She knew that she had to let me grow up,* she told me. *All she wanted was to be around to watch it happen. So, as long as I was happy, then so was she.*

9

The long days of that first magical summer slipped through our fingers like glittering beach sand. Shalto's scooter afforded us a freedom I could scarcely have imagined and the world became our playground. When we weren't mooching around the local record shop, we would head to The West End's Carnaby Street and from there to Forbidden Planet, the fantastic new Comic Book store in Denmark Street. Shalto took to my favourite superheroes like Aquaman to the ocean. And we had money to spend. He soon developed a preference for DC comics, however, while I remained loyal to Marvel, though we both rooted for The Incredible Hulk. We could pass hours arguing about their respective merits and pitting them against each other in imaginary battles. Superman always won, of course. But then no one in The Marvel universe was armed with Kryptonite. I wasn't sure what Mum made of it, comics did not exactly fit her idea of good literature, but I think she was just happy to see me getting out and about.

Now that I was older, she worked most of the week but always took one day off so that we could, at least, spend some time together. Initially, she would plan a day to ourselves at the seaside or for one of our museum trips, but as the weeks passed, she began to include Shalto in the invitation. He made her laugh and that had to be a good thing. And she never once gave him the awful customary third-degree about his circumstances, so many adults seem to feel necessary when meeting young people.

I was sorry when the holidays ended but couldn't complain. Things were going pretty well for me and I returned to school a different kid altogether. Shalto had changed too. He seemed to have perked up no end and his newfound confidence seemed infectious. It had certainly rubbed off onto me. I no longer doubted my right to take up space and even managed to strike up more than a few spontaneous conversations in the comic store. In fact, it wasn't long before I found myself on nodding terms with more than one of the regulars there.

And confidence, I discovered, was like a flower. If someone waters it then it thrives and begins to grow. Then, when it blooms other people notice and will take the trouble to water it too. Once I stopped feeling torn between feeling invisible and wanting to remain unnoticed, I gave up trying to conceal my skills with a football and just enjoyed the game. I even became a bit of a show-off which earned me a new nickname.

It happened one Thursday afternoon in double games in the closing minutes of a game of seven-a-side. I had noticed Mr Grainger, our sports teacher, standing watching me as I played and had not thought much of it. The match had been pretty close and was drawn. I was playing on the wing and had made some pretty good tackles but the next time the ball came my way, I realised that I had a shot at the goal. I wasn't sure what got into me but instead of taking a clean shot, I hooked the ball up onto my chest and then bounced it upwards, heading it rocket-like through the outstretched arms of the goalie. A moment later the ref blew the whistle. My teammates cheered and rushed over to clap me on the back.

"Here, you - Bobby Moore," called Mr Grainger as we trouped off the field whooping and pumping fists, "there's a place for you in the first eleven if you want it."

I looked around, but he could only mean me. I still resembled the great player and always would. I shook my head in disbelief. It was a moment of pure gold and one I would never forget. Not that I accepted. Not likely. I much preferred to spend my Saturday morning hanging out at the local milk bar with my best mate. But it was cool to be asked and after that, the nickname was bound to stick. I didn't complain. Anything was better than "Spastic".

It was all good. I even seemed to be getting the hang of the growing up thing However, like all lads in my middle teens, the changes in my body and mind were sometimes as baffling as they were rapid. Matters finally came to a head, one wet Saturday afternoon when the rain had confined us indoors. We were not in the mood for chess and had elected simply to listen to music. I had been lying on the rug, while Shalto lounged across my bed with his feet resting up against my Blondie poster. I can't say I was thrilled about his lack of deference for the divine Debbie Harry but knew that I would sound like an old woman if I nagged him about it.

In any case, my mind was on other things right at that moment. For the past half an hour or so, I had been grappling with how to broach a subject that had been troubling me for a while. I suspected that Shalto was probably not the best person to answer my questions, yet I had no one else to ask. And being painfully shy was not helping. I was just rehearsing in my mind how best to phrase my enquiry when the words beat me to it and somehow just slipped out.

"Here, Shalto. Does your, you know, thingy work?"

"Thingy?"

I felt myself flush. Mum might not have flinched at using the correct anatomical terms for my genitals but, me, I was all for euphemisms. On the other hand, if I'd wanted to avoid sounding immature, I had just failed miserably.

"Your dick, mate. Your pecker. You know. I'm sorry – these days I just can't seem to think of anything else. I just wondered - that's all..."

Shalto looked a bit taken aback. Swinging his legs back over the side of the bed he sat up and rubbed his head. For once, he seemed lost for words. He stared at me with a look I couldn't read and then puckered his lips as though he had just eaten something rather unpleasant. I winced, beginning to wish that I'd never raised the subject. We never talked about these things. Come to that, we never even talked about girls, which I *knew* was a bit unusual since the lads at school seemed to talk of little else.

Not that I had any wish to be included. I'd noticed that the boastful sniggering in the gym changing rooms had ramped up recently and the ringleaders had taken to bestowing the title of "school bike" on any unsuspecting girl, they managed to talk into so much as snogging them behind the gym. Most of it seemed boastful bravado as far as I could tell but then, what did I know? I couldn't even muster the courage to ask to borrow a pencil sharpener from Fiona Salmon, the girl I'd sat next to in maths for the last two years, let alone attempt any flirtation.

I looked over at Shalto, whose expression had turned unexpectedly grave. It occurred to me that I should just drop the subject but, before I could, he finally spoke. His tone was clipped and oddly formal.

"We don't replicate. At least, not as far as I am aware..."

"No shit? How do you know? I mean - if you can't remember anything about your kind..."

"Well, when people get amnesia, they don't forget how to be human, do they? They don't forget to read, or piss, do they? Really, Jonno? We've been through this before."

"Okay, I get it."

I tried to ignore the irritation in Shalto's reply and pressed on. I knew that I'd overstepped some kind of mark but had committed myself now. And besides, I really did want to know.

"So, you don't, you know, get a hard-on?"

He stared at me with narrowed eyes but remained tight-lipped.

"What, never? Really. Cos' I gotta tell you, I seem to wake up with a stiffy most morning, these days and sometimes, even at school…"

I knew, full well, that I'd be tapping into the shapeshifter's competitiveness now. Shalto had many generous qualities, but he did not like to be bested – at anything.

"Well, I could, I expect. That is, I think I could if I wanted. I might have to give it a try…"

I snorted, not at all sure that we were on the same page here. He glared at me. I cleared my throat and chose my words carefully.

"Would it feel good? I mean if – well, you know?"

"I don't see why not. I'll let you know. Now, would you mind if we change the record?"

I let it go but knew better than to hold my breath regarding any updates on the subject.

My smugness was short-lived. After he had left, I thought about what had passed between us. I wondered what Mum would have said about it and was pretty certain that she would have described my behaviour as unnecessarily insensitive, a word she seemed pretty fond of. *Whilst it might be okay to have questions,* she would have said, *Shalto was my friend and you don't put your friends on the spot.* I couldn't argue with that. There and then I made a solemn resolve to myself to respect the shapeshifter's privacy. No matter how strong my curiosity.

The topic of sex may have been off the agenda with my best friend but that in no way diminished the extent of my preoccupation with it. My head, which had always been so full of questions about the world, now hummed with enquiries of a more salacious variety.

The following week, I finally turned to Mum for illumination.

"Mum?"

"Yes, Jumbo?"

"What's a swinger?"

"I beg your pardon?"

My questions seemed to catch Mum off-balance for once.

"A swinger? And how can you swap your wife?"

"You've been reading The News of The World again, haven't you? You know what I think about that Jumbo?"

She had me there. I had discovered the weekend board sheet on the first weekend of my paper round, and it had not been long before I had come to regard it as the fount of all wisdom regarding sexual behaviour. Exposing the dark underbelly of suburban life, it would have been an education in itself, had it not used so many words whose meaning baffled me.

"Yes, I know. But – I'll be an adult soon. I need to understand these things."

Mum sighed. She reached out a hand and ruffled my hair.

"Well, not just yet, Luv, eh? But, then again, perhaps you're right. I can't protect you from life and it's probably better that you hear these things from me rather than from some gutter rag that tries to pass itself off as journalism…"

"So…?"

"Swingers are partners who enjoy variety in their sex life and achieve this through exchanging partners with like-minded couples. There's no harm in it so long as both partners are happy to do it. But it tends to provoke a lot of moral outrage in our rather bourgeoise and hypercritical society."

"But why would you want to - if you love your wife or husband?"

"Sex and love are by no means always the same thing, Jumbo, though it's great when they are. I guess people may have all sorts of reasons. Sometimes, they just get bored and are looking for a bit of excitement in their lives. It's perfectly natural when you think about it and we shouldn't rush to judge others as long as they are not harming anyone else. I'm not sure that it ultimately brings much happiness though. The fall-out can cause too many complications and hurt feelings."

She looked at me with a wistful smile.

"Now, if you insist on getting your sex education from literature, can I suggest you try Lady Chatterly's Lover or even Tom Jones by Henry Fielding? You'll find them both on the bookshelf in the sitting room. And you can ask me anything – any time. I'm being serious.

I knew that she meant what she said, but I had long ago snuck a peep into DH Lawrence's most infamous novel and, if I was sure of one thing, it was there was nothing in there that I was about to discuss with my mother.

Shalto's evident lack of testosterone was by no means the only physical difference between us. I, like most boys my age, would practically eat my weight in junk food every week. Yet, try as she might, she found it next to impossible to tempt my unusual friend with the offer of sandwiches, crisps, ice cream or any of the other treats that are generally guaranteed to make an adolescent lad salivate. Mum, however, was not one to give up so easily. We may not have had many visitors to the house but, when we did, she went out of her way to offer them - "good old-fashioned hospitality." *It was a matter of pride,* she said and the offers kept coming.

Realising that it threatened to become an issue, Shalto was obliged to resort to subterfuge and good old charm to disguise his lack of appetite for food. One such exchange took place one Saturday afternoon when Mum came up to my room with the offer of ice-cream sundaes with hot fudge sauce.

"No thank you Mrs C," smiled Shalto shaking his head. "Pardon my French, but some of us have to watch what we bleedin' eat. I didn't get this svelte-like form by stuffing down the Mars bars. I'm not like Jumbo here, who can run it off on the football field. A moment on the lips – a lifetime on the hips, as they say. Am I right?" Mum had laughed. She could hardly help herself. Yet, later she confided in me that she did sometimes worry about him. He did seem awfully skinny and hardly ever mentioned any family or anything about his home life. She wondered whether he might just need a bit of old-fashioned mothering. I told her that it was probably just his way of trying to appear cool. But my tactic seemed to backfire because after that she upped her game.

In the following weeks, she mounted a campaign of routinely inviting him to stay on for supper or lunch, or even to come around first thing Saturday morning for a good fry-up breakfast – our regular weekend treat. I found myself obliged to roll my eyes in despair and shove Shalto out of the door before he would have to find an answer.

It was rapidly becoming clear that we would have to come up with something to throw her off the scent.

"I know my mum," I said, "she's not going to be happy until she has you at that dining table with a napkin tied around your neck…"
Shalto had laughed.

"She's all right, your mum, though. I reckon she's a bit of fit bird under that scraped-back hair and those square clothes. I bet she was something else when she was a few years younger."
I frowned. I knew he didn't mean anything pervy by it, it wasn't in him. But she *was* my mum. And the funny thing was, he was right. I knew from my early "princess" memories that she had indeed been stunning. And that wasn't just me being biased. She had the looks that would turn people's heads. Only, *I* had forgotten and these days, *she* seemed determined to conceal it.

"Well, she was. As it happens. But that's not going to help us, any. We have to find a plausible explanation for why you are so finicky. We can't afford for her to become suspicious about you – in any way."

In the end, Shalto came up with the perfect excuse. His family were all vegans and had brought him up to be one, too. This was pretty out there in the nineteen seventies, even in London – or the East End of it, at least, and required explanation. Mum had listened with one eyebrow arched as Shalto explained the strict dietary restrictions and then regaled her with an earnest and lengthy sermon on the importance of maintaining the body as a temple and respecting the sanctity of our four-legged friends' lives. Mum, being Mum, absorbed it all without protest or argument. *Live and let live*, was her motto which, as I understood it, meant that it wasn't her place to question other people's values or life choices.

After that, she finally gave up on the invitation to eat with us even if I did have to dissuade her from visiting the library to look out a vegan cookery book.

Be that as it may, we had not completely made it out of the woods. A further complication arising from the shapeshifter's peculiar nutritional needs raised its head again, some weeks later, shortly before Christmas. And this time I would have a job sweet-talking Mum around.

"Jonathon. What is this?"

I looked up from my book. I did not need to see her face to know she was not happy.

"What is what, Mum?"

"This. I was upstairs in your room gathering up stuff for the weekly wash and found it under a pile of clothes. And don't even think about getting smart with me. I have eyes. I can see that it's an empty vodka miniature. What I want to know is, what it is doing in your room?"

I started at the innocuous-looking little bottle and swallowed hard. I would have to think quickly. The truth was, Shalto sometimes got peckish during his visits. He tended to get very grumpy when his energy levels dropped so often brought along a small volume of alcohol to keep him going. Generally, he was extremely careful about how he disposed of the evidence, but on this occasion, the empty bottle must have fallen out of his pocket and rolled out of view, without either of us noticing.

"I just wanted to try it, Mum. Just the once. I won't do it again. Cross my heart."

"That's all very well, young man, but you couldn't have bought it yourself. You might be tall but no one is going to take you for eighteen. Was it Shalto?"

"He didn't buy it for me, Mum. And that's the truth." At least I could look her in the eye. He'd bought it for himself.

"Okay. Well then, who?"

I looked down at my feet and pressed my lips together. Mum crossed her arms and looked at me for a minute, drumming her fingers on her elbow.

"Well, somebody bought it. And much as I respect your loyalty to the culprit, you're grounded for a week. And I promise you this, even if he is innocent in this, if I find anything like this again, I will ban you from seeing any more of Shalto. I mean it. He may not mean any harm but the age difference between you is quite significant - particularly, at this age. I can't afford to have him become a bad influence…"

"He's not, Mum. Please. I promise. He's my only real friend." I pleaded, feeling my face grow hot. I was getting upset now and Mum could see it. Her face crumpled.

"If only your father was still around," she sighed and then did something she never did – she burst into tears.

I experienced a surge of panic in my chest. I couldn't bear to see her so upset. Indeed, she could not have dreamt up a more excruciating punishment for me had she tied each of my limbs to four bolting horses. I leapt up and folded my arms around her, wondering when she had suddenly grown so small. Or perhaps it was just that I had grown so much taller. But I had grown up in other ways in the last couple of years too. As a small boy, I had hardly given a thought to how difficult it had been for her after Dad left. I had stopped thinking about him long ago and if I thought anything, it was that she had too. She rarely mentioned him by name and I'd hadn't heard her talking out loud to him in ages. She never showed any emotions about him so I simply assumed that she didn't have any. It was hard to believe that I could have been so self-absorbed. I squeezed her even more tightly.

"I'm sorry, Jumbo, but I did love him so much, you know," she sniffed into my shoulder. "And I just miss him terribly at times like this."

"I know, Mum, I know," I said stroking her hair. But I didn't. Not really. Still, for some months after, I tried my best to be more thoughtful. Yet it would be a good long time until Mum spoke of her feelings for Dad again. It was as though a window had opened and closed again just as quickly.

As for Shalto, Mum may have acted a little more cooly towards him for a couple of weeks, but it could not be long before he won her over with his cheeky charm and he was certainly more careful with his empties.

It wasn't all plain sailing, however. Much as I wanted to see my friend as just another perfectly ordinary kid, scientific curiosity finally got the better of me. That Christmas, Mum bought me a microscope. It came as a complete surprise when I opened it on Christmas morning and the gift had been an instant hit. Although my primary passion was for mathematics and physics, my fascination with how things worked nevertheless extended to the natural world.

I set to work gathering all sorts of stuff from around the house and garden and was busy making up slides even as Mum pulled the turkey out of the oven.

"Not now, Jumbo," she called over her shoulder. "Come and finish laying the table. There'll be plenty of time for that after lunch." I sucked my teeth and dragged myself over to the kitchen drawer to find the napkins. She may have been right but I could hardly wait for Christmas to be over. I was itching to show off my new piece of scientific equipment to Shalto.

"Well, I'm glad you like your present, Jumbo," murmured Mum as I begged to be excused from the table as soon as I had scraped up the last trace of Christmas pud and brandy sauce from my dish, "but perhaps, next year, we'll save the gifts until *after* lunch."

The next day was Boxing Day and Mum had invited Mrs Worth around for lunch. I'm sure she would have invited Shalto around too, had I asked her but she probably assumed he was enjoying a family Christmas of his own and, besides, Christmas is all about food and he didn't eat, so there didn't seem any real point.

Thankfully, I had more or less forgiven Mrs Worth for her betrayal back in June, though she remained pretty low on the list of my favourite people. She fell asleep in the armchair quite soon after lunch in any case, so Mum shook her head and allowed me back to my slides. It would have been a very long day without them.

Shalto's reaction, when I finally got him up in my room, did not exactly fizz with the enthusiasm I'd anticipated. *So, I had a microscope. Not exactly cutting-edge technology, was it?*
I pouted, trying hard to control the wobble in my lower lip. I should have known that this was nothing new to my friend, who if he was to be believed, had in his possession a set of lenses that had belonged to Isaac Newton himself. But I wasn't giving up that easily.

"But we could compare our blood. Wouldn't that be neat? Look I'll go first," and rummaging around in my pencil box for a pin, I pricked my finger and smeared a drop onto one of the glass slides. He watched in silence as I placed one of the little glass squares that came with the kit over it and then positioned it beneath the microscope lens. I pushed the microscope towards him

"Go on," I said encouragingly.

Shalto crouched over and peered through the eyepiece. He sat back and pushed the contraption over to me with a small grunt. He seemed to be weighing something in his mind.

"Well?"

"Well, what? It's just human blood, isn't? A little dull but a neat enough colour, I suppose."

"But we need to compare it to yours…"

"I'm not sure that would be such a good idea…"

"Why not? I know all about the blood thing - you told me, remember? And it's not as though I haven't already seen it before. But it would be so cool to see it again – magnified. C'mon, Shalto – be a sport. Just one teeny tiny drop."
Shalto looked at me and shook his head.

"I'm not sure it's allowed…"

"Allowed? By whom? Who is going to know except for you and me? Besides, I know you want me to see it, really…"
This time, Shalto rolled his eyes.

"Oh, all right then. But if I get struck off the shapeshifter's register or whatever, it'll be on your head."

So saying, he made a deft movement and pierced the pad of his thumb with the pin. A tiny of speck of blood oozed out. He dabbed it onto a clean slide and I quickly laid a fresh square of glass over it and then exchanged it with the other sample. This time, I took the first turn. I hunkered down over the eyepiece and then snapped back up straight.

"Holy Moly – it's like a bunch of tiny organisms and they're moving…"

"I told you…"

"I know but I – I never, well, I don't know what I thought…" I bent my head and looked again.

"I know this sounds crazy, but they don't look happy - almost as though they are trying to get free or something…"

"They aren't - happy I mean, and they *are* trying to get back - so if you don't mind."

I stared at Shalto in frustration.

"No need to get your knickers in a twist, mate. It's just one measly drop of blood. I just want to see what makes you tick…"

I stopped. Shalto's face was rigid with tension. I couldn't quite understand why but was about to find out.

"I'm not kidding and I AM NOT going to explain myself to some poxy little kid. The blood needs to be back with me and I'm not going to wait a second longer."

He'd spoken calmly enough but there was no mistaking the menace in the tone. The hairs that stood to attention on my neck were attesting to that. For a moment, I hardly recognised my friend at all. I shrank back. Mumbling an apology, I released the microscope's clips and passed the slide back, taking care to avoid the daggers in his eyes.

The shapeshifter shuddered with relief. Peeling back the glass cover he raised the slide and offered it to the tiny puncture wound in the pad of his thumb. I tried not to watch but could not drag my eyes away. The tiny smear of blood on the slide pulled itself back into a droplet so smartly that you could almost hear it pop. Next, it began to make its way towards the outstretched thumb, crawling across the surface of the slide like a legless flea. My mind instantly flashed back to the day I had found the finger and the way the blood had behaved then. It seemed so long ago now that I had almost forgotten how bizarre it had all been. The next moment, the blood simply vanished back into his flesh.

I stole a glance at Shalto's face. The wry and very human smile, I knew so well, was returning

"Sorry for getting a bit heavy, mate," said Shalto sheepishly. "It's not that I don't trust you. You know I *do*. It's just that, well, I get a bit anxious when some of us get separated. You understand, right?"

I shrugged and bit my lip and then looked away. I didn't understand and suspected I never could. But I had received the message loud and clear. And it was a message I must never forget - Shalto was my friend, not some science project or object of curiosity.

Next to Mum, this was the most important relationship I had ever had in my life. I just thanked my lucky stars that I had not blown it.

"I'm truly sorry, Shalto." I said hanging my head. "I just got a bit carried away. I think this is what Mum means when she says I can be a bit insensitive. I promise it'll never happen again."

Shalto reached out and mussed up my hair, exactly as my mum would when she was trying to make me feel better.

"You're okay, kid. Tell you what. Next time you come to my place, I'll show you a real microscope and we can lean on Captain for one of his fleas."

10

"What are you getting me for my birthday, then?"
I was kicking at some turf next to *our* bench in the park. Call it nostalgia, but Shalto and I still enjoyed hanging out there once the evenings began to grow longer. Just under a year had passed since the shapeshifter had revved back into my life. He wore his hair longer now but otherwise seemed unchanged. He shrugged.

"I don't really do birthdays, mate. I don't have one. All a bit of fuss about nothing. It's just a date, isn't it?"

"You can't say that."

"I think I just did…"

"But I'll be fifteen on Sunday. It's a bit deal, man. Mum says so. She always gets so excited about my birthday. Makes a real fuss of me. She says I'm almost a proper young man, now."

"Is that bleedin' right? Well, I can't be arguing with Mrs C, now, can I?"

I couldn't help chuckling. I'd noticed that he had developed a bit of a soft spot for my mum. I suddenly found myself wondering if he had ever had one of his own, a mother, that is. He'd confided that shapeshifters didn't reproduce, but surely, he must still have had someone to look after him once. Then again, he might not remember. There was still so much about that him lay hidden behind the curtain of his "amnesia". I opened my mouth to ask a question and then snapped it closed again. Perhaps this was one of those occasions when it would be a bit insensitive to ask.

I sighed to myself. There was still so much about my strange friend that I longed to know yet, Shalto or Sherton, he remained the same wary animal. And if I'd learned one thing about this particularly exotic species, it was that you had to wait for him to come to you and the slightest ill-timed or move or clumsy enquiry was enough to spook him.

"Well, what do you want?"

"Come again?"

"What do you want for your birthday? If you could have anything. What would you want?"

"If I could truly have anything? Anything at all?"
Shalto raised his eyes to the heavens.

"Yes, absolutely anything at all. What would you wish for? Knock yourself out."

"Well, if it ain't the birthday boy himself. You ready for your birthday adventure?"

Shalto pulled up outside our house to find me ready and waiting on the pavement.

"Shhh - I told Mum we were going up the Camden Markets to buy some gear with my birthday money. She won't expect us back until teatime."

"And knowing Mrs C, she won't expect us back emptyhanded either, so look, I got you this. Put it in your rucksack and tell her you bought it, will you?"

I nodded and took the bag that Shalto handed me, checking over my shoulder to ensure no one was watching. I peeked inside the bag and grinned. A David Bowie T-shirt bearing the image from the cover of the Ziggy Stardust and The Spiders from Mars album. My favourite. I couldn't have chosen better myself. Shoving the bag into my backpack, I straddled the moped behind Shalto.

"Oh, and you might as well put this on now." Shalto handed me a motorbike helmet. I placed it on my head and fastened the strap under my chin with shaking fingers.

"Thanks, mate. That's great." I grinned. "So, um, where are we going, again? And what is this other big surprise? Surely you can tell me now."

Shalto revved the engine and pushed off from the kerb with a gleeful whoop.

"Well, let's just say that - that is for me to know and you to find out. Now hold on."

Five minutes later we turned off along Wanstead Flats and headed towards the decrepit old mansion Shalto still called home. We screeched to a halt outside the great iron gates and he nodded in the direction of the driveway. Parked outside the garage stood a motorbike, its polished stainless-steel frame gleaming in the sunshine. The Royal Enfield. I knew it at once. My eyes lingered over the leather seat and shining wheel spokes. I let out a low whistle. It was even more beautiful than I had imagined. And I was going for a ride on it.

"Oh, wow, Shalto. Blinkin' great birthday present. I'll never forget this – ever."

"You're welcome – but don't you dare breathe a word of this to your mum, right? Ever. One hint that I had her precious Jumbo on the back of this and she'd never forgive me. Capiche?"

I nodded, almost tumbling head-first off the scooter in my hurry to dismount. I pushed open one of the gates and Shalto parked the Vespa. Then, dismounting he loped over to the Enfield and slung a long leg over the black leather saddle. I seated myself behind him and gripped him around his waist.

"Hold on tight, now. And remember to lean with me into the bends."

He gave the starter lever a couple of sharp kicks and the motor growled into life, drowning out the drum of my heartbeat in my ears.

"So, where are we going?" I shouted as we pulled away, but my voice was lost beneath the roar of the accelerator and the crunch of gravel beneath our tyres.

Thirty thrilling minutes later, we screeched off the road and onto a track that led into one of the little gravel carparks that line the road through Epping Forest. Shalto killed the engine and kicked out the parking strut. I half-slumped down from the seat, my legs quivering beneath me. It had been by far the most adrenaline-pumped half-hour of my life. I unfastened my helmet and drew in a long breath. It felt like the first I had taken since we had left Capel Road. I watched as Shalto secured the bike with a chain and then removed his helmet too. He smoothed the windblown wisps of his hair and looked around. I don't know what I was expecting him to say, but he remained silent. I shook my head to convey my wonder at the experience and exclaimed my thanks, but still he said nothing. I gazed about in bemusement. There had been very little traffic on the highway and here beneath the lush canopy of the forest, the air seemed thick and strangely still, save for the twittering of a few birds. I noticed that my heart had started to race again.

"Well, what now?"

"A bit of a hike, I reckon. It *is* the great outdoors and all. This way."

And without further explanation, he headed off down a footpath that disappeared into the heart of the woods. I trudged after him, my blood still throbbing uneasily through my veins, wishing that he would talk to me. But he didn't. What he did do, was pull out a half bottle of vodka from his parka pocket and tip it to his lips. I looked up at the trees as they closed over our heads and felt a knot form in my belly. I wondered why fear and excitement had to feel so similar sometimes. I wanted the knot to be plain old anticipation yet, in all the months I'd known the shapeshifter, I had never felt quite so ill at ease. Not even the first time I'd stepped inside his house. Just ahead of me, Shalto was already draining the last dregs from the bottle as he walked. I bent over to catch my breath and realised that my mouth had gone dry. Shalto turned around. He must have realised that I was no longer at his heels.

"Come on, keep up, you big fairy. Nearly there. Just need to get well away from the beaten track, as it were."

His words did little to allay my uneasiness. My mum had told me that there were more bodies buried in Epping Forest than you could properly poke a stick at and, that morning, I swear I could hear them all whispering to me. It was like seeing faces in the wallpaper at night when I was a little kid. The more I stared, the clearer the features had become. I shook my head and struggled to get my imagination under control. This was Shalto – my best friend. And this was somehow part of my birthday treat. All part of the fun. He'd bought me a David Bowie T-shirt, for God's sake. How bad could it be?

That last thought seemed to do the trick and I could feel my breathing lengthening. I looked around. We had arrived at a particularly dense part of the forest where the undergrowth lay thick and undisturbed by human feet. Shalto stopped in his tracks and held up his hand. I halted too and for a moment the birds stopped their twitter. I had never heard a silence so deep and could easily have believed that we were the only two beings left on Earth instead of a mere thirty miles from the centre of the world's busiest metropolis.

I went to speak but Shalto pressed a finger to his lips in warning. He tilted his head to one side, his face taut with concentration. Then forming his lips into a tight pout, he emitted a low, thin whistle. The whistle echoed strangely through the forest. A deep silence fell once more. I looked around. Suddenly a rustling sounded beneath the ferns quite close to us making me jump. The rustling ceased for a few seconds then started up again and a small tabby cat emerged just in front of me. I gawped at it as though I had never seen a cat before. With its ragged ears and flea-bitten coat, it was, beyond doubt, a feral cat, but I could not for the life of me work out how Shalto had known where to find it or why it had answered his summons.

I watched, half mesmerised, as the cat padded towards Shalto with a trill of greeting that suggested utter confidence. Then, all at once, the cat must have caught my scent. It faltered and sniffed the air nervously. Shalto dropped to one knee.

"There now, my old friend, don't be shy. He's with me. There's nothing to be scared of."

The cat sidled up to Shalto and rubbed its head against his shin. Shalto petted it, talking to it in a low voice but then reaching into his pocket and without warning, he produced a scalpel. It was all I could do not to call out in horror, yet instead, I clasped my hand to my mouth and watched, intrigued. Without so much as a look in my direction, Shalto grasped the creature firmly by the scruff of its neck and made a swift laceration to the tip of its ear. The cat mewed plaintively for a second but did not struggle and I could see that the wound was extremely superficial.

"Sorry, old mate. You know the drill. It's just a drop. You won't miss it, I promise."

And with that, Shalto bent his face close to the cat and licked up the bead of blood that glistened on the edge of its ear.

"There now, good as new. Thank you, my friend. Oh, and Captain sends his regards."

He set the cat gently back on the ground and, reaching once more into his pocket, produced a small dried fish that he laid before it. The cat lowered its head to inspect the reward and then picked it up in its mouth with an approving chirp. The next moment, it had melted back into the ferns as though it had never been there.

"DNA, you know. Just a basic schematic, that's all...," murmured Shalto almost to himself. But I didn't know or understand and was still reeling from the scene I'd just witnessed. I'd begun to yawn uncontrollably and wondered whether I needed to sit down. I checked my pockets for my inhaler and then let out a long sigh. If Shalto heard he gave no indication, but then he was already busy with other things.

He'd shrugged off his parka and had begun to peel off his shirt. I had no idea what was happening but his lips were clenched together in deep concentration and I did not dare interrupt. I watched silently as he lay the clothes down at the foot of a tree and began to remove his jeans. I looked up at the sun between the leaves above and suddenly realised that I had no idea how long we had been in the forest. Time might as well have congealed around us. When I glanced back, Shalto had finished undressing. He looked over at me and then was gone. Without a word. I thought I saw a flash of flesh deep in the undergrowth and then nothing. I stood alone among the silver-barked beech trees and stared at the pile of clothes, unsure what to do.

Then, out of nowhere, all hell seemed to break out. Out of nowhere a blue-jay shot out of the canopy screeching for its life. A couple of dozen wood sparrows followed, their flapping and chattering filling the air around. I clapped my hand to my chest and froze. Something was moving in the shadows. I gulped.

"Hullo? Shalto? Is that you?"

The shadow stirred again. Then, out sloped a sleek black panther, the size of a man. I felt my bowels turn to ice-water and prayed that I would not shit myself. Not on my birthday, of all days. "He won't hurt you," I muttered to myself, backing away. "It's just Shalto. Your mate, remember? And he would never hurt you."

The great black cat, meanwhile, paused a moment. A deep drumming sound reverberated from within its chest and I realised that it was purring. I held my ground and puffed the air out of my lungs to slow my breathing. The great cat continued forward. It padded softly up to me and then dipped its head and began to rub against my legs, much as the feral cat had done with Shalto. I don't know where I found the courage, but I reached down and gently touched the creature's shoulders. The fur was as soft as moss, but the muscles beneath the inky coat felt as firm as bands of iron. I stroked the head and the great cat unfurled a huge pink tongue and licked my hand. I caught a glimpse of the enormous incisors and faltered, but then I looked into the huge eyes. Yellow and split by that elliptical pupil, they appeared nothing like Shalto's, yet somehow as I gazed more deeply, I recognised him in there. My fear melted away like frost in the sunshine. This was my best friend. And allowing me into his secret world was the most wonderful birthday present he could have given me.

"So, what was all that with the cat?"

I was watching my friend as he pulled on his parka. The afternoon was turning chilly.

"Wasn't it obvious?"

"Well, I got the bit about using the DNA - but in that case why didn't you need human DNA to turn back?"

"Good question. And very sharp, if we may say so. Well, we might need it if we stayed as a cat for too long. As it is, we live in human form most of the time, so the imprint, or cellular memory is more permanent, if you will. It's a bit like the difference between a poem you memorised when you were young versus hearing a song once on the radio. We just need a little reminder or prompt to ensure a convincing copy, that's all."

I noted that Shalto was suddenly referring to himself as "we" but let it go.

"And the cat?"

"What, in the forest? Oh, yeah. Well, he was just one of them, of course. Captain used to be their leader but fancied a change. They're a great bunch. We've known the family for years, kitten and elder. That's the thing about cats. They have long memories and they don't dob you in. Not like, bleedin' dogs. Altogether too eager to please some human, as I may have mentioned before. No, cats every time, thank you. You can always rely on a cat to keep your confidence. Plus, they see the world in a very different way. Intriguing actually. They could teach the philosophers a thing or two. I'm pretty sure, one or two have tried. The rest couldn't care bleedin' less."

"So, you experienced the world as a cat, while you were one? Is that why you couldn't speak?"

Speaking of cats, I realised that my curiosity was getting the better of me. I'd done my best to reign in the questions but now they seemed to be just spilling out. Shalto squinted at me thoughtfully, perhaps wondering whether he had said too much already.

"Well, for a start, they don't have vocal-chords, now do they? Besides, you know what Ludwig Wittgenstein said?"

I shook my head and pulled a face. I'd never even heard of the guy. Shalto shook his head in despair.

"Durrrrr - only the greatest philosopher ever- well, he suggested that even if a lion could speak our language, we still couldn't understand what it said."

I stared at him.

"What? You mean like, I don't understand what you are on about half the time?"

"Something like that, mate. Something like that."

"One other thing…"

"Just one. Seeing how it's your birthday…"

"What was with all the vodka?"

Shalto smiled.

"Energy, Jonno. You'd be surprised how much we need to do this shit."

He wasn't exaggerating. By the time, we had dropped the Enfield back at his place and Shalto pulled the scooter up outside my house, it was clear to me that he was completely spent. We had only passed a brief fifteen minutes chasing each other and wrestling playfully among the bracken, but shifting shape was clearly a taxing business.

At any rate, he was in no fit state to attend my birthday tea, which was probably just as well. Mum, being Mum, had gone to considerable effort to obtain a vegan birthday cake so that my friend could be part of our celebrations. It had been incredibly sweet of her, yet I could hardly put him through the unpleasant charade of consuming it, after all he had done for me. And, Bless him, he would have forced it down rather than offend her.

Instead, I made Shalto's excuses for him. He had developed another one of his blinding migraines; we had probably overdone it a bit. I showed her the T-shirt I had bought with some of the birthday money she had given me. She nodded approvingly.

"And you'll never guess, Mum. On the way home, he drove me to Heddon Street in The West
End to see the very spot where he posed for the photo for the album cover. It was just the best."

Mum was impressed and it was not a *complete* fabrication. Shalto had shown me the famous spot once when we were up in Carnaby Street, just not *that* afternoon.

Mum said how sorry she was that Shalto could not be with us and ruffled my hair. We then spent a quiet but enjoyable evening eating birthday cake and playing chess while I happily showed off my new T-shirt. I caught her looking into my face as I blew out the candles. But, if she was looking for any signs of disappointment, there were not a scintilla to be found. It had, quite simply, been the best birthday ever.

There was, however, one small detail that bothered me and I indulged myself in one last enquiry when I saw Shalto the following day.

"So, just to clarify, Shal, 'cos it's been bothering me all night. Why couldn't you have used Captain's fur or blood, for that matter, for DNA?"
Shalto burst into peals of laughter. A rare sight and a quite wonderful sound.

"You got me, Cooper," he snorted and tapped his head. "See, I knew you were sharp up here. It's true, I could have leaned on Captain for a bit of his DNA and he, being the gent he is, would have been happy to oblige. But where's the theatre in that?"
I looked at him and blinked. He winked and then tapped his nose.

"It's all part of the pantomime, my son. And what's life without a little pantomime? You ask Will Shakespeare. Now there was a man who knew how to spin a yarn even if he couldn't remember how to spell his own name."

"Are you saying you knew William Shakespeare? Personally?"

Shalto closed his eyes and lifted his chin.

"Well, some of us certainly did."

I shook my head and twisted my mouth. My life would certainly never be dull so long as Shalto was around.

As amazing as it had been, after that, neither Shalto nor I ever referred to that afternoon in Epping Forest again. It was like a moment outside of time. An experience so secret that it to give it words would feel like a betrayal. It wasn't even as though we even discussed not discussing it. We just didn't. But the secret lay there between us and our friendship had become the closer for it.

Shalto's position in our household, meanwhile, grew more secure with every passing day. There had been no more incidents with any empty vodka bottles and the continued excellence of my performance at school was a convincing reflection of Shalto influence for good. Mum even seemed to enjoy talking to him.

The following December, when the shops were already alight with Christmas decorations, I came down from my room to catch the two of them chatting in the kitchen. I had stood and listened a little lost for words.

"Jonathon tells me that you like classical music, Shalto. Is that correct?"

"Well, more from the baroque period and earlier really, Mrs C. You know- Bach, Vivaldi, Handel and to be honest I wouldn't turn my nose up at a bit of John Dowland."

"Goodness, really? I love that earlier stuff, too. Do you play an instrument, Shalto? To tell you the truth I was thinking of getting Jumbo a guitar for Christmas, I feel young people should play something."

Shalto burst out laughing.

"Well, good luck with that one Mrs C. I've heard him sing and I reckon he's tone deaf. But you never know – he might make a good technical player. It's all about mathematics in the end…"

"Hey! I heard that," I interrupted. "I can hold a tune. And I'd love a guitar. We could start a band, Shalto and the…."

"Oh, so you *do* play? Jumbo never said," said Mum, cutting me off "But which instrument?"

Shalto shook his head shyly.

"Well, I wouldn't say I played much these days, but I played cello back in the day, and I'm pretty sure I could find my way around a bass guitar."

"No? you don't say?" breathed Mum. "I used to play the cello at school. I wasn't very good but it is such a beautiful instrument. Do you still have one?"

"Somewhere…" shrugged Shalto raising his eyebrows. "But I'm pretty sure that if cellos could rust, it would be even rustier than me."

Mum shook her head and laughed. I grabbed Shalto's arm and dragged him up the stairs. I liked it when he got on with Mum but - not that much.

"You never told *me* you could play any instruments…" I said sulkily as I closed the door.

"Well, *you* never asked," replied Shalto.

I twisted my lip. He had me there. But then he didn't like me asking questions so I couldn't win.

"Hey, guess what?" I said trying to lift the mood. "If Mum got me a guitar and we *did* start a band then I've got a brilliant name for it – Shalto and the Shapeshifters."

I won't describe the look Shalto shot me but it pretty much put an end to any aspirations I might have fostered for a career in the music business.

11

It was the Easter break. My GCSE examinations loomed on the horizon but Spring appeared to have forsaken the British Isles and we had almost forgotten what the sun looked like.

It was another damp and dreary day outside, so Shalto and I had decided just to hang out at my house. Meal times aside, he had become somewhat of a permanent fixture in our lives over the last year and Mum seemed genuinely fond of him. Of course, she'd remained blissfully unaware that he did not, in reality, attend my school or any other for that matter and nobody was about to enlighten her. She had never been one to grill him and had long since given up on making even the most innocuous enquiry into his domestic circumstances, thanks to his knack for never giving a straight answer to a question. It was a technique that never failed. Put on the spot, he would simply spin a yarn so long and complicated that she would forget the question along the way. And he did it with such charm that she never stood a chance.

On this particular afternoon, Mum had gone to work and we had the entire day to ourselves. These days, she rarely gave a second thought to the dangers of leaving me to my own devices during school holidays - I was growing up. Besides, she could depend on Shalto to keep an eye on me. He was, after all, old enough to stand *in loco parentis,* she pointed out - which tickled me no end. *Technically* Shalto was old enough to stand *in loco parentis* for anyone on the planet. Ironically, however, he often seemed less mature than I did.

"I'm bored..." he declared staring out of the window into the drizzle-soaked afternoon. "In fact, I'm the chairman of the board," he pouted, starting to writhe around the room in a hilarious imitation of Iggy Pop. "Aren't you?"

I looked at him and yawned. We were in my bedroom, reading comics and listening to music. Theoretically, I was supposed to be revising, but I had tossed my textbooks aside some hours ago.

"We could go to your place" I offered. "I haven't been over there for weeks. I'd like to say hullo to Captain."
Shalto shook his head.

"Nah. It's too cramped and, to be honest, it gives me the creeps. Besides Captain's gone AWOL again."
He must have read the alarm on my face.

"He'll come back. Always does. Just likes a bit of adventure now and then."

"You sure you haven't just shut him in the cellar, again?"

He looked thoughtful for a moment.

"Nah. He knows to scratch at the door now, to let me know."

I shrugged, all out of ideas. Shalto propped himself up on one elbow and fixed me with a mischievous look.

"You know, I've often wondered what your mum's room is like. I've never been in there."

"It's just a bedroom. I never normally go in there myself, not unless she is in there, I mean."

"You mean you've never sneaked in and had a proper look around."

"No. certainly not. Why would I have done?"

"I dunno. Just out of interest. Go on - can't we have a gander? Just for curiosity's sake, like. I just adore browsing through other people's wardrobes."

"I don't know. I'm not sure she'd like that. She's quite a private person is Mum."

"Yeah, but doesn't that make you want to have a little look around, all the more? Tell you what, you let us have a butchers' and I'll take us for a spin on the Enfield just as soon as the sun puts in an appearance."

It didn't take much to buy me. I knew it was wrong, but I knew for a fact that he wouldn't let it go until I agreed and, besides, I'd been hanging out for another spin on that fabulous bike. I checked my watch.

"Well, just a quick peek. But no touching anything. And absolutely no looking through her underwear drawer. And don't for Pete's sake move anything. She's got eyes like a hawk."

I checked my watch. Mum wouldn't be home for hours. All the same, we tiptoed out onto the landing and along to Mum's room like a couple of giggling burglars and, once there, I softly opened the door and stuck my head around just to be doubly certain the coast was clear. It was, of course. I turned to Shalto and beckoned him in.

Once inside we gazed around. I'd been in the room any number of times before but never without Mum and it felt so wrong. So wrong that it was kind of exciting. Nothing that there was anything very astonishing about the room itself, though its décor was distinctly feminine and perhaps a little on the exotic side.

Mum had told me how she and my father had travelled extensively before I was born, spending many weeks in both India and Thailand. She had adored the culture and bought back richly coloured cushions, ornate lamps and vases, most of which she kept in her room. The impression stood in such stark contrast to the dowdy clothes she wore for work and though she wore jeans at the weekend, a tied-dye T-shirt seemed the limit to any personal flamboyance.

The contradiction, at any rate, struck Shalto with some force.

"Well, well Mrs C..." he muttered running his hands over the richly embroidered cushions that were heaped on the bed. "Not what I had expected. Not at all."

Finally, He stood in the middle of the room and gazed around.

"What the Fuck?" he exclaimed suddenly blinking in astonishment at a brightly coloured canvas that huge above my mum's bed.

"It's a portrait of Mum," I observed. "My father brought it back from the United States as a present for her when I was born. Beautiful, isn't it?"

"It's a frigging Warhol screen-print," he replied. "And not an imitation, by the look of it. Bleedin' 'eck, Jonno, you never said."

I shrugged not sure why on earth I would have said anything.

"Keep your hair on - it's just a painting – now get down, this minute. I mean it, Shalto. Get off!"

Shalto had leapt onto the bed to take a closer look. He stretched out a hand to touch it but I already had him by the studded belt of his jeans. I yanked him off the bed and we both tumbled sprawling onto the carpet. I could feel my face burning.

"I'm serious, Shalto. That's my mum's bed. How could you?"

"Sorry, man," he mumbled, "but that *is* Andy Warhol's signature. Do you even know who the dude is?"

"Of course, I do. I'm not a total idiot. The soup cans and everything. Dad often went to New York. I guess he knew all sorts of people over there. He wasn't short of a penny either. I know we live in a little house, but that's just Mum – she wanted us to be independent. I'm surprised she kept it in some ways. She'd certainly never tell a soul, it's here. I suppose I'd just forgotten."

Shalto picked himself up and gazed at the portrait.

"Well, well Mrs C. You were quite a chick back then. I wonder what other little surprises you might have for us."

His eyes wandered over to the antique wardrobe that stood at the far end of the room.

"I wonder what we might find in here then."

I bristled a little and reminded him of our deal.

"Oh, come on, Jumbo. Just a little look. Andy Warhol didn't just paint any old slapper, you know. He was all about the glamour. She must have had some real style to take his fancy. Geez - I always suspected there was more to Mrs C than Marks and Spencer's A-line skirts and plain blouses. Let's just take a quick squint…"

"Yeah, well, she looked like a – that is, she was really something, back then. Now, cut it out."

I did my best to sound severe but he went ahead in any case. He tugged open the left door of the wardrobe to reveal a curtain of beige, grey and navy blouses, shirtwaister dresses and A-line skirts. Shalto kissed his teeth. A look of disappointment clouded his face. I leapt to Mum's defence. *She worked in a solicitors' office, for goodness' sake, so I was not sure what he had expected.* But either he didn't hear or he simply didn't wish to listen and had already pulled open the remaining door and was pushing aside the wider portion of garments.

"Now – that's more like it," he said letting out a low whistle. My eyes settled on the assortment of brightly coloured fabrics that hung at the far end of the rail. I could make out a couple of striking paisley kaftans, a heavily beaded jacket, what appeared to be a white crocheted tunic and there at the very end, the unmistakable drape of a long pale silk evening dress. That dress. That colour. Neither blue nor yet quite green, it confounded the senses. Fit for the princess of my half-forgotten memories and dreams.

"Well now – let's see what have we here." Shalto's long fingers danced over the hangers and settled on the dress. I was about to shout - "no," when suddenly he stiffened and then seemed to shudder. He staggered backwards slightly and turned to me, shaking his head in surprise.

"What on earth was that, Shalto? Someone walking over your grave?"

"Something like that, I guess. I honestly couldn't tell you. A whole bunch of random impressions all at once. I'm sure it was just a blip though. Let me just…."

I watched in fascination as he tentatively reached out his hand and tried again. Nothing. He shrugged and raised an eyebrow. *It was just him. Probably all the excitement over the Warhol.*

He puffed out his lips and lifted the dress carefully from the rail. He held it up. The fabric fell in soft folds of scintillating aquamarine. My heart did a bit of a jig inside my chest.

"Shot silk..." he pronounced with strange authority. "Quite irresistible, isn't it?"

"Shalto – I really don't think you..."

But he was already draping it across his body and posturing in the mirror on the inside of the wardrobe door.

"Shalto – *seriously*..."

But he had already lain it lovingly on the bed and was peeling off his jeans and sweatshirt. I felt a kind of panic but could neither look away nor do anything to stop what was happening. He slipped the dress over his head and shook out its folds, then moved to the dressing table that partially blocked the window. Seating himself on the stool, he scrutinised the make-up bag and array of jewellery and hair accessories that lay in a selection of crystal vanity dishes before him.

Picking out some kirby grips he gathered up his shoulder length hair and secured it to the top of his head. Then, rummaging through the little bag, he picked out a lipstick and unsheathed it then nodded in approval. Next, he selected eye liner and mascara and then set to work. I watched on from behind, the reflection of his face in the dressing table mirror obscured by his hands as he worked. Such deftness and confidence. He had done this before. When he was satisfied with his work, he completed the look by clipping on a pair of dangling diamante earrings. He rose, nodded to his image in the mirror and turned to me, batting his thickened eyelashes for effect.

"Well – what do you think?"

I couldn't tell whether I wanted to laugh or cry. He had not used shapeshifting powers, and yet it was as though I was looking at a totally different being. His face, always soft, looked wholly feminine. His body, always slender seemed to embody girlish grace. He was beautiful. Almost as beautiful as my mother had been. *And this was her dress.* A surge of anger trumped my confusion. I could feel my face start to burn.

"Well, granted you make a very pretty girl, but take it off. Mum will be home soon. And make sure you put everything back exactly as you found it."

It was the best I could do. I flounced back to my bedroom and slammed the door behind me.

A few minutes later, I heard a soft tap at my door. When I opened it, Shalto stood still dabbing at the dark smudges beneath his eyes with a cotton wool pad.

"I'm sorry, Jonno. Honest, I am. I was just having a lark, but I can see that I overstepped the mark and seem to have upset you. I didn't mean any harm. I would never do anything to disrespect to Mrs C. You know that. I've replaced everything just as it was. She'll never know – I promise."

I looked at him and shook my head. But I couldn't hide the tears that pricked my eyes.

"Does it ever get any less confusing, Shalto?"

"What?"

"Life?"

"Not so far as I'm aware, Mate."

That night I dreamed of my mother and father and the details were so clear that it must have been an early memory. Mum was wearing *the* dress and my father wore a dinner suit with a bow tie and silk cummerbund. My father had one arm around her shoulders and was dangling the keys of his beloved Jaguar from the other hand. I had heard a lot about that car from Mum who retained very happy memories about it. They looked so young - the picture of 1960's cool sophistication. I woke up and wondered where he was now. Something I'd neither asked myself nor anyone else in many, many years.

12

That year my sixteenth birthday fell slap bang in the middle of the examination period and provided a welcome distraction from all the swotting. Mum had ordered another vegan birthday cake and had had it decorated to look like a record player, playing an LP. Shalto, unable to escape his fate this time, had graciously accepted a slice and had even put on a convincing performance of actually enjoying it, although though he politely declined a second. How much he enjoyed the aftermath, he left to my imagination, for which I was grateful. Unlike most of the lads at my school, he remained reticent about his bathroom habits, though I had not forgotten the little he had told me a couple of years back.

I knew that I had done well in my exams and wasn't the least bit worried about the results. Maths and Physics had been a breeze. I'd had to put in a bit more effort with History and English Literature, but Biology and Chemistry had been a walk in the park. I might have spent more time playing Shalto at chess than actually revising, but I had been blessed with naturally unflagging concentration and an extremely proficient memory. I had opted to take Maths, Physics and Chemistry at 'A'-level in addition, of course, to General Studies. All in all, my trajectory to the university of my choice seemed assured.

School had certainly become more enjoyable. So much so that I actually found myself looking forward to the sixth form. Something I could not have imagined only a couple of years earlier. My friendship with Shalto continued to lend me a certain amount of street cred even though we kept ourselves to ourselves. He had ditched the parka in recent months in favour of a leather jacket and wore his dark hair down to his shoulders. He seldom ventured out without a pair of dark glasses, even in winter, and exuded an undeniable air of cool aloofness.

Not to be wholly outdone, I grew my hair as long as school regulations would allow and took to wearing ripped T-shirts and drain-pipe jeans in my free time. Hunting out new gear was a bit of a shared passion and most Saturdays, if we weren't hanging out at Forbidden Planet you would have found us elbowing our way through the crowds of kids and tourists that frequented the mushrooming array of new market stalls that was Camden Markets.

Shalto may have been the one who attracted the limelight in our relationship yet I was no longer simply the nerdy Robin to his shadowy Batman. I may not have been in the first eleven but the enthusiasm with which I participated in team sports during Physical Education continued to win me kudos in my own right. So much so that I was generally the first player picked for a side, not the last. It doesn't sound like much, but it made all the difference.

As for chess. Shalto never once permitted me to beat him yet I learned so much from him that I was not about to complain. Still, it would have been neat if he had at least allowed me to think I had bested him just once.

Once in a while, on a Saturday evening, he would also play my mum and routinely wiped the floor with her too, though she thrived on what she called "serious competition." I could never quite recall how they came to play their first match, but it cemented the odd little friendship. "You let your guard down there, Mrs C - you'll have to do better than that if you want to beat us," he would say with a wink. Mum never seemed to wonder who the "us" referred to. But there was no reason why she should. Instead, she would topple her king with a smile and shake her head at the unique ingenuity of his game. In a rare and unguarded moment, she even went so far as to remark that he reminded her of my father – the only opponent, she'd struggled to place in checkmate.

Everything might have seemed perfect had it not been for one thing. The end-of-year fifth and sixth form school dance. It may have been little more than a glorified disco but it was regarded as a rite of passage, especially for those of us, planning to stay on for 'A' levels – a chance for the girls to put on evening frocks and the boys to wear something other than school uniform. Our chance to be grown-ups for the night.

I had done my best to pretend that I wasn't interested, that it didn't matter to me but the truth was, if I didn't go then I would be the only kid among my peers who wasn't there. The real problem was that I didn't want to go alone and my chances of securing a partner for the event were significantly smaller than zero. I could have dragged Shalto along but, no matter how cool he was, I wasn't going to be the boy who took his best mate to the school dance – not for any money.

It was no big deal in the larger scheme of things. I'd watched the reports of widespread famines in Third World countries on the evening news and realised how lucky I was. But I didn't live in the third World and in my world, and through the lens of my adolescent perspective, the whole business was beginning to assume catastrophic proportions.

"I'm such a failure…" I moaned re-visiting my preoccupation with my dating status for the fifteenth time.

Shalto looked up from his Wonder Woman comic.

"I'd go to the school dance with you, if I were a girl."

"Would you? Really?"

"Why not. You're tall, good at football and not bad looking. Not to mention intelligent. What's not to like?"

"Well, you tell me. How come the only time any girl talks to me it's to get close to my cool friend with the scooter then? You know it's true. It happened again only last week after the physics exam. There I was waiting outside the school gates for you when Louise What's-her-face comes over and starts asking me about the question on Boyle's Law. Giggling and smiling. All over me like a rash, she was. And then up you pop and all of a sudden it was like I wasn't even there. I felt so used."

Shalto shrugged.

"I can't help it if they dig the more sexy mature type, can I."

"No, but seriously. What's so off about me? Huh?"

Shalto hesitated.

"Well, you gotta have more confidence for a start. Develop a bit of patter. A few chat-up lines. The moment some bird talks to you, you start mumbling on about mathematics or the world chess championships. Hardly the stuff of love's young dream, is it? Girls like you to be interested in them. But then, on the other hand, you don't have to try so hard. Let them chase after you a bit."

I pouted. I suppose I'd been fishing for some crumbs of a compliment. Fat chance of that.

"Well, if you're such an expert, how come you don't have a girlfriend, then?"

Shalto stared at me then went back to Diana Prince.

"It isn't me who needs one," he said quietly from behind his comic.

I suppose that might have been the end of it, but his taunt took up residence in my brain where it gnawed away like determined rodent. Later that day I decided to take my chances.

"You remember last Easter hols when you dressed up in Mum's clothes? You really made a very attractive girl and you carried it off so well, it got me wondering - have you ever been one? A girl, I mean? In the past?"

Shalto looked at me and shrugged.

"I'm pretty sure I was - yeah. At times, at least. And the idea seems completely natural to me. You've only seen me as a bloke, but I'm not like you, Jonno. I don't naturally have a gender. I can choose to be either sex. And to be honest, dressing up like that made me realise how much think I miss it, you know. Being a woman. The clothes, the make-up. I don't have specific memories of being female, but I distinctly recall the feeling of it and that it made me feel different somehow."

"What do you mean?"

"I don't know. Softer, maybe. More at ease with myself. But more vulnerable as well." He paused. "Hang on. Why are you looking at me like that?"

"Well, it was you who said that you would go to the dance with me if you were a girl - well, you could, you know..."

"No. No bleedin' way. Cut it out. And you can stop making with the puppy dogs eyes. It isn't happening and that's final. Anyway, I thought you'd found the whole business rather unsettling."

"Oh, that. Yeah, well, I was just being a bit silly wasn't I?" I shrugged.

"And you're not being silly now, of course?"

I frowned. Shalto could be so infuriating sometimes. I narrowed my eyes.

"Well, you know, I don't think my mum would be very happy if she found out about you dressing up in her stuff, do you? In fact, I don't think she would be very happy at all."

"Careful Jumbo, you wouldn't be attempting to blackmail me, would you?"

"Well, I wouldn't call it blackmail, exactly. Let's think of it more as a *very special* favour. And if what you say is true, it might turn out to be a bit of a treat for you too."

The chime of the doorbell just about made me jump out of my newly purchased box-shouldered jacket. I had been pacing around in my room waiting for it to sound, but still it had taken me by surprise.

"I'll get it..." I yelled, racing down the stairs to get the front door before Mum could stir from her armchair in front of the TV. I glanced at my watch. *What was I thinking? I should have been waiting in the hallway. She might easily have got to the door before me and then what?* I halted before the mirror that hung next to the coat pegs and gave the cuffs of my sleeves a final fold and wondered if the hint of

Mum's mascara I'd applied to my normally fair lashes had been a step too far. Never mind. Too late, now.

The night was by no means warm for the time of year but I had already started to sweat. I was beginning to wonder if this had not all been a huge mistake when the chime rang out for a second time.

"It's okay, Mum. I've got it." My voice rasped oddly in my ears. I ran my tongue over my lips and grasped the chub lock handle. It was now or never.

The girl who stood on our doorstep was a stranger. She was also a knock-out. No doubt about it. With golden brown corkscrew curls that tumbled to her shoulders and framed a naturally pretty face, she almost took my breath away. She wore a fine paisley shawl around her shoulders but beneath it, the pale blue-green silk of the dress clung fetchingly to her athletic frame and set off the sea-green colour of her eyes perfectly. All in all, it was as if the dress might have been made for her.

"Expecting someone else?" she asked with a coy wink.

I shook my head in half-belief. Could that be Shalto? And I knew it was. She might not look like my friend, yet there was no denying the sense of familiarity about her expression or the telling symmetry of the features.

Grinning, I placed a finger to my lips then turned and called back into the house.

"Righto, just off to the dance now, Mum. I won't be late, I promise."

"Okay, Jumbo. But aren't you going to introduce me to your date, sweetheart?" floated Mum's voice floated out from within the living room.

I pulled a face and drew the door half-shut behind us.

"Nah, sorry Mum. Sherry's kinda shy and we're gonna be late, as it is. Another time, maybe."

"Alright then. You two have fun, then. But no alcohol and no smoking- anything. You promise?"

"Course, Mum."

I closed the door sharply and whisked my companion down the path and along the pavement, only stopping when I felt her tugging furiously at my sleeve.

"Sherry? Really?" she hissed. "What kind of name is Sherry?"

"I'm sorry. It's the first name that popped into my head when I was telling Mum about you. I think we're going to have to stick with it now or I'll just get confused."

Sherry gave a reluctant shrug but was not finished with me.

"And another thing. What did you mean, another time? I told you - this is strictly a one off."

"I know that but I had to say something. I couldn't have her seeing the dress, now could I?"

My date snorted and gave a twirl.

"Well, I do think it's very me. It's a bit of a shame I have to give it back, really…"

I moaned and rolled my eyes and wondered whether one school-dance could truly be worth all this stress. In my opinion, Shalto had already made an unnecessarily big song and dance about the whole issue. Getting him to agree to my suggestion had been one challenge but the condition he had laid down, turned out to be quite another.

"I don't see the problem," I had said, once I'd mustered the courage to propose the plan. "Just one little change, just for one night. And you did say how much you missed being a girl."

"A woman – I said I missed being a woman," he'd replied. "And that's true, but I don't think you realise the effort it takes to – to…'"

"Yes, yes. I know. But you *are* a shapeshifter, after all. And it's not as though I'm asking you to change into an entirely different species…"

"Says the boy who finds it a strain to change his socks. And I wouldn't be so sure about the entirely different species bit…" Shalto scratched his head and frowned. "Okay, but I will need a dress and some shoes and stuff."

"Well, don't look at me…"

"Your mother's dress, you big dope. Oh, yes. It'll be perfect. In fact- it has to be that dress or not at all."

I had seen that same look of determination on my friend's face before. I would be wasting my time to argue and I knew it.

"Okay. The dance is tomorrow evening. I'll sneak into Mum's room in the morning and get the stuff for you and you can pick it up around midday. I presume that will give you enough time? And – just out of curiosity, will you be needing any blood for, you know…?"

My mind went back to the cat in the forest. Laying hands on a female donor would bring a whole new bag of problems.

"Oh, no. Not as it happens. Men and women share the same DNA. We just have to do a bit of jiggling...."

I looked at my friend askance. I could never entirely get my head around it when he used the collective - *we*.

And so, the next morning, once I was 100% sure that she had gone, I found myself sneaking once again into Mum's room. I felt a little sick as I pulled open one of the mirrored doors but told myself that it would be worth it. I ran my eyes along the rack of neatly hung clothes and tutted to myself. It really was all so drab and unfashionable.

Then that wonderful colour caught my eye. The colour of my childhood longing. I felt my eyes water and it wasn't from the faint whiff of forgotten mothballs. I reached out and stroked the dress with my fingertips. The memory of how sophisticated Shalto had looked in it danced before me and I hoped that it would not be a bit too posh for a school dance. I lifted the dress from the rail and lay it carefully on the bed. Lying there, it didn't look so posh after all. The elegance of the design lay in its simplicity. It was the colour that worked the magic.

I nodded. Now, I would need some shoes. Strappy sandals, I thought, flat for dancing. I examined the row of shoes that lined the bottom of the wardrobe and selected a suitable match for the dress.

"Make-up, next." I noted out loud. Shalto had not mentioned any such thing, but even a teenage boy understands that a girl needed her lipstick and mascara. I moved to the dressing table and picked through my mum's make-up bag. There were so many little compacts and lipstick cases, I doubted she would miss them, but I took a couple of items from the bottom, just in case, picking out an aqua eye shadow and black eye line pencil. I couldn't recall having seen Mum wear such brightly coloured make-up in many years, favouring as she did more subtle shades of green, yet the colour matched the dress exactly. Then, frowning in concentration I popped the top off a lipstick and wound it upwards. It was a soft peach my mother often wore. I was not sure what colouring my date would have, though had sort of assumed that she would be a feminine version of Shalto. I stared at the peach lipstick. It would do. Anything darker might look a bit tarty. The last thing we needed was for Miss Shalto to look like a cheap hooker. She would be drawing enough attention as it was.

I tucked the make-up into my pocket, gathered up the dress and shoes and closed the bedroom door. I would put them back tomorrow while Mum went to Stratford to do the weekly shop and she would never even know they were missing. Suddenly, I remembered the brassiere. Shalto had not needed one but his female counterpart surely would.

"Oh bugger...."

The words "gross invasion of privacy" flashed neon bright into my mind. My mother's underwear was not exactly forbidden territory to me. I had unpegged her smalls from the washing line when rain had threatened often enough. Still, something about this felt very different. However, the idea that I could persuade Shalto into shopping for lingerie seemed extremely unlikely and it would be too late now, in any case. I would have to go back in there.

I pulled open the top drawer of her dressing table and reached in. There, on the top of the carefully folded under-garments lay a couple of plain everyday bras. I hesitated. The absence of either one would be too readily noticed. I reached into the back of the drawer, hunting for an alternative and pulled out a pink lacey brassiere, one I assumed my Mum kept for best. I unfolded it to take a closer look and a small wad of photographs fluttered to the floor.

I bent to retrieve them turning them over to look at them. I knew that this was Mum's private stuff but couldn't help myself, somehow. The first picture was a black and white photograph, I had seen before, though not for a number of years. It was of my mother and father on their wedding day and must have been taken outside the registry office where they had married. I studied it, struck by details I had never noticed as a younger child.

Mum was dressed in a white crocheted mini-dress with matching white patent-leather lace-up boots. Her hair was done up in a bee-hive bun and impossibly large white hooped earrings dangled from her ears. She wore the heavy black eye-liner that had been fashionable in the early sixties and looked impossibly glamorous and happy at the same time. In one hand she clutched a simple posy of lily of the valley and in the other her husband's hand. Julian. My father. It felt strange to see him. A bit like a remembering a long-forgotten dream. Tall and self-assured, with that closely cropped beard, carefully shaped moustaches and a thick thatch of hair that fell over his face. Red hair, I thought, though you couldn't tell from the monochrome photo. And his suit, so stylish and sharp. No wonder Mum had fallen for him - he had looked like a young Douglas Fairbanks Jr.

I turned the photograph back over. *February 2nd 1965.* Just four months before my birth. He would be gone before I turned six. I felt a sudden constriction in my chest and shook my head. Mum had always denied that I was a mistake but perhaps she had only said that to spare my feelings. After all, he hadn't even been around for my birth. Mum said it wasn't his fault. They hadn't expected me to arrive until the following month and he'd had unavoidable business commitments in New York. Still, I could barely remember him, something that struck me as rather odd as I looked at the photograph, as I could remember my first day at school well enough. But then I supposed I'd been at school ever since.

The next photograph was something quite different. A snapshot of the two of them seated aloft an elephant, she in a paisley kaftan and my father in a white linen suit and a Panama hat; they could have easily passed for a couple of film stars. Undated but, I suspected, taken well before I arrived on the scene. Mum looked so young. She had told me stories of their travels around India when I was a little boy, painting such a vivid picture of the markets with their jewel-coloured silks and exotic spices that I could almost smell them.

I sighed. She had certainly led a more glamourous life back then. I shuffled the photos and gaped in surprise. The third photo was a slightly faded Polaroid of my mum with her arms draped around the neck of a young tiger. I searched her face for fear, but her eyes only sparkled with happiness. The tiger must have been tamed for the benefit of tourists. I had heard of such things, but even so, she must have had some balls. I wondered why my father was not in the photo, but perhaps he had not been quite as game as she had. Or perhaps he had kept that souvenir for himself. It seemed odd that I had never seen the photo before, but perhaps I had and had simply forgotten. When I thought about it, it had been years since I had heard her talk about the past.

And then, there it was. The fourth and final photograph. The one of my mother and father posing together at some posh do. She, the fairy-tale princess of my childhood memories in the aquamarine dress, and he, film-star handsome in his bow tie and dinner jacket. And there, from his hands, dangled the keys to his beloved jaguar. I turned the photo over to see if there was a date, but there was none. I scratched my head. I had always thought that this was my *one* vivid memory of the two of them together, but perhaps I had just been remembering a photograph, after all.

I was still sitting staring at it when I heard the sound of the key in the front door. I stuffed the bra inside my T-shirt and quickly replaced the photographs. Then scurrying into my own room, I closed the door with a pant of relief.

"Hello? Jumbo? You up there? It's only Mum. I've got the most terrible menstrual cramps, so they sent me home. Be a love and fill me a hot water bottle, I'm going to have a lie down."

I sucked on my inhaler. That had been a close call. I skipped down the stairs to where she stood in the hallway. Her face was white and drawn.

"C'mon, Mum. You get yourself to bed. I'll put the kettle on and bring you some of those new pills the GP gave you. The I just need to pop over to Shalto's, if that is okay?"

"Of course, it is, Jumbo. And thanks. You're such a good boy. I'm sure I'll be fine by this evening. After all, it *is* your big night."

I wasn't sure what I'd been expecting but the school hall looked amazing. Someone had gone to town with the with fairy lights, balloons and streamers and, as I looked around, I felt as though I'd walked into one of those American prom nights I'd seen in the movies.

And that was just the beginning. It's astonishing what a carefully styled hair-do and a bit of make-up can achieve and there were fit looking girls everywhere. As we entered, a particularly foxy-looking young woman in a figure-hugging black backless dress flashed a smile at me and realised that it was the same awkward girl I had sat next to in English for the past two years. Even the lads had polished up well. Or, most of them, at least.

Best of all, no one looked more stunning than the stranger at my side. All eyes had turned to us as I had guided my date through the vestibule and, for the first time in my life, it had been a great feeling.

And she knew how to move too. Never one for dancing in public, I had steered us towards a couple of seats and would have been quite happy merely to sit and watch everyone else. I soon realised, however, that if I did not dance with my partner, somebody else would. Sherry draped her shawl over the back of the chair and placed her bag (a small beaded antique evening bag, I presumed she had found in the house,) behind her legs. We had just made ourselves comfortable when I caught sight of a prominent member of the school's rugby team making a beeline for us from the other side of the room.

"Oh, Christ. It's Gareth Evans..." I sighed covering my face with my hands.

Gareth was a strapping and surprisingly mature-looking lad for his age and was considered quite the catch among fifth and sixth-form girls. Or at least, that was what he boasted. He fixed his gaze on Sherry from the other side of the dance floor and winked. She smiled back and then looked away with a far-from subtle flutter of her eyelashes. I jabbed her in the side with my elbow.

"What are you trying to do?" I breathed under my hand.

"Well, I didn't come here to sit on my arse all night, did I?"

I felt my cheeks begin to burn. There was only one thing to do. I rose abruptly to my feet, blocking Gareth Evans' advance in the process, and then jerked my head towards the dancefloor in invitation. Sherry rolled her eyes but then looked over my shoulder and smiled sweetly at Gareth who was hovering behind me. "Sorry," she mouthed. Evans scowled and turned away. If she did not want to dance with him, there were plenty of other fish in the sea.

Sherry stood up and smoothed out the wrinkles in her dress.

"I hope you dance better than you flirt," she teased, holding out her hand. I stared at it. It looked so small and delicate. So delicate, that I found myself wondering what her touch would feel like on my skin. I shook my head and declined to clasp it.

I turned and marched determinedly to the dance floor and began to shuffle self-consciously from foot to foot to Duran Duran's Planet Earth, thankful that no one expected us to do the waltz or foxtrot any more. The less physical contact we had the better.

Sherry trailed behind and then valiantly tried to mirror my movements. Goodness knows how we must have looked, but it can't have been good. Sherry was doing her best to maintain her smile. I knew very well that she was trying to make eye contact with me but I wilfully avoided her gaze. I couldn't imagine what on earth had possessed me to think this could ever be a good idea.

Soon enough, Sherry too, seemed to have had enough. She leaned into my shoulder and said something into my ear. I spread my hands, unable to hear her above the booming bass of the music.

"Let's get a drink," she mouthed, miming a drinking motion. This time, I nodded and gestured towards the refreshments table. She placed her hand in the crook of my arm and followed me. I shrugged my elbow free. Sherry shot a glance at me but did not seem to take undue offence. At the table, she surveyed the variety of soft drinks on offer and then filled two plastic cups with the fruit punch.

"Here hold these. Lucky, I bought some supplies," she giggled. Then turning away from the rest of the room she reached into my mum's lacy bra and fished out a miniature bottle of vodka. Unscrewing the cap, she emptied the little bottle into one cup and pushed it towards me.

"It's not much, but it'll take the edge off and I have more in my bag…"

"No, Shalto - I mean, Sherry. You know, I promised my mum."

"For Gawd's sake, Jonathon. Stop being such a big girl's blouse, will you? We're not going to get you kaylied, just a bit merry. You'll be stone cold sober by the time we get you home, I promise. C'mon we're not the only ones - I can tell you that much."

I frowned. She was right. I'd already spotted a couple of lads reaching into their jacket pockets and slyly taking a swig from concealed hip flasks. I shrugged and put the punch to my lips. It had a sharp kick but wasn't horrible. I drained the cup and grinned. She took a sip from her own, wrinkled her pretty nose in distaste and immediately set it down.

"That's better. Now, just keep your eyes on me and follow what I do. And try to look as though you're enjoying yourself."

I followed her back to the dancing couples, rather wishing she that had not issued the instruction about keeping my eyes on her. She might have been trying to help but it was precisely *the way* she moved that bothered me. Even when she was only walking. I watched her hips as she began to sway to the rhythm of the music. So effortlessly fluid. Sensuous without shoving it in your face. I'd expected my friend to make a pretty companion. I had not prepared myself to fancy the pants off her. And yet I only had myself to blame. I watched her closely, trying to distract myself from the discomfort of the situation by concentrating on the task of trying to mirror her moves. And then the alcohol must have kicked in. All at once, it all seemed so easy. I had rhythm - I'd always loved music - and didn't need to dance like a broken plank. And I didn't need to mimic someone else, either. All I had to do was give myself over to the beat of the bass that throbbed through my body.

And, just like that, Sherry and I began to move as one. I'm not saying I was Micheal Jackson, but we must have put on a good show because I saw at least a couple of girls who sat watching nudge each other and smile. And it was not to poke fun. I could see how their cheeks flushed and their eyes sparkled.

Sherry grinned at me and gave me the thumbs up. I returned the gesture with a broad grin. I was all right. In fact, I had never felt better.

The DJ was an absolute wizard, a master brewer of teenage dreams; his magical concoction - a heady mix of disco, glam and Status Quo with just enough punk to remind the teaching staff who were there to supervise, that this was a new and different generation.

Swept along on a cloud of do-no-wrong bravado, we boogied, bopped and even did the funky chicken. And never once did our fingertips so much as touch. This was the eighties. Dance was about strutting your stuff - striking an attitude and even the characters in Jane Austen's novels had enjoyed more bodily proximity. I knew, because I has slogged through Pride and Prejudice for GCSE English.

The evening flew past. We stopped only once for a brief sit down and another fruit punch. I looked around the room with a warm glow, while Sherry fished under her seat to retrieve another miniature from her bag. This was it. I was in the pond. After all the fish-out-of-water years, I had finally made it into the pond. Okay, so it was only a small pond but we were all still only small fish.

"Having fun?" asked Sherry, her eyes still dancing.

I gazed into her face, trying to focus.

"Thank you so much. I mean it. I'm having the best time ever. Really. And you look *so* good. I never even dreamed…"

But she was already urging me to finish the punch.

"C'mon Fred Astaire, less dreaming more grooving - I love this Police track."

I puckered my brow and winced. *Don't Stand So Close To Me.* The lyrics had never made so much sense to me before. I hauled myself up off the chair and followed her as she threaded her way into the centre of the crowded dancefloor. I blocked out the vocals and focused on the beat. Maybe it would have bothered me more if I had been completely sober but, so long as we kept our distance, I could have stayed on the dancefloor all night.

But it was getting late and the evening was drawing to its close. The lights dimmed and the music softened. The unmistakable introduction to The Commodores' *Three Times a Lady* oozed out from the speakers and wrapped itself around us. Sherry looked up at me with a hesitant smile. I noticed how the kohl had smudged around her eyes and felt a surge in my heart rate. I grabbed my inhaler from my jacket pocket and headed for the seats in mortified silence.

"What *is* wrong with you?"

Sherry was next to me in an instant, her eyes flashed with indignation.

"Nothing. I'm just knackered and hot. Aren't you?"

"Listen, chum. These are the last three dances. If you don't dance with me, someone else will…"

She jerked her head to the left. On the far side of the hall, Gareth Evans, was already lumbering in our direction. I had noticed him sneaking nips from his hipflask and leering at Sherry from his corner near the refreshments table all evening. Evans. It would be Evans. It had felt good to be the object of his envy but now it was just alarming. He wasn't known for taking no for an answer at the best of times and now he looked half-cut.

I looked at Sherry. Her lovely face was suddenly tense with fear.

"Jeeze. The guy's a gorilla. Do you want to cause a scene? I've seen his kind before. We have to dance, Jonno. Just play along for God's sake."

I took a long puff from my inhaler and then stuffed it back into my pocket. I stood up. My legs were wobbling beneath me but I knew what I had to do. I reached out my hand to Sherry. Our hands clasped just as Evans was barging past a couple who, entwined in each other's arms, had drifted across his path. But the simple gesture had been enough to stop the full-back in his tracks. Muttering an obscenity under his breath, he made a clumsy about-turn and lurched unsteadily away from us.

Yet, there on the edge of the dance floor, I hardly noticed him go. The world and everything else in it had become a blur around me. Everything except for Sherry's hand in mine. A bomb could have gone off right then and I wouldn't have cared. All that mattered was the feel of her cheek against mine as she wrapped her arms around my neck and I pulled her in close. I felt a chain reaction of prickly pleasure ripple through my neck and spine and down into my groin. Sherry giggled yet I didn't pull away or attempt to stutter some mortified apology.

On we danced, swaying, pressed against each other, in perfect unity to the strains of Lionel Richie's soulful baritone. I had never been a fan of cheesy ballads but all at once the sentiments seemed to make my head swim. I groaned softly. This was bad. *If only I had not consumed that last vodka.* Sherry heard the protest and lifted her cheek away from mine. My chest constricted. Her lips were so close to mine now and all I could think about was touching them with my own. *Yet this was Shalto, my best mate.* I tried to get a grasp of myself but resistance, as the baddies in the films say, was entirely futile. I suppose I could blame the vodka or even the testosterone but it wasn't Shalto I kissed and it wasn't Shalto who kissed me back.

It would, however, definitely be Shalto, I had to face later.

"I never want to see you again..."

Minutes later I was striding out of the school with Sherry trailing in my wake. Right then, I didn't want her anywhere near me. The kiss had been amazing but somehow, just as the song had ended so had my momentary insanity. Pushing Sherry away from me, I looked around me in horror and fled from the dance floor, barely giving my date time to grab her shawl and bag on the way out.

"I don't understand," she called after me. "We're best mates. I only did what you asked me to..."

I stopped and turned. It was the least I owed her - him. I was so confused.

"Not Shalto. I mean, you – like this - Sherry. This was an incredibly stupid idea. How could
you have let me go on with it? I don't know what we were thinking."

"Hey, cool it, man. It was just mucking about. No harm done. I'll get off home, now - you'll never have to lay eyes on Sherry again, I promise. But hey, what's the problem? It worked, didn't it? I would say your street cred went up a few hundred per cent back there."

"Are you kidding me? We kissed, for Fuck's sake."

"Bleedin' hell. So what? I always thought you humans made entirely too much fuss and bother about all that stuff. Just a bit of theatre. It didn't mean a thing..."

I nodded.

"Nice though..." she added.

"Piss off, Sherry – or Shalto, or whoever the fuck you are...'"

We walked to the end of the street in silence. I knew that I was out of order but could not bring myself to apologise. We continued on down the main road, passing our bus stop and ignoring the buses that trundled by. I just needed to walk. To get my head straight. Sherry meanwhile had the sense to let me be.

It was a long hike but by the time we had reached the parting of the ways, I had cooled down enough to be civil, at least. I turned to my companion.

"Well, this is it. Thanks for everything, then."

"See you, tomorrow then, mate."

"Yeah, usual place. Oh, and make sure you bring the dress and stuff back, eh? I need to get it back in mum's wardrobe as soon as possible."

"Did you have a good time, Darling? I wasn't expecting you home so early. Didn't you want to see your date home?"

Mum was waiting up when I got home. I had expected that she would want to hear all about it the following morning but hadn't expected that.

"Nah. Sherry can take care of herself."

Mum pulled a face.

"What did that mean?" I asked, feeling my cheeks beginning to burn.

"Well, I thought you were going on the bus. It's a bit late for young girl to be walking the streets alone. In my day, a young man escorted his date home, made sure she got there safely…"

"She got a taxi-cab…" I lied.

"oh, well, that is okay, then. But you had a good time, did you?"

"Yeah, great, thanks. It was good."

"And - are you going to see her again? Sherry, I mean?"

"M-um." I protested.

Mum shook her head and smiled while I escaped to my room as fast as I could.

The next day I woke up late. My head ached and someone seemed to have lined my mouth and throat with blotting paper during the night. Still, there'd be no school today, so at least I would be spared the task of fielding the inevitable teasing and questions that would inevitably follow.

Mum had obviously decided to let me sleep in because she had left a little note in the kitchen saying she was feeling a lot better and had gone shopping and would see me later. It was a bit of relief, really. I didn't feel in the least bit like talking. Everything just seemed out of whack. And I knew it wouldn't feel right again until I had seen Shalto.

I'd made myself a mug of coffee and was just pouring the milk onto a couple of Weetabix when the doorbell rang. Shalto. I puffed heavily and pulled my dressing gown around me. I padded barefoot into the hallway, not knowing what to expect. I opened the front door and there he stood, just as he always did. I stared at him with a shake of my head. I had never felt so relieved nor so disappointed to see my best friend again.

He nodded back to me and I noticed his eyes. They looked different. Dull somehow. As though something had knocked the wind out of his sails. Neither of us spoke a word as he handed me the hold-all and all that remained of Sherry, though we both took care to avoid brushing one another's fingers in the exchange. I led him into the kitchen and pointed to a chair then set the bag on the worktop. We sat on either side of the kitchen table while I stabbed at my Weetabix with an awkwardness that would have seemed preposterous only a week ago. I wished *somebody* would say *something* yet neither of us seemed eager to make the first move and we seemed to have reached stalemate.

And then, at last, and quite out of the blue, Shalto smirked and pointed at me in gleeful delight.

"Man, you should have seen yourself, getting on down like John Revolting..." he said pouting his lips. Then, as if to make his point, he sprang up and began to strut around the little kitchen, grinding his hips and throwing his best disco moves.

"Well, you can talk," I guffawed and pushing back my chair, I started to mince around, batting my eyelashes and giggling with exaggerated bashfulness. On we cavorted, whooping riotously and sending ourselves up royally while my coffee turned cold. It was five minutes of hilarious relief. But it didn't change anything.

When we finally slumped back down in our seats I looked over at my friend and shook my head with a sad smile.

"It wasn't just a kiss though, was it? I had a boner. Don't tell me you didn't notice."

"Oh? And I just thought you had a gun in your pocket..."

"Don't laugh, mate. I've got no one else to talk to about his stuff. Seriously, d'you reckon it makes me a queer?"

"God, no. You've got it all wrong, Jonno. Not that it would matter. If you were - I mean. That's another thing you lot get all out of proportion. This either-or thing. It's so limiting sometimes. But if it makes you feel any better - when I'm a bloke, I'm a bloke and when I'm a woman, well, that's what I am. All woman. Technically, we're neither one nor the other, I suppose. Or we're both, maybe. Not sure you can even think about it those terms. Cool, eh?"

"Pretty cool, I guess. But I'm not one of you, and right now I'm pretty bloody confused. The way I see it, when I'm with you, *Shalto* – it's like you're my best friend, the most important person in the world, next to my mum, of course. And, hey, you're kinda neat and all, but you don't make me want to get my rocks off - you know what I mean..."

"But..."

"Well - as Sherry - you were the same person underneath, right? But it felt entirely different somehow. I don't understand."

"Well, I was and I wasn't. I can't explain it very well. It's not quite a matter of being the same underneath, like putting on a costume or disguise. As Sherry, I'm still me, but I'm also different. People around me react differently. The world I inhabit seems slightly scarier somehow. I see things a bit differently. Feel more exposed, perhaps. Like with that oaf at the dance. Shalto - Sherton even, they could have dealt with him, no problem. But suddenly I just felt so vulnerable. Don't get me wrong. It felt good, as well - getting noticed in that way, by you and some of the other lads there, but it's not something you can control and that is the scary bit.

And thinking about it, last night, that feeling seemed very familiar, somehow. I know I can't remember much about the past, but my sense is that I did spend a lot of time as a female and I think I do kinda miss it. I reckon I've probably opted to live as a male these past years primarily because it does just feel safer when you are alone in the world."

His words struck home. I thought about how scary Capel Road must be for a young girl alone and in the dark, and I hung my head.

"Shalto, I'm so sorry I left you to walk home on your own, last night. It was pretty low, I know. But I wasn't thinking..."

"It wasn't the most comfortable thirty minutes of my life but, I must admit, it did get me thinking about all of this stuff..."

I didn't know how to reply so we sat in silence and somehow it felt okay. I'd never heard the shapeshifter talk so openly before and realised how deeply he must trust me. How deeply we had come to trust each other.

At length, Shalto spoke again.

"Would it be so bad, anyway?"

"Would what be so bad?"

"Being queer. A pouf - as you young lads like to call it these days."

"Not as bad as it might be," I conceded. "Mum has always been very open-minded about these things. She loves Bowie and that whole velvet underground scene. She always said it was fine to be whatever you were. She's great like that. On the other hand, I'm not sure the rest of the world is quite so accepting, so I wouldn't wish it on anyone. But no - it's more the confusion that's bothering me. Messing with my head, as they say."

"Well, the last thing I wanted was to mess with that head, like it is isn't messed up enough already. So, let's agree to put it

down to experience, turn the page and close the whole sorry little chapter, shall we?"
I smiled.

"No argument here, Mate. It's ancient history as far as I'm concerned. And it was my idea, after all, so don't beat yourself up about it. Now, be a chum and put the kettle on. Mum'll be back from Sainsburys soon and I need to put her stuff back where it belongs. And I don't know how much vodka you gave me, last night, but my tongue feels like the bottom of a blinkin' parrot's cage this morning."

13

I tried my hardest to follow Shalto's advice and draw a line under the whole Sherry episode, yet it was not as easy as he had made it sound. I was generally quite adept at simply shutting things out of my mind when I chose to. So much so that Mum referred to it as my "talent for compartmentalising." I'd never quite known what it had meant but it sounded very organized and I liked that. Making it work for Sherry, however, was proving to be a real challenge.

It seems almost impossible to shake her from my thoughts. I found myself daydreaming about her at the oddest moments and it wasn't only sexual, though God only knows that was trying enough. My penis had persisted in developing a will of its own and seemed to delight in popping up and betraying me at the worst possible times. I had no idea what was normal and suspected that I was growing up to be some kind of sexual pervert. Shalto, of course, had been no help and I had no one else to compare notes with.

It had begun to worry me so much that I had almost considered talking to Mum about it. *Almost. She* would not have minded but *I*, unfortunately, did. Very much. In the end, a chance conversation with our new GP helped put my mind at rest. I'd needed to renew my prescription for my inhaler and, as I'd turned sixteen, Mum encouraged me to go alone. My asthma symptoms had troubled me less and less as I'd grown older and I tended to carry an inhaler for reassurance as much as anything else. Indeed, our former GP had gone so far as to suggest that my symptoms may well have been psychological in "aetiology". It was a neat word but it didn't impress my Mum who promptly had me transferred to a different doctor.

Dr Jenkins turned out to be a bit of a natural when it came to adolescent lads. Having listened to my chest, he had grunted with satisfaction and fixed me with his clear eyes. *And was there was anything else bothering me?* I don't know whether he had somehow picked up on my anxiety or just remembered what it felt like to be a teenage boy. Either way, I came away from that appointment feeling a lot less deviant than when I'd arrived. He also agreed to renew my prescription but encouraged me to try and do without the inhaler, if I could.

Still, there was more to this Sherry thing than feeling turned on. I found myself longing for both the physical *and* emotional closeness we had shared in the fleeting moments of that last dance. In our own way, Shalto and I had grown as close as any friends could be, closer perhaps, but that night the connection between us had been something else altogether.

From time to time, I would catch him looking at me from beneath his lashes and wonder if he felt the same way. He never brought it up, but something had changed between us and we both knew it.

For weeks, we continued on as though it hadn't. School had broken up for the summer holidays and, under normal circumstances, days of carefree sunshine and companionship would have beckoned. This year, however, I managed to find myself a summer job working as a kitchen storeman and porter at The Mile End Hospital; a fact I somehow failed to mention to Shalto until the day before I started.

He couldn't exactly object. I hated having to ask Mum for money and wanted to contribute. I still had my paper round but that was just pocket money, really. This would give me a chance to earn some real dough. We would still have the weekends and occasional evenings but not enough time to begin to get on each other's nerves.

Shalto shrugged it off saying it would give him some time to tidy the house up a bit. I wondered if he was joking, but with Shalto, you could never be sure. Whatever the truth of the matter, neither of us complained too bitterly about the situation.

The weeks passed. My new job involved early starts, long hours and a fair amount of heavy lifting. There were daily deliveries of tinned goods and groceries by the crate to unload and hundredweight sacks of potatoes and flour to heft from the stores into the kitchens. It did wonders for my physique but, by the time I got home, all I wanted to do was do was collapse in front of the TV with my tea. At least that is what I told myself.

Shalto and I continued to meet up at the weekends. We played chess, read comics and larked about in the same old way. We even bought ourselves skateboards and hauled them down to The South Bank where all the best skaters hung out. But it all seemed like hard work. We had lost the casual easiness of just hanging out and neither of us seemed to know how to get it back.

Meanwhile, life around me was becoming less predictable too. Despite her dodgy hearing, Mrs Worth, had always been very passionate about choral music. In fact, I could remember her listening to all sorts of fancy singing by people with strange names like *Verdi* and *Puccini,* though had never really thought much more of it. Recently, however, she had learned that a local community choir at started up on a Tuesday evening. She was very keen to join but was a bit shy about doing so alone.

Finally, after weeks of hints and not so subtle wheedling, she managed to persuade my mum to go along with her. It had not been easy. Mum was not a complete social recluse, (she would attend work functions), but believed in keeping herself to herself and skirted pretty close to it at times. In the end, Mrs Worth pointed that it would not be that long before I spread my wings and flew the nest. And where would that leave Mum then? It was a low blow but proved effective, or so Mum told me. Besides, she said, it would be good for me to have the space as well.

Mum had not regretted it. The group had made them both very welcome and from that first night onwards, I had the pleasure of hearing her singing around the house as she tried to memorise the songs.

It did make me think though. I was so used to regarding my mum as an unchanging certainty in my world that it was easy to forget that she had a life outside of mine. I remembered the photos I had found and suddenly found myself wondering what it must have been like for her when she met my father. She had never told me what had caused the breakdown in the marriage and perhaps I was still too young to understand, but she had made no secret of the fact that the two of them had been very deeply in love. If my feeling could be so strong after one evening with Sherry then I could scarcely imagine what that must be like.

I seemed to recall that she had spoken more about him when I was very young and I couldn't work out why that had changed. It had though. As far as I could remember, she had only ever told me about the good times. In fact, I could not recall her ever having said a bad word about him. Not to me, at least.

I wished that I could remember him more clearly but he remained an obstinate blur. Perhaps I should have found a way of asking her more about him but it all seemed so hard somehow. She had, after all, taken care to hide those photographs. I knew her well enough to realise that had she any wish to talk to me about why he left, she would have done.

Then came the day that the GCSE results were posted. I'd taken the morning off work and had hightailed it around to my school as soon as the gate opened. A handful of other students, mostly the class swats, were milling around already, waiting their turn. You could just about smell the anxiety in the air. I puffed my cheeks and tried to regulate my breathing. It wasn't fear for me, exactly. I knew

I'd done pretty well - it was a matter of *how* well. Still, my thwarted anticipation was great enough to get the better of my manners. Shouldering my way through the pack of giggling girls who were gathered in front of the notice board, I looked up and scanned the sheet for my name. There it was. A row of 'A's save for a 'B' for Geography - and I didn't care about that. I pumped my fists and looked around, half-hoping that Shalto might have remembered and turned up to show his support. But there was no sign of him and I felt suddenly foolish, for thinking he would. After all, what could a bunch of stupid exam results mean to someone like him.

On the way out, a couple of other kids stopped and slapped me on the back in congratulations. A few years earlier the same gesture would have meant the world to me, but today it seemed to count for little. The one friend I wanted to share my success with was nowhere to be found.

I didn't have to be at work until after lunch so hopped on a bus and headed to the offices of Skynner, Sykes and Skynner. At least Mum would be over the moon. I wasn't sure which of us had been the most keyed-up that morning, though she had tried her best not to let it show.

"That's fantastic. I always knew you were a budding genius," she breathed, her face lit with pure pride as she hugged me. Joan got to her feet and hugged me too, planting a big moist kiss on my cheek. I was just recovering when something very unusual occurred. Mr Skynner Jr emerged from his office, peered down out me through his half-moon spectacles and shook me warmly by the hand.

"Well done, my boy. You have done us all very proud."

I blinked in confusion and then muttered some words of thanks. He nodded, made an about-turn and disappeared back behind his office door as promptly as he had materialised. I looked at Mum and raised my eyebrows. I could only recall ever having seen him once or perhaps twice in my life. Since when had he become "us"? Mum shrugged and smiled in pleasure.

"We're all one big family here, aren't we Joan?" she said with a wink and an odd little smile.

"Oh, yes, indeed," sniffed Joan, who seemed to be struggling to hold back her tears. "And we couldn't be more thrilled, Jonathon. Really, we couldn't."

"I think that will probably do, now," said Mum in a low voice. "Jonathon doesn't like a lot of fuss, do you Sweetheart? But you don't look all that chuffed yourself, Jumbo, Luv. Are you sickening for something?"

She held me at arm's length and scrutinised my face with a frown and then the placed the back of her hand against my forehead.

"Come to think of it you haven't been yourself for a while. I *had* hoped it was just the stress of the examinations. I know you've done brilliantly and how hard you've worked but, honestly, academic success is not worth making yourself miserable or ill over..."

"Don't fuss, Mum. I'm just tired..."

"Hmmm – well, I tell you what. I reckon a proper celebration is in order. What say you ask Shalto to come round this evening? We'll have fish 'n' chips, (he can eat chips at least,) and I'll buy a bottle of bubbly on the way home. You're old enough to drink at home now so I think we can push the boat out. Or why not invite that girl you took to the dance? I know you haven't mentioned her lately, but you said you had a great time with her..."

"Mum - *please*. She's gone away for the summer. Besides, I don't think it's going anywhere..."

"Well, Shalto, then. It seems ages since I saw him."

I nodded and kissed her on the cheek.

"Thanks Mum. I'll give him a bell when I get to work."

The evening passed pleasantly enough. Shalto had sounded genuinely very pleased for me when I spoke to him on the phone and seemed positively touched by the invitation to share in our celebration. He said that he'd needed a bit of good news as Captain seemed to have gone wandering again and, this time, he had a feeling that the cat would not be back. I tried to reassure him but I couldn't help feel like a bit of a heel as I replaced the receiver. I knew how empty he found the house when Captain was not around and, no matter how I tried to justify it, I had been neglecting him. He would never have said as much, but it didn't take much to work out how alone he must have been feeling since I had started work at the hospital.

As it turned out, I felt happier to see him than I had in weeks and I Mum seemed happy to see Shalto too. She greeted him with a warm smile and was pleased when she did not need to press him to accept a glass or two of the champagne she had stowed in the fridge. I could tell that she would have liked to see him eat a little more, but then he so rarely ate with us at all, that she let it pass. Much as she privately fretted about his nutritional welfare, he wasn't going to starve to death in one evening.

I, on the other hand, tucked into my cod and chips with gusto. Perhaps it was the champagne but, for the first time in ages, I felt relaxed. I began to chatter cheerfully about the subjects I planned to take at 'A' level. Maths, Physics and Chemistry. And then everyone had to take General Studies, so that would make the fourth.

Mum listened with a smile and then turned her attention to Shalto, who normally had so much to say for himself yet had barely spoken a word for nearly fifteen minutes.

"What about you, Luv? You must have sat your 'A' levels, this year? The results come out in a couple of weeks, don't they? And then off to university, I guess? It must be pretty exciting, huh?"

Shalto and I exchanged an awkward glance. I had forgotten that Shalto was supposed to be a couple of years above me yet had made no mention whatsoever of him sitting any exams to Mum. And now she had well and truly put him on the spot.

"Oh, you know," he drawled, "it hasn't been going so well. I'm not sure bleedin' university is right for me, if you'll pardon my French. I'm thinking of dropping out for a year or two. Yeah, I was thinking of starting a little business, actually. Something in the antiques line - it's a bit of a hobby of mine. Maybe start with a stall in Camden market or, you know, just pass pieces I find at rag markets and junk shops onto the dealers in Islington, maybe."

My mum raised her eyebrows in a kind of first-I've-heard-of-it surprise. I watched her face and said a little prayer to myself. She was a dab hand at spotting deceit once her suspicions were alerted. She was going to see straight through this one.

"Oh? I see. But Jonathon is always telling me how smart you are – at maths and everything. It seems such a waste of your talents. What do your parents think about all this?"

Shalto shrugged his shoulders.

"Not sure they really care either way…"

He looked away, giving me the opportunity to catch Mum's eye. I shook my head meaningfully and did my best to look grave. Thankfully, my mum took the hint. Undoubtedly regretting her lack of tact, she made some noises of consolation and then let the subject drop.

I, however, did not. Later on, as he was leaving and Mum had retreated to her bedroom, I cornered Shalto in the hallway.

"What the hell was all that about? Selling antiques for Pete's sake? You were making her ask too many questions..."

"Well, we'll need some cover story for me not going away to university come the end of September and, besides, it was just nice to have someone pay me a bit of attention, for a change. You certainly seem to have lost interest since Sherry came on the scene. I'll bet you'd find a chink of space in your oh-so busy week to make some proper time for her."

I stared at my best mate in disbelief.

"You know how crazy that sounds, don't you?" I hissed. "You *are* Sherry. Sherry *was* you. How can you be jealous of her?"

Shalto glared at me and then closed his eyes and tilted his head to one side. He bit his lip and then stared me straight in the eyes. I shook my head and covered my face with one hand.

"All right. I miss her. Is that what you what to hear? Sherry, I mean. I know it sounds daft, but I can't stop thinking about her – you. You as her. It doesn't make sense and it's freaking me out. But that's the way it is."

Shalto did not react at all as I had expected. He reached out and squeezed my shoulder.

"I know, mate. I know. You won't believe it, but I miss her, and *us* when I'm her, too."

14

The following weekend, Sherry walked back into my life.

It started with a simple date. A trip to Leicester Square to see a matinee showing of that summer's hit movie - *Raiders of The Lost Ark*. A later viewing had been out of the question. I'd had the discussion many times before and, as far as Mum was concerned, travelling all the way back from the West End by tube and bus at my age and at that time of night was asking for trouble.

"And you needn't look at me like that, young man," she would say. "You have no idea what the world is like come closing time. You'd be lucky if all someone did was throw-up all over you."

I wasn't sure if she was talking from personal experience but she had done a good job of putting me off night buses, at least for the time-being. And it did mean that we would be able to stop off at MacDonalds afterwards where I would be able to treat Sherry to the sight of me slurping down an extra thick chocolate milkshake.

When Saturday came, I was so excited it must have shone from every pore.

"So, who is she?" asked Mum. "I presume it *is* a girl you are meeting as you *never* make this much effort for Shalto and you certainly don't wear cologne. What is that? Hi Karate...?"

I froze like an escaped convict in the glare of a searchlight.

"It's Sherry, the girl I took to the dance," I garbled. "She's a little bit older than me, Mum. But ever so well brought up. She goes to church and everything."

I could tell that Mum was struggling to keep a straight face but at least she held her tongue. Grabbing her purse, she wished me luck and held out a couple of pound notes. I raised my hands in refusal.

"But Mum, I'm earning my own money now. You don't have to..."

"No – I insist. Let it be my treat, Jumbo. For doing so well in your exams. And if it's any good and that Harrison Ford is as cute as he looks, you can take *me* next weekend. It's a very long time since I went on a date with a handsome young man."

My face burned as I closed the front door but it wasn't from any embarrassment my mother had caused me. The ridiculous words I had blurted out were ricocheting around my head like ball bearings in a pinball machine. *Sherry a regular churchgoer?* The fabrication had not sounded remotely convincing, even to my ears. I couldn't think what had possessed me to concoct such a story. Mum was no fan of organised religion and made few bones about it. But, of course, the answer was obvious.

No sooner had I let slip the words "a bit older than me" than I had scrambled to repair the impression. After all, an older girl was more likely to lead me astray than someone my own age. I took a punt that the mention of church would imply that Sherry, God bless her, was unlikely to be sexually active. It sounded really daft when I had the time to think it through but, if I was being honest, I was just trying to avoid another one of *those* conversations. The kind where my mum would refer candidly and anatomically correctly to parts of our bodies, I personally felt were best left unmentioned, while I sat silently praying that the bedroom floor would just open up and swallow me whole.

The date was great. The movie was ace and by the end of it, I wanted to *be* Indiana Jones, or at least own a whip like his. Sherry and I got on like a house on fire. And there was this kind of electricity between us. A bit like when you touch something statically charged and feel that funny little thrill. Nevertheless, Shalto and I had agreed to hold back on any physical contact. Neither of us wanted things getting weird too fast. But it was thrilling enough just to hold hands.

It was not long, however, before my impetuosity backfired on me. Things seemed to be going really well. I hung out with Shalto during the week and met up with Sherry at the weekend. We stuck to our commitment to take it slow and I hadn't so much as attempted to introduce my "girlfriend" to Mum. That seemed altogether too fraught with pitfalls, plus - I didn't want to appear overkeen. Yet Mum knew me well enough to recognise that something was very different and if I thought that I'd been able to hide the depth of my feelings from her, I was mistaken.

A couple of weekends later, I found myself listening in to a phone conversation that my mum was having with uncle Roy, one of her brothers. I wasn't proud of myself but it was a genuine accident. I had sneaked into Mum's room to use the phone extension in her bedroom to call Shalto whilst she prepared Sunday lunch. It wasn't something I generally did, but things had become a bit tricky between us since Sherry had appeared on the scene and I preferred to make our plans out of earshot. I had just hung up when I heard Mum pick up the kitchen phone. I suppose that I should have simply hung up myself but I was afraid that she would here the click and realise that I had been on the line. Instead, I covered the receiver with my hand and tried my best not to breathe. The number rang out a couple of times and then a voice replied confirming the telephone number. I could hear the chatter of the racing commentary on a TV in the background.

"Hi, it's Margot."

"Good grief. Has Christmas come upon us, already?"

"Okay. I deserved that. But really, how are you, Roy? And how's the family?"

"Well, I've got the house to myself, just now. Cynthia's nipped around the corner to a local jumble sale and the kids…"

Mum made little sounds of acknowledgement as Roy rambled on, but even I could tell that she was hardly listening. Uncle Roy must have caught on too. He paused.

"And what about you, Sis?

"To tell the truth, I was kind of hoping you could help me out. Jumbo's got a girlfriend and it seems to have become rather serious very quickly. To be honest, I'm just not sure how to play this one…"

"Aye, well. He's at that age now, Sis. All raging hormones. It's only natural. All you can do is make sure he knows what he's doing and that he doesn't end up getting the poor lass up the duff. Still, I do wish you'd think about what I said and come back and live up here. You need your family. It's very hard for a lass bringing up a nipper all on her own. Especially a lad."

"Roy. We've been through this many times. This is our home. I just want a bit of help."

"Do you need me to talk to the young man?"

"Well, it's not quite that Roy. I've never been embarrassed to talk to Jonathon about the facts of life or contraception, for that matter, and I know he's at that age when they start to experiment – and that is all perfectly natural. It's just that …"

I listened transfixed as my mum opened the sluice gates and it all came tumbling out. Her anxieties, her fears and the predicament in which she found herself.

It wasn't my sexual development, that worried her, it was the danger that I might jump into a precipitous commitment like an engagement before I'd had time to "discover myself". She loved my sweet nature but feared that it made me vulnerable to falling heavily for the first girl who showed any genuine interest in me. The prospect of early nuptials was far more likely with a so-called "good girl" who would insist on waiting until the wedding ring was on her finger. Her logic, though different to mine, was faultless. Talk about hoist with your own petard? My story about Sherry going to church seemed to be blowing up in my face and there was nothing I could do about it.

I clasped my forehead in my hand but mum was far from finished.

"Look, Roy. I know I'm getting ahead of myself but nobody knows better than I how powerful first love can be - or how devastating the fall out is when it goes wrong."

Roy grunted.

"The less said about that, the better, Sis, and it wasn't as though we didn't try to protect you- but, well, you always had a mind of your own. But, if I've learned anything from having bought up bairns of my own, it's that the more you tell 'em not to do summut, the more they'll bloody do it. Give 'em a long leash and turn a blind eye. If it's the lad's first girlfriend, chances are it'll be a flash in the pan. Blokes have a pretty short attention span at that age. You remember what I was like, Margi - different bird every month..."

Mum laughed and remarked that she certainly did. She had always said that, as much as she adored him growing up, Roy had been loud mouthed and as vain as he was handsome. He had had his pick of girls and took it, while his own feelings never seemed to be in danger.

"Yet Jumbo couldn't be more different," she sighed.

"Aye, that's true enough. But I'll give you ten to one, you'll only make him keener by placing obstacles in their way. You know what they say about forbidden fruit. If Jonathon is serious about this girl, you may find that a blanket of approval may be the best way to smother the flame."

"Oh, Roy. Thank you - I think there may be something in what you say. When did you get to be so wise? I'll let you get back to your sport, now."

"Aye, well. Anytime – you know that. Just don't leave it so long next time and promise me you'll come up for Christmas, this year. We've missed you both."

My mum made her farewells and I heard the line go dead as he hung up. I tapped the receiver against my head and then set it back on its cradle. As if things weren't complicated enough already. I tiptoed back to my own room and lay on my bed, unsure whether to feel freaked out or relieved.

15

The summer holiday always seemed to last forever when I was younger, but this one had passed in a flash. All the same, I returned to school a whole new person. I had grown up a lot; both physically and emotionally. I was in the sixth form now and even though I was just about the youngest in our year, I was now amongst the tallest and fittest looking kids in the school. My experience of working in the real world, though brief, had bolstered both my confidence and my piggy bank, to say nothing of my muscles. I'd had a taste of what it was to be a grown-up. And it felt good.

Most importantly of all, in addition to a cool mate, I now had a girlfriend as well- a circumstance that had boosted my standing in the school's social ranking even further. And it got better. Most of the other kids who had stayed on for the sixth-form were just as keen to get into a good university as myself. My stellar achievement in my GCSE exams shifted my status from swat to boffin overnight. It wasn't as though everyone suddenly included me in their weekend plans, but I did become the go-to guy for anyone who needed a helping hand with a thorny maths theorem or to spot the error in an equation. I never minded. I had Shalto. I didn't need another friend.

At home, Sherry's introduction into the order of things seemed to have gone as well as it could. Sherry had turned up to our house, that first time, dressed in her favourite jeans, vintage baseball jacket and Converse basket-ball sneakers. And no make-up. She looked so effortlessly pretty with her corkscrew hair tumbling down around her face that I couldn't see how anyone could resist her.

Be that as it may, Mum, while doing her bright and cheerful best to make my "new friend" feel welcome, remained a little reserved. After a while she seemed to thaw a little but, at times, I could see the question marks in her eyes as she gazed at Sherry. I tried not to let it make me too anxious. Mum was used to being the only woman in my life and it was only natural that she might be a little over-protective. And then there had been that conversation with Uncle Roy. We would just have to keep playing it cool.

Sherry, for her part, handled the whole nice-to-meet-you thing with surprising sensitivity. But then, she did already know my mum, pretty well. She was funny and bright whilst remaining respectful and polite. And she never took liberties. Or talked about religion, which was a huge relief, given the misapprehension I had misguidedly planted in my mum's mind.

Then one Saturday morning, while Sherry sat in our kitchen waiting for me to finished my toast and marmalade, things got suddenly complicated.

"Where are you two off to this time, then?" asked Mum.

"Camden Market. I told Jonno we need to get there early before it gets too bleedin' crowded, if you'll pardon my French."

Mum stared at Sherry, her face creased in thought.

"I'm so sorry. I didn't mean to swear…" stammered Sherry.

"No, don't apologise. A bit of colourful language never did any harm. It's just that I keep thinking that there's something familiar about you. And now I know what it is. I'm not sure why, but you remind me of Shalto, somehow – you know, Jumbo's best friend."

Sherry didn't even look at me which was just as well.

"Oh, really? It's funny you should say that. Shalto's my cousin. Once or twice removed, I believe. But who keeps count? That's how we met. Didn't Jonno mention it?"

I glared at her, trying to disguise a rising sense of panic. I still wasn't very good at this.

"I thought you two met each other at an Interschool Chess Tournament?"

"Oh, that? Well, yes, we did. Meet that is. But it came up that Jonno knew Shalto and that's how we got chatting. And then, Shalto set up our date for the school dance."

"Oh, yes. I see. He's a good lad and a good friend to Jumbo. But, tell me, what does your family think of Shalto just giving up on university and this whole wild antiques scheme?"

Sherry shrugged.

"Well, you know Shalto. He always was a law unto himself. He'll probably end up richer than the rest of us put together."

I took a large bite of my toast and tried not to choke.

"Well, I hope you are right," commented Mum with a thin laugh. "I'm afraid, I know only too well what happens when you give up an opportunity for real career. Not that I would have it any other way." And with that she smiled at me and tousled my hair. "Now, I really need to get off to the shops. You two have a lovely day. And don't get carried away."

By the time the half-term break came around, the complications seemed to be increasing exponentially. School was fine. In fact, it remained the one place where things felt remotely normal. It was everything else.

My relationship with Sherry was growing increasingly close and, each time we parted, I could hardly wait to see her again. The status of my relationship to Shalto, however, had taken on a new and somewhat vexing complexion.

He was still my best mate, but it had begun to feel as though I had to twist his arm before he would agree to let me see Sherry again. It started to become a real pain. Shalto and I had always got on brilliantly, but now, even when I thought we were having a great time his resentment simmered just below the surface. He was convinced that I would prefer to be with his alter ego and his insecurity was beginning to sour our friendship.

Sherry, meanwhile, simply doted on me whenever I saw her, which completely did my head in. I had no wish to make Shalto feel bad, but I was falling heavily for Sherry and I knew it. The whole situation was beginning to feel a bit on the surreal side.

Things really turned pear-shaped when Mum overheard Shalto and I arguing one afternoon. She took me to one side for a quiet "chat about things" and said she was worried. I told her that I had no wish to talk about it and must have come over like the typical moody teenager, though there was hardly anything typical about the situation. But Mum refused to back off. She wasn't going to stand by and watch me wreck the only friendship I'd ever had without saying something. She drew my attention to the dangers of allowing *the giddiness of my first romance* to jeopardize another equally important relationship. She had noted that the three of us (Shalto, Sherry and myself) never seemed to hang out together and wondered at the wisdom of this. *It was*, she said, *little wonder if Shalto felt his nose had been put out of joint.* I listened as patiently as I could and then retreated to my room, my head throbbing. I don't think I had ever wanted to confide in Mum so much as at that moment. But the risk was just too great. The idea of losing Shalto had always been bad enough. But now, I would rather have died than never see Sherry again.

Things came to a head not long after the half-term break had ended. Thanks to Mum's words of wisdom, the week off school had turned out to be a blast. I had spent some wonderful days with Sherry but had also made time to do some cool stuff with Shalto too, visiting our old haunts and tearing around Camden Town on the scooter. It seemed to make him happy though I couldn't help noticing how wan and drawn he appeared. He had always been very pale but now his skin looked positively waxen. It didn't help that he had decided to "dye" his hair jet black. But so had most of the dudes who hung out at our favourite places. So much so that my own blonde curls had become a constant source of misery to me. But I wasn't even going to go there with Mum and besides Sherry said she loved them.

With mum at work, Sherry and I had found ourselves alone in the house more than once. We had fooled around a bit but had agreed not to sleep together. It would only make things weirder. I knew that we were right to hold back although I wanted to and, sometimes, it seemed as though I could think of nothing else. Shalto told me that, in his opinion, I was too young. I'd like to have told him to piss off and mind his own business but, in a way, it *was* his business. And, as strange as it sounds, I really did think that he had my best interests at heart.

It was a wet Sunday morning. Mum and I had just sat down to have a coffee together when Shalto turned up with a stack of LPs under his arm. We had recently both got into Punk and New Wave and music seemed to be the one thing about which we could safely agree. Mum took one look at his spikey new haircut and the safety pin through his ear and rolled her eyes.

"And how's the antique business, Shalto?"

"Bustin', Mrs C. Thanks for asking. Oh, and, now that you mention it, I've got something just for you. Found 'em, down Greenwich way."

He ferreted about in one of the many pockets in his combat trousers and pulled out a little velvet-covered box and handed it to her. Mum raised her eyes brows and thanked him with a surprised smile. I stood up and peered over her shoulder. She opened the box to reveal a pair of beautiful aquamarine-coloured glass drop-earrings.

"Why, Shalto. They're stunning. They're Art Deco, aren't they?"

"Right you are, Mrs C. Spot on. Well, a little bird told me it was your birthday last month and then I recalled you saying how much you loved the period, the other day, so when I saw 'em, I couldn't resist, could I?"

"Wow. Thank you." She lifted the earrings out of the box and held them to the light. "These are just exquisite, Shalto. You really do have an eye for it, don't you? But when did I mention it? I don't recall..."

I caught his eye and shook my head silently, mouthing – "no."

"Ah, well. No. I wasn't actually there at the time – but Jonno, here, happened to mention that you had been talking to Sherry about it, so I just thought…"

"Well, that was so sweet, though but you shouldn't have. But I love them. Thank you again and I shall treasure them forever." And with that she kissed him on the cheek.

"You're very welcome, Mrs C. You've always been so very kind to me and I just wanted to show you how much I have appreciated it. Perhaps they can be something to remember me by."

Mum smiled again and trotted off to try the earrings on in the hallway mirror. I looked at my friend and frowned. A crowd of worrying thoughts had begun to flood into my mind like fans into a football stadium, but I shook my head and parked them in my deal-with-it-later basket.

"There, what do you think, Jumbo?" asked Mum returning. I shook my head.

"They are *so* your colour, Mum. Nice one, Shalto."

Up in my bedroom Shalto unsheathed one of the albums and placed it on the record deck. He dropped the stylus into the groove and turned up the bass.

"We need to talk…" he announced, struggling to make himself heard above the din of our favourite Clash track. I stalked over to the record player and adjusted the volume and then looked at him. He lowered his voice and spoke through gritted teeth.

"I can't keep splitting myself in two like this. I just can't. You have no idea how exhausting it is, Jonno. Zero. It takes every bit of cellular energy that I possess and a crate load of vodka. I knew it was a crap idea. I should never have let you talk me into it…"

He started to pace about the room, most of his words still lost beneath the throb of the music. Finally, I stepped into his path and squared up to him. I had no time for this.

"Oh, boohoo. Poor Shalto. You *like* being Sherry, just as much as I like you being her, you know you do, so don't give me that."

Shalto's eyes met mine. He sank to the floor and slumped against the bed. He looked deflated. Like an air-filled Santa Claus you see lying in a heap in someone's garden, once Christmas is over. I plumped myself down next to him. He turned his face to me.

"I know, I do." He said sadly. "I love being with you when I'm Sherry, but I feel so vulnerable as her when I'm alone. And I am alone, mate. All the time you are at school or here with your Mum at night. Especially since Captain took it into his head to just piss off altogether. I'm just all alone in that big freakin' house. And I don't think you appreciate the effort it takes to make the change…"

I plucked at my collar, feeling my throat constrict a little. The idea that Shalto might pull the plug on Sherry made me reach into my bedside table for my inhaler. I drew in a puff and tried to speak calmly.

"Look, I'm sorry. I realise this is difficult for you. And I never meant for it to turn out like this. But I don't want to think about a life without Sherry, either. Surely you feel that all that effort is worth it when we *are* together? It's like a perfect fit. C'mon, Shalto. I know you feel it too. Besides, it's not as though you have anything better to do all day except lie around and drink vodka to recharge and wait for me to get home from school. You don't have a life outside of being with me. Not really - you know you don't…"

Shalto interrupted me with a small groan. The strange regularity of his features crumpled and he buried his face in his hands. I could not have jabbed my friend more sharply, had my words been needles.

Shalto, meanwhile, cleared his throat and looked up. I met the cold gleam of steel in his eyes and saw that I had gone too far. I screwed up my eyes and cursed my lack of tact. It never had been a strongpoint. And then he let me have it.

It was all true. He was a shapeshifter, for fuck's sake. Surely, he should be doing something a bit more meaningful with his life than this? Instead, he had allowed himself to become some kind of add-on to a teenage boy. It would have turned his stomach if only he had one that actually functioned.

I felt the sting of tears in my eyes. I'd have to find a way to pull it all back, somehow.

"Look, Shalto, you know I didn't mean that, mate. You've always meant the world to me, whether you're are you, Sherry or Sherton. You know that. I'm just so confused. I just don't want to have to choose between you."

But the chill in Shalto's expression did not thaw.

"No? Well, you might just be better off without any of us."

And with that, he sprang to his feet, flung open the bedroom door and then ran down the stairs and out of the house. I didn't follow him. There didn't seem any point. I recognised stalemate well enough. But as I lay on my bed going over the whole strange morning, the memory of the earrings and the odd words that he had spoken to my mum came back to me. And then it hit me. This was no spur of the moment gesture. Shalto had already decided to go - and he had no intention of coming back.

16

Two long weeks dragged past and I saw neither hide nor hair of either Shalto or Sherry. I tried ringing the house but, no matter what time I called, the line was engaged. I didn't need to be Sherlock Holmes to deduce that someone had intentionally left the phone off the hook.

I kept replaying that last conversation with Shalto in my mind but could not accept that it was over. I toyed with the idea of simply turning up at the shapeshifter's house but something held me back. I very much doubted that either Shalto or Sherry would open the door to me, no matter how long I knocked and my persistence might only attract unwanted attention from curious neighbours which would be the last thing either of them needed. I wanted to go though, and it took all the willpower I had to resist the impulse.

By the end of the first week, Mum began to comment on how quiet our little house had suddenly become. Worried that she would start to ask difficult questions, I invented a harmless fiction about Sherry travelling up to Norfolk to visit relatives. Mum remarked that this seemed a bit odd given that it was term time, so I was forced to further embellish my white lie by muttering something about an aged grandparent being on their deathbed, adding that since Sherry attended a private girls' school and her parents paid her fees, they could pretty much do as they pleased. It was a bit of a reach but at least Mum bought it. But then, she had no cause to suspect I was making it up.

Afterwards, I sat in my bedroom and mulled things over. I hadn't planned what to tell Mum if I did not make things up with Sherry, mostly because I didn't really want to think about it. After all, I hadn't technically fallen out with *Sherry*. Although, she wasn't answering my calls either. And that's when it hit me. In my mind, Shalto and Sherry had become two distinct individuals. But they were not. They were the same person. I yanked at my hair. The whole thing did my head in. My heart simply would not accept what my brain knew to be a fact. No wonder Shalto found it all so draining. He had tried to tell me that I could not have both of them in my life at the same time but I had not wanted to listen. Now I had neither.

It was Shalto's absence that Mum most noticed. She joked that she missed her "Shalto fix" and hoped we'd see him again soon. She seemed to have missed the hint he had dropped when he gave her the earrings but he hadn't mentioned any travel plans, so using that as an excuse seemed out of the question.

Unable to come up with a convincing explanation for his sudden absence, I resorted to outright subterfuge. I went out to "meet him as usual" at the weekend and spent a miserable morning in my own company, mooching around the record shop. Then, the following week, I simply pretended that he had been at round at ours while Mum had been out at choir practice. If nothing else I was getting good at this whole double life business.

On the plus side, Mum and I got to play a few more chess matches than we had in ages, though my poor concentration must have been a bit of a giveaway that something was up. I left my king wide open a couple of times and made a handful of ridiculously risky moves which caused her to raise her eyebrows and frown. Even so, she kept her mouth shut. If there was something wrong, I would tell her in my own time. She was never one to pry. She was always really cool like that.

By the end of the second week, however, I was becoming a wreck. Worry was turning into desperation. At night, instead of sleeping, I had lain awake, ruminating on the same depressing question - *What if the shapeshifter never contacted me again?*

And then on Thursday night, just as the clock clicked onto midnight, a new thought popped into my head. *But what if they were somehow waiting for me to make the first move?* I might not want to risk going around to the house on Capel Road, but that didn't mean that I simply had to sit on my hands and wait.

So, Friday morning, just after dawn, I dragged myself out of bed and stole downstairs. I tried phoning for the hundredth time. The line was engaged as usual but I hadn't expected anything else.

Thinking as calmly as I could, I found the pad of Basildon Bond and an envelope in the sitting room dresser and then crept back up to my room. I sat at my desk and chewed the end of my biro and then shivered. The central heating would come on soon, meanwhile, it felt as though we were in for an early winter.

I willed myself to concentrate on the task in hand. I had written the letter a hundred times during the night, yet now I had the pen in my hands the words refused to flow. I made several beginnings, all of which ended in the bin but, in the end, I folded the single sheet of paper into the envelope and scribbled the address. I nodded in satisfaction. My words had been brief and to the point.

I don't care who you choose to be. I just want you in my life. Yours forever, Jonathon.

I was lying though, and this time to myself as much as anyone else. If the enforced separation had shown me anything it was that Sherry was the one I wanted - wanted so badly that it didn't even feel like a real choice. Every day, it was as though some invisible cord that connected her to me became tauter and more uncomfortable. Our separation was becoming physically painful and I could only hope she felt it too.

With the letter written, I pulled on some jeans and a jacket over my pyjamas, helped myself to a first-class postage stamp from the drawer in the hall stand and slipped out into the cold dark morning. *Please, please, please,* I whispered as I crept along the street to the post box on the corner. *Please, please, please,* as I held the letter to my lips and then fed it into the slot. I double-checked the collection times, one more time. It would definitely catch the first post. It should be in Shalto's hands by the evening or first thing Saturday morning, at least.

An hour or so later, I sat in the kitchen, aware that Mum was watching me as I prodded my Weetabix in appetiteless agitation. I could almost feel her eyes as they lingered on the dark circles under my eyes. Then, out of nowhere, I heard what sounded like a choked-back sob. I looked up but she had turned away. I got to my feet and reached out to touch her shoulder.

"Don't cry. Mum."

She turned her face and a large tear rolled down her cheek.

"I can't bear to see you so unhappy, Jumbo – and then I remembered what it was like and I suddenly wondered if – well, I wondered if Julian still thought about me sometimes. I'm sorry."

I wrapped my arms around her, in tears myself now.

"Don't be sorry, Mum. I know you must miss him, but I never really realised what it must feel like.."

"Until now, huh?"

"I guess so. And, I'm sorry for not talking to you. I think I'm in love, Mum. Does that sound ridiculous? I expect you think I'm a bit young for all that?"

She blotted away my tears with her handkerchief and brushed my hair out of my eyes.

"Well, so was Romeo and no one ever questioned the sincerity of his passion."

"Is it always this hard, Mum?" I sniffed.

"It can be, Luv. But when you find real love, it's worth all the pain – even if you lose it again. You'll see. Now, get yourself off to school and the rest will take care of itself. I promise."

The following day, bright and early, I heard the doorbell chime. Mum was in the kitchen and got to the door first and I heard the relief in her voice as I bounded down the stairs.

"Well, Good Morning Sherry. Aren't you a sight for sore eyes."

"Hello, Mrs C. I know it's early and it's the weekend, but is Jonathon up yet? I have to talk to him."

17

Autumn turned to winter bringing damp fog and charcoal grey skies yet whenever I stood at the window waiting for Sherry to arrive, I found it difficult to believe that it would ever rain again. Sherry. Beautiful, funny and devoted Sherry. To me she was perfect and just being with her was enough to make me feel pretty special too. Not that she ever made a big thing of her looks. During the week she would hang out in her favourite oversized jumper and jeans, her face bare of any make-up and her spiralling locks pulled back in a scrunchy. But I think she knew what a kick it gave me to see her all dressed up, and I know she enjoyed it too, so whenever we went out at the weekend, she would throw on a rah-rah skirt with tights and legwarmers and just go to town with her hair and make-up. Then, as often as not, she would top off the look with Shalto's old biker jacket and a pair of lacey fingerless gloves. The overall effect was irresistible and she wouldn't have looked out of place in a Bananarama video. She certainly turned some heads in Camden Town.

I couldn't have claimed to match her as boyfriend material, but I had shot up in height, and with my head of golden curls and the signature smudge of eye-liner I'd adopted the night of the school dance, I looked a lot less like the sixth form nerd I truly was. I did toy with the idea of growing my hair long for a while but Mum was not exactly encouraging. *After all*, she said, *it wasn't as though the world needed another Roger Daltry.* She had a point. Corkscrew curls might have looked great on Sherry and the late and great Marc Bolan, but I tended to resemble an unkempt poodle once my hair grew over my ears.

Camden Town was an exciting place to be that year. Twelve months had passed since I'd first blagged my way in to a pub with Shalto and no longer felt nervous about it, while Sherry could easily pass for twenty when she was all doled up. Half the kids who hung out in the dark corners of The Dublin Castle were probably under the legal drinking age but, so long as they didn't cause any trouble, the bar staff turned a blind eye. It was the best place to see new bands and enjoy the anarchic vibe that was sweeping the UK. We had, of course, been obliged to stick to the early evening sessions, but there were so many would be bands looking for their big break that the gigs ran all afternoon on Saturdays.

It could get pretty raucous at times but we didn't care. Spitting and the hurling of obscenities was all part of the fun of going to watch Punk and New Wave bands, as was the hurling of empty beer bottles. Most of it was harmless though and Sherry and I always took care to get out of the road the moment any sign of a genuine fight broke out. In fact, we felt a little cheated if no one kicked off at all.

I'm not sure that Mum fully appreciated the nature of our weekend entertainment. But she had been young once herself and was no stick in the mud. She did however remain unmovable about her late-night travel curfew, which meant we had to leave Camden pretty early to get home. However, since I had saved up loads of money from my holiday job, Sherry and I got into the habit of taking a taxi back from Stratford which saved us a heap of time. It also saved us from the worst of the late-night vomiters and the hairy walk back to her house from the bus stop. I guess it also put pay to long goodnight snogging sessions on her doorstep but, given the obvious temptations, that was no bad thing.

Mum may have not been as permissive as the parents of some of the kids we mingled with in Camden but she still allowed me a considerable amount of freedom, given my age. I could pretty well do as we pleased at the weekends, so long as we stuck to the rules. No smoking, drugs and soft drinks only. And she could be firm. I once made the mistake of arriving home with the smell of lager on my breath and she promptly grounded me for a month. I never made that mistake again. From then on, I only ever drank alcohol at the start of the night. Until, of course, I discovered that vodka was virtually undetectable.

But we didn't have to go out to have a good time. Sherry loved listening to music, playing chess and reading comics as much as Shalto had, though she brought a different perspective to it all. She also relished a good maths problem. Best of all, she could make me see the funny side of anything. Though witty, Shalto had been a cynic at heart. Sherry's cheerful optimism was like a breath of fresh air.

At Christmas, Mum kept her promise to Uncle Roy and dragged me away to spend Christmas up north with him, Aunty Betty and the cousins. I made a tentative effort to wriggle out of it but Mum pointed out that Christmas was for families and, since Sherry had her own, she imagined they would be glad to see her for a change. Besides, she was fairly sure that we could both survive a couple of days' separation.

The problem was, Sherry's family was purely mythological and so I felt terrible about the idea of leaving her in an empty house alone all over Christmas, especially since Captain had, it appeared, indeed abandoned ship. Still, we could hardly change the script now.

As such, I had broken the news with a great deal of trepidation and a string of abject apologies. Sherry, however, surprised me. *My Mum was right, of course, and she was having none of my pity or my guilt. It was only a couple of days, and we would make up for lost time over the Christmas holidays.*

It turned out to be a real family get together, as Uncle Trevor and Aunty Laura bought their two kids over for Boxing Day. I say kids, when in fact, both were in their early twenties though still living at home.

Not wishing to leave us in Uncle Roy's bad books by racking up a huge bill from long distance phone calls, I had snuck out of the house to the phone box up the road and called Sherry as often as I dared. I suppose I thought I was being subtle about it, but it's difficult to slip away unnoticed with three inches of snow lying on the ground, and no one was going to turn a blind eye and deny themselves the opportunity to embarrass the shit out of me.

"Young love, eh Trev?" sighed Uncle Roy as I snuck back in after tea when everyone was dozing, my face glowing from the cold air. "Those were the days, eh? Here, Jonno. You know I loved your Aunt Betty so much when I first met her, I wanted to eat her. We've been married twenty-five years come the Spring and now I wish I bloody well had."

Uncle Trevor had chuckled heartily as they watched my already pink cheeks turn as red as Rudolph's famous nose.

"Aye, well. Never you mind, lad. If you don't eat her now, there'll probably be a lot more of her to eat later." He winked and nodded over to where my Aunty Laura sat snoozing, her plump arms folded across her enormous bosom.

I shook my head and escaped to the kitchen where my cousins had just concluded a heated round of Trivial Pursuit and were preparing for a new game. Their faces fell as I walked in.

"Oh, no. Just when I thought I had a chance of winning, for a change..." quipped cousin Tim.

Teasing apart, I didn't have a horrible time. It was interesting to see how much my cousins had grown up and I really liked Tim, who had just completed an apprenticeship in mechanical engineering and loved to build all manner of little contraptions for his own amusement. He wasn't bad at chess either.

There was mountains of food, lame party game and plenty of alcohol and even I was permitted a couple of lagers. And, as happens in most homes over Christmas there was plenty of reminiscing about old times. I'd never known my grandparents, but my Mum and Uncles shared endless happy memories and anecdotes of their family Christmases together. It all sounded perfect. Nobody once mentioned Dad though which seemed a little sad for Mum, though she never showed it.

And Sherry had been right. The couple of days apart may have been rough, particularly for her, but the time spent cuddled up on our sofa watching daft old Christmas films or playing Scrabble with Mum more than made up for it. Sherry even got into the spirit of things and nibbled at one of Mum's mince pies, though I suspect most of it ended up hidden in her napkin.

During this time, however, the little matter of Shalto's sudden absence in my life hung over our heads like an unbalanced equation obliging Sherry and I to put our heads together and come up with a convincing explanation for it. In the end, I told Mum that, over Christmas, he had simply thrown everything up and taken himself off travelling. It had all been very sudden, but then that was Shalto all over. The antiques business had not, apparently, been going very well so he had just said What the Fuck and splurged out on an Interrail ticket.

Mum, it turned out, was not wholly surprised. She recalled what he'd said when he had given her the earrings and assumed, in hind sight, it had been his way of saying Goodbye. She only hoped his absence might cause his parents to appreciate more fully what a remarkable young man they had bought into the world.

Getting Shalto out of the picture was one thing. Sustaining his absence was quite another. Sherry and I were obliged to think up one last twist in the plot. Whilst he was away in Europe his parents would make the move to the USA for work and Shalto would decide to go with them. He would phone me once or twice but, eventually, we would lose touch. It happens.

Six weeks later, we put the plan into action. Much to my relief, the scheme required only a couple of carefully stage-managed phone calls and passed off almost without a hitch. Mum seemed to buy it, at least. Nonetheless, his unexpected flight to the New World left a Shalto-shaped hole in our lives, which neither of us quite knew how to articulate. He'd spent a lot of time in our home and Mum had grown very fond of him, in her own way. As I realised, had I. He could be a bit of a spanner in the works at times – you never knew what he was going to come out with, but that was all part of his charm. And it had certainly worked on my Mum. Whether it had been persuading her that I was perfectly safe on the back of his scooter, or allowing me to accompany him to pubs to see bands when I was obviously underage, he always managed to talk her round.

"You'd think Shalto might at least have sent a post-card," complained my mum, one teatime, à propos of nothing in particular.

"Oh, I think post cards are a bit uncool…" I commented, rising swiftly from the table to place my plate in the washing-up bowl. But I almost wished that he'd send one, myself. It was a very odd thought indeed.

Whatever my misgivings about the loss of my oldest friend, I soon learned to keep them to myself. Sherry had dropped enough hints that she did not wish to be reminded of her former incarnation, but her strength of feeling about it became crystal clear one Sunday afternoon, as we sprawled on the sofa watching a cheesy Elvis movie.

"Hey, Shez. Remember that time we spotted that busker who was the spitting image of Elvis down Carnaby Street."

"Don't, Jumbo - please. I never saw him. *That* wasn't me. I've told you," she snapped, pulling away from me.

I sighed. It sounded a touch crazy to me. *After all, we'd shared so many happy times together, why would she want to wipe that out?*

"Let it go. Please."

"But I don't understand. Is it the memory thing, again? Has shifting identities caused you to forget a lot of the stuff we did together…?"

"No, no. You're right - you *don't* understand. The memories are all there, fully intact, so to speak. But you don't get it, do you? It's like method acting. If I want to pass as Sherry, I have to immerse myself in being her. I can't afford to get it all mixed up."
I started to nod but then shook my head.

"Hang on a minute though. The only person you have to "pass as Sherry" with, really, is me. And I know all about you."
Sherry rolled her eyes.

"Sometimes, Jonathon, I think you're still soaking wet behind the ears. There is your mother for a start – and later, well who knows? Don't you get it? What do you think would happen if anybody else found out? I can't afford to be bleedin' careless. And neither can you. You made your choice and it was me, so now Shalto has left the building. For good. Are we clear?"

I let it go, but not without some internal head-scratching. I suppose I had made the choice in my heart, but I'd had taken pains not to force that choice upon the shapeshifter. It had been Sherry who turned up in response to my note and Sherry who told me she needed to be with me. So, even if the sentiments were correct her accusation seemed a little unjust. But then, when I mulled it over a bit more, I was forced to concede that, in the end, it didn't signify who made the choice. Sherry and I seemed to have been made for one another and it had all worked out.

Things were never quite the same between Mum and me after that morning when she had shed those tears for my father. But in a good way. Perhaps it was just that I was finally growing up, but since then, I had tried harder to see things from her point of view and pay a little more attention to her feelings. Whatever the catalyst, the change worked in our favour and Mum attributed my newly discovered maturity to Sherry's gentle influence. Tossing aside her reservations about me settling down too young, she began to go out other way to make Sherry feel welcome in our home. *If I was happy,* she said, *then so was she.* And I was, without doubt, the happiest she had ever seen me.

The upshot of this, however, was that Sherry, all at once, found herself fielding repeated invitations to stay for Saturday tea or come to Sunday lunch. Initially, she managed to scrape together a range of ingenious yet plausible excuses. She was abstaining for Lent or recovering from a tummy bug; her mother had invited an old maiden aunt for the weekend. Inevitably, though, we ran out of ideas. Shalto's mysterious vegan diet had worked like a dream but now we were stumped.

"What about saying that you're diabetic?" I suggested in desperation, one afternoon. "Don't they have to stick to a severe regime of what and when they eat?"

"Maybe – but it doesn't sound very plausible after all this time and besides, I can see that leading to all sorts of unnecessary anxiety and complications. You know what your mum is like. She'll be off researching it at the library before we know where we are."

I nodded. She had a point. But I was all out of ideas.

"It's no good," sighed Sherry, "I'm just going to have to swallow the food and then regurgitate it at the first opportunity."

"Regurgitate…?" I wrinkled my nose. Wasn't that something owls did?

"Vomit. Hurl, barf - throw up. I'm sure you've done it, Jonno. Never pleasant, but I assure you the alternative is even less so…"

I stared at her. Sherry wriggled her bottom and shook her head, twisting her mouth with distaste. I shrugged.

"So what? Even the Queen does her share of sitting on the throne…."

"Oh, no, no. This is worse, believe me. And if there is one thing worse than regurgitating undigested food, it's having it lie around inside your body for hours until, you know – well, you can't even imagine…" She shuddered.

"If you say so." I sniggered, pulling a face. "But you clearly haven't visited our bathroom the morning after curry night."

Sunday lunch together at our house proved a success. Sherry did not eat a great deal but was gracious and subtle about it. She complimented Mum's cooking and took her time to savour each mouthful. She made her excuses to leave the table as soon as we had finished dessert but was not absent long enough to raise any suspicions. On returning, she insisted that Mum put her feet up whilst she dragged me into the kitchen to do the washing up. Once mum was settled in the front room, I turned up the radio and gave reign to my questions.

"Here, Shez, can you actually even taste the food? Or was that all part of this amazing charade you've got going on."

Sherry blushed. She took the plate I held out and polished it with the tea towel.

"Well, the more I eat, the more I seem able to discern the different flavours. It's quite fascinating, really. Pleasant almost. But tell me you didn't hear me throwing up - I tried to keep it as quiet as possible."

I gave her the thumbs up then grinned.

"But next time, if you're just going to waste the lemon meringue pie, you could at least leave a bit more for the rest of us."

Sherry opened her mouth to protest but instead laughed and took a swipe at me with the tea towel.

"Oooooowwww…" I shrieked.

"Hey, you two. Keep it in down in there…" called Mum from the next room. But it was in her happy voice and I knew that the day had been a success.

Some weeks later, a quite different mood descended on our little household. Out of the blue, Sherry and I had our first falling out.

It had been a perfectly ordinary Saturday afternoon. It was late Spring but the weather had turned very cold again so Sherry had come around to ours to hang out. She popped her head around the door of the living room to say Hi to Mum, who was watching some sentimental black and white movie on the TV. Mum returned her greeting but then shushed us and returned her gaze to Humphry Bogart and Ingrid Bergman, directing us to help ourselves to the chocolate digestives in the biscuit tin. We thanked her, stopped off at the biscuit tin and then headed to my room as usual.

"I'm assuming I can have your share of the bickies then?" I joked as we tumbled up the stairs, exchanging kisses.

"I would be eternally grateful…" she giggled.

"See. I knew you were my perfect match."

Sherry flopped down on the bed and propped her cheek up on one elbow while I set down the packet of digestives and kicked off my trainers. I padded over to my desk, hoping she would notice my old microscope which sat on my desk. I'd come across it whilst I was looking for a sock under the bed, that morning, and had almost forgotten it was there. Sherry, however, had picked up the new Spiderman comic I had been reading and was flipping through its pages. I coughed.

"Hey, Shez. Do you remember when Mum first gave me this microscope and we looked at our blood under it?"

Sherry stiffened a little. She put down the comic but seemed reluctant to answer. I supposed it was the Shalto/Sherry thing again and was just about to change the subject when she sighed and made a reply.

"Yeah. Seems a long time ago, now. You were so young."

"I suppose I was. But I've never forgotten how amazing it was…"

"Yeah, well, you know…" She shifted uncomfortably and sat up, turning towards me.

"I'd love to see it again – d'you think you could just…"

"To tell the truth, I'm not really comfortable with the idea…" She began to swing her legs like a cat that thrashes its tail in irritation.

"But you didn't mind then? So why object now?" I ploughed on, failing to take the hint.

"Well now, that's odd because I seem to remember that Shalto *did* mind. In fact, he minded rather a lot."

I felt silent. The Shalto/Sherry thing really did confuse me at times. I pouted and looked away.

"I'm sorry, Jonno. I guess I just don't want you to think of me as different, you know. Like I'm some kind of freak or something..."

"C'mon Shez. You know I'd never think of you like that. It's just – well, you're, you know, so fascinating. I mean back then I didn't know much about all this stuff, but the more I think about it, well, it's just mind-blowing, really."

Sherry was on her feet now.

"It? What do you mean - it? I'm not an *it*. I'm me and why this sudden fascination? What's changed?"

"Nothing. Nothing has changed between us. It's just that, well if you think about the things your body can do, well, if we only understood a tiny part of it, think what we could do – for the human race, I mean. When you get injured, you regenerate, you don't age the way we do..."

Sherry was staring at me. Her face seemed oddly blank.

"And saving the human race is suddenly so important to you, is it?"

"Well, I've been thinking. Mathematics- it's all very well, isn't it? But where does it get us in the end? But if I were to study Microbiology – that would be an entirely different matter. I could easily get a place at university with the subjects I'm doing and – just imagine. With what I could learn from you - well, who knows what discoveries I could make?"

This final snippet of grandiosity was lost on her. My girlfriend was already halfway down the stairs before I'd even had the time to realise what a total arsehole, I was making of myself. I followed her out onto the upstairs landing as the front door slammed shut, shaking the whole house. The next moment, Mum stepped into the hallway.

"What on earth was that all about? I've never seen Sherry so upset."

"I'm an idiot, Mum," I whined. "A complete idiot. I've done something really, really stupid and, to be honest, I'm not sure if I can *un*do it."

18

I stood on the doorstep of the old house on Capel Road, prepared to eat the biggest piece of Humble Pie in the history of Humble Pie consumption.

Cursing my socked feet, I had run back upstairs to pull on my discarded trainers and then charged back down and out through the front door, but Sherry had already disappeared from sight. I sprinted all the way up Upton Lane to the Romford Road without getting so much as a glimpse of her ahead of me. I didn't think she had that much of a head-start but then she could really move when she wanted to. I would just have to keep on running.

By the time I got to Forest Gate station I was knackered. I bent over and held my knees, gasping for breath. I didn't have a snowball's chance in hell of catching-up with her so I might as well forget it. I would just have to go to the house. I thought about the risk I might pose if I made any sort of scene at her place, but I promised myself to stay calm. I would knock quietly on the door and refuse to go away until she let me in. I didn't have another choice. I very much doubted she would answer the phone and I could hardly expect a note to work a second time, no matter how low I grovelled. So, I would simply stand my ground. For as long as it took. Even if that meant camping out on the doorstep.

The old house stood looked as desolate as it always did. I opened the gate and stepped into the driveway. Out of nowhere, a rather cross-looking blackbird swooped and flapped its wings at me in warning. I jumped and yelped in confusion and then shook my head at my overreaction. So much for maintaining a low profile. I glared at it and clenched my fist. It must have had a nest in one of the gutters.

I stood chewing my lip and scanning the façade of the building. Paint was peeling from the window frames and the screens, as ever, blocked any view of what lay inside. I wondered how Sherry could bear the claustrophobia of it all.

I held my inhaler to my mouth then grasped the door knocker. I tried to knock gently but the clang of iron on iron reverberated through the house causing the blackbird to flutter anew. I cursed myself for my ham-fists and then looked around. There was no one around to hear it. Then everything fell silent. I knelt down and pushed open the brass flap of the letter box. It creaked uneasily.

"Sherry, c'mon, please. I know you're in there. Look, I know I'm an idiot. But I'm the idiot that loves you - surely that gives me at least one get-out-of-jail-free card?"

Nothing stirred within the house. I remained on my knees with my ear pressed against the door. I was loath to knock again but equally loath to move. I squeezed my eyelids together and rapped my forehead against the doorframe, trying to calm the rising panic I felt in my chest.

Suddenly, a touch on my shoulder sent me sprawling off the doorstep in alarm. I landed facedown with my nose against a pair of Converse basketball boots. I looked up. A pair of jeans-clad legs, a sweatshirt and that face I knew so well.

"Sherry - thank God."

"Did you really mean it, Jonno?"

"Mean what?" I panted, trying to smile. "Shit, I'm so glad to see you. Thought I'd really blown it, this time…"

"- that you love me? Did you mean it?"

"Oh, Shez. Do you really have to ask?"

"No. Perhaps I don't. But *you* really have to *tell* me…"

I scrambled to my feet and wrapped her in my arms.

"Sherry, I love you. I love you now and, in a way, I've loved you for almost as long as I can remember. What's more, I'm pretty damn sure I'm gonna love you for the rest of my life. And that would be the case whether you were a shapeshifter or just made out of the same boring old flesh and blood as me. I'm truly sorry, I got carried away with that other stuff. I just got overexcited and wasn't thinking straight."

Sherry kissed me then put her lips to my ear.

"I love you too, Jonno and if you love me, then that is enough. I'm sorry I let my paranoia get the better of me. I'd trust you with my life, truly I would. But you are still so young in so many ways and I'm not sure you can truly understand what it might mean if anyone else so much as…."

"No, I do. I get it, now, honest, Shez. I would die rather than endanger you in any way and I certainly never meant to upset you, but I can see how I did. You must believe me. I give you my solemn promise that I will never again act like such a prize prick."

Sherry stepped back and held out her hand with a wink.

"Well, in that case. Come in. I know we don't often spend much time at my place but I was rather hoping for the right moment. I think this may be it."

Inside, I gazed around the hallway. It looked as dingy as ever, but something was different. The passageway was a good deal less cluttered than on the last few occasions that I had visited and even the few boxes and frames that remained had been sorted and neatly re-stacked. Something else was very different too. I noticed the shapeshifter's cotton gloves hanging on their hook near the front door as we entered, but Sherry left them where they hung.

"Don't you need them?" I asked as we passed.

Sherry took my hand and tapped the side of her nose.

"I'll explain all, presently."

We passed the first reception room, which lay in darkness, and I assumed that Sherry was leading me down to her den in the kitchen. I was mistaken. Instead, she paused at the end of the hallway and indicated that we were going to head upstairs.

"Watch your step, Jonno. I managed to clear most of the stuff off the stairs but the carpet is old and worn in places and it's all too easy to trip."

I shook my head, impressed. I knew that Sherry had been selling the occasional item to raise cash but had no idea of the extent to which she had taken the old place in hand. We tramped up the staircase. The upstairs landing of the first floor seemed almost empty, save for a couple of paintings in heavy ornate frames that still leaned against the ancient bannisters. I peered up through the stairwell to the next floor, but that seemed as chock-a-block with random items as ever.

"It'll take me while to get up that far, I'm afraid," commented Sherry following my gaze.

"Nevertheless, someone has certainly been busy. I'm surprised you even knew where to start."

"Well, it was about time and, after all, I have to do *something* while you are at school, don't I? I've only sold the odd bit of crap, really. Nothing of any real personal or historical value."

I looked at her, struck by a sudden realisation that I had never really showed that much interest in how she spent her time when I wasn't around. Not if I was being honest. I went to say something but she placed a finger to her lips.

"Never mind all that, now. Come on. I wanted to show you something in particular."

And, so saying, she led me along the landing and opened one of the great panelled doors. The antiquated hinges complained vociferously but the door opened unimpeded by the mountains of assorted stuff that had formerly filled the space behind it. Sherry held up a hand and then disappeared inside. I heard a couple of clicks and a welcoming glow of light spilled out into the landing. I stepped inside.

I couldn't help but gasp. In the centre of the room towered a magnificently carved oak four poster bed, complete with a silken canopy and curtains that were embroidered in heavy golden thread. The floor was carpeted in soft thick red Turkish rugs and on either side of the bed stood two exquisite standard Tiffany lamps that glimmered like jewels. The bed was made up with huge pillows and crisp linen sheets, that had been turned down.

"Jeez - Sherry. This is amazing. How old is this?"

"Very old, Jonno. But I think you are missing the point..." she had closed the door and was peeling off her sweatshirt.

The moment I had dreamt about had finally arrived and all I could feel was crushing paralysis.

"What about the gloves?" I asked stunned by my own ineptness. "I thought you couldn't touch this stuff without, you know, getting all these memories?"

"I told you - I'll explain it later. Now are you going to come over here and lie next to me on this bed or are you going to stand there asking stupid questions."

"I don't know what to - I mean I know what to do *technically*, but I haven't a clue, how to ..."

"Relax. Neither do I. I – that is, Sherry is a virgin just like you. I was rather hoping we could solve the mystery together."

She moved over to the bed, kicked of her basketball boots and wriggled out of her jeans.

I moved up next to the bed, fumbling to unfasten my belt.

"Sherry?"

"Yes, Jonathon?"

"You wouldn't by any chance have any of that vodka on you, would you?"

"Come here..." she whispered pulling me close and brushing her tongue across my lips. "Trust me. You are *not* going to need it..."

Mum was busy in the kitchen by the time I returned home.

"Sorry about earlier, but it's all okay, now. We made it up..." I grinned, leaning against the doorpost.

"I can see that," she smiled back. "In fact, I would say from the big soppy expression on your face that you two did a little more than just kiss and make-up."

"Mum..." I wailed hardly knowing which way to look.

"Now, listen Jonathon Cooper, your mother is not some old prude, whatever you might think. (Though if you did, I would only have myself to blame, I suppose). But then, neither am I some old hippy chick so I'm not going to wax lyrical about the magical connectivity of sexual congress…"

"Mum – please."

"No, Jumbo. Hear me out, please – I'm not trying to embarrass you, but this is an important milestone in your life. You turn seventeen next month, and as far as I'm concerned that makes you an adult so I am going to treat you as such. Sherry is welcome to stay over anytime you please and the two of you do not have to creep around like criminals. Is that clear? All I ask is that you are careful. Too many lives have been ruined for want of a condom."

I nodded, doing my best not to cringe. I could tell that Mum would have liked a hug right then, but it just wasn't going to happen. I gulped.

"Right-o. See you in a bit then. I'll just head up to my room and um- finish a couple of – um things."

"Are you sure? I thought we could have a little drink to mark the occasion. Just the two of us. I've got that malt whiskey left over from Christmas."

"Nah – you're all right. I really should, you know…"

"Okay, Jumbo. But I'm going to pour myself one, even if my son is too uptight to share in the celebration."

"Mum? You're not going to get all weird on me and mention any of this to Sherry, are you?"

"Really, Jumbo. As if I would. I'm just trying to get my head around the fact that my little boy is a man now. And I don't have anyone else to share it with."

I saw the tears well up in her eyes and relented.

"Not too much of a grown man for a hug, though?" I said spreading my arms.

"Never, Jumbo. Come here."

Up in the sanctuary of my room, I lay on my back with my hands clasped behind my head. I thought about what Mum had said. I *did* feel different, in a way. Not quite a man, but I somehow knew that my childhood lay behind me now. I closed my eyes and sighed. Our lovemaking had not exactly moved the earth and we certainly hadn't broken any records, yet I had never dreamt that you could feel so close to another being or that exploring each other's bodies could be so much fun. And we were just beginners.

I blushed when I recalled my mum's warning about unwanted pregnancies. For all her talk of me having grown up, it had been the last thing on my teenage mind. Still, her no-nonsense caution had raised an interesting question. Shalto had told me that shapeshifters did not reproduce but what if they mated with a human? *Was it possible that Sherry could become pregnant? And if so what on earth would that mean?*

In some ways, it was yet another of the redacted paragraphs that filled the pages of my life. Like the gloves. Or rather how Sherry suddenly seemed not to need them. I didn't visit the old house all that often, but I had never before known her to leave them off before. She had said that she would explain but then it hadn't seemed important as we both lay grinning in the wreck of the bedsheets. I knew she didn't like me asking questions but I had a feeling that this one wasn't going to go away.

19

Things between Sherry and I could not have been better. It was like dropping a kid into a toyshop and telling them they could have all the toys for free. I couldn't get enough of her, though I was sensible enough not to lose my head. This was a big year for me at school and I couldn't afford to screw it up – in any sense of the word.

Despite Mum's invitation Sherry and I preferred to do our courting, (her words, not mine) around at her place. It was just more conducive to the mood. There is nothing very sexy about a sixteen-year-old boy's bedroom and nothing more likely to dampen your ardour than the knowledge that your mum is asleep in the next room. Sherry's amazing bedroom became our secret love-nest, her bed our private wonderland where we could be anyone that we wanted – literally, as it turned out.

It was the last weekend in May. Sherry and I were sprawled on her bed. I had been stroking her back when she remined me that it would be my birthday in a couple of days.

"You're going to have to force a bit of cake down," I joked. "You know what Mum is like."

"Well, I will - but it'll be coming straight back up. Hey, I wonder what shape it'll be this year?"

"Oh, don't." I groaned. "A double bed, I shouldn't wonder. She gets so excited by it all - my birthday, I mean, not us – you know…"

"Making the beast with two backs, as old Will Shakespeare used to say."

"Yeah, that would be weird, huh? No - but seriously, she's always made such a big deal of my birthday."

"And so, she should. You're lucky. I don't even have one, as far as I know," she complained.

"Well, then we must pick a day for you – make it your official birthday, you know like the Queen. What month do you fancy?"

"Well, I'm rather partial to September. That way, it breaks up the year a bit. How about the first - like yours and that would make it easy to remember."

"Consider it done. I'll put it on the calendar when I get home and then every year we will celebrate your birthday, too."

"Thank you, Jonno. I don't think anyone ever gave me a birthday before…."

"You are very welcome…"

"And what about you? What would you like for your birthday? Or rather, who would you like?" She lay back on the pillows head and winked. "I can arrange to be anything you desire. Just for the night. Blonde and voluptuous like Marilyn Monroe, perhaps? Sexy as hell like Debbie Harry? Or dark and ferocious like Grace Jones. Or even a beautiful androgenous man like David Bowie – no one would ever know. It can be your wildest fantasy come true. I can't replicate them exactly without their DNA, but it'll be close enough, believe me. It would be the ultimate birthday wish."

"Stop it, Sherry," I giggled, blushing all over. "You know I don't want anyone but you."

"But this is fantasy, Jonno and it would *still* be me – come on, tell me your secret desire..."

"Oh no," I pronounced, wagging a finger at her. "You're not catching me out that way. The moment I suggest someone, it would be – *what's wrong with me, then*? I'm not falling for it. Besides, I can't think of anyone I'd rather make love to. Honestly. I'm crazy about you, Shez and you know it."

She shrugged and then looked at me intently, the mischief all gone.

"I want to be everything to you Jonno. I mean it."

"But you are. Can't you see? And, in any case, I thought you found the shapeshifting thing all too exhausting."

"Well, it is. But once in a while is different. And I know it sounds contrary, but I do kind of miss it sometimes. I don't expect you to understand..."

"Maybe I can't. Not really, but I can imagine what it would be like to have this incredible ability and never use it. I'll never forget that day in Epping Forest and if you ever want to do something like that again, for you, I mean, then I'm in. But as Billy Joel says – *Don't go changing to try to please me* - because I really do love you just the way you are."

If I entertained the smallest regret about passing up the opportunity to spend a night with Debbie Harry's double, I kept it to myself. Curiously enough, it would be the first and last time Sherry made any such offer and, though I had no doubt that she would have seen it through, I couldn't help feeling that I passed some kind of a test, that day.

I got into the habit of spending Saturday night at Sherry's, especially as we had generally been out for the evening. However, I tried to make a point of getting home in time for Sunday lunch with Mum as I knew how was important it was to her. And even if I dragged my feet, Sherry would turf me out of bed herself. *The last thing she needed was my Mum to start resenting her poaching her Jumbo.* I also rarely stayed over on a school night, though I sometimes got home pretty late. Mum was cool with that so long as I didn't neglect my homework and got a decent night's sleep. I tended to spend the whole evening at Sherry's on a Tuesday when Mum went out to her choir practice and then on a Thursday when Mum would often enjoy a *night to herself*. Otherwise, Sherry and I always had the afternoons after school to ourselves and were not averse to what she quaintly termed *a little afternoon delight*.

Nevertheless, staying at Sherry's had taken a bit of getting used to. Spending an entire night in that gloomy old mausoleum of a house, the first time, had put me in mind of Scooby-Doo my favourite cartoon and when I woke up in the small hours and had crept along the landing in search of a bathroom, I half-wished I'd held back on the lagers. I didn't believe in ghosts but then I hadn't believed in shapeshifters. Though only metres away, it was one of the longest walks of my life. I flinched at every shadow and creaking floorboard. The bathroom when I found it was, at least, functional. Sherry had thought of everything.

She had stirred as I'd clambered back into bed next to her.

"Are you awake?" I whispered.

"Uh-huh."

"Can I ask you something then? Have you ever seen a ghost in this old house?" I asked.

"Depends what you call a ghost..." she yawned and fell back to sleep.

Not quite the answer I'd hoped for. I stared up at the ceiling and wondered where Scooby and the gang were when you needed them.

Meanwhile, spending so much time in the house prompted me to pose the question that had continued to bug me.

"So, what happened to needing to wear the gloves? You said you would tell me."

"Oh, yeah. So, I did. Well, I *do* still need them when I go into many of the rooms, especially upstairs and down in the cellar. But we found that once we had handled something in the first instance, the effect was not nearly so overwhelming the second time. And some of the stuff, well it hardly affected us at all. We couldn't go on living in such chaos so we decided we would sort it out."

"We?"

"Well, Shalto started it. He'd begun to sell things that were old but did not seem to hold particularly strong sensory information.

That freed up some space and gave us some cash. We also decided to move quite a lot of the storage cases into the garage, which freed up quite a bit more. Now and then, I come across something with a particularly powerful kick and then I put the gloves on and move it to an upstairs room. I'm doing my best not to throw too much stuff out, but it's my home and I need space to live and I can't be creeping around in terror that I'll accidentally make contact with something and get freaked out."

"I guess so. But is it still so overwhelming? Can't you make any sense of the things you experience?"

"No – and I suppose I don't want to. It's too confusing. It feels like I'm going crazy or something."

"I could shift stuff for you – if that would help. It doesn't seem to affect me." She smiled and shook her head.

"That's kind, Jonno. But I feel it's my job, somehow. It might sound daft but it's like I'm meant to be a bleedin' museum curator or something. And even if I can't remember how or why I came to be in this position, it's time for me to accept the responsibility and stop going on as though I'm living in some kind of a squat."

I shrugged. It made an odd sort of sense.

"And is the Enfield still out in the garage?"

"It most certainly is, though that was more Shalto's thing. But look, it would be fun, so I promise we'll take it out for a spin this summer – though I reckon your Mum would skin us alive if she ever got wind of it, so keep it under your helmet, yeah?"

My seventeenth birthday turned out to be vintage Mum. When I got home from school, I found a cake in the shape of a green Mini Cooper with a white roof sitting on the kitchen table. Mum was there too and she watched as I stared at it, a little puzzled. I would not have described myself as being especially into cars.

"Not that impressed, eh?" she teased.

"No – sorry, Mum. It's great. I love it. Really. It looks just like the real thing. Thank you."

"Come now, Jumbo. You don't fool me. But perhaps you might be more impressed if it were a little bigger. Oh, and would you mind taking a quick peek out of the front the window, I'm expecting a delivery."

"M-um…"

"Go on…"

I traipsed into the living room and pulled back the net curtains, wondering what on earth had got into my mother. There, parked on the opposite side of the road stood a green Mini Cooper with a white roof. I hurtled back into the kitchen to find Mum standing swinging a set of car keys from her fingers. She smiled and dropped them into my hand.

"You're seventeen now, Jumbo. That's old enough to get your driving licence. So, while the car is technically for both of us, I've booked you in for a weekend's intensive driving tuition for the end of term. Meanwhile, I'm a bit rusty myself but we'll find an empty car park one Sunday afternoon and you can have a practice.

My mouth must have dropped open.

"Can we go and have a look, now?"

"Of course, we can and as soon as Sherry gets here, we can all go for a little drive, if you'd like – there are some lovely pubs out Chigwell way. We can have a drink to celebrate. I can't guarantee a terribly smooth ride though, I suspect that I'm a bit out of practice with the gear stick, but if you don't mind a bit of bunny hopping, we'll be golden."

20

Mum's bunny hopping notwithstanding, the little green mini turned out to be a gamechanger. My weekend's crash course, (no pun intended), had been exhausting but the results spoke for themselves. I passed my test first time, only a week later, and the day I removed the L-plates and chucked them in the dustbin was easily my proudest moment ever. I had wheels now. I truly was a grown-up.

What's more, the acquisition of transport galvanised my mum into yet another bold decision. It had been a good-few years since we had gone away on vacation and she decided that a holiday by the seaside was long overdue.

As a small kid, she'd made a point of taking me to the seaside for long weekends but, somehow, we had fallen out of the habit. As I grew older, London with all its attractions beckoned and Exhibition Road in South Kensington soon became our preferred holiday stamping round. I adored all the great museums although The Museum of Science was, of course, always top of my list. Mum loved the V&A and though I was into all things scientific, even I could spend an hour lost in the splendours of the past with their magical colours and textures and extraordinary workmanship. Occasionally we would venture into magnificent halls of The British Museum. The sheer size of the place could be pretty overwhelming but I doubt there is a young boy alive who would not thrill at the sight of real mummies. I still remember grabbing Mum's hand in terror the first time I laid eyes on "Ginger" the first dead body I had ever seen, though he became quite the old friend over the years.

As I entered my teens, I began to tire of our old haunts, or find them less cool. I know that Mum would have loved to take me abroad to places like India or Thailand, but air travel was still a luxury that lay outside the reach of her modest budget and the idea of a package holiday to the Costa del Sol was her idea of hell.

Then Shalto had appeared on the scene and I suppose I made it fairly obvious that I preferred hanging out with him to trailing around after my mother.

The idea of a proper holiday, therefore, came somewhat as a surprise. I'd like to think that I had grown up enough to see how nice it would be for my mum to have a proper break and for us to spend some quality time together, but I was never put to the test.

Never one to delude herself, Mum automatically extended the invitation to include Sherry. I guess that she knew that I would only mope around missing her if she did not.

Broadstairs, she suggested. *We could rent a little apartment overlooking the bay. Self-catering. We would be able to swim, sunbathe and eat ice cream, all we wanted. Having a car meant that we did not have to deal with the tiring business of heaving luggage onto trains with the added advantage that we could explore the coast a little. We could share the driving. It would be fun. Furthermore, it would provide a chance for Sherry and her to get to know each other a little better. In short, it would be perfect.*

Sherry and I could find no objection to the plan. London became so dull and overcrowded in the summer. Besides, Sherry claimed that she had always adored Charles Dicken's writing and jumped at the chance to frequent his old stamping ground. "I have the first editions of most of his novels," she had whispered to me in private "and I have a feeling I might have attended one of his readings once, though it's all very hazy, of course."

I had merely shaken my head. I didn't care for Dickens but had always loved the ocean. And then there was the attraction of Sherry in a bathing suit. It all seemed irresistible.

"Just one thing, though..." Mum had added, frowning thoughtfully. "I really think that I ought to meet your mother before we whisk you away, Sherry Just to reassure her that you'll be in safe hands, you know. I know you're virtually an adult, but I'm sure that I would appreciate the same courtesy, in her place."

Sherry had opened her mouth and then closed it. Fortunately, Mum had not been looking for a direct response right then, and seemed preoccupied with placing the slices of bread she had covered with cheese, under the grill.

"What the bleedin' hell are we going to do?" hissed Sherry, once we were safely up in my room with a plateful of warm cheese on toast.

"We could say your mother is too busy, but I'm not at all sure how well that would go down."

"*Your* mum can certainly be very persistent when she gets an idea in her head," conceded Sherry. "I doubt it's something we'll be able to head off forever..."

"Well, what if we were to make it possible then?"

"Sorry?"

"Make it possible for her to meet *your mother*, I mean. Or, at least a woman who *says* that she is your mother. After all, if she meets her once and they don't hit it off, she never has to meet her again, does she?"

Sherry stared at me with wide eyes and then the penny suddenly dropped.

"Oh, I see – well, just the once perhaps. I suppose it would rather kill a lot of birds with just one stone."

Later that week, a certain Mrs Audrey Matthews phoned Mum to say that she was rather busy at present but could squeeze in lunch at a local hostelry the following week. I was in the kitchen at the time of the call and listened as my mum participated in a what appeared to be a very one-sided conversation. Finally, she replaced the receiver and looked at me with and raised eyebrows.

The Mathews' residence, she informed me, *was currently undergoing extensive renovations and Sherry's mother could not think about entertaining at home at the moment.* She had, it transpired, suggested that they meet for lunch in the little Italian restaurant in Wanstead. This was by no means so convenient for Mum, but was on the Central line, which meant that Audrey Mathews could whisk in from her office, thus eliminating the need to squander her, apparently, extremely valuable time, doing whatever it was she did as CEO of a financial something or other.

"I had no idea that Sherry's mother was a person of such consequence," she concluded with a twist of her lips. In other words – Sherry's Mum had sounded like the biggest snob she had ever had the misfortune to encounter and the sooner it was over with the better.

Nice one, Sherry, I thought, *now let's see if we can pile it on a bit more.*

"Oh, well," I chipped in, "I guess she is *terribly* successful, but she hardly ever speaks to me, even when I stay at their house, which is in a bit of a state by the way. As a matter of fact, she doesn't strike me as the least bit interested in Sherry as long as she gets good grades. Just a word of warning though. Don't whatever you do ask about Sherry's father. It's a bit of a sore subject at the moment."

Mum sighed. That was probably a relief. After all, I doubt she wanted to talk about *my* father either. They would have to look elsewhere for common ground.

The lunch meeting when it took place, turned out to be every bit as uncomfortable as I'd hoped.

"She turned up in classic Chanel and pearls, Jumbo. Can you believe it? And carrying a handbag that probably cost six months of my salary. I wouldn't have minded, but you should have seen the way she looked down her nose at me. She didn't even try to hide it. The woman spent the whole first course banging on about her portfolios and then sent the main course back. I don't think she ate more than a half dozen lettuce leaves during the whole lunch. Her questions about my life bordered on the impertinent, not that she bothered to listen to the answers. She didn't seem to have the smallest clue about Sherry's interests and kept referring to you as young John. And she drank like a fish. I began to feel really quite sorry for your Sherry, really, I did."

"So, you two aren't about to become best chums then, I take it."

Mum glared at me.

"Well, you needn't laugh. When we *did* finally get around to discussing Sherry coming along on holiday with us, she made two stipulations…"

"Oh, and what were they?" I asked, feeling suddenly worried.

"That Sherry absolutely has to have her own room - and that she and Sherry's father pay the entire cost of the accommodation – to make sure it is of adequate standard for their darling daughter. Just like that. No negotiation or consideration for my pride. The woman is used to getting her way in everything, I suspect. I'm sorry, Jumbo, I like Sherry, truly I do, but I don't care if I never lay eyes on that windbag again."

"And did you accept?" I asked quietly.

"Not yet…" she sniffed. "But I've said that I'll get back to her…"

"Shit, Sherry. You don't think you might have gone just a little OTT there, with the Chanel and all. And what's this about separate rooms and paying for the accommodation? You're kidding right?"

"Hey, I think it worked very well. She clearly hated me and did not, I might add, make much effort to conceal it. Not after the first thirty minutes or so, anyway. Well, not after I said that, in my experience, most children raised by working mothers who did not employ nannies turned out little short of feral…"

"You said WHAT to my mother?" I could feel my hackles rising.

"Not me, silly - my mother. Mrs Audrey *stick-up-her-arse-*Matthews You wanted to make sure they didn't get too pally, didn't you? And as for the separate rooms - if I'm paying, three rooms mean will mean a nicer place anyway. I have the money, or I can sell something, and this way we can give your mum the treat she deserves. We could rent somewhere overlooking the sea, something really swish..."

"But you know how proud she is...."

"I do, but you know as well as I that she always places you before her own feelings - and if this means I can go, I reckon she'll swallow her pride and accept. It'll all work out. We'll make it our business to spoil her to death, I promise."

"Hmmm, I never knew you could be so crafty...."

"Well, I've been around, as they say..."

"One more thing. Where did you get the Chanel? Mum was most impressed though she would bite out her tongue before she'd admit it."

"Turns out I have a wardrobe full of the stuff in the attic. Honestly, Jonno, you wouldn't believe what I've unearthed since I started trying to sort the old place out."

"Well, I can see just one tiny fly in the ointment. I intend on keeping you in my life for a long time to come. What if they have to meet again? I mean if we decided to marry or something, some day – I mean."

Sherry's playful brightness drained suddenly away.

"Oh, Jonno, Luv. Think about it. We can never be married. I don't even have a birth certificate. Technically, I don't even exist. Not as a human being. We can be happy without a piece of paper. But you're right. Even I cannot be me and my mother at the same time so any family get-togethers will have to remain off limits. Meanwhile, if your mother is somehow insane enough to want to foster a relationship with a woman who so clearly patronises and disrespects her, well we might just have to arrange for a little accident to befall Audrey Matthews and take her back out of the picture."

"Oooh, matricide. You wicked girl. I love it when you're naughty."

Sherry's plan worked like a charm. Mum put aside her scruples and accepted the deal on the table with all the good grace, she could muster. Four weeks later, we packed up the mini and drove down to Broadstairs and made ourselves at home in a spacious and tastefully furnished three story Victorian house on the main esplanade for a week. The living room boasted French windows that opened onto a really cool veranda with unimpeded views of the sea and a gated pathway that ran directly down to the beach.

The weather turned out to be perfect, the sea warm and the sunsets every bit as spectacular as one could have wished. We did make a couple excursions around the coast to Cliftonville and the famous Dreamland amusement park in Margate, but mostly enjoyed all the traditional seaside pleasures Broadstairs had to offer.

Mum was happiest lying on the beach reading and getting a tan. Except for when she was obliged to bat away the advances of the occasional hopeful Romeo. *What did she expect?* Sherry had teased. *She was still one stunning looking woman. It was just that she generally did her best to hide it.* Mum had shaken her head and told her not to say such silly things but even I had to concede that she did look pretty hot in a swimming cossie - and that, really is the last thing a kid my age wants to admit.

Sherry and I, meanwhile, passed the time building sand castles, splashing around in the sea on an inflatable lilo, we bought from one of the little shops on the esplanade, or chucking handfuls of coins into the slot machines in the innumerable amusement arcades. Then there was the pier to explore and Bleak House and all the fascinating Victorian nooks and crannies. We never had time to get bored.

In the evening we'd all sit on the veranda with a drink and watch the sun melt below the shimmering horizon then scamper off to the chippy to get fish 'n' chips, piazza or an Indian takeaway for dinner. Sherry and I wouldn't hear of Mum cooking. It was her holiday too. She didn't complain, though I suspect she was hanging out for fresh vegetables by the end of the week.

Later, if we were not all too tired, we would venture out to one of the nearby pubs and listen to live music. Sometimes we even had a dance and though Mum did not have a partner, it was clear that she would not want for offers. It was quite eye opening in a way. I got to see a side of Mum I never really knew existed and realised, for the first time, that she was by no means over the hill. Not that she allowed it amount to anything. But there is nothing like a little harmless flirtation to add a spring to the step and a sparkle to the eye.

On the whole, our vacation by the ocean turned out to be pretty plain sailing, though it did not pass without the need to navigate the occasional sea mine.

One major danger was the amount of time we found ourselves thrown together. This was not a problem *per se*, Mum and Sherry were hitting it off very well and I could tell how much Mum liked her, perhaps even more since meeting the terrible woman who claimed to have mothered her. But idle hours foster curiosity, and Mum, who up until had veered away from cross-examining either Sherry or Shalto, succumbed to her inquisitiveness. One of the most awkward questions popped up over drinks one evening.

"So, Sherry. Are you looking forward to getting your 'A' level results next month? And have you decided which university you want to go to? Jonno tells me so little. But you know boys, useless about that sort of thing."

Sherry spluttered on her vodka and tonic and then swallowed hard.

"Sorry about that. Went down the wrong way. Well - no. in fact, I'm staying on an extra term to do the Oxbridge entrance exam. I wouldn't care myself, but Mum is really keen. So, I won't be going anywhere, for a while anyway."

Mum nodded. It probably fitted with the picture of Sherry's life she had already constructed for herself.

"Well, I hope it's what you want as well. It's not for everyone. All that privilege and entitlement. But then, perhaps you're more used to it. What are you hoping to read?"

Sherry looked at me. I didn't step in. I was too busy enjoying the show.

"Well - philosophy, I thought and maybe economics…"

"Really? That seems very adventurous. I thought your thing was maths and physics, like Jonno?"

"Oh, well yes. But then, well economic theory involves a lot of maths. And as for philosophy – I love physics but I guess, I'm interested in the bigger questions."

My mum sat back. I could tell she was impressed. She raised her glass.

"Well, here's to you Sherry. You strike me as a rather remarkable young woman. I'm sure that you will go far."

"And here's to tangled webs…" I mumbled under my breath, clinking glasses with them both.

"What was that, Jumbo?"

"Oh, nothing. Just an acknowledgement of the richness of life's great tapestry

A couple of days later, we steered perilously close to another potential explosive topic and this time I was obliged to defuse it alone.

Mum, being Mum, paid absolutely no attention whatsoever to where either of us chose to sleep and she never entered either of our bedrooms without first being invited. As chance would have it, there were two smaller bedrooms and a bathroom on the upper floor and one ensuite master bedroom on the first floor. It made sense for mum to take the ensuite room, which was just as well, as there was the small matter of Sherry's digestive peculiarities to navigate, not to mention her dietary requirements. Mum may have been broad minded but even she would have baulked at the quart of vodka, Sherry had smuggled into her room. She had taken the precaution of decanting the stuff into a large plastic bottle, which appeared for all intents and purposes as though it contained water, but nevertheless the ruse was not without risk.

It was not however the vodka that attracted undue attention. Mum caught me by the elbow in the kitchen one morning and drew me aside.

"Jonathon, I know you will tell me to mind my own business, but is everything okay with Sherry?"

I shrugged and replied that Sherry seemed as happy as I had ever seen her. Mum crinkled her brow.

"It's just that – well, I've heard her in the bathroom a couple of times. The walls here aren't as thick as they look, but – anyway, I rather wondered if she might be bulimic?"

I stared at her and tried to speak but I couldn't seem to unstick my tongue from the roof of my mouth. Finally, I managed to stammer out a "no."

"Well, okay. If you're sure? I did wonder if she might be, you know, pregnant but I'm pretty sure it isn't morning sickness. Have you thought that she might have an eating disorder, though? To be honest, after meeting her mother I wouldn't be surprised if, well, that isn't fair of me to say that, of course…"

My head felt as though someone had stuffed it full of cotton wool. I dug my hands into my pockets, wracking my brains for a plausible cover story. Mum looked at me in expectation. I swallowed and did my best to sound as casual as I could.

"It's just a bit of a tummy bug, Mum. She probably picked it up from swimming in the sea. You know what it's like. She didn't want to mention it because she didn't want to spoil the holiday. It's just made her feel a bit nauseated and, well- you know. I'm sure she'll be right as rain in a day or two. To be honest, she is a bit susceptible to these things, but she doesn't like to talk about it…."

"Oh? Is it that horrible Irritable-Bowel Syndrome thing? I read an article about that in one of my magazines. Seems very wide spread in young people, these days. Well, do tell her to let me know if there is anything I can do?"

"Actually Mum, I think it'd be better not to mention it. She can be very sensitive about these things…"

"As you wish, Jumbo. You know her better than I do. But I do hope she feels better soon. Such a pity if it ruins her week."

After that, Sherry took a little more care about her bathroom habits, but she had seemed well impressed with my handling of the situation.

"Quick thinking, there, Jono. After all, I understand that IBS is a chronic condition so you have also furnished me with a ready-made excuse for picking at my food and being a little over-fussy whenever I have to eat."

"Well, you're more than welcome. I think we make rather a good team. Don't you?"

"I most certainly do."

21

The Broadstairs sunshine and carefree days which followed set me up brilliantly for what would be my final year at school. Mum had discouraged me from finding holiday work, insisting that I should just enjoy being a kid while I still could. I'm not sure that I appreciated her categorizing me as a kid but didn't argue as it meant I could spend more time with Sherry.

Once term began, however, I set my nose firmly to the grindstone, despite the obvious distractions. Fortunately for me, Sherry understood and did not take the change in my priorities personally. Camden Town and its attractions still beckoned at weekends but only so long as it did not impede the important business of study. I was on a mission now and nothing if not determined to distinguish myself in my 'A' levels.

"I'm going to be top of my field," I enthused to Sherry who smiled patiently. It was easy to forget that she could easily run rings around me in mathematics. She certainly never made a point of it. On the contrary, if she saw me struggling with a maths problem, she would just quietly point me in the right direction with her questions and it was only later that I would realise how helpful she had been.

"I want a PhD by the age of twenty-three and a research fellowship after that," I would gush. MIT in the states or maybe Caltech? The sky's the limit."

Sherry would squeeze my arm encouragingly, probably grateful that I had dropped the notion of Microbiology as that field and returned to my first love - physics.

One evening, however, when I had started to bang on about my glorious future yet again, she suddenly and unaccountably burst into tears.

"Shez?" I asked in alarm. "Whatever is the matter. I thought you wanted me to do well?"

"Of course, I do Jonno. You know that. It's just that – well, I don't want to pour cold water on your dreams - but I'd rather hoped to be part of them."

She wiped her cheeks with the back of her wrist and I watched transfixed as her skin absorbed the droplets of moisture like blotting paper. I shook my head and looked into her face.

"But you are, Shez. I can't imagine us not being together, you know that."

"Really, Jonno? Think about it. I'd never be able to travel to the USA. I have no passport or documentation and their background checks are notoriously thorough. Don't you see? I know you love me, but I also know how much all these opportunities mean to you and, well, I don't want to be the one who holds you back, Jonno."

I could, of course. See what she meant, that is. And any future I envisaged had *always* included her. I just hadn't thought it through. I did my best to brush the issue aside. Still, I wasn't at all sure my reassurances that I would find just as many exciting opportunities right here in the UK convinced either of us.

Feeling a little peeved I went on the defensive.

"Bloody Hell, Shez. I don't get it. You've got this amazing mind – you're always twenty moves ahead of my game in chess and can grasp complex new ideas in half the time it takes me. I know you've had a few hundred years head start on me, but still. Just what do you do with it? Why are you wasting time clearing up an old house when you could be – well, anything?"

Sherry looked away in distress. For a moment I thought she was going to cry again. When she replied it was in an unusually small voice.

"Jonathon, I know you just accept me for who I am, but that same wonderful thing about you makes you forget that it's not that simple for me. In many ways I'm a fugitive - a fugitive hiding in plain sight. I don't always feel safe out in the world. Not without you at my side."

Her words could not have hit me harder had they been pasted to the front of a freight train. I took her hand and, raising it to my lips, planted a kiss on her palm.

"Sherry, you're right. I can't understand, not really. But I promise you this, so long as I am around, I will never let any harm come to you."

I never mentioned MIT or Caltech again but continued to study hard until the time came to make choices about applying for university the following year.

One cold Saturday morning Mum came downstairs into the kitchen to find me huddled over my porridge and poring over an UCCA Handbook. She moved to fill the kettle and coughed.

"So soon?" she commented. "I've been bracing myself for the idea of you leaving school and then home, but you look so young sitting there in your pyjamas and dressing gown. It seems only five minutes ago you sitting under the table playing with your Lego."

"Mum. Pleeeease. You're the one who is always reminding me that I'm an adult now and besides, we've discussed this."

"I know. I guess I'm having mixed feelings – probably not something you Vulcans understand."

"Oh, ha ha! I can't help it if I have a logical mind."

I ignored the face mum pulled and took a few spoonsful of porridge while Mum busied herself with a mug and boiling water. I wrinkled my nose. It had gone cold. I reached over for the golden syrup, hoping that would make it more palatable. Much better.

"Well, what do you reckon then?" Mum set her coffee on the table and sat opposite me. I looked up from the handbook and shrugged. My lack of enthusiasm didn't faze her. Mum, it seemed, had her own ideas.

It was exciting and terrifying all at the same time, she gushed. *There was indeed a lot to take into consideration. Hull had a rising reputation but Manchester, of course, was considered the birthplace of nuclear physics. So, if it was good enough for Ernst Rutherford it would be good enough for her son. And how exciting would it be to be working in the same labs where the atom was first split? Or waking through the same corridors as Alan Turing?*

I grunted and scraped up the last vestige of oatmeal from my dish.

"I was thinking Imperial College, perhaps," I suggested, licking my spoon. "Or St Mary's, even. They had a great physics department now and Mile End is so close, I could still live at home..."

My mum's face fell. The next words she spoke were tentative and considered.

"But Jumbo - the whole point of going to university is to get away from home. To cut loose and spread your wings. Maybe even go a little wild. It's the parties and the staying up all night talking about life and the meaning of it all. I mean, I know you'd be there to learn but, truly, it should be about so much more..."

"Nah. All sounds a bit overrated if you ask me. You know me, Mum, I've never been outgoing socially."

"But this will be different, Sweetheart. You're going to meet like-minded people who share your passion. It's not going to be like school. Not one little bit, I promise you..."

I folded my arms, hoping to signal that the discussion was at an end. But Mum wasn't giving up, so easily.

"Well, what about Sherry? Where is she hoping to study? I thought she was applying for Oxbridge. What became of that – you're always saying how brilliant she is?"

I shrugged.

"That's what her mother wanted but I'm pretty sure she feels the same as me, Mum. We live in the greatest City on the planet. Why would we want to go anywhere else?"

Mum fell silent and frowned. A moment or two passed during which I sincerely hoped she had let it drop. I was wrong.

"Look, Jumbo, if you're worried about me – you don't need to be. Really, I'll be fine. I've made a few friends at choir and, believe me, once you're out of my hair, I certainly don't intend to sit around waiting for the phone to ring. Why, I may even take some time out from work and go travelling. I've even thought of returning to college myself, so..."

I rolled my eyes and sighed.

"I don't doubt it, Mother. Now, can we please change the subject."

"Okay, Jumbo. But one last thing. If it's the money you're worried about, well you don't need to be - that is all taken care of. Your father saw to that, at least. I'll talk to you about all that when the time comes, but just know, the financial side will never be an issue and so, even if you do choose to stay in London, well, I shall insist that you do so in a flat of your own. Are we clear?"

I gaped at my mum in bewilderment.

"And you needn't look at me like that, Jumbo. I couldn't love you any more, you know that. But sometimes, I think I've been a tad overprotective. Perhaps I should have pushed you a little more firmly into the outside world. You turn eighteen soon and one of us has to cut the apron strings. University seemed like a natural opportunity. But, if you're not going to do it yourself, then I will just have to do it for you."

That was my Mum. Full of surprises. And when she said something, I knew that she meant it.

22

The day before my eighteenth birthday turned out to be a Tuesday. Not that there is anything very significant about that apart from the fact that the next day would be a Wednesday - early-closing day for some of our local shops. I was at home on exam leave which meant I could take it easy. The 'A' level examinations were almost over. I had one remaining maths paper to worry about and that was not scheduled until the following Monday. There wasn't a great deal of revision involved. It was more a question of familiarising myself with a couple of theorems, I hadn't used in a while and applying the correct strategies to solve my mental roadblocks.

Mum had arranged to take the Wednesday off. *It would, after all,* she said, *be a big day for her too.* I had raised an eyebrow but let it go. All the same, we had not made over-elaborate plans to celebrate my birthday. The idea of any kind of a party was out of the question. After all, it wasn't as though I had a host of friends queuing up to attend. Besides, I wanted to remain focused and since Sherry loathed going out for big meals, a quiet night at home with cake and bubbly seemed just the ticket. Mum had insisted that we at least invite Mrs Worth to join us for a slice of cake and a celebratory drink and I could hardly object, though that was more for Mum's sake than my own. She hadn't seemed her usual perky self for the last couple of days and, that evening, something a little peculiar happened.

Sherry had been around earlier in the day but had decided not to stay over, (as she sometimes did on weeknights, following our holiday), and had muttered something about having to organise a birthday present for a certain party. Late that evening I had been in my room going over a few equations. Normally, I would listen to music, but that night all I wanted was peace and quiet and a clear head. It had been a scorching day and had turned into a sweltering night and I had left the door open to let some air in.

I was writing out a rather tricky geometric proof when I heard a mumbling coming from my mum's room. I dismissed it as the radio but then pulled myself up and listened more closely. That was no radio. I slipped off the bed, tiptoed to my door and opened it a little wider. The voice was my mum's all right. And I could tell that she wasn't on the phone either. I cocked my head to one side. She could only be talking to herself. I hadn't heard her do it for ages and, for some reason, this sounded different to me. I'm not sure whether I was motivated by concern or plain old nosiness, but I crept up to her door, which stood slightly ajar, and held my breath.

She was seated at her dressing table mirror and I could just see the back of her head. But she wasn't looking at herself in the mirror, she had her head bowed. Then it became clear. She was talking to a photograph.

"So that's it – tomorrow, our little boy will officially become a man."

I put my hand to my mouth. It must have been one of the photographs of my father.

"Not that we're going to mark it in any style, and don't ask. I've no idea who he inherited his homebody disposition from, it wasn't you, and it *certainly* wasn't me, my Love. To be honest, I'm not sure he'll ever truly fly the nest."

I felt myself flush. I had exceeded all expectations in my mock "A" levels and had received offers from all the universities I had listed on my UCCA form, but I had resolutely stuck to my guns regarding remaining in London. As had Mum.

I knew that I should go back to my room but I couldn't tear myself away. My mum almost never spoke *about* my father and here she was talking *to* him.

She sighed and I could see she was stroking the photograph with her fingertips.

"Look at us, I was giddy with love for you. So many years. I wonder if you still look the same or whether I would even recognise you now. I'll bet you don't look a day older. Vanity always was your – *our* biggest flaw. It wasn't our fault. It was simply the way it was. We tried to give each other what we most needed. But in the end, vanity and love are like oil and water. You thought I made a choice between being a wife and being a mother but, you never really understood the contest and for that I'm deeply sorry. It doesn't mean that I don't miss you, though. So, wish me luck, Julian, wherever you are. Tomorrow is going to be a difficult day."

With that, she opened the dressing table drawer and replaced the photograph. Fearing she would turn around, I backed away, creeping silently to my room and closing the door. Parents? Who knew what had gone on between them? I certainly had no mental space left to try to work it out. My head was full of problems that could be solved and *they* were always the best kind.

The following morning, I slept late. I had long since forsaken my newspaper round and it was my birthday, so Mum indulged me with a lie in. Maybe I dreamed about my father, but if I did, the dreams faded too quickly for me to remember them.

It was getting on for eleven-thirty, (which was very late for me), when I finally emerged from my bedroom, woken by the delicious aroma of bacon wafting up from the kitchen. Mum must have heard me stirring and called up the stairs.

"Happy Birthday, Jumbo, Darling! Come straight down. I'm making your favourite breakfast. Bacon with scrambled eggs and American pancakes with syrup. Don't let it get cold."

I stumbled down to the kitchen, belting my dressing gown around me.

"Smells great, Mum. Thanks…" I yawned, slipping onto a chair where she had laid a place at the table. Mum kissed me on the cheek and squeezed my shoulder, nodding towards a small stack of cards and envelopes that lay stacked on top of a manilla file next to a large glass of orange juice. I blinked in surprise. Her old wedding photo lay on top of the pile. I picked up the photo, while Mum turned back to the frying pan. I stared at it and then lay it to one side without saying anything and began to open the cards.

The first couple were from Uncle Roy and Uncle Trev and contained a couple of record tokens. I grinned. *Nice one, guys.* You could never have too many of those. The third was from Mrs Worth and boasted a book token. I raised an eyebrow. She never forgot my birthday, but this year she had been particularly generous. Being eighteen was *clearly* a big deal. I made a mental note to thank her later.

The large card on the bottom was from Mum and, as I opened it, a fifty-pound note fell out. I had never actually seen one before and gaped at it for confusion for a moment before stammering:

"Crumbs, thanks Mum. But it's too much."

"Not for you, Luv. Not on your big birthday." Her eyes sparkled. She planted a kiss on the top of my head and placed my birthday breakfast on the table before me.

"Now, eat up. We've got lots to talk about and I'd prefer to get it all out of the way before Sherry gets here…"

I picked up a fork and dug into the pancakes. The taste of maple syrup filled my mouth, making me smile as I ate. I thanked her, speaking with my mouth full. Something she normally abhorred. She ruffled my hair in that way of hers and then sat opposite me with a cup of coffee and watched me enjoying my meal.

By and by, she began to drum her fingers quietly on the table. I looked up and wondered why she suddenly seemed so anxious but her face was set in a smile. She reached for the photograph, I had discarded and tapped it on the table.

"Now Jum - I mean Jonathon, there are things I have to tell you. Things you are old enough to hear and understand, now. Things about your father and about you, really..."

"Please, don't mum. I don't want to hear about that loser. He left us and couldn't have cared less..."

"Now, Jumbo, that is *not* entirely the case. And it's one of the things I wanted to talk to you about. It was far too complicated for you to understand, back then, and I'm not sure that it isn't still. Your father did leave us, it's true. But that never meant he didn't care and it didn't mean that he didn't try to make it right. As right as he could. He made sure that we would never want for anything. He paid off the mortgage on this house, and left me some besides - and I've always known I could ask for money if I needed it. It's just that I wanted to remain as independent as - oh, never mind. And, well here's the thing - he placed a large lump sum of money and shares in trust for you and now you are eighteen, well it's all yours.'

She reached for a manilla folder and slid it over to me. I stared at it and curled my lip.

"How much?"

"£10,000."

"Shit! But I don't want his money. I don't want anything from him - nothing, do you hear?" I shoved my plate away. I could hear my voice getting louder. And the look on Mum's face changed.

"Now don't get angry, Jumbo. You're not a child anymore. This isn't something you can pretend isn't happening. The money is yours. It'll help you through university or you could save it for a deposit on a home of your own if..."

I scowled. Mum took a deep breath.

"Well, never mind that now, Jumbo, there will be plenty of time to think about it all later. What I need to talk..."

The shrill ringing of the phone interrupted her words.

"Oh, darn - just a minute, Jumbo." She sprang up to answer. No one ignored a phone call back then, especially one that you were not expecting. I heard her say our number and then -

"Oh, my goodness. Really? How silly of me to forget. I'll be right there if you could just hang on a couple of minutes. Oh, thank you, so much. And thanks for ringing. You've really saved the day."

She came back and raised her eyes to the clock with a sigh. It was five minutes to midday.

"I've got to rush out Jumbo, got to pick up your cake. Silly me. I forgot that Ingles closes at midday on a Wednesday. Good job they called. I'll shan't be two ticks. Gosh, I only have a couple of minutes, better get a move on. Happy Birthday again, Sweetheart." With that, she grabbed her handbag and bustled out of the kitchen and out through the front door.

I didn't want to think about Dad and I didn't want to think about this money. It was my birthday and I just wanted to enjoy it. I picked up the photograph and slipped it into the manila folder without looking at it and then pulled back my plate. Spearing the last pancake, I stuffed it into my mouth and concentrated on the salty sweetness on my tongue.

I felt better by the time I had cleared the plate. Clearer in my mind. Not so tight inside. Another moment passed when there was a soft knock at the front door. I wiped my mouth and got to my feet, wondering if Mum had forgotten her keys in her haste. But it wasn't Mum, it was Sherry. She stood on our doorstep holding a bottle of champagne and a fistful of decorated balloons that were emblazoned with the number eighteen.

"Happy Birthday, Jonno. Blimey, you are still in your PJs? Sorry, I know I said that I wouldn't be around until after 2 pm but, you know me - I couldn't wait to see you."

She leaned in and gave me a lingering kiss. I took her arm and pulled her inside before the neighbours started twitching the net curtains.

"Come in. You just missed Mum. She forgot to pick up the cake."

Sherry rolled her eyes.

"Another Jumbo birthday special? Well, I'll just have to suck it up, I suppose. And then a meal tonight. You know I'd only do this because it's your birthday and I love you…"

"Golly, you're such an old romantic…" I kissed her again. "You know, I would have offered you some of my pancakes and bacon but I'm afraid you've missed the bus, so you'll have to find another way to prove you love me, for now."

I led her into the kitchen and sat down. She put the champagne in the fridge and then set the balloons, which were attached to a weight, in the centre of the table. I picked up the manila folder and placed it on the worktop.

"Actually. I'm glad you came early. You were just in the nick of time. Mum was trying to have one of her serious talks." I pulled a face.

"Well, I like to be of service."

We sat teasing each other a while. I wanted nothing more than to take her up to my room but that seemed out of the question. I looked at the clock, wondering what was keeping Mum. The bakery was only just up the road around the corner.

A loud knock on the front door made me jump.

"I'll get it," I said with a grin. "If it's The Jehovah's Witnesses my PJs might scare them away. I ambled down the hallway and opened the door. A woman stood before me holding a square white cardboard box. I recognised her face but couldn't quite place her.

"Can I help you?"

"Hi, yes. I think so. I'm from Percy Ingles. Mrs Cooper ordered a cake for today. She told me that she would be right there, but something must have held her up and we were closing. I pass your house on the way home in any case, so said I would drop it off – are you the birthday boy?"

I must have given her a strange look because she suddenly burst into tears. I didn't know what to do so I just stood there.

"I'm so sorry," she sniffed, "I'm just feeling a bit shaken up. There was a dreadful accident just outside the shop, just as we were closing, and I had to walk past. A woman was hit by a delivery lorry, I believe. There are police and an ambulance there now – Goodness, are you okay, Luv?"

I was as far from okay as it is possible to be. Mum! I could not even form the words. I elbowed the woman and her box to one side and tore off up the road, still in my dressing gown and slippers.

What happened in the following ten minutes is all a bit of a fog. I raced up the road and then heard a lot of screaming and crying and realised it was me. There were police and ambulance workers and a crowd of shell-shocked-looking onlookers. I felt as though I was watching it all from somewhere up on a roof. It must have taken a while for them to calm me down and then I'm not quite sure what happened, because the next thing I knew, I was back outside our house, half-propped up on the arm of a young WPC who seemed to have escorted me back home.

Sherry was standing on the doorstep looking out for me. She must have taken the cake in and there was no sign of the woman who had brought it.

"Oh, Sherry. It's Mum. She's gone."

Sherry placed her arms around me and hugged me to her. I could feel a trembling but couldn't tell whether it was Sherry or me.

"She was over the road from the bakers. They reckon she must have slipped off the kerb. Her handbag was open so they think she may have been looking inside it as she walked and missed her step. The lorry driver never saw her until she was falling and by then it was too late. I don't know what to do."

"I'll take care of you, Jonno. And I won't ever leave you - I promise. Now come inside and get some clothes on, while I make you a hot cup of tea."

The WPC who had been standing to one side nodded and then made a small cough.

"I got the impression there wasn't another parent around?"

Sherry shook her head. The WPC sighed.

"Thought as much. Look, I know it's a big ask, but if he *is* the next of kin, we need him to officially identify the body – unless you know of anyone else?"

This time, it was I who shook my head. There were my uncles, but they were a half a day's travel away and besides, she was *my* mum – and I was an adult now.

"I'll do it…" I mumbled. "It should be me."

Sherry squeezed by arm.

"Okay. But I'll go with you and, Jonno, you will need to get yourself dressed."

The next morning, I rose early. Sherry had stayed with me, but she rarely slept more than a few hours per night in any case. The two of us had lain awake whispering and holding each other until the first streaks of dawn were beginning to brighten the sky when I must have finally drifted off.

When I came to, she lay sleeping next to me. I watched her for a while, touched by how pale and beautiful her skin looked in the half-light, like one of those marble statues I had seen in the British Museum. And then I noticed that, just like them, she hardly seemed to move at all. For a horrible moment, I thought she had died too, but when I reached out my hand, her flesh was warm to the touch. Nothing like that of the body in the morgue yesterday.

For the first time, it struck me that since she didn't eat then maybe she didn't really need to breathe either. If that was so, then perhaps it was true that she never would die. If that was so then, perhaps *she* might be the one person able to keep her promise and never leave me.

I decided to leave her sleeping and tiptoed downstairs. The sun had already climbed well above the rooftops and was pouring in through the Venetian blinds in the kitchen, a harsh reminder that the world carries on turning no matter what happens in our insignificant little lives.

Suddenly, I noticed the cake box next to the draining board where Sherry had left it. I moved over to it and lifted the lid. It was perfect. An immaculately rendered fondant chequered chess board with eighteen black and white candles that had been exquisitely modelled into full-size chess pieces. There couldn't have been a better cake in all the world. I folded the lid right back and gazed at it, wondering where on earth they had found the candles.

"Oh, Mum. You've surpassed yourself." I whispered. But I wanted her – not a cake, no matter how fancy. Without thinking, I batted it away from me, sending the whole thing crashing to the lino tiles where it burst into pieces, flinging waxy chessmen into every corner of our little kitchen. I stared at the crumbled mess at my feet and collapsed next to it with a howl.

"Damn you, Dad. Where were you? You should have been here to protect her…"

The next moment Sherry was next to me, squeezing me tight and picking bits of sticky cake and icing off my pyjama bottoms.

"Hold on, Jonno. I'm right here. I don't know how we're going to get through this, but I promise we will - together.

23

"I can't do it, Sherry. I just can't. I can't think straight. I'll just fuck it up. I know I will."

It was late afternoon on the Sunday following the accident. Uncle Roy had just left. He had travelled down, first thing Friday morning, to help with the funeral arrangements and I had never been so glad to see him. His support turned out to be invaluable since neither I nor Sherry would have had the smallest clue where to begin with all the official stuff. I'd told him that he could crash at our place but he could see I needed my space and had found himself a nearby bed-and-breakfast.

"You've been a real tower of strength," I said to him as he shook my hand and then hugged me. And I meant it. So much so that I pretty well crumbled once he had gone. Especially as I was facing the prospect of my final 'A' Level maths paper the next day.

I had managed to hold it together while he had been around but now that we were alone again, I felt my courage desert me. Sherry hadn't left my side for more time than it took to fetch a pint of milk and a loaf of bread from the corner shop and was doing her best to comfort me, yet all I wanted was to curl up in a dark room and sleep

"I just can't face it, Shez. It's all too much."

"C'mon, Jonno. Don't be so hard on yourself. You know this stuff like the back of your hand. Just trust yourself."

"That's easy for you to say," I pouted. "You've no idea what I'm going through. You never even had a mum, so what would you know about it?"

Sherry looked away and I knew that I had gone too far. I begged her forgiveness. *I hadn't meant to lash out at her. My brain was so scrambled, I hardly knew what I was saying.*

Sherry took my hand in hers.

"I know, Jonno, I know. But, look, I'm sure the school can make some sort of appeal to the examination board in these cases, can't they? Or perhaps you should postpone it until resits…"

"What's the point of that? What's the point of anything, for that matter? Mum wanted this so much for me - and now I can't even do this for her. I don't want to fail and I don't want to be treated as some special case. But I just can't think straight." I buried my face in my hands. I wasn't exaggerating. I'd barely had more than three hours sleep a night, in days, and the haze in my brain felt denser than a London fog. The thought that I would blow my 'A' levels seemed like the last straw.

Sherry looked at me and chewed her lip. I buried my face in my arms and wished I was somewhere else.

"Of course, there might be a way…"

I looked up at her.

"- for Jonathon Cooper to sit his examination and pass with flying colours, I mean. That is, someone calling themselves Jonathon Cooper…"

"You've gotta be kiddin'?" It must have been the first time I had smiled since my birthday breakfast. "Are you saying that you'd pretend to be me? And take the exam for me?"

"I wouldn't call it *pretending*. Not really. It would be more like doing it by proxy when you think about it. You and I both know that you would ace that paper, under normal circumstances. And I'd make sure that I answered the questions the way you would. No one would ever know. How could they? It'll be a piece of piss, if you'll pardon my French."

"How do you mean- *the way I would*?" I frowned.

"Well, you know - make a couple of errors, fluff a couple of equations. Just minor points."

"Fair enough. And you'd have to show your working out. We can't afford to arouse suspicion of any sort. Though what anyone could suspect, I can't imagine."

"Exactly," replied Sherry, "And the beauty of it is, I wouldn't have to talk to a soul. I'll just walk straight into the exam hall, sit at a desk and Bob's your Uncle."

I shook my head.

"But I'd be cheating, Shez. I would. There's no escaping it."

"Hey, forget that. I'd say the universe owes you one, wouldn't you? Besides, wouldn't you get just a little kick out of meeting yourself?"

She couldn't have pitched it better. That idea alone was irresistible. Even in my sorry state.

"I'll say. Of course, you'd have to wear my school uniform and don't whatever you do talk to anyone who might know me…"

"I know, Jonno. I'll even make sure I leave before the exam is finished. That way I could avoid anyone who might want to speak to me. And don't forget, I've been to the school before. The examination hall is where they had the dance, isn't it?"

I nodded.

"It would be a weight off my mind, Shez. It really would."

I'm not sure who was the more nervous the next morning. As soon as we were out of bed, I gathered together my school clothes. I held them to my face and wrinkled my nose. The shirt needed a wash but that's what happens when you don't have a mum around anymore. Sherry looked at me and rolled her eyes. I handed her the bundle.

"Oh – and I'll need this…" she said yanking a hair from my scalp with a look of dreamy determination.

"Ouch!" I squawked rubbing my head.

"Hey, that's the only bit *you* have to do…" she teased as she headed to the bathroom.

"Let me watch, Shez. Oh, please, let me watch," I begged, the fierceness of my curiosity momentarily piercing the dull canopy of grief that had engulfed me. But she remained adamant and closed the door in my face.

Ten minutes later, the bathroom door opened and I came face-to-face with a perfect replica of myself. It was like looking in a mirror but with a whole extra dollop of freakishness.

"Whoa," I exclaimed in disbelief.

"Ditto!" exclaimed my reflection in a voice I hardly recognised, yet knew to be my own.

I made him turn around, assessing the whole astonishing picture.

"Jeez, you're a full-on Doppelganger. I wish you had let me watch…"

My strange alter ego shook his head.

"No, Jonno. I'm sorry but much as a part of me would like to, a shapeshifter shifting their shape is something so private, so intimate, that I couldn't even entertain the idea of letting you witness it. Besides, believe me, it would gross you out. Seriously. I'm pretty sure that you'd never be able to look at me the same way again."

"What? You mean the way I am looking at you now?"

"No stupid. The way you look at Sherry. But what do you reckon, since you mention it?"

"Well. I didn't realise I looked so young, for starters. But I guess I'm kind of cute even if I do look rather sad."

"C'mon, Jonno. You're entitled to look sad right now. Now, buck up and find your examination identification number for me – the minicab will be here any minute."

According to Sherry, it all went without a hitch. Taking the cab meant that she avoided bumping into anyone I knew on the bus and she had arrived in time to avoid anything but the brief wait in line to be admitted to the exam hall. I hadn't informed the school of my loss and was sort of hoping that it would go unnoticed. As luck would have it, however, the accident turned out to have been fairly big news around Forest Gate and word about my mum gad already got around. Not surprisingly, Sherry's arrival attracted a fair amount of attention, all of which was unwelcome given the circumstances.

All the same, the little gaggle of sixth-formers who had congregated in the corridor outside the exam hall that morning had shown nothing but genuine sympathy, murmuring words of condolence as they filed into their respective examinations. One of the girls even squeezed her arm whilst another put a handkerchief to her nose and sniffed loudly. Sherry, however, could not allow herself the luxury of acknowledging their attention. She had kept her head lowered and sailed on straight past them without meeting anyone's eye.

The test paper itself had, of course, turned out to be the easy part. Sherry had completed it as planned and then left ten minutes before the end without having to encounter another soul on the way out.

Back at home, I almost cried with relief when I heard her key in the front door and had never felt so pleased to see myself. I tried to coax her into the kitchen for a debriefing. The novelty of hanging out with my identical twin, no matter how temporary, seemed a welcome distraction from my other darker thoughts. Sherry, however, was having none of it. She shook her head and made directly for the bathroom. Once she was back to her old self, she sat me down with a pad of paper and went over the entire exam paper, question for question. When she finally laid the pen to one side, I felt my eyes fill with water. I took her hand and thanked her. There was no doubt about it - with my normal head on, the paper would have been a breeze for me and I knew, without a shadow of a doubt, that I would have achieved top marks. We may have cheated the system but at least I had not cheated myself.

After that, all we had to do was await the results. Thanks to Sherry the easy part was over. What came next would be the real test.

24

The coroner released Mum's body later that week and Uncle Roy was able to confirm the following Thursday as the date for Mum's funeral. Meanwhile, he had promised that both he and Uncle Trevor would return in time to help out with the wake, which we agreed should be held back at our house after the service.

Joan had turned up on Monday evening and still looked visibly shaken. Whilst Mum had never referred to her as being a particularly close, they had known each other for years and had always struck me as a bit of a double act whenever I had popped into the office. She said she hoped that I didn't feel she was intruding but wanted to do anything she could to help. Sherry and I gladly accepted her offer. Neither of us had the foggiest idea about how you went about arranging a wake and mostly sat in the living room like two abandoned kids in need of a parent.

Joan, on the other hand, seemed exactly the kind of person you needed in a crisis. Used to organising other people's affairs, she started by placing a notice in the local paper and then took herself off to the local off-licence to purchase several bottles of sherry (for the ladies) and whisky (for the menfolk). Whilst she was at it, she took the opportunity to hire a box of wine glasses for the day. *So much classier than paper cups,* she claimed.

Sherry and I looked at the amount of alcohol and wondered just how many guests she was expecting. *You'd be surprised how many people a funeral brings out of the woodwork*, commented Joan, as though she could read our thoughts. *Margot may have kept herself to herself but she was very highly regarded around these parts.* I told he that I was pleased to hear as much and asked how much I owed her – for the booze etc. Joan, however, would not hear of such a thing. *It's the least I can do,* she sighed - *the very least.*

Mrs Worth had also stepped up with the promise of cakes and sandwiches and the loan of her best bone-china tea set. Mum did have one herself, but seeing that Joan had us catering for the five thousand, it seemed like a good idea. Meanwhile, our old neighbour also made it her business to see that the two of us, (or me, at least) were properly fed. Not wishing to intrude, she took to ringing the bell and leaving piping hot shepherd's pies and the like on the doorstep of an evening. I think she suspected that as nice as Sherry seemed, she was not much help domestically. I, for once, was grateful for her interference. I hadn't eaten a proper meal in days and had already had to make an extra hole in my belt to keep my jeans from falling down.

She even came over to help clean and tidy the house on the afternoon before the funeral and never so much as raised an eyebrow in criticism of the state of the kitchen or front room, which lay strewn with used cereal bowls and discarded glasses. If she thought that girls, at least, should know better, she certainly kept it to herself.

Sherry may not have been taking care of me, in the traditional sense, but I honestly don't think I would have gotten through any it without her. She hardly left my side for days and seemed to know when to talk and when to leave me to my thoughts. And between the two of us, we did at least figure out how to use the washing machine. I had never thought about it much before, but Sherry never generally needed to wash her clothes. Not unless she spilt something on them and then she would generally just throw them out and buy something new.

We played a lot of chess that week. It engaged my brain and was a welcome diversion from the turmoil of my thoughts and the numbness that gripped my heart.

Then, on the Tuesday morning, I noticed the manila folder still lying on the kitchen workbench, where I had left it. I didn't want that to be my last memory of Mum and hadn't even mentioned it to Sherry. And I certainly didn't want to have to think about my father. I tucked the folder between a couple of Mum's old cookbooks which took up one end of the kitchen shelf and did what I did best - put it out of my mind.

Sherry, meanwhile, was not at all her usual self either. She was frequently restless and easily distracted; to the point where I very nearly placed her in a couple of easily avoided checkmates. She laughed it off and said that she'd reckoned I deserved a break, but I wasn't convinced. At other times, I would catch her staring down at her hands and twisting her fingers as though trying to solve some unspoken puzzle. I guessed that she was just worried about me.

Uncle Roy arrived back the Wednesday evening, accompanied by Uncle Trev. Once again, they both declined my invitation to stay with us and said that they would book into a guest house. There were plenty dotted along the Romford Road and we were just discussing which to try first when Mrs Worth turned up. Whether it was by luck or neighbourly nosiness, I couldn't say, but in any case, she refused to hear another word about paying for lodgings and promptly offered to put them up for a couple of nights as her guests. *It wouldn't be any trouble and she had a couple of spare bedrooms lying empty.* Uncle Trev and Uncle Roy accepted, quite overcome by what they called "southern hospitality." She also insisted on laying on an evening meal for all of us, around at her place. It was the last thing I wanted, but I thought about what Mum would have said and knew it was the least we could do to replay our old neighbour's kindness.

Both Uncle Roy and Uncle Trevor seemed to take to Sherry straightaway. Nevertheless, it turned out to be a stilted and rather awkward meal. Neither Sherry nor I had much to say and Mrs. Worth, who was usually a chatterbox, seemed to become a different person in the presence of her two strapping northern male guests.

Roy and Trev, for their part, were far less relaxed than they had been on their home soil. They repeatedly expressed their sincere regret about their virtual estrangement from their sister and the opportunity they had lost in watching her only child grow up.

"There's no substitute for blood, Jonathon," remarked Roy. "We lost our parents when your Mum was still just a girl. As the eldest, I tried to look out for her, as a father would, but she was always wilful, was Margot, and I guess she resented a mere brother trying to throw his weight around."

"Aye," agreed Trevor, "- blood is thicker than water at the end of the day. My only comfort is that we had at least begun to build bridges in recent years and can pull together as a family now when it really counts."

I said nothing. I had enough pain to deal with and wasn't interested in shouldering theirs as well. I'd never had a sibling, but I did have Sherry. She wasn't my blood, but she meant more to me than they ever could.

When the meal was over, they invited me to the *black and white* pub up the road for a couple of pints. They'd spotted the old Spotted Dog on their way to the house and suspected it might offer a good range of *real* ale.

"Is it a genuine Elizabethan building?" asked Uncle Roy. "It certainly looks as though it is."

"Oh, I'll say," replied Mrs Worth with obvious pride, " - older, even. It belonged to Ann Bolyn's father and Henry VIII himself used to stay there. Used to hunt all around here, he did. Of course, this was all forest back then and that's how this area got the name Forest Gate. It's thick with history around these parts."

My uncles couldn't have been more impressed. They looked at me but I declined, making some excuse about being tired. Which was true in any case. I know they meant well, but I was never so grateful as to thank Mrs Worth for her kindness, get out of that house with Sherry and close our front door behind us.

Later, I went to bed so exhausted that I had the best night's sleep, I'd had in days. I woke up willing it all to have been a horrible dream and wishing that this Friday would turn out to be like any other. It wouldn't of course.

I lay in Sherry's arms for a while until we remembered that we had the wake to think about. I showered and dressed but couldn't force down any breakfast, except for a mug of coffee. Sherry and I did our best to arrange the furniture in readiness for the gathering and then wandered about in listless silence, stopping only to stare out of the front room window. It looked as though it was going to be a hot day. I felt like kicking something.

"I just want this day to be over, Shez," I moaned, tugging at my hair.

"I know, Jonno, I know," whispered Sherry slipping her arm through mine. "And it will be - very soon."

The doorbell rang at half past ten and there stood Joan with a large cardboard box full of wine glasses and a shopping bag full of mixers for the whisky. She still looked pretty dreadful and almost sobbed into my ear as she embraced me.

"I can't stay," she apologised, "I need to get to the crematorium to check the flowers and music. But Mrs Worth has everything in hand and will be here shortly. Chin up, Jonathon. We'll all be there for you." And with that, she was gone. I hefted the box and bag into the kitchen and looked around. It was all beginning to feel very unreal.

Uncle Roy and Uncle Trev arrived at eleven, weighed down with shopping bags full of paper plates, plastic forks, pork pies, fruit cake and a quart of fresh milk. I told them that I didn't think we were expecting many guests, but they insisted it was better to be prepared. Mrs Worth soon followed, bringing with her enough sandwiches, home-baked cheese scones and Madeira cake to sustain a pack of Boy Scouts.

She was dressed all in black and I realised that it was the first time I'd ever seen her dressed in anything other than her old floral house coat. She'd brought an apron with her though, and tied it around her waist, as soon as she had set down her load.

In addition to the buffet, she provided a rather old-fashioned hand-embroidered tablecloth which she spread out across the living room table, smoothing it flat with her wrinkled old hands.

"Be a love and fetch the tea set round," she said to Uncle Roy. "I've left it in a box next to the front door." Uncle Roy set off, pleased to be useful in what had suddenly become a woman's world.

I watched as she laid out the plates full of neatly cut triangular sandwiches. There was salmon and cucumber, ham and pickle and egg and cress. I shook my head. *Better to have to have leftovers than to run short*, she sniffed. But I was simply wondering what all this was doing in my Mum's living room. And then it struck me that I ought to have offered her the money to cover all this, long since. I went to the kitchen to find Mum's purse and then approached her, but she had closed her hand over mine before I could even open it.

"No, Jonathon. Let me do this for her," she whispered, her old eyes tearing up. "I never had any children of my own and came to look upon her quite as the daughter I never had."

And I could see she really meant it. When I thought about it, she had always been there for Mum. Whether it was minding me or putting the world to rights over endless cups of tea, she probably had been my mum's closest friend and support. The truth was, I'd never quite forgiven her for telling on me, that day I got on the bus with Sherton Myam. But that was over five years ago now and, looking back, I could appreciate how young and vulnerable I had seemed.

As angry as I had felt back then, I could see that she had only had my best interests at heart. I bent down and hugged her. She smelled the way her house used to. She kissed my cheek and reached for her lace handkerchief.

I looked around for Sherry but she seemed to have vanished.

"Now, if you want to make yourself useful," suggested Mrs Worth, "perhaps you could unpack the box of glasses that Joan dropped off and put them on the kitchen table next to the refreshments. And mind you give them glasses a wipe with the tea towel. You never know where they've been."

I nodded, grateful to have been given an occupation. The hands on the clock on the mantelpiece were creeping ever closer to one o'clock and I had begun to feel cold all over, despite the warmth of the day.

Ten minutes later, I had just set the last glass on the little table where I had eaten so many of Mum's breakfasts and teas when I I felt a hand on my arm.

"The hearse is here, Jonno."

It was Sherry. And Sherry as I had never seen her. Plainly dressed in a smart black dress and sling-back sandals, I recognised as my mother's. I had told her to help herself to anything in Mum's wardrobe but had not been prepared for the jolt it gave me to see her standing there, literally filling my mum's shoes. My feet and ankles turned to sponge beneath me. It must have shown because Uncle Roy stepped forward and placed his arm around my shoulders.

"You can do this, lad..."

We filed out of the front door. The great black hearse stood at the pavement and behind it, waited two black Limousines.

My eyes flicked to the wooden box that lay in the hearse. *How could that be my mother? How could she be lying in a box? It couldn't be true.* I looked around in a kind of panic. Sherry was next to me now and I grabbed her hand.

"It's okay, Jonno. Just keep your eyes on me. Do you have your inhaler?"

I tried to answer but my mouth was too dry, so I licked my lips and nodded. I hadn't needed it in months but had slipped it into my pocket, just in case.

The driver of the first Limo opened the passenger door for us and Sherry and I slid onto the forward-facing leather seat. Then Uncle Roy and Uncle and Trevor took their places and the door closed. I caught a sudden acrid whiff of tobacco. I had never seen either of them smoke but one or both had clearly had a crafty puff in the last fifteen minutes.

Uncle Roy tipped me an *I've-got-your-back* wink. But I could see that his face was rigid with suppressed emotion. I felt my lower lip begin to tremble and looked away. So long as I could hold it together for the next hour, surely the day could not get any worse.

The funeral procession crawled up and around Upton Lane, past The Princess Alice and along Woodgrange Road towards Manor Park Crematorium. Talk about making painful progress. I gripped Sherry's fingers, wondering why we had to move so slowly but that was the way it was, back then. Everything slowed down for a funeral and it was hard luck for anyone in a hurry who found themselves stuck behind a hearse. Mum had always said that it was a sign of respect that funeral processions moved so slowly – a reminder to everyone to slow down and reflect upon the fleeting span of our time on this earth. Horse-drawn hearses were still popular in our neck of the woods and she would have us go out and stand on the pavement in silence whenever they passed. I'd always reckoned that it was a touch melodramatic but had loved to see the beautiful black horses in their plumes and finery, all the same. All at once, I felt angry with myself. Why hadn't it occurred to me to insist on such a send-off for Mum? She would have loved it. But it was a bit too late for that, now

I gazed out of the limo window appalled that the shops and houses still looked as they always had when nothing would ever be the same again. I'd looked away as we passed the offices of Skynner, Sykes and Skynner. It was all wrong. She should have been there right now, filing cases or chatting to Joan. Not lying in some poxy box. And then there was Percy Ingles – the bakers. The exact spot where she had lost her life beneath the wheels of some stupid fucking delivery truck. I had not been up this way since that day I ran howling up the street in my dressing gown. My head began to swim. I felt the burn of bile in my throat and fought to keep it down. I clenched my hands into angry fists.

"Jonno. My eyes. Look into my eyes."

I felt a pressure on my thigh. I turned and looked into Sherry's face and remembered to breathe.

I'd assumed that I would always have a mum, but that was just a childish fantasy. Now that she was gone, I wondered why anyone would ever willingly expose themselves to the kind of loss I was experiencing. Yet, as I gazed into Sherry's eyes and thought of the years ahead, I knew that I would never have to feel this pain again.

I closed my eyes for the rest of the journey and only opened them as we drew to a halt outside the Crematorium. I clambered out of the limo and felt the familiar crunch of gravel beneath the soles of my best shoes. I knew the little chapel well, or its exterior at least. When I was little, Mum and I had spent hours exploring the extensive graveyard and had even memorized some of the names on its oldest gravestones and memorials. Mum had loved the carved stone lilies and ubiquitous statues of weeping angels but had expressed firm views about burial.

"Whatever you do, Jumbo, don't let them bury me. No matter what anyone says. I simply couldn't bear it."

At least, I'd respected her wishes in that respect. She may have been brought up as a Catholic but had always laughed off any notions of an afterlife or of having an immortal soul. She did, however, have a positive aversion to worms and all creepy crawlies of any description, so I could at least spare her that.

We seemed to wait an age for things to start moving. I gazed around and it suddenly dawned on me that that we were less than a stone's throw from Sherry's house in Capel Road. I had never thought of it before, but the far side of the historic cemetery must have backed right onto her garden. I was pretty sure that Sherry rarely ventured into the garden herself, but the thought that she and Mum would now be neighbours made me smile.

Just then, Uncle Roy cleared his throat. The Undertakers had unloaded the hearse. It was time to move. Sherry and I followed the coffin through the old doors and down the narrow aisle. My uncles both helped to carry the casket. They had asked if I would like to be one of the coffin bearers but I had shaken my head and declined. I wanted to keep as far away from that strange-shaped box as possible.

Neither had I been to view the body. Not since that dreadful day when I visited the hospital mortuary to identify my mum's remains. *It would be a way of saying my final goodbye*, Mrs Worth had suggested. But I wouldn't hear of it. I'd seen enough of the inert body that had lain beneath that white sheet on that metal table. I had barely been able to confirm that it was Margot Cooper and any trace of the vital being who had been my Mum was long gone.

Just the memory of it was enough to make my ears buzz. I looked around, hoping to grasp upon something that would nudge the image back to the periphery of my thoughts where it had set up camp since the afternoon of the accident.

The pews of the neat little chapel were fuller than I had anticipated. Joan had been right. A number of her colleagues from Sykes, Skynner and Sykes had made it their business to pay their respects, including a couple of the senior partners themselves. I spotted Joan amongst them. She was wearing a frumpy black frock and an oddly jaunty black pillar-box hat. She met my eye as we passed and I noticed that she had already managed to smudge her mascara. She gave me a tearful little smile. I nodded back, thankful for the familiar face amid a sea of others, I would be hard-pressed to name - others who were, indeed, perfect strangers to me.

I couldn't work out who the two dozen or so women filling the pews were at all, until I caught sight of a plump Afro-Caribbean lady with a heavily freckled face and smile that her grief could not wholly suppress. Mrs Reynolds. The leader of the Community Choir to which my mum had belonged. It had to be. And then I remembered that they had volunteered to perform a cappella version of Mum's favourite choir pieces as part of the service.

I'd never paid much attention when Mum spoke about what they were doing at choir practice. It wasn't my kind of music and seemed terribly old hat. And I'd considered it far too uncool to attend any of their concerts, even at Christmas. But something about the way my mother spoke about Mrs Reynolds had made an impression. She had, or so my mum claimed, a voice to make the angels weep with envy and a laugh so infectious, she could have the whole choir in stitches within minutes and, somehow, looking at her then, I could believe it.

I looked away. My mum had a nice voice too and I wished that I had told her. I wished that I had gone to one of her blasted concerts. It wouldn't have killed me and now it was too late.

The pallbearers reached the front and set the coffin down on a structure that looked more like a conveyor belt than something that belonged in a chapel. I stumbled slightly as my knees threatened to buckle beneath me. Sherry caught my elbow and ushered me to our seats in the front pew.

The service began. The chapel had become very stuffy and there didn't seem to be enough air. The buzzing in my ears got worse and I began to feel as though I was watching a foreign film in slow motion - minus the subtitles. The Minister stood up to deliver a eulogy. I recognised Mum's name and then my own, but apart from that, he might as well have been speaking Martian.

Towards the conclusion of the service, the women from the choir rose to their feet and gathered on either side of the coffin and I saw Mrs Worth for the first time since we had arrived. Mrs Reynolds hummed a note and then moved her hands and they struck a song in unison. The wonderful harmonies of *Amazing Grace* soared into the highest eaves of the chapel. Maybe it wasn't my kind of music, but for the first time that morning, I felt the tears begin to stream down my face.

Sherry placed her arm around my waist and passed me a handkerchief. The singing came to an end. The ceremony was moving to its close. The soft hum sound of a motor started up and the coffin began to rumble forward into an opening in the wall. My heart all but stopped. The congregation stood in unison. For one awful moment, I had the strangest sensation that I was floating adrift, up among the rafters, watching myself, just as I had done on the day that Mum died. But just then, more music started and Bob Dylan was singing *Just Like a Woman – the track I had chosen*. My mum's favourite. Something about that "voice of sand and glue" tugged on me like an anchor and I felt myself returning to body, once more.

I became aware of Sherry's hand stroking my back and smiled down at her, mouthing the lyrics even as the tears dripped off the end of my nose. *Breaks just like a little girl.* I Buried my face in my hands. That was my Mum. I had always thought of her as so supremely sorted - unshakeable in her dependability. And nothing like unbreakable. But she broke, right enough. Right beneath the wheels of a stupid bloody great lorry, of all things.

The music stopped and a curtain moved automatically concealing the opening in the wall. That was that, then. There was a shuffling and low murmur from the pews behind us as people prepared to make their way out.

Sherry slipped her hand through the crook of my arm and we stepped into the aisle to leave.

"Oh, my God..." I gasped, stopping dead in my tracks.

Next to me, Sherry had stopped too, rooted to the spot like one of the marble angels in the grave yard. My uncles, who had been sitting next to us, heard the exclamation and looked around.

"Well, would you look at that? And still looking like one of the Kray brothers, even now. Look at that suit. Where does he think he is?" Uncle Roy's lips curled in contempt as he spoke. And now Uncle Trev was chiming in, his voice directed towards the back of the chapel.

"Have you no respect, Laddie? They, neither of them, lay eyes upon you for nigh on twelve years and then you have the gall to turn up now when it's all too bloody late. Shame on you."

A deep hush fell over the congregation. The man standing near the entrance to the chapel gave my uncles a withering look but remained silent. Uncle Roy and Uncle Trev moved over to embrace me and then strode purposefully out to show their disgust. Several mourners took their cue and began to exit the chapel in an orderly file. Joan hovered nearby for a moment and then left too, glancing back over her shoulder with an expression I could not read.

I stood in silence, too stunned to move. The remaining occupants of the pews behind me filed out until only Sherry, myself and the man, who still lingered at the back, were left. I gaped but could find no words. *Julian.* The face from the photo. A face from the place where memory had become indistinguishable from dreams. With hair and a beard the colour of a fox's and the smile to match. And barely looking a year older.

My father approached and held out a hand in greeting and then suddenly his eyes flashed. His gaze moved from my face to Sherry's with the slightest shake of his head.

"Why, Sher-Ton My-Am," he exclaimed and the name sounded strange, almost like Japanese, the way he pronounced it. "What a bonus. It's been the longest time. How lovely to see you again, my dear friend."

"Don't come any closer, Julian, I mean it…" Sherry rasped.

I stared at her in confusion. She seemed almost to writhe like an animal in a snare.

"No, no…" She staggered back, clapping her hands over her head.

"Oh, yes – you're starting to remember now, aren't you, my Dear? Come, all you have to do is take my hand…"

I stepped forward, ignoring the extended hand. I took a deep breath and drew myself to my full height.

"Look I don't know what you want with me, or how you know Sherry. But we don't want you and we don't need you - so piss off back to under whatever stone you crawled out from."

The smile took on an extra curl of mischievousness. He raised one eyebrow.

"Fine words and valiantly delivered, though not exactly the reception I'd anticipated, I'll grant you. But I'm pretty certain that *you will* indeed want to hear what I have to say. It strikes me that your mother, may she rest in peace, never got the chance to have that talk with you. The one she'd been saving for your eighteenth birthday. It's one you really can't afford to miss. Meet me at the Spotted Dog tomorrow for lunch. We can make that a liquid lunch if you prefer. And Sher-Ton My-Am, good to see you again, by the way. You simply must come along, too. I promise I will keep my distance."

The drive back was easily the most awkward ten minutes of my life. Uncle Roy commented on the number of people who had shown up to farewell his sister, but apart from that, we sat in silence. No one wanted to mention the elephant in the limousine, least of all me. My head was bursting with a thousand questions, yet I would have to keep them to myself. Sherry sat next to me with her head bowed and might as well have been a million miles away. And it was not about to get any easier.

When we got home, the living room was filling up with people I hardly recognised. The afternoon had turned uncomfortably warm and the daintily cut sandwiches were already beginning to curl. Mrs

Worth took one look at my face and immediately took charge. She directed Sherry and me to the sofa with instructions to stay put. She didn't require us to mix and make small talk, but from there, we could accept condolences and thank people for coming. Meanwhile, she enlisted Joan to supervise the refreshments and then disappeared into the kitchen to see to the tea.

I collapsed onto the sofa with a sigh. It was the last place I wanted to be but I owed it to Mum to behave like an adult and I was determined not to let her down. Sherry sat next to me and clung to my arm like a beaten kitten and I couldn't even ask her what on earth was wrong.

Uncle Roy opened the malt whiskey, handed Sherry and me each a small tumbler and then set to filling glasses for the guests. I drained the glass in one and coughed, screwing up my eyes as my throat burned. Sherry took a sip and then shrugged.

Over the following half hour or so a series of people I barely recognised drifted past, shaking my hand or, in the case of the women, kissing my cheek, and muttering their sympathy. In between times, they chatted to one another and ate sandwiches and cake. Uncle Roy and Uncle Trev, who really only knew each other, were knocking back the Scotch and were starting to become rather loud.

By and by, Joan appeared with one of the partners from Skynner, Sykes and Skynner, I hadn't met before, a portly balding gentleman with a cleft chin. He clasped my hand with a graceful bow of his head and then invited me to contact the office to arrange an appointment at my earliest convenience. I thought him rather a stuffed shirt until he cleared his throat and declared in a voice, I was sure he must generally reserve for the courtroom -

"Words cannot express how greatly we will miss your mother, young man. She was the beating heart of our operation. The beating heart, I say." At which Joan burst into floods of tears.

Things did not exactly go downhill from there, but neither did they improve. It made me proud to hear the lovely things that all these people had to say about my mum, but I still just wanted them all to go home so that I could be alone with Sherry.

Uncle Roy and Uncle Trev had gotten into their stride, by this time, holding forth about when they had all been kids to anyone who would listen. Ordinarily, I would have got a kick out of hearing their good-natured yarns. Mum seldom talked about the past or her childhood and it had been a favourite part of the family Christmases we had managed to spend together. But that afternoon, I struggled to hear what they were saying above the clink of tea cups and the drone of polite conversation. What I did notice was that neither of them seemed to make any mention of my father. Not, that was, until they came themselves to make their farewells, at which point they made no bones about how angry they felt with him.

"As though losing your mother was not enough for you, lad," sighed Uncle Trev, "the last thing you needed today was the appearance of your useless absentee father…"

"Aye. We should have sorted that bastard out, years ago when we had the chance…" muttered Uncle Roy. "But let's not make this afternoon about that waste of space. Now, you two kids take care of each other and let us know if there is anything we can do. Anything. Remember family is blood, and blood is thicker than water."

I shook their hands and wished them a safe journey home.

Thankfully, most of the remaining mourners followed their lead and took their leave, though the pair of us were beginning to resemble wilting pot plants by the time the house was quiet again.

Joan stayed on to help Mrs Worth clear away the leftovers and insisted upon washing up the plates, glasses and tea things before she went.

I was looking around at the empty living room when Mrs Worth walked in to retrieve the few remaining cups and saucers. I got to my feet and shook my head.

"I'm so sorry. I failed her, didn't I?" I groaned. "You only get one wake and I should have said something, at least…"

Mrs Worth wiped her hands on her apron and then placed them on either side of my face.

"Don't upset yourself, Jonothon. It's a big thing for someone your age. And in the end, it was just one day. You were her whole world and meant everything to her. She never struck me as either lonely or unhappy. And you always made her so proud. You had enough on your plate with your father showing up like that. I know how much your mother missed him, but it must have been such a shock for you…"

"Thank you, Mrs Worth. I can't say I care, to be honest. About Dad, I mean. Mum never wanted to talk about him and *I* certainly never missed him."

Mrs Worth blinked at me with a small frown. I thought she was going to say something but she seemed to change her mind. Instead, she winked at Sherry.

"You look done in, Dearie. We'll just finish up and then we'll be out of your hair."

When it came for Joan to leave, she asked me if I would mind carrying the box of glasses out to her car so that she could return them to the off-licence. It was no problem but as I finished closing the boot of her car, she caught hold of my hand and suddenly kissed it. I looked at her, a bit taken aback. Her eyes were brimming with tears again but she just nodded, got into the car and started the engine. I watched as she drove off up the road and then tramped back into the house.

That just left Mrs Worth.

"Well, just you two take care of each other. And let me know if there is anything I can do for you," she said patting my hand as opened the front door. "You know where I am."

As kind as she had been, Sherry and I heaved a loud sigh of relief as finally closed the front door behind her. And it wasn't just that the whole wake thing was finally over. The fact was, despite the enormity of what had occurred at the crematorium, we'd had zero opportunity to discuss it until then.

I didn't need Sherry to tell me that she had formerly been acquainted with my father or that the unexpected encounter had shaken her to her core. I'd never seen her so rattled. So much so that I felt a little cautious about how to approach the matter. Still, I had to know.

As it was, I had spent every free moment that afternoon turning the pieces over in my mind and once I had started, random snippets of memory started to fit together - Sherry's reaction; her agitation over the last few days. And then there was that picture I had first seen hanging on the wall in Sherton's house, all those years ago. Now that I thought back to it, the glamorous woman in the shot was Sherry to a T. And the man photographed from behind – the one who seemed so oddly familiar. It was Julian. It had to be. I couldn't believe that I hadn't seen it before, but then I hadn't been looking. I couldn't work out what the hell was going on but a dreadful idea was forming in my brain.

I told Sherry to remain where she was and ran upstairs to Mum's room. On my return, I poured out a tumbler full of vodka, handed it to Sherry and then set the snapshot of my mother and the tiger in front of her on the coffee table.

"Julian …" she breathed, closing her eyes.

"What the fuck, Sherry? Did you know about this – about him?"

"No – yes. Only very recently. You have to believe me, Jonno. I never imagined – that is, not until the other day when I saw the picture in that folder. I know I shouldn't have looked; it wasn't as though it was any of my business and even when I saw it, I couldn't remember, not properly. I knew it meant something but it was just a jumble of feelings. Like that time with your mother's dress. Do you remember? I could sense him when I touched it. I had no idea what had happened and I guess I just pushed it to the back of my mind. But it started to make some kind of sense when I saw that photo. But then, I didn't want to upset you – not after, well you've had enough to deal with. And I couldn't have told you anything coherent, anyway – not until this afternoon when – when I finally came into direct proximity with him."

"And you can tell this is him, right? This tiger? Just from a snapshot?"

"Oh, it's him, all right. Couldn't be anyone else."

"So – does that mean my mother knew? Is that possible?"

Sherry shrugged her shoulders and drained her glass in one gulp.

"I don't know Jonno. But I don't see how she could *not* know, really, do you?"

I fell silent. Mum had been going to tell me something the morning of my birthday. Something about my father. And then there was the little matter of his effect on Sherry. What the hell was all that about, anyway?

I looked at Sherry and was suddenly all questions. She did her best to answer but spoke like someone waking from a dream, her thoughts jumbled and disjointed. *The moment that Julian had drawn close, a tidal wave of memories almost knocked her off her feet. The sensation had abated with distance from Julian but had left her confused and disorientated.*

"The memories have already faded but I can't tell which were mine and which were somebody else's. It felt like all that junk in my house had tumbled down over me, burying me beneath it all. And another thing. I felt this pull, like gravity, almost – and yet I knew that if I so much as touched that – that man, that would be Sherry, gone – finished. It terrified me and yet, somehow, I wanted it too. You won't let him though, will you Jonno? Take me away, I mean."

I stared into her face. I had never seen her look so lost or so helpless.

"Whatever he was to you, or me, in the past, Sherry – we belong to each other now, and no one is going to take that from us. No one."

That night we clung to each other like shipwrecked survivors on a life raft. In the morning, I awoke to find Sherry sitting up and gazing at me, but I couldn't tell what she was thinking. I yawned and scratched my scalp.

"Did you get any sleep at all, Shez?"

"Jonathon. I think I've worked it out. The memories - our kind, we are unlike you in so many ways. You know that our physical beings are made up of a collective of autonomous "cells," for want of a better word – well, I think we might share a collective mind, too. Those thoughts and feelings I experienced when I was close to Julian, well, thinking about it, I'm pretty sure they couldn't have been my memories alone; I had flashes of memories of myself from another person's point of view. Like watching myself on film, I mean. It all receded so quickly, once I backed away, but the more I think about it, the more it makes sense. Don't ask me what it all means, though."

I had listened in silence. What she said would make sense. Indeed, given the strangeness of the last twenty-four hours, anything seemed possible.

I dragged myself out of bed and pulled on some clothes. I didn't feel much like eating but Sherry insisted and I allowed her to play Mum. After all, I no longer had anyone else to nag me. I ate a solitary breakfast, watching her through the kitchen window as I munched on my marmalade and toast.

She stood at the washing line in the garden, pegging out the tea-towels from the previous day's little gathering on the washing-line. She looked so ordinary in her sweatshirt and jeans and it was such a normal thing to do. Then, as she stretched up, the early morning sun lit her hair like a halo and I felt my chest constrict. Some ordinary. But then, I had often thought the same about Mum. She had always looked ordinary to most people yet I had always known that she was anything but. She had been a beautiful princess. I paused and wondered what that made my father and then twisted my mouth. *It rather looked as though he could have been anyone, he damn well pleased.*

I drained my coffee mug and slammed it down a little too hard on the table. I wondered at the wisdom of going anywhere near Julian again. Perhaps we should just both carry on as we had been. We'd been happy enough so far. I'd had done perfectly well without a father for most of my life and Sherry certainly seemed more anxious about the idea of meeting him again than anything else. Julian hadn't shown an iota of interest in either of us for years. Perhaps if we failed to show up for this lunch date then he would simply leave us be, now.

Still, I hated unsolved equations and there were two questions that really niggled me. Julian had mentioned the fact that Mum had intended to talk to me about him on the day of the accident. How had my father known this? (And why did the fact that he knew seem to bother me so much?) Secondly, and perhaps more to the point, if Julian was my father, what on earth did that make me? Some kind of hybrid freak? I didn't feel special in any way. But how would I know? I'd never fitted in, that was for sure. Could this be the reason?

There was, of course, a last question which did not concern Julian so much as Mum. I rose to my feet and began to clear the breakfast things away, shaking my head at Sherry as she came in from the garden.

"Sherry, given the Julian thing - do you reckon Mum ever twigged? About you, I mean?"

She responded with a wry shrug of the shoulders.

"I never got the feeling that she suspected anything. But I could be wrong. The eating thing may have been a bit of a giveaway. She did remark upon it that once, didn't she?"

I nodded. She had indeed. Yet she had not pursued it any further or taken the opportunity to prepare me for the truth about Julian. Much as I hated to admit it, the one person who might be able to satisfy my curiosity was Julian. I curled my lip.

As easy as it would have been to steer well clear of The Spotted Dog that day, I guess both of us knew that our need for answers had already decided the matter.

25

I tugged at my collar as the Spotted Dog came into view, wondering if my choice of a shirt and tie had been such a good idea after all. My mouth and throat had grown suddenly dry and it was difficult enough to swallow, as it was. The ancient pub seemed suddenly foreboding. I must have passed the timber-framed black-and-white building a thousand times, though had never, to my knowledge, been inside before. Mum had often told me that it dated back to Henry VIII's time, a fact that made it seem unimaginably old to my young mind.

The car park looked to be pretty empty as we drew near and we could hardly miss the sleek maroon Jaguar, parked close to the entrance.

"That'll be him," I breathed, "he always was a sucker for flashy cars."

"Why are you whispering?" asked Sherry. "I don't think he can hear you out here."

I shook my head and clasped Sherry's hand with a grin.

"I guess, I'm kinda nervous. More so than I had anticipated, if you must know…"

"Oh, I *know*. You brought your inhaler, right?"

I nodded again then stepped resolutely towards the ancient front door, ducking to avoid the ancient and unusually low lintel, with Sherry in my wake.

Inside, the bar seemed almost as deserted as the car park. There was no sign of Julian so we made our way through a narrow lobby and along to a wooden door with a sign saying "Lounge." I peered through the little glass window in the door. There, alone at one end of a long wooden table in the far corner of the room, sat the unmistakable figure of my father. I nudged Sherry and spoke beneath my hand.

"Thank goodness he didn't choose one of those tiny tables. Stay as far back from him as you can, and don't hesitate to make your excuses and leave if you have to. I'll understand."

I blinked in surprise as we entered. Either my eyes were deceiving me, or he was tucking into a large toasted sandwich. The hinges of the door creaked noisily behind us as it swung closed. He looked up and rose to his feet in welcome, putting his lunch to one side.

Chewing and smiling at once, he looked even more fox-like than before.

I acknowledged him with a curt greeting and was taken about when he suddenly laughed.

"Your face, it's a proper picture. Not expecting your old man to be enjoying one of these, eh?" He picked up the toasted sandwich, took a large bite and then continued with his mouth full. He turned his gaze to Sherry. "Still squeamish about the whole digestive thing, huh, my dear? You don't know what you're missing. But then you never did."

Sherry shuddered. I squeezed her arm. It had not been a promising start.

Thirty minutes later, my father was holding forth. Sherry seemed to be coping by sitting at the furthest end of the table to him but, for all the strangeness of our little company, I doubt an observer would have noticed anything out of the ordinary about us.

Those first few minutes had been a little tense but then, as soon as Julian had finished his meal, he went to the bar, bought us all a round of drinks and immediately launched into a rambling soliloquy. From the number of glasses on the table, I reckoned that it was his third double vodka and, if I had not known better, I would have sworn that the guy was becoming inebriated. Then again, perhaps an audience was all the stimulant he needed. It's not often a shapeshifter gets to share their story.

"God, The Spotted Dog. I haven't set foot in the place for years. Mind you, I knew it when it was Nan Bullen's father's hunting lodge. That's Ann Bolyn to you. As it happens, Henry and me, we were mates. He knew all about us. I used to stand in for him at court sometimes so he could go whoring. Sat on the throne and everything. Absolute git of a human being, but a lot of fun. Course, we would all have been burned at the stake if that sanctimonious old twat Thomas Moore had got wind of it. Though he would have had to catch us first. And no one ever has - at least not for long."

I sighed and crossed my arms. My father was a motor-mouthed gasbag. Sure, he had some tales to tell but he seemed to be enjoying the spotlight, and the sound of his own voice, a little too much. I glanced over at Sherry. She was sitting sideways on her chair and had placed her handbag on her lap as though in readiness to make a bolt for the door. But, where I expected to see a look of exasperation on her face, I discovered something very different. An expression of riveted fascination. Suddenly she spoke. Her voice sounded more tremulous than usual, but it rang with an eagerness that took me entirely by surprise.

"I can remember it. His face – so white and puffy and the rings on his fingers - and the smell of him…" She pulled a face. "We share the memories, don't we?"

"Ah, Sher-Ton My-Am. You were always on the ball. We've missed you."

Julian's lips curled into that fox-like smile of his, but there was a dark edge to his voice, I didn't much like. Sherry, however, seemed enthralled, almost.

"But I forgot it all. How did that happen? Can you tell me?" My father fixed her with his eyes but the reply sounded almost casual.

"We have to maintain proximity, don't we? At least every few years or so. You went your own way and we lost radio contact, as it were."

"You lost me?"

Julian seemed to consider this and then winked.

"Don't worry, I always knew where to find you, my dear. I knew that you would not stray far from that dreary little mausoleum of yours."

"But I searched everywhere for my own kind. For years…" Julian shrugged and spread his hands in a kind of what-can-you-do gesture.

"I figured you needed to learn the lesson…"

Sherry fell silent. She seemed suddenly lost for words. I blinked. I had so many questions of my own but could see how important this was to her. She had spoken to me about it often enough. Lose your memories and you struggle to hold onto your identity. Lose your identity and you're looking at a world of trouble. It wasn't rocket-science.

"What happened to the others then?" I asked on her behalf. "They can't all have broken radio contact, as you call it. Sherry seems to feel that there had been many more of you at one time."

Julian stared at me, now. I swallowed hard. His sobriety seemed to fully restore itself.

"So, there was. But that was a very long time ago. Most of them left for the New World over a century ago. Those of us who remained hung on for a while but many decided to follow the others. We need physical contact to merge our consciousness so that proved a problem for many years and I won't deny that it was tough. Of course, it's different now, what with your Concords and all, it's only a matter of hopping on a flight. And believe me, money has never been an object for us. But really, who needs to be dragged down by old memories? I've always...."

He stopped mid-stream. The mention of money had caused Sherry to startle. Julian seemed to read her thoughts.

"Don't worry, the vault, your little stash. Let's just say you were keeping some things safe for some friends of ours – not that they'll be needing them now," he smirked. "As for the rest - well, you always were quite the magpie. Had an eye for the shiny objects, but never really got the hang of money, did you? Always the same. You don't even have a bank account, right?"

Sherry mumbled something about having managed all right, thank you.

"Is that so? And who do you think paid your bills? The council rates? Water rates? All of it. These things don't pay themselves, you know."

Sherry turned to me with a quizzical frown and then looked away in embarrassment.

"Old Skynner of Skynner and Sykes, and his old man, and his before that. They've managed our properties and portfolios since - well, I don't care to remember, right now." He looked at me this time. My astonishment must have been written all over my face.

"Yes, you heard me correctly. The Legal Partnership your mother worked for. Of course, she should have been a solicitor herself, she was keen as a knife, but well..."

"You mean they know...?"

"Well, I wouldn't put it like that. They manage business for a Trust. I'm not saying they've never had their suspicions, but a lawyer's job is to follow instructions – not to ask too many questions."

"And Joan?" I heard myself mumble.

"Who, Joan? Ah, that pathetic old tart. Is she still there? That's right, I saw her at the crematorium. She always thought the sun shone out of your mother's – well, never mind. I think Margot always had a bit of a soft spot for her. That was all. She was just the receptionist."

I drained my glass. My head was beginning to spin. Having suspicions had been one matter, hearing it straight from a horse this dark's mouth was beginning to feel like quite another.

"So, my mother? She did know all about this – about you?"

My father ploughed on, seeming to relish such an attentive audience.

"Margot, she was brains as well as beauty. I first saw her, quite by chance, when I was up North on business. She was just sixteen and the most beautiful female I'd ever seen and I'd seen a few. Her parents had gone and those brothers of hers guarded her like bull terriers. She had been a bit of a school swat, but she was hungry for life. I persuaded her to apply to The London School of Economics and move down here as soon as she left school. The Brothers Grimm didn't like it one bit, but she was ambitious, back then at least. And what a head, on what a pair of shoulders. There was nobody like her, I mean it, Jonathon, ever. She truly was something else and she was the love of my extraordinarily long life - until she got broody. I hadn't counted on that.

Still, for those first few years, what times we had. Margot loved the glamour of it all. You should have seen her. She was spectacular- made Julie Christie look average. Everyone wanted her at their party and there wasn't a door that was closed to us. It wasn't such a big change. We were used to hanging out in all the best clubs back in the old days, weren't we Sherry, baby? But with Margot, I began to move in quite different circles."

I noticed that Sherry had begun to fidget in her seat. Her face was creased in concentration as though she was trying to work something out. She shuffled slightly closer and then closed her eyes. But then, my father suddenly addressed me.

"Don't tell me you've forgotten, Jonathon. I seem to recall, you used to love to see us all dressed up for night on the town."'

I looked away. The memory of Mum in that aquamarine dress flashed into my mind - the dress Sherry had worn for the school dance.

Julian paused and reached inside his jacket pocket. He drew out a black and white photograph and handed it to me. It was a studio portrait of Mum. Scarcely older than I was then, and made up in the heavy eyeliner and mascara of the day - and completely stunning. Mum and not Mum. Certainly not the straightlaced legal secretary she had become.

The photograph seemed worn and a little faded and I wondered if Julian carried it around all the time. I sniffed and hesitated before handing it back, reluctant to let it go.

"And me? Surely you remember me, Jumbo?" There was a sudden tenderness in my father's tone but I recoiled at the intimacy of the name.

"Jumbo?"

"Yes, Jumbo. It was me who gave you the pet-name. You were enormous as a toddler and lumbered around when you first started to walk. Your mother said it was an awful thing to call you, but it was *cute* and *you* were so cute – so in the end, it stuck."

I shook my head.

"I don't remember any of that…"

"But you must remember me teaching you to play chess.? What you don't? Well, it sure in hell wasn't you mother. You could already beat her by the time you were four years old. She was very bright in many ways, but chess was not her game."

"That's not even true. She frequently beats me," I protested, momentarily forgetting that she would never get the chance again.

Julian smiled.

"You learned pretty early on to *let* her beat you, Jumbo. Because it pleased her. I was the same. We'd both do anything to make her smile. Don't you remember?"

His voice had become gentle, pleading almost. I buried my head in my hands. I'd preferred his cockiness to this fake sentimentality. And then a light bulb lit up in my head. The chess-board birthday cake Chess had often been the glue that. held us together through our ups and downs, but perhaps the cake had been a nod to my father at the same time. I shook my head. It was something else, I would never know.

Across the table, Julian had replaced the photograph and lit up a cigarette. If my failure to remember anything of our alleged former closeness had offended him, he did not let it show and he seemed determined to fill in the blanks in my knowledge. It felt as though it was going to be a long afternoon.

I wasn't wrong. An hour later, my father was still yakking on. I was trying my best to take in all that he said but my head was reeling and I could feel my eyes glazing over. Later I would think of a million questions about it all but, right then, I was in a state of information overload. I looked over at Sherry. The excitement from earlier appeared to have vanished and she was beginning to look agitated, instead. I guessed that she was beginning to struggle with the effects of her proximity to Julian. I looked at my watch and grimaced.

Julian must have caught the look. He paused and produced a small business card from his wallet. Then, drawing an expensive-looking fountain pen from his jacket pocket, he scrawled a telephone number on the back and slid it over to me. I picked it up and stared at the gold embossed script - *Julian Cooper - International Entrepreneur.*

The entrepreneur cleared his throat.

"It's getting late, now, and it's been a lot for one day. I get that. Call me, if you want to learn more. Or if you need anything. Or not. I will leave it up to you."

With these words, he stood, straightened his tie and extended his hand to me in a gesture that struck me as oddly formal. I shook it with a respectful nod. I hardly dared refuse. He made no such overture to Sherry, however, who sighed with relief and stepped back as he made his way to the exit.

I reached for her hand as we fell in behind him, but before I could grasp it, Sherry turned and looked back at the table where we had been sitting. Then, pulling one of her famous cotton gloves out of her handbag, she doubled back and deftly seized one of the shot glasses – one from which Julian had been drinking - and slipped it into the bag before anyone except me could notice. If she saw my raised eyebrows she pretended not to. After all, this was hardly the time or place for explanations.

Back out in the car park, Julian gave us both a curt nod and slid into the front seat of his Jaguar. The engine purred into life and he was gone.

"What now?" I wondered, turning to Sherry.

"What indeed?" she replied, slipping her arm through mine and guiding me back toward the road.

"I don't know about you, but I don't feel like going back to the house, just now. I could do with getting away from it all for a little while."

"Well then, let's just keep bleedin' walking, shall we? After all, a bit of fresh air never hurt anyone and we've both been sat on our backsides far too long, of late."

26

"He's not telling the whole story – Julian, I mean." Sherry lifted her head from my knee and looked into my face. She was sitting on the floor next to the sofa where I had lolled flaked-out in silence for most of the evening. We had gone for a long stroll following our meeting at the Spotted Dog but had mostly walked in relative silence. Neither of us had felt quite ready to talk about what had happened. Sherry struck me as a little shell-shocked, whilst for me, there was just too much to process. I'd bought a kebab on the way home and had washed it down with some of the leftover whisky from the wake. I wasn't a fan of the stuff, but it certainly did the job. For a couple of blissful hours, my thoughts had felt like ants in syrup – and it was a strange relief. But I could feel them shaking the stickiness off, even as she spoke.

I yawned and gazed through the net curtains of the bay window. The sky outside had begun to turn black with rain clouds, casting the room into heavy shadow. The air felt thick and hot. I wouldn't have been surprised if we were in for a storm. I cocked my ears, half expecting to hear the sound of Mum's key in the lock at any minute. It took me a moment to realise my mistake.

"What do you mean?" I placed my hand on her shoulder to prevent her from slipping sideways and righted myself. She'd given me a few hours to digest what had passed in the Spotted Dog, but it wouldn't wait any longer.

"I've worked it out. My memory loss and then this overwhelming torrent of images and memories that assails me when I get too close to him. It's as though I'm the memory bank and he is the key. His proximity unlocks the memories inside me and allows him to access them at the same time. That's the reason why he suddenly seemed to get such a buzz when he started bragging about Henry VIII and all that. He can't remember that himself but when the place triggered the memories inside me, he was able to access them. But the thing is, whilst I just experience them as a jumble of random sense impressions, *he* is somehow able to pull it together and make sense of it all.

I have this house full of stuff, right? And when I touch it, I get triggered, but the impressions are very fleeting and I can't usually retain them in my mind. Perhaps because there is just so much of it, or perhaps because my function is only ever to release the memories."

"Go on – I think I get what you are saying – a bit like, *you* store memories the way parts of my brain do but the part that *thinks about* the memory is in a different part of the brain."

"Yes – it must be something like that. I think that we can both retain memories of recent events, in so far as they continue to be relevant. For example, you and I - I can remember everything that has happened since I met you because it is recent and ongoing. But, given the length of our lives, the quantity of our memory impressions far exceeds anything the human brain has to store. Perhaps that led us to evolve a vastly more sophisticated system. A memory network, if you will – or a hive mind. And a highly organised hierarchy at that. A bit like bees or ants.

Now, I'm pretty sure that Julian is a way more powerful being than I am. I've no idea as to the true extent of that power, but if you do think of our kind as hive members, I'm pretty sure he would be something akin to a Queen Bee. What's more, I believe he has the power to choose how much current memory is available to the rest of us, that is, he can decide how much we need to remember."

"Christ - that's one hell of a power trip…"

"I know, but bear with me. It would explain how I lost my memory of who I was and what I was doing in my house. My amnesia served two purposes. Firstly, it ensured that I remained in the house and, more importantly, it ensured that that I could not spill any secrets. I retained enough knowledge of *what* I was to ensure that I avoided unnecessary interaction with humans and the chances of exposure. And, of course, mathematical knowledge and the ability to play chess, for example, involve different systems. They don't depend on the retention of sensory impressions.

And, the thing is, it worked for quite a few years until I met you. It worked just bleedin' fine. But he didn't take into account how alone I felt or just how badly I needed to belong to something or someone."

"It sounds pretty cold-blooded when you put it like that," I put my hand over my mouth to stifle another yawn. It wasn't that I bored just completely knackered.

"True. But, without trying to defend him, when did the Queen Bee ever worry about the fate of a worker? It's just the way it is. I was a part of a living museum of our kind- a memory keeper."

"And all the time he knew you would be there, waiting, if and when he needed to remember. But what about the rest of them, the shapeshifters, I mean."

Sherry paused. I squinted.

"What is it?"

"There is something about that which does not add up. Julian said most of them had gone to the New World. Why would they do that? If we function as a hive, I mean. This is what has had me thinking…"

She got up and walked over to the chair where she had slung her bag. Unzipping the top, she slipped on her glove and fished out the shot glass.

"You see this. Julian was drinking from this and that means he should have left a trace of himself on it. The way you might leave a lip or fingerprint. Only, we are shapeshifters, don't forget, and that residue, no matter how small, remains connected to us. So - that thing about proximity triggering memory. Well, I reckon it must work both ways; that is why I knew what he was remembering when he spoke about Henry Tudor and everything. But then I was so busy trying to keep my distance and not get overwhelmed by his consciousness that I didn't think to try and find out more myself. Besides, he would probably have been aware of me trying to access his recent memories and I've no doubt he could easily block that. The trace on this glass is so small that, even if I tap into the information he left here, it's probably not going to disturb the current of his thoughts, or at least not sufficiently for him to realise what is going on."

I grimaced. This was all starting to sound very bizarre.

"Oh, I know - I know that it sounds crazy. But you remember how we met, right? The finger and the eye? I know you've gotten very used to me as just Sherry, but this is who and what I, no – we are."

I shook my head and sprang from the sofa to embrace her. *I didn't care what she was. She should know that by now, and nothing about that would ever change.* Sherry kissed me on the cheek and sat back down on the sofa with the glass in her hands. She went to touch it with her ungloved hand but hesitated and then looked up at me, her face tense.

"I don't know if I can do this…" she whispered. "It might hold the answers but, the truth is, I'm not sure I'm truly ready for them…"

I knelt next to her and took the glass from her hand and then placed it on the table next to the sofa.

"Look, Luv, we've both had a bit of a day of it. You don't have to do anything until you are ready. Come to that, you don't have to do it at all – not unless you truly want to. We've managed all these years without knowing all this stuff, we'll be okay. Let's sleep on it, huh? I don't know about you but I have a splitting headache and I could do with an early night. I feel as though I could sleep for weeks."

Sherry sighed and nodded. We turned on the landing light and headed for bed. Halfway up the stairs, I turned back, worried that I had left the glass for Mum to clear away when she got in. And then I remembered once more. She wasn't coming home - and she would never be coming home again.

My hopes for a decent night's kip proved sadly misplaced. It was not, however, Sherry's theorising about shapeshifter memory and culture that kept me awake, or even the thunder that had indeed to roll around the skies outside. No, it was Julian's revelation concerning my origins. I'd managed to avoid thinking about it all evening, but that night, stone-cold sober and alone with my thoughts, the words I'd been trying to forget swarmed back into my mind as clearly as if I had captured them on my tape recorder.

"Back then, I ran a couple of private gambling clubs, Ronnie and Reggie became regulars, not the clientele you'd generally want to boast about, but it drew all kinds of film stars and models who found that kind of thing glamourous. Bobby Moore and his wife Tina began to frequent the club I ran over Mile End way and we became good mates. Bobby brought the whole bleedin' West Ham team and their wives along and later, he even introduced some of the lads from the England Team - when Alf, or I should say - Sir Alf, wasn't on their case. It was a heady mix. Made sure it never got ugly or out of hand like, though later of course there was that business with Bobby running up gambling debts and the kidnap plot - but that was never anything to do with us."

I shook my head and stared at him.

"Wait right there. Ronnie and Reggie? As in Ronnie and Reggie Kray? Are you kidding me? Are you insane or something? You put my mother in the way of the Kray Brothers?"

"What can I tell you? Living for hundreds of years, well you tend to crave a little excitement, now and then. And what did human morals mean to us? Your mother was young and a bit reckless back then, I guess. But I would never have let any harm come to a hair on that woman's head. Never. I worshipped her. You have to believe that. Besides, The Krays were never that smart. I could always handle them. I impersonated Reggie for a whole weekend once while Ronnie was a temporary guest of Her Majesty's, and his own twin brother never even twigged, even afterwards. He just thought Reggie was messing with his head when he claimed he had been locked up all weekend.

We didn't play by their rules. Didn't need to. I could have run rings around them if I'd wanted. Plus, I had some very powerful friends."

At this point, he'd paused and stared into the distance. I sat dumbfounded. It was Sherry who seemed to find her voice.

"If this is so, how come I couldn't remember her - Margot, I mean. I spent many hours in close proximity to her and it never triggered anything – well, except once, but that was just a strong sense of you."

"I kept you all away. You might have seen her once, fleetingly, but that is all. As soon as I met her, I knew. I didn't want the complication. I got you to run the Romford club. I took over the one at Mile End and when I wasn't there, we spent most of our time up West. It wasn't difficult."

"So, what went wrong?" asked Sherry throwing a glance my way.

"She had an extraordinary life with me but she chose an ordinary one with your boy here – end of story."

"Your boy, too…" I piped up.

Julian and Sherry exchanged a look and that was when Julian had come out with it—the knockout blow.

"You're not my son, kid. Not technically at least."

I must have gaped or something because Sherry reached for my hand.

"We can't procreate, Jonno -remember? Not with other species, leastways. You can't be Julian's child. I'm so sorry Jonno, I never realised…"

"She was going to tell me. The day she died - my eighteenth birthday. She was going to tell me that I was adopted…"

Julian had pursed his lips.

"Well, no - not exactly. Margot was your biological mother, straight up. I knew this Doctor up Harley Street ran a clinic for women, couples really, who had fertility issues. He fixed things up for us."

"You mean - sperm donation. So, my father could be, anyone - just some random stranger?" The news was not exactly getting any better.

"No - not altogether a stranger. Calm down. I didn't want that and so, well, I made a list of friends - healthy, athletic, successful footballers, most of them. Men who owed me a favour, you could say. Well, I had them all make an anonymous donation and then, well, we picked one at random. That way, no one knew who the donor was. Sort of a guarantee that years later you couldn't go knocking at their door."

"Bobby Moore," I gasped "He's my father, isn't he? Everyone has always commented on the resemblance. It was him, wasn't it?

"No, no. You're barking up the wrong tree there, son. I empathetically deny that it was Moore. He'd had a little trouble in that department. Believe me - it wouldn't even have been possible for the poor bastard. Now drop it."
I'd looked across at Sherry who shrugged.

"Sorry, Jonno. This is all news to me. But it's public information that Moore underwent treatment for testicular cancer in his early twenties, though, so…"

"But what about you? I demanded looking at Julian. "Was Mum going to tell me about you? What you truly were, I mean. It's a pretty big secret for one woman to keep."
Julian replied with a shake of the head.

"I can't really answer that, I'm afraid. I suspect not, though. I reckon she thought you'd be better off not knowing. I know she was planning to tell you about your parentage and about the money I had placed in trust for you, but I hadn't spoken to her directly in many years. And that was the way she wanted it. I never really understood why."
He looked suddenly deflated.

"The truth is, we spent six extremely happy years together before you came along. Travelling and leading a life of hedonism most people only dream of, free from the petty moral constraints and morality that shackle most of this dull little island. And then you came along and it all began to change. She wanted to be a *proper* mother and started wanting us to act like a *proper* family with *proper* bleedin' family values.

Believe me, Jumbo, I tried my best to be a father and a regular husband. I did. I loved her and wanted to make her happy. But, in the end, it just wasn't in me. Don't get me wrong, I was crazy about you. You were such a smart, amusing little chap and I'd never had a kid before. But I guess eventually the novelty wore off and you -the pair of you - were not enough for me. At least that's the way Margot saw it, I guess."
I closed my eyes and sighed.
"But look here," he continued, "I may be a shapeshifter, and you may not technically be my offspring, but a big part of Margot lives on in you and for that reason alone, you will always be very important to me. Especially now. You don't have to believe me, but I loved that woman more than I ever loved any other being. And the way I see it, we can make a life where we find a space for each other or you can walk away. And who knows? Maybe it is no accident that you and Sher-Ton My-am, here, hooked up. Maybe it could be the start of a new chapter for all of us."

The following morning, I awoke to find the bed empty and the smell of coffee wafting up from the kitchen below. I sat up, shook my head to dispel my sleep hangover then clapped my hand to my mouth with a low groan. The image that had haunted my dreams, when at last I'd finally managed to drift off, flooded back into my mind and with it a new and disturbing comprehension. Swearing softly under my breath I took my dressing gown off the hook on the door and tied it around my waist then looked around. Now, *where the fuck were my slippers?*

Down in the kitchen, Sherry took one look at my face and asked what on earth was troubling me. I slid onto a chair at the kitchen table and stared up at her, unsure how to start. I swallowed hard.
"I had a dream last night. I dreamed of Mum and Julian. They looked just as they did in an old photograph Mum kept in her room. I've had the dream many times before but, this time, I knew that it was an actual memory. In the dream, Julian was dangling his keys to his Jaguar and they were laughing, as though they were sharing a joke; a joke I couldn't possibly have understood. I was what, only just four years old perhaps, back then - but suddenly it all made sense.
All that stuff he said about the fertility clinic and the anonymous sperm donors - it was just a cover. To protect Mum, I guess. They were swingers, Sherry. All that hot air about not being

constrained by living by bourgeois morality, the parties, it all adds up. This was the swinging sixties for Christ's sake. Mum was very open-minded, but she was brought up very traditionally. No wonder she didn't want any part in it, once I came along…

Do I sound insane, Shez? This is my mum, I'm talking about. I feel dirty just saying it. And if that is so, was I just some accident, after all? The consequence of some split condom in a drunken orgy. Honestly, I think I might puke - please say something. Anything. You knew Mum. I feel so ashamed to even be suggesting such a thing, but - have you seen my inhaler?"

Sherry reached up to the shelf where I kept a spare and set it before me. She knelt next to me and took my hand.

"No, Jonno. No. I don't think you're insane – or misjudging your mum, though you are coming across a tad judgemental. Last night, I - well I couldn't get the glass out of my mind. So, I came back down. And I sat with the glass in my hands. And it worked. Please don't be cross with me for not waiting for you. It was just something I needed to do alone.

Well, turns out, I was right. He wasn't telling the truth, not the whole truth, at any rate - and your mother is at the centre of it all, Jonathon. D'you remember when he made the remark about not wanting to be dragged down by the past- old memories? Well, it was more than that. He didn't just leave me in the house. He cut me off. He cut us all off. Because he wasn't lying when he said that he'd never loved anyone the way he loved your mum. The way he felt about her made him want to put us all behind him. To start afresh in the twentieth century, as it moved towards the next millennium. He had no real intention of connecting with me or the house ever again – and he has left the rest of my kind wondering the world adrift from their history and deeper sense of identity. I can't see that he has had any interaction with any of them for well over a decade - all that talk about international travel. I think it was bullshit."

"But didn't he say that they needed the connection to survive?"

"Exactly. In which case, he left them all to perish…"

I shuddered.

"So, none of them has survived?"

"I honestly don't know Jonno. I could never find a trace of any of them. But, then again, I'm not sure that I tried that hard. I spent most of the time skulking in that bleedin' house feeling sorry for myself. It was not until I met you that it even occurred to me that it could ever be different. And now it turns out that the house with all its memories, no matter how muddled, may have been my salvation."

"And you got all of this from one little shot-glass?"

She nodded.

"Of course, a lot of it was pretty jumbled and I might have missed something – but there's no mistaking the fact that he cut us all adrift…"

I looked at her and did the math. I had lost a mother but Sherry may have lost her entire race. Logic suggested it was the greater loss. Half an hour earlier I had been fully resolved never to lay eyes on Julian Cooper again but now that resolve seemed suddenly less solid.

"Sherry, I'm so sorry. I've been so wrapped up in my own stuff that I hadn't even considered it from your point of view. Never mind about whether Julian is or isn't my father – he is one of your kind - and may even be the last one. I know he's been an arsehole, but in a way, he is still *your* family. If you want him in your life – *our* lives, I can live with that. More to the point, it sounds as though you might need that connection to survive, in the long term, at least."

Sherry shook her head.

"I don't know, Jonno. I certainly don't feel the need to be anywhere Julian again because I have you, and you are the whole world to me. Maybe he is wrong and that is enough. Maybe we can exist without being connected to one another, so long as we find a human who can accept us for who we are. Perhaps that is what he found with your mother and why he felt he no longer needed it himself.

And there's something else. If I did get close to him again, eventually, all those memories would start coming back, and the very fact of them would change everything. Perhaps I wouldn't even be Sherry, anymore. In fact, I'm pretty certain, I wouldn't be. I'm guessing I'd be a whole heap more complicated."

"I'd still love you, Shez…"

"Would you? You can't know that for sure. And you know what? I like being Sherry. Being Shalto was fun, but being Sherry - *your* Sherry is so much better. I don't need to think about it. I don't want Julian in my life and I'm absolutely convinced that I don't need him. I can't tell you what to do, but I have the feeling that it is *he* who needs *us*. Having said that, I don't believe either of us will hear from him again unless you want it."

We both fell silent. Perhaps she was right. But I still had questions of my own. I asked what else she had learned from the glass. *About my mother, for a start. Had she truly wanted a child, or had that all just been a crock of shit too?*

"No. As far as I can tell, that much was the truth." Sherry smiled. "She tried very hard to conceive. And Julian wanted it too. Their lifestyle was a little wild and unconventional by some standards, so they took advantage of their access to a healthy gene pool and then left things to chance."

"So, what about Moore?"

"As for that, who knows? You *do* look a lot like him, but again, Julian was being truthful. Moore was a handsome man with a bit of a reputation, but he certainly didn't father you. So, perhaps we'll never know who did. But I can tell you this much, Jonno - bullshit aside, Julian did love you. I felt it as strongly as anything I have ever felt when I've experienced such memory impressions. There was absolutely no doubt that he wanted to be a father but, who knows? Perhaps in the end, he simply wasn't able to change and wasn't able to make the sacrifice, your Mum could. And then there was something else. It all seems very muddled, but he wasn't being entirely transparent when he said that he'd never really understood why your mum severed all contact with him. But one thing's for sure, however it *did* happen, I sensed that it hurt him more than he could admit."

I looked away. Is that why he had turned up at the funeral? The one person who could explain it was gone now and I would never know.

I stroked Sherry's cheek.

"You looked drained. Was it so awful?"

"More weird than awful, I guess."

"Do you think Julian will have had a sense of it - you tapping into his memories, I mean?"
Sherry shrugged.

"I don't know. If he is as powerful as I suspect then I think that it *is* quite possible. But I've no idea what he would make of it and, frankly, I don't much care."

Later that day, Mrs Worth popped around with a toad-in-the-hole, she had made for us. She didn't stay long but stepped in for a minute to give us instructions on how to heat it up. She stared around the kitchen with a sigh until her eyes settled on the familiar old dent in the cabinet door. She smiled and looked at me.

"I remember the day you did that, Jonathon, don't you?"

I looked at her blankly.

"Oh, I know, it seems difficult to believe now - you grew up to be such a mild lad, but goodness you had some tantrums back then when you first moved in. Such a wee thing, you were, but such a little bugger at times. I could hear you from my front room. I don't know how your poor mum coped, some days. But she loved you to bits and, thankfully, it was just a difficult phase."

I shrugged. It didn't ring any bells with me and I wondered if she was confusing me with some other neighbour's kid. She *was* getting on in years. I smiled and thanked her for her kindness and saw her to the front door.

"What was all that about?" asked Sherry when I returned to the kitchen.

"Search me. Maybe she's finally losing it."

That evening, after I had polished off the admittedly delicious toad-in-the-hole, I made an announcement.

"Sherry."

"Huh?"

"I've been thinking. I don't want to see him again. Julian, I mean. Maybe I won't always feel that way, but I don't want to see him now - not so soon after Mum. It's all too unsettling. But if you decide you *do* – I'd never stand in your way. You know that, don't you?"

"Thanks, Jonno. But I've made up my mind, too. As far as I am concerned, it's just you and me. And nothing and nobody else matters."

27

The weeks following Mum's accident felt a bit like finding getting stuck in a giant motorway traffic jam. I couldn't turn back, no matter how badly I wanted to, and yet I couldn't seem to move forward either. The only thing to do was to sit it out and try to find ways to pass the time. Thankfully I did not have to do so alone. Whenever I needed her, Sherry was there. She had pretty well moved in with me following the funeral and neither of us had seen any reason for her to move back out.

Whilst Julian may have quit the scene, he nonetheless continued to play a role in our financial affairs. First of all, there was the manilla folder my mum had handed me on my birthday. I had left it tucked away amongst Mum's cookbooks in those first few days following her death but had, in the end, found myself obliged to deal with it. Mum had mentioned something about a Trust but I had no real idea what that even meant. When I finally opened the folder and examined the documents inside, it soon became clear. I stared at the cover letter. It had been signed by Skynner Senior of Skynner, Sykes and Skynner, no less, and summarised the intent and powers of the legal papers enclosed.

Julian Cooper had, it transpired, ensured my financial independence for the foreseeable future. Not that I would be rich, exactly, - but comfortable - comfortable enough to pursue any direction in life I chose. The information, which at any other time would have overjoyed me, seemed about as palatable as damp cardboard. Right then, I was just a little boy who would have swapped every last penny in his piggy bank for one more hour with his mother.

I'd pushed the letter away in contempt with a loud- *Fuck you, Julian.* But then, I supposed, it was the least he could do. He had twice robbed me of a father. He must owe me something.

I calmed myself down and looked a little closer at the legal paperwork. The Trust had been set up in the months following my parents' separation. As such, the endowment spoke little of my father's current sentiments but referred to his strong sense of parental responsibility. *Except, he wasn't my father and never would be,* I thought angrily. If I had the slightest sense that he had tried to do the right thing by me, I certainly wasn't going to admit it to myself.

A week after the funeral, I took up Mr Skynner Junior's invitation to arrange an appointment with him and climbed the familiar stairs to his offices. That was easy enough in theory, but I'd been forced to pass the spot where my mum had been killed on the way which made it a huge deal.

Joan greeted me with a sad smile and I did my best to hold it together whilst she fluttered around me, offering me a cup of tea while I waiting. I knew she meant well but I just wanted to bang my fists and scream.

My Skynner betrayed no such sentimentality. He repeated his condolences in a quiet voice and then got down to business. Given the nature of his involvement in the management of the Cooper estate, he had been able to circumvent probate and had overseen the seamless transfer of the deeds of the house into my name. He had also opened a bank account for me and had deposited the ten thousand knicker that had been held in trust until my majority, which in this case had been eighteen. He ended by saying that I was to call upon him any time I needed anything or had any queries. I thanked him and left his office in a kind of daze, just about managing a curt nod to Joan on my way out. I heard her burst into sobs as I closed the door behind me.

A few weeks later, a very unusual event occurred. Sherry received some mail in the afternoon post. We happened to be at The Myam Mausoleum, as Sherry called it, at the time. Sherry liked to keep a close eye on the place and was still eager to sort the old place out a bit more. As such she would often drag me round there with her to lend a hand, though I suspected her primary motive was to prise me out of the house for a much-needed change of scene.

We were shifting a large marble bust of some long-forgotten dignitary into the hallway when we heard the creak of the letterbox and the slap of an envelope as it hit the floor. Sherry tripped lightly towards the front door and went to toss the unsolicited missive onto the pile of colourful advertisements for the new pizza takeaway and invitations from Reader's Digest to anonymous claimants inviting them to claim the fabulous prizes they had somehow managed to win, but instead, she paused.

"It's addressed to me, Jonno. Miss Sherry Matthews." She touched the address with her gloved index finger and shrugged.

"Well, open it then, Silly."

"You don't understand. No one writes to me - no one. Who would even know I'm here?"

"Well, there is only one way to find out," I teased.

But she looked pretty worried. Shaking her head, she took the envelope and carefully tore it open. Inside, she found a copy of the deeds to the house and a formal letter from none other than Skynner, Sykes and Skynner. The letter was brief and to the point. They were pleased to inform her that the deeds of the property on Capel Road had been transferred into her name, including the entirety of its contents. Meanwhile, it would be their pleasure to continue to manage the estate, should that suit her requirements and they remained her obedient servants etc etc.

We looked at each other in confusion. It had to be Julian behind this, it couldn't be anyone else, but there had been no mention made of him by name nor of his motivation for such an act.

"I can't believe it's pure goodwill, he doesn't strike me as the goodwill type," I offered a little sourly. And yet there was no obvious angle. There didn't seem to be any strings attached in the way of conditions or contractual obligations. The old house was simply Sherry's property now.

"Perhaps it is his way of finally washing his hands of the past," she mused. "Then again, perhaps he simply acted out of a sincere desire to see his adopted son settled and happy."

Despite my resentment of him, I had to admit that I didn't know my father well enough to be an unbiased judge. Two things had however become clear – Sherry now had a legitimate claim on The Myam Mausoleum and neither of us would ever want for money again.

A little later that afternoon, Sherry came into the front room where I had been stacking some tea chests and looked at me with a big soppy grin on her face.

"What?" I asked.

"I've been thinking. You've had such a rotten time lately and I wanted to do something to cheer you up, just a little bit. Now that all this is legally mine, I can give you a gift."

"Oh, no. Not that old bust, please."

"No, you idiot. Something, I guarantee you're going to want. Come this way."

She led me out of the front door along to the garage and slid back the door. I gasped. The old Enfield.

"I want you to have it, Jonno. I know how much you love it. Look, the idea of you riding it would have worried your mum sick, but it can't worry her now and someone should enjoy it. But you will promise me to be very careful, won't you – for her sake?"

I shook my head. Only Sherry could have lighted upon the one thing that could have brought a smile to my face at such a time. And for a long while, zooming along the roads through Epping and Ongar at top speed on that old bike proved to be the only reliable respite from the crippling torpor of my sadness.

Mum's little house, meanwhile, had become mine to do with as I pleased. As it turned out, Mum had also taken out substantial life insurance so with that, and the lump sum from my trust fund, money had become the least of my worries. It seemed cold comfort at the time but I could have found myself in far worse straits.

My uncles continued to offer their support but were a little too apt to phone with unsolicited advice. They considered me too young to shoulder such financial responsibility and made no bones about it. In their eyes, Mum had babied me and left me unprepared for the real world. They badgered me to move up North to be near them, just as they had Mum.

It irritated me but I didn't hold it against them. I would have been the first to admit that I was immature for my age. Apart from my one summer holiday job, I had seldom been anywhere or done anything on my own. Also, despite Mum's liberal attitudes to sex and a whole raft of other social issues, she had seen to it that I remained closely tucked beneath the shelter of her wings. To me, it had seemed a natural enough maternal response to my childhood solitariness and the struggles I experienced trying to fit in with the other kids. However, on learning of my parents' surprisingly close acquaintance with the underbelly of the East End, perhaps she'd more reason than most to shelter me from the realities of the adult world.

In some ways, I might have been better off closer to my family, but the idea of leaving our little house appalled me. Its bricks and mortar seemed the only solid and enduring certainty in a world that had turned upside down. My days as a school kid had ended and I had managed to lose an already absentee father. Even the girl I loved lacked conventional permanence. Everything around me was changing, including my body, which contrived to torment me with a belated spurt of growth that had me tripping over feet that seemed to have grown clownishly large and ungainly almost overnight.

University beckoned but I simply did not feel ready. My exam results arrived and were outstanding, assuring me a place at any college I cared to pick. Yet, I couldn't even feel excited. Instead, all I felt was anxiety and self-doubt. I was a fake. True, it had only been one paper that had not greatly affected the overall mark, and true, from Sherry's completely accurate recall of the paper, I knew that I could have completed it with my eyes closed but I couldn't seem to let it pass. The irony was, I wouldn't even need a bloody "A" in maths to get into Imperial College - they had made me an offer that required a mere four grade Bs. It was enough to do my head in.

Worst of all, my memory decided to double-cross me. The image I had always carried in my head of Mum had always been crystal clear. Within six weeks of her death, it had begun to blur around the edges like an out-of-focus photograph. The idea that I should lose it altogether just about sent me into a tailspin and the more panicky it made me, the hazier my visual recollection became.

It was at this point that Sherry stepped into my mum's metaphorical court shoes and took charge.

"I want you to consider applying for a deferral, Jonno. You know, take a gap year. It shouldn't be a problem with your grades. You've been through too much and need to give yourself more time –you've had an awful lot to get your head around. You were always the youngest in your year at school and so twelve months now wouldn't exactly set you back, would it? And it wouldn't have to be wasted. We could spend the year doing the place up. Nothing major, until you feel ready – but make it our home, you know, the way we'd like it. We could even do a bit of travelling - just around the UK. There are plenty of beautiful places to see. Meanwhile, you could even do a couple of units with the Open University if you wanted to keep your hand in. We could even do them together That might be fun. Anyway, what have you got to lose? After all, it's not a race, is it?"

Her words made perfect sense to me. I never made a big deal about it, but I'd always been ambitious. I was determined to reach the top of my field and anything less would simply feel like failure. I wasn't firing on all cylinders and knew that I risked jeopardising the trajectory of my academic advancement if I started my undergraduate studies in my current state. I knew nothing of grief or how to deal with it, but everyone said that time was the great healer. Well, I'd give it a chance. It wasn't as if I had many other options.

So, as Autumn set in, and after much discussion and not a few minor disagreements, the two of us embarked on a major renovation of the house.

At first, we had shared the workload. The physical exertion helped pass the time and there was something satisfying about working together, with Radio 1 in the background. Sometimes we even managed to have a little fun, singing into our scrapers and brushes and dancing around when our favourite records came on. It felt good. I hadn't exactly been a barrel of laughs all summer even though we had spent a few weeks touring around in the trusty mini. I even began to think that I was finally turning a corner.

Just few days later, however, something changed and I found myself snapping at Sherry for no good reason. At first, I wondered whether we had just been overdoing it. I was still not sleeping very well and had gotten into the habit of sitting up until very late watching mindless TV. Anything to delay that moment when I laid my head on the pillow and my thoughts would inevitably turn to the Mum-less bed in the room next door.

Then, one afternoon, the explosion came. Sherry had been on the upstairs landing, soaking an area of wallpaper with a sponge. I had been watching her when suddenly an odd little patch of colour caught my eye. It was a scribble I had made in wax crayon as a young kid and had been there so long, that I no longer saw it. I bent down and stroked it with my finger. All at once, I experienced a vivid memory of Mum scolding me and threatening to confiscate the crayons. It was not a bad memory. Quite the opposite. "But it's a picture of you, Mummy," I had pleaded. She had tried to be cross but couldn't keep a straight face and kept smiling to herself for hours afterwards. She had never been able to bring herself to paint over it. Not in all those years.

I stared at the scribble and felt my face grow hot. My ears began to ring and then all I could hear was screaming. My screaming.

"Leave it alone. Don't touch it. Don't you dare touch it…"

Sherry turned and looked at me, her eyes wide with shock. I threw down the scraper I was holding and stormed off down the stairs and into the kitchen. I clasped my head and looked around in desperation. I just wanted to smash it against something to stop the throbbing. Or lash out and hit somebody. In the end, I clenched my fists and launched an almighty kick at the cabinet door. I heard a thud and then a cracking sound and suddenly my head cleared. I stared at the cupboard door. The kick had landed on the exact site of the old dent – and this time it had broken through the wooden panel of the cupboard door, leaving a jagged hole.

My hands were shaking so I took some deep breaths and then drew myself a glass of water, spilling half of it down my front. I frowned and remembered Mrs Worth's remarks about my temper tantrums as a child. Perhaps she had been right, after all.

Taking another few breaths, I slunk back into the hallway and peered sheepishly up at Sherry, who was hovering nervously at the top stairs.

"I'm so sorry, Shez. That was bang out of order. I didn't mean to frighten you. But you know it wasn't you I was angry with, don't you?"

She nodded sadly.

"I know, Jonno, I know. And you don't have to apologise to me, but look, I think this part of the job is for you and you alone. I'll help out again once the archaeological excavations are complete."

I nodded. I didn't wholly understand what she meant but didn't want to argue. I certainly didn't want to lose my cool again.

"Just one thing, though. We *really* will have to have a new kitchen, now."

From that moment on, I spent every spare moment stripping walls and rubbing down paintwork by myself. And, as time went on, the meaning of Sherry's words became clearer to me. Each shred of wallpaper I removed seemed to reveal a fresh childhood memory and every surface I rubbed down took me back to another time – a time when I could barely rest my chin on the landing bannisters or reach the bathroom sink. I saw my mum's smile in the repeating pattern of blue and mauve hydrangeas (her favourite flower) that lined the stairs, the roll of her eyes in the Sellotape marks that defaced the once beloved Thomas the Tank wallpaper in my bedroom when I began to stick up posters of Blondie, Bowie, Farrah Fawcett Majors and later the Sex Pistols. It was as though everything I touched suddenly had the power to transport me to another time.

One afternoon, I had been sanding the rails of those same upstairs bannisters when I suddenly remembered sitting with my legs through them, swinging my feet and listening to Mum moving about downstairs. It had been late and I was supposed to be in bed, but there was something so warm and comforting about the feeling that it brought tears to my eyes. I'd wiped them away and looked at the gaps between the rails with a shake of my head. It was difficult to believe that my legs had ever been that tiny, but they must have been.

"It was awesome," I'd gushed to Sherry, later. "It all came back – exactly as though I was back there."

"Tell me about it."

"Oh, my God. Of course. It must be a bit like it is for you…"

"Well, perhaps we are not so very different after all. But I also get the feeling that you might be ready to talk about your mum, now. What d'you reckon?"

Sherry was, as always, right. From that day on, after I had finished work for the day, she would sit and listen quietly as I shared my memories over a cup of tea. She rarely asked a direct question but, little by little, I found myself able to put my feelings into words and - sometimes those words did sound angry. But it was okay and I needed to say them.

All through that winter, the renovations progressed apace. Once I had completed the prep work, Sherry would check that I was ready and then bring out the heavy book of wallpaper samples and colour charts. Together, we would leaf through them and she'd ask me how I thought this pattern might work here, of that texture there. Only when she was satisfied that I was ready for the change, would she help me to hang the new wallpaper or paint the window frames and skirting boards. And little by little we began to make my house *our* home.

Naturally, we left Mum's old room until last. I knew that it made sense for us to take it as our bedroom - it was larger and lighter and altogether more suited to a couple's needs - yet it would be many more months before that room was ready to relinquish its ghosts. They gathered around me the moment I set foot in there. My mum in her long pale lilac nylon night dress and negligee in front of her dressing table; me sitting on the bed on Mother's Day while she enjoyed the burned toast and weak coffee, I had made for her; cuddling up to her in her bed when I had earache or had simply had a bad dream.

Memories huddled in every corner and lay in ambush upon every surface. The souvenirs from her exotic travels. The wardrobe full of her clothes and *that* dress. Her dressing table and the little things I couldn't begin to imagine parting with. Like her silver-plated hairbrush and the little square bottle of Chanel No 5. I had only to remove the rectangular glass stopper and release that magical fragrance to feel her lean over my shoulder and ruffle my hair.

And then there was the Warhol painting. Gazing down from above her bed, it looked more like the icon of a saint every time I stepped in the room. Or a princess perhaps? The Mum of my childhood longing.

"I'm not sure I'd be comfortable putting it up in the living room," I mused one day. "It'd be far too valuable to have on general display. But it could hardly stay where it is if it became our bedroom."

"I don't see why not," said Sherry, with a shrug. "It's a beautiful image. I don't think I'd have a problem with keeping it there."

"Hmph. Well, *you* might not have a problem with my mum staring down at us in bed, but believe me, *I would*."

"Well then, perhaps we could move into your room and turn that into a study. Design the colour scheme around it, even. You wouldn't mind her watching over you as you studied, now, would you?"

I smiled. That didn't seem such a bad idea when the time was right. Still, Mum could stay where she hung for a bit longer. There was no hurry and replacing my single bed with a double suited us fine for the time being.

Sherry, meanwhile, embarked on a project of her own. The day after I'd lost my cool about the scribble on the wallpaper, she had taken herself off to the house in Capel Road for a few hours. She returned in a state of quiet excitement. *She had formed a plan*, she told me, *because if I could move on then so could she.*

She had resolved to take The Myam Mausoleum in hand. And she was not talking about a cursory tidy-up and reorganisation. No, she had decided to undertake a complete inventory and classification of every last artefact and piece of furniture that had been stored away there. She realised now that it was her duty. She had not seen it before because she had failed to understand the function of the house. It was a House of Memory, the collective memory of her kind, or some of them at least. After all, if Julian had somehow divorced them from any access to the memory of their past, then, surely, someone should attempt to record it for perpetuity. Even if she did need Julian's proximity to make sense of the memories, she could still experience the fleeting cascade of sensory and cognitive impressions every painting, rug, vase or piece of furniture evoked. And if she could manage to record them, then you never knew - perhaps she too could start to piece together the parts and create a narrative.

I was rather taken aback, at first. I'd rarely seen her quite so animated. But then, when I thought about it, she did seem to have been drifting rather aimlessly these last years and even as Shalto, the shapeshifter had spent a great deal of time just sitting around waiting for me to be free. Shalto's brief foray into the antiques trade had changed that to some extent but that was something Sherry seemed to have abandoned.

Purpose, I decided, suited her. *So long as she was careful*, I told her, *I thought it was a great idea.* And The Project, as we came to refer to it, was born.

So, whilst I continued to paste paper and paint ceilings, Sherry took to spending hours, and later entire days, sorting and cataloguing the hundreds of items that still filled many of the rooms in the old house on Wanstead Flats, as well as those she had already stored in the garage.

"So, how is it all going?" I asked the first time I had gone over to lend a hand shifting some of the heavier furniture. It felt odd to be back in the old house and I realised that I had missed it. Those stolen hours we had spent in that great bed. When life was all still a great adventure and it had not yet dawned on me that you could lose the things you most loved. That the world could suddenly turn to shit.

Sherry pursed her lips.

"Okay. There's a lot of stuff. But I think I am beginning to make some headway."

"You are being careful, aren't you, Shez? I understand more than ever how disorientating some of this stuff can be for you."

"Oh, don't worry." She grinned tugging at her gloves, "I'm fine as long as I keep these babies on. And I'm pleased to report that I'm getting the hang of managing the sensations better when I do remove them. It's slow progress, but I think it'll be worth it."

I frowned.

"I've been thinking about the Julian thing since he is such a big part of all this. I meant what I said about supporting you if you want to contact him again. Truly. It's your call."

Sherry looked at me for a while. Perhaps she could tell that I was not being entirely open with her. I had witnessed first-hand his power over her and the truth was, I feared she might never again escape his orbit, should his gravity draw her any closer. I'd already managed to lose two parents - the idea of losing her as well seemed unbearable.

She shook her head.

"The way I see it, Jonno - I can be a small cog in the engine that drives the juggernaut of Julian's ego or I can be with you, someone to whom I mean the whole world. I don't believe it's possible to be both. It's not much of a bleedin' contest, is it now?"

I can't pretend that I wasn't relieved. And something told me that Sherry had hit the nail on the head. No matter how it seemed now, she would somehow end up having to choose between Julian and I.

Julian, for his part, remained as good as his word. Months passed and neither of us heard so much as a peep from him though I always had a feeling that he was never far away. It wasn't a feeling I enjoyed. All the same, I kept the card he gave me though I couldn't, for the life of me, have explained the logic behind that one.

28

"I think we should treat ourselves to a little holiday," announced Sherry one weekend the following Spring. "We've both worked hard all winter and I reckon we both deserve a bit of a break."

She had a point. Christmas had come and gone. We had survived a couple of days up North with my uncles and Mum's house, (I still thought of it as that), was coming along at a great pace, whilst Sherry was beginning to make real headway with The Myam Mausoleum.

And I was in an altogether better place. As the days grew longer and the supermarkets began to stock their shelves with Easter eggs, I began to feel the weight lift from my chest and a lightness returning to my thoughts. As such, our trips out on the old Enfield regularly extended down to Rochester and we had even ventured as far afield as Canterbury one beautiful Sunday, but the idea of some proper time away seemed particularly inviting.

"But where?" I asked. "We may not be short of money but neither one of us has a passport and, unless you have a birth certificate, I don't see you getting one, do you?"

"I know. But what's wrong with England – or Wales, even? Look what a great time we had in Broadstairs with your mum."

"Yeah, we did, didn't we…"

"We could go back there if you like."

I shook my head. Too many memories.

"Well, how about Cornwall then? Not too many tourists this time of year. The kids are still at school and it's still a bit chilly at night. But they are forecasting an early summer, this year, so daytime should be great for walking and swimming even, if we get a heatwave. We could hire a cottage. You know, with a clifftop view and a real fire. I've seen adverts in the Evening Standard. We could drive down in the car and maybe hire bikes once we get there."

"Bikes? As in bicycles? Are you serious? I've never seen you so much as look at one…"

"Doesn't mean I can't ride one, Mr Clever Cloggs. You know that they say you never forget. C'mon Jonno. It could be like Two Go Mad in Cornwall. Wizard fun and all that. All we need is a little dog…"

"Hmph. Okay. But we are *not* getting a little dog," I protested.

"Fair enough. Can't stand them, anyway. Snappy little bleeders."

That evening we scoured the classifieds and found a little holiday cottage for rent that seemed to fit the bill exactly. And, to our great delight, it turned out to be every bit as snug and remote as the neat little ad had suggested.

Situated just outside the historic and picturesque fishing village of Looe, it perched in romantic solitude on a low outcrop of cliff and was as isolated as any young couple in love could wish. Compact, but not so small that it felt pokey, it was just right for two people. The sitting room was a bit old-fashioned but overlooked the sea. It also had an open fireplace with a basket full of logs on the hearth and a good supply of wood out the back. Next to it stood a kitchen that, though tiny, was certainly as well-equipped as the two of us would ever need. There was an ensuite bedroom upstairs that featured an ancient and somewhat lumpy double bed but boasted a view of the sea below that bordered on the spectacular. It was all a bit on the Laura Ashely side but neat and clean. Just what the doctor ordered, in fact.

The owners had left the keys under the flowerpot next to the backdoor along with a little note wishing us a pleasant break and advising us to light a fire as soon as we had made ourselves at home. To air it out, they said. These old cottages tended to feel a little damp in the Spring months if they had not been occupied for a week or two. Sherry and I had looked at each other and laughed. Neither of us had the foggiest idea of how to build a fire. All was not lost, however. Sherry may have lost any conscious memory of building a fire but appeared to have retained the skill, all the same. She simply did what came naturally to her and soon had a cheerful blaze burning in the grate. I couldn't remember ever having seen her look quite so chuffed with herself.

Once we had made ourselves at home, we stepped outside into the little back garden which boasted a small redbrick patio and table and chairs.

"Perfect for the warm evening," declared Sherry.

"You do know what time of year it is?" I joked.

"I don't care. What's a little evening chill? We can rug up and sit out here, anyway. It's perfect."

Best of all, a steep but sturdy flight of wooden stairs ran directly down from the cottage garden to a private cove, at the foot of the low cliff, where we discovered an upturned rowing boat, complete with oars.

"Oh, Jonno. I think we've managed to wind up in heaven," breathed Sherry as we looked out over the waves. "D'you think we could go out for a row?"

I grinned but did not feel quite so keen. I'd never been what my Mum called a *water baby*. I could just about swim a length of the local pool but that was it. Boats rocked about a lot and tended to make me nervous. I'd spotted a tatty-looking life-buoy on the rail at the bottom of the path but it had done little to allay my fears.

"I dunno, Sherry. We'll have to see. It would have to be very calm. We don't want to find ourselves *literally* in Heaven, do we?"

Sherry pouted. I knew she found me a bit of a stick in the mud sometimes but I reckon I'd rather be stuck in the mud than swept out to sea.

Hiring bikes also proved to be a bit trickier than we had hoped and, in the end, we had given up. It looked a bit too hilly to me anyway, though I did not admit as much to Sherry. Still, there were some wonderful clifftop walks and we had the car when we felt like exploring a bit further.

The days passed pleasantly. The weather was warm, without being hot and quite often we would spend the whole afternoon just lying on the sand of some sheltered little cove, watching the sea and the locals who came to enjoy their favourite swimming spot or build sand castles with their kids.

One particular afternoon, I caught Sherry staring at a young mother and her toddler who were exploring some nearby rock pools. She wasn't smiling the way that women often do when they look at little children. Just watching. Exactly as a zoologist might observe a new species. I didn't say anything but, in the end, the intensity of her stare had begun to make me feel so uncomfortable that I'd nudged her with my elbow to make her look away. Later that evening, she asked me what it had been like to be a child. I shrugged not knowing what to say. But then, I couldn't imagine what it must have been like *not* to have been a child.

The truth was, I had watched the mother and her child too, though for entirely different reasons. I still missed my mum and often reminisced about her playing with me or sitting cuddled up in front of the TV whilst we ate cheese on toast and watched silly old films. It wasn't as if I spent a lot of time daydreaming about what lay ahead for me but, watching that mum with her kid, I realised that I'd never once pictured a future that didn't include a child of my own.

Looking at Sherry, I recalled that this would never be an option for us.

Not that I could complain. I was with the most extraordinary woman in the world and she loved me. It seemed greedy to want for anything more. Not that that stopped me from experiencing a pang of sadness though.

On the fourth morning of our stay, we had risen early and made our way down to our little beach for a stroll when I saw something bobbing up and down near the rocks. I yelped and pointed.

"Sherry, quick, look. It's a seal - look, out there, just to the left of that big rock. It was seal - I'm positive."

Sherry shaded her eyes and followed the line of my finger.

"Oh, wow, Jonno. I think you're right. I knew this place was heaven. Do you reckon we could buy it?"

"What, the seal? I'm not sure they're for sale, Shez..."

"No, you plonker. The bleedin' cottage. Can you imagine, being able to come here whenever we wanted?"

I wrapped my arm around her shoulder and squeezed her to my side. The seal dipped below the surface and was gone.

"D'you know. I don't think that idea's as daft as it sounds. I've got a heap of spare cash sitting in the bank and it would be an investment, as well as a holiday home. Maybe, not this one exactly, I doubt they'd want to sell it. But I'm sure we could find one like it..."

Sherry's face lit up. She kissed me and then pulled off her sandals and waded into the shallows, the salty water lapping at the hem of her shorts. I watched her as she followed the shoreline around to where the beach met the crumbling outcrop of the cliff. She looked back and waved, calling me over to see the anemones and tiny crabs that scurried around the shallow rock pools. I waved back and smiled to myself. She seemed so young - it was impossible to believe that she was so old.

I kicked off my sneakers and waded in after her, puffing at the coolness of the water against my thighs. She was poking around at something when she suddenly stopped and let out a loud gasp.

"You okay, Shez?"

She nodded and held up a bedraggled lump of matted fur. I wrinkled my nose.

"What is it?"

"Not sure, but I think it's seal fur. The pups must rub-up against the rock to scratch or something - and voila. Cool, huh?"

I curled my lip. I wasn't sure about cool. I could smell it from where I stood downwind.

Sherry shrugged her shoulders and stood staring at the fur. I yawned and turned back to the beach. And then she was splashing back through the shallows, squealing and leaping as a couple of small waves broke against her legs.

"I don't know about you but I fancy a bacon sarnie, for breakfast," I said reaching for her hand.

"Well, okay. We'll head back, then."

I grinned. I knew she would only nibble on a piece of toast and marmalade whilst I tucked into my bacon sandwich, but it all felt so comfortable and natural.

Neither of us had ever referred to the fact, but I'd noticed that she made an enormous effort to eat "properly" since that day in The Spotted Dog with Julian. It was partly to keep me company, I missed Mum most of all at mealtimes and had continued to lay a place for her at the kitchen table almost automatically for many weeks after she had gone. But I think part of it was to appear normal. Sherry seemed determined that if Julian could do it, then so could she. She still only really ate like a sparrow but it also meant that we could do more of the things couples ordinarily enjoy together socially, such as going out for a pizza or an Indian meal. Shortly before Christmas, she had even asked Mrs Worth to teach her how to cook properly, which had pleased our old neighbour no end. It was also just as well because I was so useless at it, I could have burned boiling water.

The change had been a huge deal but I knew she didn't like to discuss it so, like so much else between us, neither one of us ever brought up the subject. Vodka, of course, remained her primary source of energy but that had become so natural to me that we both occasionally became a little careless about the number of bottles we left lying around the house, and it would take a raised eyebrow from Mrs W to remind us to hide them away.

Sherry gazed longingly at the little rowing boat as we made our way back to the cottage.

"Do you think we could take it out?"

"I think that would be a very bad idea, Luv. Just look at that chop. We don't even have a life jacket. I don't know about you, Shez, but I'm not the strongest swimmer and Cornwall is famous for its rip tides..."

She kissed her teeth.

"And you reckoned Bobby Moore might be your father..."

"What?"

"Oh, nothing. I just don't think it would do you any harm to take a risk now and then..."

"Hey, look I take a risk every night eating my own cooking, so don't give me that..." I lunged for her and she shrieked.

"Well, no one said you had to cook..."

"But if I didn't, it wouldn't make it much of a holiday for you, would it, now?"

"Jonathan Cooper - I do love you."

I seized her wrist and pulled her down into the sand.

"Well, I should bloody well think so. Now kiss me and I might let you win at chess this evening."

"But *I* always beat *you* at chess."

"See, that's how much I love you..."

That night, a full moon shone in through the little bedroom window, bathing the sheets and pillows on the bed and turning them silver. Sherry stood wrapped in the cotton kimono I had bought her last Christmas, staring out across the bay below. I climbed beneath the covers and patted the bed next to me but Sherry seemed miles away.

"Hey, Shez. I'm over here and I've got nothing on under these bedclothes. What can you see that competes with that, huh?"

"Just looking at the light on the water. It looks so beautiful from here..." She leaned forward suddenly and gasped.

"What is it, Shez?"

"I just thought, I saw - oh, never mind. It just looks so tempting..."

"The view from *here* looks pretty tempting to me."

Sherry shook her head and giggled shyly.

"Well, you know what they say about temptation ..." she said turning and shrugging off her robe. I caught my breath. I would never quite get used to how beautiful she was. And under that cool light, she reminded me of one of those marble statues my mum had taken me to see in the British Museum. A goddess of beauty.

"You truly are the most incredibly beautiful thing I have ever seen, Shez. I mean it. I know I'm not great with words but you could make a poet out of me..."

"Oh yes, please. Byron, I hope - mad, bad and dangerous to know? Actually, he wasn't all that. I think we met him once. Now scoot over you silver-tongued devil - 'pardon my French, but it's bleedin' freezing out here."

Some hours later, the sound of a door creaking broke through my dreams and I blinked open my eyes. The sky outside was grey and streaked with the fiery red tendrils of dawn. The bed next to me was empty but still warm when I leaned across.

"Sherry?" I whispered, "Where are you?" I strained my ears to catch the tell-tale sound of movement but the cottage lay silent and completely still. The only thing I could hear was the rustle of waves on the shore and the distant call of the waking gulls, carried by the breeze. I scratched my head and rolled out of bed.

"Sherry, where the hell are you?"
Something besides the chill of the early morning air made me shiver. I cocked my head and headed to the window to scan the garden below. Nothing moved in the graininess of the gloom. Then, suddenly, out of the corner of my eye, I sensed more than saw a shadow flitting across the beach to the water's edge. Could it be Sherry? I strained to see. There was someone there, right enough, but I couldn't tell for sure that it was her. I watched spellbound as the figure entered the water and then disappeared beneath the waves. And then the fear set in.

"SHERRY!"
I pulled on my jeans and sweatshirt and made my way downstairs in my bare feet, checking the bathroom as I went. The kitchen and living room lay in complete darkness. I flicked on a light and padded to the back door. It was unlocked. Sherry was out there. I had to find her.

Outside the sky seemed brighter and I began to see more clearly as my eyes accustomed themselves to the low light. I cautiously picked my way down the wooden steps to the little beach and stared around. Dark shapes hunkered in the shadows, rocks I supposed, though they had looked far less ominous in the daylight. A patch of colour caught my eye. There, over the boat, hung a piece of cloth. Sherry's kimono. I picked it up and held it to my face. It was still warm. She must be close but, surely, she could not have gone into the sea. It would be freezing at this hour. I turned and ran over to where the waves lapped at the edge of the beach and stared out across the water. The water looked cold and black except for the dancing glints of red reflected from the sky. A sliver of cold neon orange gleamed on the horizon. It would soon be dawn.

I could feel panic rising in my chest. I called out.

"Sherry. Sherry. Come back, please…" But all I could hear was the rhythmic breathing of the sea.

Then, all at once, I saw a movement among the waves. That same bobbing action we had seen earlier in the day. The next moment I spotted another, heading in towards the shore. I watched transfixed. The two bobbing shapes came together. Seals. They were playing, chasing each other, twisting every which way and slapping the water with their tails and flippers. And I knew that one of them was Sherry. Closer and closer to the shore they gambolled until I found myself wading into the freezing foam, just to feel part of the fun. And suddenly I was close enough to see their shining round eyes and pale long whiskers. I clapped my hand to my mouth to stop myself from whooping in delight. I must have been grinning like a maniac. The sunrise, the water, these remarkable animals. It was a piece of pure magic. I had wanted to be cross for the anxiety she had caused, but I couldn't begrudge her this.

The sun continued to ooze its way out from behind the horizon, edging the clouds in rosy gold. Then suddenly, another dark bulbous shape seemed to appear out of nowhere. It was a big - scarily big. A fully mature bull. From the size, it had to be. I heard myself cry out a warning. There was a ferocious growl and then an unearthly shriek. The bull had lunged at one of the smaller seals. It gripped it by the scruff of its neck, shaking the animal like a ragdoll. Yet that was no animal. It was Sherry, it had to be. The bull was attacking the interloper and I was helpless to stop it.

I let out a howl of horror and then remembered the boat. I couldn't hope to get it into the water in time but I raced over and seized one of the oars, then racing back again I strode chest-deep into the water and began to batter at the bull as hard as I could. My third blow met its target with a terrible thud. The bull screamed and thrashed but let go of its prey and swam away, growling and spitting. But then the next moment it seemed to rally and was turning. Bellowing like a buffalo, it headed directly towards me. I lashed out again in warning and did not pull my punches. The oar hit the water with a tremendous smack. The next one would need to meet flesh. I had never harmed an animal in my life. But this was Sherry. This was life and death. Realising that I meant business, it recoiled and headed off towards the open water, followed by the other smaller animal.

The mauled seal lay half submerged in the shallows. I could see angry-looking wounds glistening in its flesh. I dropped the oar and dived towards it, gasping as the shock of the freezing water knocked the air out of my lungs. Seizing the animal by its flipper, I towed it back to the shore and staggered onto the beach, dragging it clear of the waterline with my last ounce of strength. The seal shuddered and gave out a little whimper. I tried to tug it further up the beach but was so cold that I could no longer feel my hands or feet. I was fighting for breath and losing. I looked around in despair. I knew that we needed to get off the beach. If the bull recovered and came after us, we would be next to defenceless. I sank to my knees, panting heavily. My vision began to darken around the edges. I looked into the seal's great dark eyes and shook my head. I was losing my fight for oxygen. I used the last of my strength to wrap my arms around its body and drifted into unconsciousness.

The sun was hanging well above the line of the horizon when I came too. Sherry was lying naked in my arms. The gash in her neck had closed but there was a dark bloodstain trailing back down the beach. I stroked her face and she awoke. She met my eyes and blinked back her tears.

"Jonno - I am so sorry."

Angry relief flooded my brain.

"For Christ's sake, Sherry. What did you think you were doing? These are wild animals not fucking selkies! Never mind. We need to get you back to the cottage. Can you stand?"

She nodded so I wobbled to my feet and helped her up, turning homewards.

"No wait, Jonno. We can't afford to lose so many cells. We have to…"

She knelt back down and splayed out her fingers on the blood-stained sand. She shuddered and the sand began to ripple. The dark stains were moving towards her fingertips. I had seen something like this many years before and remembered Sherton Myam's waxy finger. When the nearest patch had disappeared, she stretched her back and hobbled down towards the water's edge, repeating the same movement as though in a trance.

I watched transfixed for a couple of minutes then made myself move and padded over to the upturned boat to fetch her robe. When I returned, every last trace of blood had gone and Sherry stood staring forlornly out across the sea.

I slipped the kimono around her shoulders and took her face in my hands.

"Are you okay?"

"I will be, Jonno, but I'm afraid I'm going to need a bit of help to get back up those bleedin' stairs. So many of us were swept away in the current and it'll take us a while to recover. I'm so sorry for being so thoughtless. You could have been injured or even killed and it would all have been my fault."

I winced a little at her use of the word "us" but put a finger to her lips. We were both safe and so long as we stayed away from the ocean, I planned for us to stay that way.

Back in the cottage, I got us some towels and poured us both a large vodka. Once we were out of our wet clothes, I hunted out a thick blanket and wrapped Sherry up in it and then did my best to get a fire going. When all was done, we huddled together on the sofa and Sherry rested her head on my chest. I smoothed her hair and silently marvelled at how quickly her injuries had healed.

"Jonno?"

"Hmm?"

"What a fucking-selkie?"

I snorted.

"You mean a *selkie*. I don't think you need to include the expletive."

"Okay. A selkie, then. What did you mean?"

"I thought you of all people would know. My mum used to tell me about them when I was a little kid. They are seals at sea but take on human form on land. I've got an idea the legends come from Scotland. There are some beautiful and very sad stories - Jeez, Sherry. Do you think she was trying to prepare me in some way?"

"Who knows? Perhaps she was trying to let you into their world a bit. I'm sure a big part of her must have wanted you to know…"

I cut her off, regretting I had brought the subject up.

"Yeah, well, as I said, those were no selkies last night, and seals may look cute but the males can be incredibly aggressive. I get it, Sherry. I do. You have this amazing ability and it's only natural that you want to use it sometimes. I would, if I were you. But promise me that you'll never do anything so reckless again."

"I'll be more careful, I promise. But Jonno, it's not an ability - something I can do - it's who I am. I want so badly *just* to be Sherry for you, but I can't always deny this fundamental aspect of my nature. Please tell me that you won't let it come between us."

I drained my vodka. I knew what she meant but had no wish to go there. My father had left us because he could not adapt to the demands of being merely 'normal'. I couldn't lose Sherry, as well, not now.

"Well, last night you came dangerously close to being *just* a mangled and dead seal. So, I suggest we restrict the self-expression for remote parts of Epping Forest and the safety of our own home, shall we? And we'll say no more about it, okay?"

Sherry took my hand and pressed it to her lips. I hugged her to me but I was still shaking inside.

It took Sherry another couple of days to fully recover but we returned home at the end of the week and quickly settled back into our usual routine. I'd genuinely resolved to leave the subject in the past, but something about the whole episode had unsettled me. At first, I presumed it was just the trauma of it all, but in the following weeks what had begun as a minor niggle somehow burgeoned into a major preoccupation – a major preoccupation that quickly caused me to become grumpy and resentful.

"For Goodness' sake, Jonno, what is eating you?" demanded Sherry when I had snapped at her once too often. "You've been biting my head off for the last two weeks. Now spit it out."

I looked at her in astonishment. *Had I?* And, I thought that I'd been doing such a great job of playing it cool.

"Just now," she explained. "All I did was put the spoon back in the fork rack and you called me stupid. And yesterday, when I forgot to close the fridge door, anyone would think I had committed a capital offence. C'mon, out with it, Jonno. I know you only act like that when something is stressing you, so you might as well tell me now."

I looked at my hands. The fingers were balled into fists. She might have had a point.

"Why?" I asked in a quiet voice.

"Why, what?"

"Why didn't you tell me you were going to swim with the seal that night? And why don't you shapeshift when I am around anymore? I understand that it's part of who you are, yet you don't seem to want to share that part of you any longer?"

"Any longer?" She pulled a face. "I've never done it very regularly, Jonno, as you well know."

"Yeah, because you were worried that you would lose your memories. But now you know that's not the case. I don't get it?"

Sherry looked away. I could tell she was upset but couldn't work out why.

"Look, Jonno. I don't know how to make you understand this, but I'll give it a try. *You* are the most important thing in the world to me and I just want you to think of me as your partner –

your partner in a completely normal relationship. No different to you, really. Just someone who loves you the way I hope you love me. And that is *all* that truly matters. The other stuff is just, well, incidental. I don't want it becoming a *thing* between us."

"But Shez, I've always thought of you that way. You know that. I didn't become friends with Sherton or Shalto or you, for that matter, because of what you can do. We became friends because we had a connection. It was only ever that. I know I made that goofy cock-up about the blood and the microscope and everything, but I was just a silly kid back then."

"Oh, I know that, Luv. And I know the hang-up is more mine than yours. You've always just accepted me. You have. But I can't imagine wanting to go on living without you and I'm so afraid that, in the end, it will drive us apart. Look at Julian and your mum. They loved each other but it wasn't enough."

"Have you met Julian?" I asked with a smile.

"Point taken. Well, listen. I'll try to be a bit more relaxed about the whole shape-shifting thing if you promise not to take my need for privacy about it personally."

"Great. And I'll try not to be such a grumpy twat. You know sometimes, I suppose I wonder what on earth you see in me and that's a bit scary, if you must know."

"Well, Jonathon Cooper, you're just fishing now and if you want to catch anything you're going to have to use some slightly less obvious bait."

I looked at her with a smirk. I didn't always *get* metaphors but this one, I understood. The question of what exactly *she* saw in *me* did scare me though. When I thought about it. Which, luckily was not too often.

29

"Had a good day, Sweetheart?" Sherry's voice rang out from the sitting room as I stepped through the front door and wrapped itself around me like a welcoming hug. I smiled and slung my bag down in the hallway and then smiled again. Old habits die hard. I remembered how as a schoolboy I had tossed my battered old satchel into the same spot. Except that back then, the house had all too often been empty; the hallway cold and silent. Not that I'd minded. I had always known that Mum would be back to make it feel like home, soon enough. I sighed. It had been over two years since she had passed away. I was getting on with things though the void, she had left in my life, felt only marginally smaller than it had a year ago.

"Good, thanks. No. Wait. Better than good. Great, in fact. I'm finding this series of lectures on Gauss and the Prime Number Theorem completely fascinating. I thought the first-year introduction was interesting, but this - kinda blows your mind, as they say..."

I slumped down next to Sherry on the sofa and we exchanged a soft kiss.

"And you? How's your day been?"

Sherry wrinkled her nose.

"Oh, you know. There's only so much afternoon TV you can watch. Still, I've whipped up a storm in the kitchen..."

"Ooh, great. What's for starters..."

"This..." said Sherry, leaning across and giving me another kiss; this time long and lingering.

"Well, if that's for starters, I think I might jump into the shower right now. Care to join me?"

"Behave. You know you told the guys to get here for six. You promised Kevin a chess match, remember?"

I rolled my eyes.

"What *was* I thinking? The poor bugger will lose as usual, and then we'll all have to put up with him sulking for the rest of the evening. He keeps trying to memorise these obscure moves and games but then takes his eye off the ball entirely. He's developed this real thing about beating me. He should try playing you. That'd fix him. Honestly, I know he has us in stitches sometimes but he can be so competitive. He could do with a good woman if you ask me. Oh, and that reminds me, Andy asked if he could bring a friend - nudge nudge, wink wink..."

Sherry smiled.

"The more the merrier. I must have cooked enough to feed the whole faculty. Smells great, too. Almost made me want to eat it rather than just push it around my plate."
I frowned.
"You don't have to, you know. I really appreciate it, but it must be hard – and we could always get a takeaway."
"No. Don't say that, Jonno. I love that you have friends now. You've been a different person since you started at Imperial. We actually have a social life and, this way, I can feel a useful part of it too. Not just a spare wheel. Besides, it gives me something to do."
I shook my head.
"You're bored out of your brains, aren't you? Seriously? And you're brighter than any of these tossers. Sorry. I know they're not tossers. It's just that I feel so helpless to make things better for you. But I have to go to lectures and tutorials..."
"C'mon, Jonno. We've been through all this before. I can't go to college or even work. I'd need a national insurance number at the very least and it wouldn't be worth the risk of working somewhere that wasn't legit – I simply can't afford to draw attention to myself. That's just the way it is. Look, I got by for years. And I've always got The Project. I'm not complaining, truly, I'm not..."
"I know. I know you're not. But we're young, we have means – the world should be our oyster. Wouldn't you love to travel to India, or Morocco or even Paris?"
"But we love Broadstairs and Brighton and look what a wonderful time we had in Cornwall – well, up until I got into a fight with the marine life, anyway. That *was* a bit of a dampener..."
I frowned. I hadn't meant to make her think that she was the one holding us back but I couldn't stop myself.
"Look at Mum and Julian – they got around, travelled all over the world. I'm sorry, Shez. I'm just saying. It can't be impossible..."
"But look who they hung out with. Some of their associates must have been well dodgy. Look, back in the day, I'm pretty sure I would've known how to get my hands on fake identification but we don't move in those circles. You're a maths student for God's sake and I – well, I'm not even sure what I am."
"You're right, of course – we don't know anybody who could help us. But d'you know what? I'm willing to bet we know somebody who *does* know someone..."

"No. Not Julian, Jonno. It's asking for trouble." Sherry was shaking her head, her brow creased in apprehension.

"Don't worry, I have no intention of inviting my dear father back into our lives. I had someone quite different in mind…"

The evening turned out to be enjoyable albeit a tad overly boozy. Kevin, as predicted, tipped his king after only forty minutes of play but managed to limit his sulking to an irritated snort. Andeep's new squeeze, Morag, proved a welcome addition to our group, delighting us all with a string of uncensored observations about everybody and everything we knew, until we were unsure as to whether we should laugh or feel offended.

She and Andeep made an interesting couple. Physically, they could scarcely have been more different. Morag, who was thick-waisted and must have stood nearly six-foot-tall in her stockinged feet, dwarfed Andeep with his fine hands, delicate Sikh features and graceful physique. And, despite her long black hair, she was as pale as he was dusky. Dressed in black from head to toe, her vivid red lipstick made me think of Morticia Adams. Strangely enough, she and Andeep appeared to be wearing identical pairs of heavy-framed glasses and I wondered if this is what had drawn them together.

She was one of those people my Mum would have described as "larger than life." Everything about her was written in capital letters. I'd certainly never met anybody quite like her and imagined that she could be quite a handful at times. I liked her, though, and it seemed to me that her natural animation and garrulousness provided the perfect foil for Andeep's gentle earnestness. I wasn't so sure what Sherry would make of her, however, and that was what mattered to me. I loitered around the kitchen when Morag offered to lend a hand clearing the table, curious to see how they would hit it off.

"You mustn't mind my bluntness," trumpeted Morag, "I'm reading Philosophy and like to call a spade a spade. No confusion that way. People obfuscating their meaning – that's what causes all the trouble in the world if you ask me.

Fuck me, no wonder you're so slim. You hardly ate a thing during dinner. You want to watch you don't fade away. I know we're all meant to look like matchsticks these days but you can take it too far…"

The frankness of Sherry's response took me by surprise.

"Oh, no need to worry about me. To be honest, I don't like eating in public. It's just a bit of a hang-up with me. I just get too self-conscious. I'll probably stuff my face later…"

"And now Big Mouth here is just making you even more self-conscious, I suppose. I do apologise…"

"No, really, you're okay. It's just a thing I've had since - well, forever really."

"Tell me about it. I don't suppose you noticed, but I have to eat everything in a particular order- it's a bit of an obsession of mine. Plus, I don't like things touching on the plate, though I've had to learn to live with that a bit…"

"Oh, I'm so sorry. I would have served…"

"Hey – no need. It's a good challenge for me. Time was I would simply have avoided supper invitations like this, but I reckon I'm doing quite well, don't you?"

Sherry nodded and smiled.

"You know what? You are. And I'm glad you came. I hope it works out with you and Andy. It's nice having another girl in the picture if you know what I mean."

"Oh, I most certainly do. These Maths undergrads. They talk a load of horseshit most of the time; think they are being really deep. They've just listened to too much Prog Rock, if you ask me."

Sherry laughed and then stooped to pull the crumble out of the oven, directing Morag to the jug of custard on the side. I caught her eye as she straightened up and she gave me a big wink. I returned the wink and made myself scarce. It'd be neat for her to enjoy the company of another woman for a change, although I half hoped that she would put our newest acquaintance right about the Prog Rock. It had certainly never been my scene.

"I like her," she announced later after we said Goodnight and were clearing the remaining dishes and glasses from the table. "I think she will winkle Andy out of his shell. And she is so upfront. People seldom say what's on their minds. I found it very refreshing."

I raised my eyebrows.

"I see what you mean. But she's pretty full-on. And she's no oil painting, either."

"Jonno! How can you be so shallow? Besides, Andy may be cute in a dinky kind of way but he's no Adam Ant, for that matter. I think they're very well-suited. I hope it works out, anyway. I reckon we could all be friends."

I chuckled. Sherry put her hands on her hips.

"What now?"

"Adam Ant, eh? Well, he's certainly a pretty boy but I didn't realise, he was your dream man. I'm not sure where that leaves me, though."

"Well, I have some eyeliner and white pan-stick in my make-up bag, maybe we could find out?"

30

Little about the offices of Skynner, Sykes and Skynner seemed to have changed since my last visit, least of all the entrance The dinginess of the peeling wallpaper combined with the perennial whiff of stale urine catapulted me straight back to the days when I was just a little kid sidling shyly up those stairs to check in with my mum.

I wrinkled my nose and wondered why someone did not simply invest in an air freshener. The type they sold in solid blocks and were guaranteed to neutralise nasty niffs. Still, if the initial impression was less than inviting, nothing could have been more welcoming than the reception I received. Joan positively glowed with pleasure at my appearance and was still beaming when I left. She wanted to hear all about my university course and declared, more than once, how proud my mum would be. And when I asked whether she was still a member of the lovely choir that had sung at Mum's funeral she virtually melted with gratitude that I had remembered.

Mr Skynner Junior's greetings, though more reserved, struck me as no less heartfelt.

"Why, young Master Cooper, it *is* good to see you. We miss your poor mother dreadfully. More and more with every passing day, indeed. Such a dreadful business. Such a waste. But, tell me what can we do to be of assistance. Is it a matter pertaining to the Trust?"

I took a seat and cleared my throat. The old solicitor peered at me through his half-moon spectacles and tilted his head in expectation.

"Ahem. In your line of work, I suppose - that is, I'm guessing that you know of people who can, well, arrange papers and such like…"

"Papers?"

"Birth certificates, NI numbers, passports even. New identities to be specific."

The old man stared at me for so long that I began to wonder if he had nodded off. Finally, he formed a reply and I got the impression that he chose his words with exquisite care.

"Well now, I can't say that I would know of such an individual personally, though I might have an idea as to the generalities in such matters. And I am assuming that this enquiry is in aid of research for some assignment with which you have been tasked?"

"Assignment?"

"Why yes - University assignment. You *are* a student? I would be correct in guessing your enquiries are along the lines of academic enquiry, would I not?"

I looked at him searchingly for a moment before I finally twigged.

"Ah, of course, sorry, I should have made that clear. Yes, academic enquiry. A little hypothesis I'm putting together on, ahem, the use of algorithms to establish unique identifiers with the aim of, ahem, preventing Identity fraud. Though of course, first I need to understand how such things are done within, um, existing, systems, so to say. For example, at present, how would I - that is, how would someone go about obtaining a fake – I mean, bogus identity."

The old solicitor seemed satisfied. He folded his arms and stared up into the corner of the office.

"Well now, I suppose that person would need to supply details of gender, age - not too exact you understand and maybe a photograph, if they were after a passport. Add to that a willingness to maybe try out a new name; the most successful identities are those made using the birth certificates of deceased infants of approximately the age of the candidate."

I nodded.

"I see, I see. And where might one find the kind of specialist who deals in this kind of service, shall we call it?"

Mr. Skynner appeared to weigh his next words still more carefully than the last.

"Well, of course, I couldn't say for sure. I had a chap who did some time for forgery back in the early seventies. Well-known in his day, he was. Common knowledge and all. Don't know what became of him but rumour has it that he still hangs about The Blind Beggar in Whitechapel. Used to be the best. Allegedly, that is. He might be just the chap to give you some historical perspective…"

"I don't suppose you can give me a name?"

"Young man, such a thing would be a complete betrayal of client-solicitor privilege. Now good morning, to you. And be sure to let me know if we can be of further service."

I thanked him and rose to my feet but before I could turn to leave Mrs Skynner raised one hand and, with an odd grimace I might almost have mistaken for a wink, executed a most bizarre wave.

I walked out mimicking his actions with my hand, calling my farewell to Joan as passed. I was halfway down the stairs before it clicked. "Fingers…." I exclaimed as I stepped into the street. "His name's bloody Fingers."

I must have loitered outside The Blind Beggar for a good five minutes before plucking up the courage to go in. I parked the Enfield at the curb-side and removed my helmet. It would have been just as easy to drive over in the mini, but I had reckoned that my motorbike leathers would lend me the kind of raw edge, required by such a venture. Sadly, it also increased my tendency to perspire, a factor I had not reckoned with. I flapped my arms and hoped it was cooler inside.

As pubs go, it didn't have much to recommend it, at first sight, though its notoriety as the bar once frequented by the Kray Twins no doubt accounted for its popularity with tourists and students of an evening. Which is why I found myself there at four o'clock on a Thursday afternoon. Drinking time for ne'er-do-wells, hopeless dipsomaniacs and serious betting men in need of a refreshment break from the bookies.

Several weeks had passed since I had spoken to the old solicitor, during which I had been half-paralysed by indecision about the whole idea. I had been willing enough in spirit but the rest of me was frankly a little terrified. The fact was, I would have felt more at home stepping onto the bridge of The Starship Enterprise than strolling into the heart of east-end gangland and attempting to rub shoulders with a convicted felon.

Sherry had even offered to go with me but I had put my foot down. I didn't want her anywhere near that world again, not if we could avoid it, at least. So, there I was. It was now or never. I took a deep breath and stepped in through the doors, lingering a moment on the large coconut-hair doormat and trying hard to feign a casualness, I didn't feel.

I glanced around. Rumour had it that you could still see bullet holes in the walls from an infamous gangland shooting that once took place there, but I was far too preoccupied with trying to breathe to look for them, just then. The pub was empty, save for a handful of old men studying the racing form, a middle-aged couple who seemed much the worse for a prolonged liquid lunch and a small gentleman of South Asian appearance who sat in the far corner, nursing a glass of some dark spirit.

It did not look terribly promising. Suddenly, the whole idea that the guy I was seeking would somehow just happen to be there seemed absurd. Nevertheless, I mustered my courage and sauntered over to the bar as casually as I could. A solitary barman stood polishing glasses with a towel. I set down my helmet and directed a nod his way. He eyed me with a slight squint and, slinging the cloth over his shoulder, greeted me with a cordial "afternoon, Guv'nor."

I swallowed hard and tried to work up a bit of saliva, but none seemed forthcoming so, doing my best to prise my tongue from the roof of my mouth, I blurted out the first thing that came to mind. The barman licked his lips and set to pulling a half pint of lager. I drummed on the counter and studied the row of optics above the bar as he added a splash of lime. He set the glass before me and then handed me a bag of pork scratchings. I thanked him and offered up a pound note, taking a sip of the larger whilst I waited for the change. It was very cold, very sharp and very good. I felt my body temperature drop a couple of degrees. I wiped my lips with the back of my hand and cleared my throat. The barman returned and placed a couple of coins into my open palm. I mumbled my thanks and flashed him my most charming smile.

"I wonder- that is, I was just looking for Fingers. Has he been in, this afternoon?"

"You mean Fingers The Mauritian? Yeah, maybe. Know him, yourself like, do you?"

"Kind of…"

"Oh yeah? Well, if you did, then you'd know that he is the geezer sitting over *there*, then, wouldn't you?"

I felt my mouth turn dry again and took another gulp of lager. I looked over to where the gentleman I had taken for Indian or perhaps Pakistani was lighting up a cigarette. Seeming unaware that either of us was observing him, the fellow turned his head, twisted his mouth and blew an impressively large smoke ring into the corner. I noticed that the small glass in front of him was empty.

"Goodness, so he is. Thank you. Can't see a hand in front of my face without my bloody specs. What's he drinking?"

"His usual…"

"Great. Make it a double then, if you don't mind."

The barman rolled his eyes but took a glass and held it up to a bottle of rum. He placed the glass in front of me and tilted his head.

"And one for yourself, by all means," I added with forced cockiness, offering up a five-pound note. The barman thanked me with a mirthless wink and returned to the cash till to fetch my change.

Gathering up the drinks, pork scratchings and my helmet, I made my way over to the corner. As I drew nearer, the small walnut-skinned man struck me as more distinctive than I had first thought. With slicked-back wavy hair and pencil moustaches, he seemed at once shifty and exotic. I examined the wide pin-stripe of his brown double-breasted suit and noticed the Cuban heels. The guy would have looked more at home in an old black-and-white film set in Rio or Panama than here in a shabby east-end pub. On closer inspection, however, the suit seemed a little greasy and a couple of sizes too large for him. Either the wearer had shrunk or it had been made to fit someone else. I was curious to know. He seemed naturally small yet seemed to belong to that suit as much as it belonged to him.

He was surrounded by a fog of tobacco smoke that made my eyes smart. I coughed a little but he appeared not to notice me. I leaned over and, setting the glass of rum down on the table, nudged it towards where he sat.

"Mr Fingers, is it, Sir?"

The little man looked up and stared at me. I stepped back. His eyes were the colour of icy Thames water.

"Mr Fingers, Sir?"

"I am indeed, he. But what business is it of yours? That's what I'd like to know. You don't look like the Old Bill, though you're young enough. They all look like school kids to me, these days."

If the paleness of his eyes had been a surprise, then the pitch of the man's voice threw me completely. It seemed still more shrunken than the rest of him, a half-whispered falsetto twisted by a faint lisp. The lines of my well-rehearsed spiel completely deserted me and, somehow, I found myself burbling on about how Julian had been my father, the exact information I had been aiming to conceal. The response however did not begin unfavourably.

"Lor' love us. Julian Cooper's lad, eh? Would you Adam and Eve it? I ain't laid eyes on him in donkey's. My word, them were the days. We used to 'ave us some high times, back then. 'Ere, 'as anyone ever told you you're the spit of Bobby Moore. Such a gent, that one. Used to pop in here now and again, back in the day. Nice family, too. Course, I 'ad nothing to do with that kidnap attempt – not my bag, was it? Besides, I was inside at the time. Animals - I say. Animals wot would even *think* of doing such a thing to them little kiddies of his."

His voice had risen to a pitch that threatened to have every dog within half a mile howling. Fearing it would become a squeak, I held my hands up.

"Please. I'm sure no one would ever think you had anything to do with any of that, whatever it was. Really, I was just wondering if you could help me out. That's all."

"Oh yeah. 'Ow would that be, exactly?"

I heaved a sigh of relief. My companion's voice seemed to have settled back into the audible range.

"Well, I hear you are quite the artist when it comes to creating, shall we say, facsimiles…"

This flattery may have been transparent but it achieved the desired response. The Mauritian's small face broke into a huge grin, revealing an impressive array of gold teeth. He held up his hands with a gleeful chuckle.

"I weren't called Fingers for nuffink. Tools of my trade, ain't they? And that's ink, see. Indelible see like the stuff on your five quid note. Won't come off no matter how much I scrub 'em. Good as a bleedin' tattoo, it is."

I winced. His fingers did indeed look as though they had been trapped in a vice, although on closer examination, I suspected the yellow had more to do with the pile of cigarette butts that had already accumulated in the ashtray next to his glass.

"The very man for the job, by the sounds of it. Could you then? Help me, I mean.? I need to create a new identity for someone – and a passport would be nice, save all that bother with background checks and what have you. I think I've brought along everything you will require."

Fingers pursed his lips and then closed his eyes for a moment. I held my breath. My heart began to thump a warning. It was all feeling too easy. And suddenly he flashed that golden grin again.

"For Julian Cooper's kid? Why not? I reckon as how I owes him a favour or two and it never 'urts to pays them as is due. Though it may take a week or two and it'll most certainly cost you. Specialised jobs like this don't come cheap these days…"

"What are we looking at?"

"You got any dosh on you, now, like?"

I nodded, glad that I had come prepared.

"Let's say a pony now and a monkey when I deliver…"

I did my best to keep my jaw from hitting the floor. Five hundred pounds. It was a lot of money. Still, I had the twenty-five I needed for now. And it would be worth it. I held out my hand to shake the ghastly fingers, tucked my helmet under my arm and reached into the back pocket of my leathers.

Fingers turned out to be every bit as good as his word and had not lost his touch, as far as I could tell at any rate. Only a couple of weeks later, I laid a bona fide birth certificate, NI number and a completely kosher-looking passport before Sherry and watched her face. It was not quite the reaction I had anticipated.

"Sarah Woodall?" she frowned.

"Okay, so you're going to have to go by the name Sarah Woodall, now. It may not be the most interesting name in the world but it's a small price to pay for a genuine identity. Besides, Sarah - Sherry? You can still use the name Sherry as a nick name. It's just that a new identity can open so many more doors for you."

Sherry nodded and cuddled up next to me on the sofa, stroking the birth certificate with her index finger.

"Of course, you know what else this means?" I added.

"We can travel...?"

"We can get *married*."

"*Mrs Sherry Cooper*. Now, *that* name certainly has a nice ring to it."

31

"Why on earth would you want to get married? It's just so archaic. The whole idea is predicated on the notion that a woman is little more than a chattel. Her father gives her away to another man, for Pete's sake. She belongs to him – and don't even get me started on the vows…"

I winced. Morag's rebuke was not exactly the response Sherry had hoped for on breaking our good news.

Six months had passed since Sherry Matthews had stepped into Sarah Woodall's shoes and the previous week, passports in pocket, we had finally made it to Paris. I had taken Sherry up to the top viewing platform of the Eiffel Tower and there, as we gazed down over the City of Love, I had got down on one knee and made my proposal official. Sherry had squealed in delight when she saw the ring I had bought, as well she might. I doubted many undergraduates could stretch to a full-two-carat diamond solitaire, but then there was not another woman in the world as rare and precious as the one I planned to wed.

It was all coming together. Sherry was legal now and I had all but completed my degree. The acceptance of my PhD proposal was looking like a mere formality and there was nothing to stop us from planning a small wedding for the summer. And when it came to a honeymoon, this time, the world truly would be our oyster. Sherry had already brought home a stack of brochures for luxury holidays in the world's most exotic destinations. "I want to travel in comfort," she had joked. "None of your backpacking for these honeymooners."

Our only sadness was that my mum would not be there to share in our happiness. My father wouldn't be there either, but then I hadn't the smallest clue who he was. Still, it would have been nice for someone close to us to share in our joy. Which is why I didn't exactly appreciate Morag sticking her size nines in it.

"But I want to belong. I want to belong to Jonathon. Is that so wrong?"

I could tell that Sherry was hurt but held my tongue. She seldom thanked me for intervening when it came to Morag.

"Not wrong so much. Just a slap in the face for a whole bunch of women who have been busy burning their brassieres for the last fifteen years. Really, Sherry, have you never read The Female Eunuch?"

Sherry shrugged.

"You know very well that I'm not big on reading and I'm sorry but I really don't see the point of burning your underwear. I don't really need to wear a bra myself, but I rather feel for those rather well-endowed women who need the support. Look at you. Your boobs are fabulous and I envy them, but even if you don't feel the need for foundation garments now, that could all bleedin' change, if you'll pardon my French. Gravity can be very unkind as a woman gets older..."

Morag stared at her and then burst into peals of laughter.

"God, Sherry. You see -this is why I love you. You're just so refreshing. Intellectually, I can out-argue every other person I know, but you always – well, never mind. Of course, if you're happy then I'm happy for you - it's just that I worry that you are underselling yourself..."

"*I beg your pardon?*" I really could not hold back now.

"Nothing personal, Jonathon. You know that. You're a nice enough guy, but it's okay for you -you're following your dream. I just think Sherry could have more. I know she didn't have a so-called academic education but she's so bright. Yet it's almost as though you both try to hide it. Andy told me, she played him at chess once, just the once, mind you. He said it was pretty damned impressive. He reckons that Sherry plays better than Kevin or even you, Jonno. And yet she almost never plays. What's going on there?"

"Hey, I am here, you know. Stop talking about me as though I'm not." Sherry looked cross and began to fiddle with the cuff of her sweater. Morag reached out a hand and placed it on her arm.

"Shez. I know we've only known each other for a bit over a year, but you're the best friend I ever had. Other people don't get me but you, you just take me as I come. It's just that, well I think you could do so much more than spend your time sorting out an old house and waiting hand and foot on some guy."

I went to protest but Sherry held up her hand. She turned and looked at Morag. I felt the hairs on the back of my neck prickle.

"Look, Morag." She said quietly. "I know that you're entitled to your opinions and there is certainly no shortage of them. But Jonathon means the world to me and so does that old house. I had rather hoped that you'd want to be part of my happiness, that's all. If that's too much to ask then I can see that I have been mistaken in thinking of you as my friend."

Morag shook her head and then covered her eyes with her hand.

"See there, I did again," she sniffed. "Me and my big gob. I just dive in without thinking and now you hate me. What the fuck's wrong with me? Of course, I want to be part of your wedding, if it means that much."

"So, you will do it, then? Be my bridesmaid, I mean. It'll be perfect because Jonathon is going to ask Andy to be his best man. I know it's only a tiny wedding, but I want to make it as special as I can."

"If you'll still have me. Though you know, traditionally a bridesmaid is supposed to be a virgin..."

"Well, technically so is the bride, so I think it's safe to say that both bleedin' horses have long since bolted from those particular stables..."

I looked at them and shook my head. That was Sherry and Morag all over. At first, the fact that they had become best friends mystified me, but the more I saw them together, the more it made sense. As a rule, Morag tended to dominate the space she inhabited and her choice of clothing made her appearance all the more intimidating. She always wore the same plain black polo-neck sweaters, long black skirts and Doc Martens. In addition to which, she always wore extremely heavy eyeliner and that garish red lipstick of hers. The whole effect stood in stark contrast to Sherry's tom-boy casualness, natural prettiness and inclination to blend into the background.

Yet, appearance was only the half of it. Morag clearly took pleasure in exercising her formidable intellect and little escaped her curiosity. From that very first evening, she had struck me as determined to *see* Sherry. And to draw her out. It had alarmed me at first and I had even thought of warning Sherry off. Morag had a passion for solving puzzles. Things could prove very tricky if she became too determined to solve the enigma of my girlfriend.

I'd done my best not to panic. Sherry was adept at spinning a convincing enough back-story about her life. On the other hand, I had never seen anyone subject that story to any *serious* scrutiny.

Neither Kevin nor Andy had come remotely close to posing such a threat. Their chief interests lay in chess and maths, and people, especially those of the opposite sex, generally came a poor third. Since Sherry shied away from revealing her talents in either, they took my undeniably pleasant girlfriend at face value and she had had no more intrinsic pull on their interest than Match of the Day.

Morag, however, was a very different kettle of fish. She liked to ask questions and seemed to lack any concept of tact. On more than one occasion, I'd watched with my heart in my mouth as Morag took the opportunity to corner Sherry and interrogate her about what she had been up to all week.

As it turned out, I'd got it all wrong. Despite the fact that her curiosity often came over like an inquisition, I noticed that she would back off the moment Sherry declined to answer. On top of that, Sherry always greeted Morag with particular warmth and generally seemed much more relaxed when she was around. I was obliged to formulate a less sinister hypothesis. Morag had taken an instant liking to Sherry and was simply trying to show an interest.

Be that as it may, I'd barely known the woman a week before she'd begun to get up my nose. I couldn't deny the size of her intellect but she made no attempt to hide it and seemed to revel in taking us lads down a peg or two whenever she could.

One evening, after they had all gone, I gave vent to my frustrations.

"God, Sherry. Your mate Morag. Does she really have to bleat on about Simone de Blah Blah Beauvoir the whole time? Nobody gives a rat's arse, if you ask me."

"Well, I do," replied Sherry with a puzzled frown. "It makes a pleasant change to have someone challenge the *status quo*, in my opinion, and besides, she makes me think. Something we could all do a bit more, if you ask me."

On another occasion I took another tack, expressing my surprise that the relationship with Andeep had lasted more than a month, especially given their religious and cultural differences. *Andy*, I joked, *must simply be too terrified of her to dump her*. The joke fell flat. Sherry stunned me by jumping to Morag's defence.

If I must know, she said, *she rather relished the brutality of her frankness. Since Morag held nothing back, Sherry always knew where she was with her. Indeed, she was beginning to believe that it was entirely possible that they would end up being firm friends.*

Well, that was telling me.

Twelve months later, Morag and Andy were still together and Sherry's prediction seemed to have come true. Morag and Sherry had become best mates and I would simply have to make my peace with the idea of her being part of my life. It raised an interesting question, though. One that it took me a few weeks to frame.

"Sherry?"

"Hmmmn?"

"You wouldn't tell Morag, would you? About what you are, I mean?"

Sherry had looked at me thoughtfully and then replied.

"No. She's too old. She wouldn't be able to deal with the truth without freaking out. It was different with you. You were still very young. You simply accepted who I was because it did not challenge any fixed worldview."

I nodded. It made sense. That's the thing about little kids. Spider-Man himself could have sat next to me on that park bench and I would have been cool with it.

"But, what about Mum? She didn't meet Julian until she was in her late teens?"

"Ah, but *she* fell in love," she said with a shrug.

"And love conquers all, right?"

"Or is blind. You decide."

Our marriage, when it did finally happen, seemed to echo that of my parents. A stripped-down Registry Office affair with few guests, it took place in the Victorian splendour of Newham Town Hall, on the Barking Road, a building way too grand for its postcode.

Sherry and I had been to look at it and apply for the marriage licence a few weeks before. We had stood outside and looked up with open mouths and I had suddenly remembered that Mum had once described it as "an eccentrically glorious sore thumb sticking out above the dinginess of East Ham High Street."

I squeezed Sherry's hand.

"It's a bit over the top, isn't it? I hope you didn't mind us getting married here instead of a church, or something."

"Are you kidding? It's completely bonkers," she declared. "It doesn't belong and it doesn't give a hoot. I can't think of anywhere more perfect."

The only official guests turned out to be our witnesses, Andy and Morag. Kevin appeared to have gone AWOL since the Easter break and I couldn't honestly say that we missed him very much. He'd notched up the level of his competitiveness since Morag had arrived on the scene and it had become very wearing. Besides, I'd begun to resent his attitude towards Sherry and was no longer willing to turn a blind eye to the casual putdowns he threw her way. I guess he'd begun to feel as though he was the odd one out, with the rest of us being in couples, but it was no excuse.

We had thought about inviting my uncles and their family, but things being as they were, it would have made the guest situation all lopsided. They both understood at once and generously sent us a couple of cheques as wedding gifts. A little *Something to get you started*, wrote Uncle Roy. But really, we had everything we needed and were probably better placed financially than either of them. I guess it was their way of trying to be there for their sister's only child.

We had, of course, both wanted to invite Mrs Worth. I had not forgotten her closeness with my mother nor her kindness to us in those early months following Mum's death. She had, however, fallen and broken her hip just a couple of weeks before and was languishing in hospital. I'd been to see her a couple of days before the big day and had jokingly promised her a piece of wedding cake. It was, of course, a bit of an empty promise, since we had not planned to have one. But then I remembered how much those fancy birthday cakes had always meant to Mum and I, and resolved to pick up an iced party cake from Ingles on the way home. It seemed the least I could do.

There was one other surprise guest sitting in the waiting room when we arrived - Joan. She was wearing a rather posh-looking frock and jacket, and another odd little hat with a small veil. She even wore a neat floral buttonhole. "I hope you don't mind," she said, blowing her nose into a lacy handkerchief, "-only, I went to visit Gladys Worth in hospital and she told me about it. I knew she couldn't make it and, well, I felt I owed it to Margot that *someone* was there to see her little boy..." at this, she had dissolved into tears. I looked at Sherry who shrugged. Fair enough. Joan had been in the background of my life since I could remember. I guessed that Mum would have been pleased.

"You are very welcome, Joan. In fact, we're all going to a pub out Epping way for the reception, afterwards - if you would like to come along..."

"Oh, no thank you, Jonathon. That is very kind. Very kind. But they are expecting me back at work, this afternoon. And it wouldn't do to let them down."

The wedding turned out to be just perfect. Sherry wore a cream vintage Chanel suit, (she seemed to have a hoard of them somewhere in that house), and something on her head, she told me was called a *fascinator*, which matched. I didn't care what it was called. To me, she looked as glamorous as a film star. I couldn't wait for our life as husband and wife to start. I'd made sure I'd scrubbed up okay in and had splurged on a three-piece suit. I think we must have made a striking couple because we certainly attracted some stares.

Morag stuck to her black, though forewent her perennial Doc Martens and appeared the picture of grace in a pair of heels. Andy also looked surprisingly dapper in his graduation suit and striking flamingo pink turban. He seemed to have taken his best man responsibilities seriously and even had the sense to remember to bring a camera. Something Sherry and I had entirely forgotten.

The sun was kind to us so we posed for a few snaps on the steps of the Town Hall and then in the garden. We were all smiling. Even Joan, once she'd finally managed to stop weeping. But then, we had a lot to smile about.

When we were done, we said Good bye to Joan and all clambered into the mini and repaired to our favourite pub. The one Mum had driven us out to that day she had bought the little car. Andy had promised to drive home. Although he didn't adhere to complete abstinence from alcohol, he did subscribe to self-discipline about the volume he consumed and could always be relied upon to get the rest of us all home safely. It promised to be a great afternoon.

"You happy, Luv?" Sherry asked as she nestled close to me in the back seat. "I know you would have liked Mrs. Worth to be here and I'm sorry we seem to have fallen out with Kevin."

I kissed the end of her nose.

"It's fine, *Mrs Cooper*. The people who matter are here. Well, those who could be. Though, would you mind if I don't call you Mrs Cooper again, like that. Not just yet. You are my wife and the love of my life, but Mum is still Mrs Cooper in my mind and it doesn't sound right. Not just yet. I'm sorry."

Sherry took my face in her hands.

"Don't be. I get it. Truly, I do. Names don't change people, Jumbo. I know that. I have everything in the world I need, so long as I have you."

"By the way," chipped in Morag from over in the front seat. "What's with the name *Woodall*? I thought you told me your surname was *Matthews*?"

"Did I?" replied Sherry, grimacing to me. "Well, Woodall is my surname, technically, but Matthews was my mother's maiden name, so I took it on after I lost her…"

"Oh, yes, I see," nodded Morag. "Good for you. And for your information, if you had married a Sikh, you would automatically get to keep your own name. A bit more equality there, huh?"

At this, Andy turned his eyes from the road ahead and shot her a telling glance. Sherry and I met each other's eyes and stifled a giggle.

I wasn't completely sure what Morag was driving at, but I had news for her. Our friend may have stretched the boundaries of some Sikh customs, but I happened to know that his family had extremely traditional views on marriage.

32

"So, this little museum-thing, you curate, when do I get to see it?" Morag asked, changing the subject. I suppose that it was quite possible that she and Andy had heard enough of Goa with its pristine beaches and azure waters, and to be fair, Andy was already beginning to nod off in the corner. Still, it was the first time we had all met up since Sherry and I had returned from our honeymoon so you could hardly blame us for wanting to bask in the smugness of our mutual happiness, just a little.

It was getting late. We had taken our coffee into the sitting room. Sherry had conjured up one of her wonderful meals and I for one was feeling stuffed to the gunnels. Morag had forsworn alcohol for some reason and seemed the only one amongst us intent on making more conversation.

"Oh, The Mausoleum? I wouldn't call it a museum, more a private collection. And it's not in a fit state for visitors just yet, I'm afraid." Sherry rose to her feet and started to clear away the coffee mugs.

"Really? You've been working on it ever since I met you…" Sherry looked around and then down at her watch.

"Well, I guess that's true. But only part-time. And some of the stuff is very fragile and just all jumbled together so it's a rather painstaking business. Look, sorry Morag. I hadn't realised it was getting so late, we've got an early start tomorrow - the first day of term and all that. It's a big day for Jonno. He starts his doctorate. Got to make sure he gets a decent office."

"Oh, yes. Of course. Me too. Thank God, you reminded me," she yawned. "I'm teaching a tutorial at 10 am and have a G.P. appointment at 8.30 am. But tell me again, who exactly owns this mu– sorry - private collection of yours."

Sherry weighed the mugs in her hands. Her ears turned a little red at the tips.

"Don't ask me. It was arranged through a local solicitor. I've never actually met the owner and don't even know their name. I suppose that might seem odd, but I never even give it any thought now…"

"All sounds very Dickensian, to me…"
Sherry laughed.

"Yes, I suppose it does, in a way - but then again so does ending up in the workhouse, so I guess plus ça change, as they say." Morag grinned and threw a cushion at her sleeping lover.

"Here, Rip Van Winkle. Time to go. The old married couple need their beauty sleep."

Sleep however eluded us both that night. Sherry had been unusually quiet since we had finally closed the front door behind our guests. She lay completely still next to me, but I could tell that she was still awake. Me, I was obsessing over the same stuff that had filled my brain for the last month – my choice of subject for my PhD and where it might lead me. The journey would begin in earnest in less than eight hours and it was beginning to feel like the ascent to Everest, daunting and exciting in equal parts.

Choosing an area of research had been excruciating. So much seemed to hang on the decision and the field was so wide open. Narrowing it down to a research proposal seemed next to impossible. In the end, I had done what my tutor had suggested. Gone with my gut and opted for the topic that most excited my scientific curiosity. It would, after all, be a long slog and I would need all the passion I could muster.

It had to combine my interest in quantum physics and mathematics. Time after time, I came back to one thing – quantum computation. The dream of developing a quantum computer was edging ever closer to becoming a reality and now might just be the time to ride the wave.

By the end of sixth form, Richard Feynman had pretty well supplanted Spider Man as my personal hero. He had singlehandedly reignited interest in the field back in 1981 with his keynote speech Simulating Physics with Computers. Then, just as I was starting my undergraduate studies, David Deutsch formulated a description for a quantum Turing machine. The race was on to develop quantum algorithms and I wanted to be a part of it. I had always been fascinated with Bell's theorem and its potential applications in quantum computation. But what if the line of research I had chosen led to nothing but dead ends and failure? Worse still, what if someone got there before I did? It happened. Indeed, given the flurry of interest in the field, the probability that it would happen suddenly seemed unpalatably high. And then it would be years of study down the toilet. Perhaps I was an idiot for not choosing a less competitive area of research. I stared at the bedroom ceiling.

"Why do you think she is going to the G.P?" asked Sherry out of nowhere

"I dunno - people have doctor's appointments all the time."
"Do they?"

"Yes. Particularly women. You know. Women's things. Go to sleep, Shez We both have an early start in the morning."

We lay in silence for a few minutes but I could tell Sherry was still wide awake.

"Did you notice she wasn't drinking?" she whispered suddenly.

"So? It's a free country. Maybe she wasn't thirsty," I yawned.

"You know what, Jonathon Cooper. For someone so smart, you can be surprisingly dense, sometimes."

"That will be the effects of sleep deprivation…"

The next morning, I returned to the Imperial campus as a PhD candidate and placed my foot firmly on the first rung of the ladder to academic recognition and a stellar career. It was heady stuff. That afternoon, however, I unexpectedly found myself at a bit of a loose end. I had been allocated a perfectly acceptable office with two other pleasant and equally eager first-year PhD students who graciously gave me first dibs on my choice of desk. Unlike myself, they were both new to Imperial so had disappeared for the afternoon to undergo the orientation tour.

We hadn't really had any time to discuss their PhD proposals but there would be plenty of opportunities to get to know each other later. I never liked the business of having to forge new relationships, but maths is after all the universal language and, in my experience, once we had all had the chance to scrawl some equations up on the whiteboards that lined the walls, social formalities generally became redundant. And if all else failed I had a backup plan. I opened my rucksack, took out my chess board and set of chess pieces and placed them on my desk. I was yet to meet the maths nerd who did not play.

I looked around the little room that would be home for the next four or so years and sighed. That seemed as much as I could achieve on my first day. The idea of spending the afternoon in the library held little appeal. It would be humming with new students all week and nothing irritated me more than people whispering in the background whilst I tried to concentrate. I decided that I might as well bunk off early and pay a surprise visit to Sherry at The Mausoleum.

An hour or so later, I let myself into the house on Capel Street and stepped hesitantly into the hallway. The lights were already on yet the house seemed silent. I stood on the doormat, feeling a little unsure. I had wanted to surprise Sherry but suddenly wondered whether it would be such a good idea. She had insisted that I should have a key of my own so that I could just let myself in but I still regarded it very much as her private domain.

"Shez, you around?" My voice seemed to echo down the passageway.

There was a sound of rustling and scraping of furniture from down in the kitchen and then I heard her call out.

"Oh, yes, Jonno. Come on through. What a lovely surprise. I wasn't expecting you."

I made my way down the hallway. It had been a couple of months since my last visit and I let out a low whistle. I would scarcely have recognised The Mausoleum as the same house Sherton Myam had once inhabited. Sherry had already made great strides in clearing and organising the first two floors of the old building, but this? I peered around the door into the first reception room. The transformation was remarkable and I could not resist stepping inside. It reminded me of one of the old antique shops, I had used to visit in Epping with my mum. The furniture I had once stacked up in piles had been arranged neatly around the room, forming little walkways. Objects of every description lay on any available surface and I noticed that each bore tags or stickers, on which a number and sometimes a letter had been inscribed. Carefully labelled paintings and photographs crowded every last square inch of wall, while rich brocade curtains framed the shuttered windows. The fabulous chandelier that had once hung neglected and dust-covered from the ceiling sparkled with a new brilliancy whilst the rich Persian rugs that had used to loll rolled up in the corners lay stretched out beneath my feet.

I shook my head and picked up a small flask from the sideboard. The glass was yellowed and bubbled. I turned it over in my hand and then picked up a crackled ceramic dish bearing the tag "5C." I was no expert but these things were old, some of them very old.

"Jonathon? What's keeping you?"

I replaced the dish with care.

"Sorry, Shez. Just couldn't resist. I can't believe what you've accomplished here. It's incredible." I bounded through the entrance into the kitchen and planted a kiss on Sherry's lips. "Seriously, though, you shouldn't be trying to shift some of those really heavy pieces around by yourself. You know I'm more than happy to come over and help, any time."

Sherry grinned shyly.

"I know, but your time is precious and besides, I can be a bit of an Arnold Schwarzeneggar when I have to be."

I looked at Sherry and made a face - the kind you make when you have just tasted something very unpleasant.

"O-kay, then," I said holding up my hands and backing away. "But, promise me that YOU WILL NEVER mention that particular detail again."

Sherry snorted and raised her eyebrows.

"It's a deal. But I'm glad you're here, in any case. As it happens, you couldn't have timed your visit more perfectly. There's something I've been longing to show you, and it's not the size of my muscles, I promise. Now sit down there a moment. Help yourself to a vodka."

I declined with a wave of my hand. No matter how regularly Sherry consumed the stuff, I had never quite come around to the taste. Especially neat. Sherry meanwhile crouched down and pulled open the bottom drawer of the kitchen dresser. I watched as she lifted out an ancient-looking leather satchel and a couple of thick ledgers and then laid them on the kitchen table. She looked at me and then closed the drawer.

"Go on. Take a look," she said, pushing one of the ledgers towards me.

I grinned and opened the first volume at a random page. My eyes fell on a carefully drawn-out table of columns, each filled with tiny spidery writing. Sherry leaned over my shoulder and pointed.

"See, I give each item a number and in this next column a physical description of the item, and here, in the next box a detailed account of the sensations and memories it triggers. Later I plan to cross-reference the entries to try and get a bigger picture."

"But there must be hundreds of items here...."

"There is, there is. This volume is for items that remain in the house, or the garage. That last column lets you know whether it is on display, in which room and if not, where it is stored. That second volume is for the stuff we have placed in the rented lock-up over in Leyton, I have a third for the items I've decided to sell. I know I couldn't include some of the stuff we sold a few years back, but I don't think it was anything too important. I would have felt it. Anyway, what's done is done. At least by the time I've finished, every article in the house will be recorded and catalogued."

"But how?"

"Well, as you know, I always keep my gloves on when I first handle something, but once I am ready, I clear my mind, remove one glove and then lightly touch the item. To begin with, it was just a confusing jumble but, Jonno, as I've persevered, the impressions are gradually becoming clearer and less overwhelming. I've started with things I think are fairly *quiet*, if you like. And I don't fight and try to understand whose memory I am experiencing, I just observe. It's much better that way."
I shrugged.
"Look here. I'll explain."
She pointed to item 297 and ran her finger across to the next column which contained the words - "one pewter chocolate pot." The entry in the next column suggested that it could be found on top of the kitchen dresser. I looked up and sure enough, I could see what looked to me like a very old coffee-pot.
"I've stowed it away up there for a good reason," she smiled, "as you will see if you read on."
I shifted my gaze to the next box and read the words out loud.

The great fire of 1666? Impression of running through narrow alleyways, embers falling all around, the chocolate pot in my arms. People screaming. Thick smoke and heat all around. Chaos. Rats running across the cobbles trying to escape.

I noticed her shudder.
"Are you okay, Shez?"
"I'm fine. But it was so vivid..." she breathed. "Just as though I was there. Of course, I'm only guessing it was the fire of London, but other items, cross-referenced here, look, in this column, seem to support the hypothesis. And I can't be sure whether it was my memory or somebody else's although it sure felt like my experience, and not one I'd be keen to revisit. And that's why I have placed it up there – out of reach. It's one sure way to avoid any unnecessary or accidental contact with it."
I frowned and looked back up at the chocolate pot.
"And yet it looks so harmless, doesn't it?" I commented. "I wonder anyone took the trouble to save it. It doesn't look especially valuable."
"I asked myself the same question. But perhaps the true value is in the strength of the memory. Don't you see, everything in this house was carefully preserved for some reason and it wasn't necessarily monetary value. The collection may have been neglected in recent years, but some of these artefacts are many centuries old

and someone took care they survived wars, fires and God knows what else. That pot certainly has, though to be fair, it is probably the worst entry you could have picked. Try again and let's see if we can find something more cheerful."

I closed the ledger and then, letting the pages fall open again, stabbed my finger halfway down a page.

>Item: *Velvet hat with feather.*
>Impression: C 1600? The Globe Theatre. Onstage. Play unknown. Crowd is cheering. Strong stench of alcohol, urine. Making a speech. Laughter and applause. A man with a red beard. Julian? See items 307 and 339

Sherry broke into a grin.

"Oh, well done. This has to be one of my favourites. I was a member of The Lord Chamberlain's Players, I'm pretty sure of it. Or, I was in the memory, at least. It was thrilling. I've found a couple of other things that tie into it. I don't have any recall of Shakespeare himself, but no one would have thought of him as anyone very special at that time in any case. So, I could have been on the stage with him and thought nothing of it. And who knows, perhaps he was one of us. That would explain quite a bit, if you think about it."

"The fact he couldn't spell his own name the same way twice, you mean?" I chuckled. "Hey, could you recall if you were male or female?"

"*Jonathon Cooper.* That is a very good question. I should make a point of including that in the description box. I had a clear impression of being constricted. A corset maybe? And of being swathed in volumes of velvet fabric. Thinking about it, that probably accounted for the strong smell. I doubt those costumes got washed very often. So, a woman, I guess."

"Well, actually no. It's far more likely that you were a boy. Women were forbidden from appearing on stage at that time. So, if you were in a dress, it would have been as a boy *dressed up* as a woman."

"Oh, this is *good*. I really must get you over more often."

She scribbled a couple of notes in the description box. I smiled. It was good to see her so absorbed and excited.

"Have you got anything more recent?"

"Oh, yes. In this second leger. I started off trying to keep things in some kind of historical order but it proved impossible. I just have to record items as I come across them, and I don't always know *when* they are from. Ordering them correctly will have to come later. That said, I have at least tried to include the items, I figure are from this century in here.

I let the cover fall and stabbed again at random. My finger landed on an entry for a gasmask box. I read the description and associated memories to myself and then looked. I could feel my eyes tearing up. Sherry looked at my face and shook her head

"Well, the memories were not quite as traumatic as those triggered by the chocolate pot, but they were powerful, nonetheless. I did say that some of his stuff had survived wars. I'm beginning to wonder if the war was the reason, it all ended up here, just thrown in a big jumble. Perhaps the place where it originally belonged was destroyed in The Blitz. It's as though someone just parked it all here and then left the place to fall into neglect."

"You mean Julian? Except that, he also dumped the money and guns. Not to mention The Enfield."

"You're right. But if he did mean to break from the past, why bother to keep it all? And why leave me here with it?"

"Well, Shez, maybe it was an insurance policy, in case he had a change of heart. You saw how much he enjoyed himself in The Spotted Dog when you put him in touch with the memories of Henry VIII. It's a hell of a lot to give up when you think about it. But perhaps he finally made his peace with it. After all, he did give it all to you, didn't he?"

"I guess. Though I can't say I find that as comforting as perhaps I should. Anyway, there was something else I really wanted you to see. Look at this."

Sherry took a pair of gloves from the dresser and slipped them on. Then, reaching for the leather satchel, she lifted the flap and carefully withdrew an extremely ancient-looking tome. She placed it in front of me with a nod. I opened the stiff leather cover and touched the page. It felt remarkably smooth beneath my fingertips.

"It's vellum," whispered Sherry. "- not even paper. Very, very old. I found it in an old casket up in the attic, it must be five weeks ago, now. I know I haven't finished the upstairs room yet so it wasn't very methodical to be looking up there, but I guess I just got curious. It was pretty well the first thing I came across."

The page was covered with symbols—script of some kind by the looks of it, but none that I had ever seen before. I shook my head.

"What language is this?"

"I couldn't tell you, for sure. I've been to the library and cross-referenced it with every modern language I could find. I even went to the British Museum but couldn't see anything remotely like it. Of course, I didn't dare show it to anyone..."

"Because you think it may be *your* language."

"I don't see what else it can be, except maybe a code, but even then - I get the strangest vibes from it. Nothing I can even put into words, yet strangely familiar."

"And you can't read any of it?"

Sherry shook her head. "

"Not a syllable. It might as well be, I don't know – the tracks a spider left after it fell in the ink pot."

"We need a primer..." I muttered, thinking aloud. "Or some kind of key, at least. And if there is one then there is a good chance it will be here, somewhere. Another book, or a tablet or something. Maybe even some pattern woven into some cloth. You know, hidden in plain sight."

"You're a genius," she breathed throwing her arms around my neck, but then she suddenly pulled back and looked at me aghast.

"Oh, but Jonno, I'm so sorry. Here I am banging on about an old book and I haven't even asked about your first day," she suddenly exclaimed.

"Oh, that," I laughed. "I bagged the best desk in our study room and the other chaps seem nice enough, but apart from that, nothing quite as exciting as your discovery - not yet, at least."

"They'll be time enough for that, Jonno. Just wait and see. I have a good feeling about it. Meanwhile, I'd better get myself up into the attic, my guess is, that if there *is* a primer, that's where I'll find it. There's a mountain of clutter up there, but that would make it the perfect hiding place because unless someone knew what they were looking for, they might easily overlook it."

"And then, of course, there is just the little matter of translating it..." I teased.

Sherry rolled her eyes. I laughed. If there was one thing, I had learned about Sherry, it was that once she got her teeth into a problem, she would be like a dog with a bone.

I wasn't wrong. In the weeks that followed, Sherry spent an increasing number of hours in The Mausoleum. The mornings she would devote to the main task of organizing and cataloguing the contents of the remaining rooms, but come the afternoon, she would pull down the loft ladder and clamber into the attic spending hours sorting through a miscellany of old trunks and tea chests.

My days were becoming busier too but whenever I managed to get away early, I would let myself in and drag Sherry out for some fresh air. If the weather was fine, we would sit on one of the benches around Wanstead Flats and watch the world go by or saunter over to the pond to toss a bit of bread to the ducks. It was a good time for both of us. I still missed Mum but life was comfortable and full of promise and we didn't seem to have a serious care in the world.

33

The new university term had cranked into full swing and the days began to grow as short as they were chilly. Bonfire night came around. None of us, except Sherry, liked fireworks very much. Altogether too noisy and alarming. So, when Andeep proposed an "It's not Guy Fawkes Night in this Dimension" party, its appeal caught our imagination. Obsessed, as he was, with Everett's many-worlds interpretation of quantum mechanics, he seldom missed an opportunity to drag us all into a discussion about alternative realities where every possible outcome of an action played out in infinite variations.

"There must be a world where Guy Fawkes never plotted to blow up parliament, or was never captured and, therefore, there would be no Guy Fawkes night and hence – no fireworks. Let's have a party where we all stay warm indoors, turn the music up and imagine we are there."

Morag and I had cheered but Sherry was not so easily convinced.

"Hold on, Andy. There's a bit of a flaw in your logic, there," she pointed out. "Guy Fawkes didn't invent fireworks, now did he? Who's to say they don't celebrate something else with fireworks on the fifth of November in this universe?"

"I tell you, what," I cut in, "How about we inhabit a world in which no one ever invented loud fireworks at all? So even if Guy Fawkes did plot against Parliament, it was using good old-fashioned arson or something. We could still have Bonfire Night, but without the loud bangs."

"But I like fireworks..." pouted Sherry.

"Hey, no buts – and no loud bangs. Neither exists in this dimension. And that could be a recipe for world peace, as well. But – oops sorry - so, I tell you what, if you're really good I'll let you light a sparkler in the garden when it's all over."

"And how about this? In this dimension – the definition of a party comprises only a very small group of friends who already know each other?" suggested Morag, raising an eyebrow.

"Oh, now I definitely want to live there," smiled Andeep. "It all sounds so much easier going.

The night of the" party", Morag and Andy came round before the sky had begun to light up. We had heard one or two crackers explode but a heavy drizzle threatened to put a dampener on any private bonfire celebrations kicking off in the next few hours.

"I don't think we need to worry too much, anyway" observed Morag as she handed Sherry her voluminous black trench coat and scarf. "Have you seen the price of fireworks in the supermarkets this year? I don't think many people in this neighbourhood can stretch to that kind of extravagance, you might as well put a match to your weekly pay packet. I think most people will just go to the council-organised events at the weekend. Bread and circuses, eh? Got to keep the populus' mind off the real issues. God forbid they might start to wonder whether Guy Fawkes really was the villain, after all."

Sherry was struggling to make a response when Andeep stepped in.

"Now, now, Morag. He didn't exist in this world, remember? Or didn't have access to gunpowder, at any rate. You've got to observe the rules, or there's no point."

Morag looked at him and then rolled her eyes.

"Fair enough. The world in which gun-powder was never invented and there are no fireworks or loud bangs. Beam me up, Scottie."

Andy scowled and went to open his mouth but must then have decided to let it go because he shut it again without saying a word. I smiled. Sherry and I might have been an odd couple but, in our little circle, that by no means marked us out as unusual.

"Oh, by the way," I announced. "I did invite Ian and Brian, the guys who share my office, but I think they may have had better offers. And, it's a bit far east for a lot of people. So - you know."

Sherry dipped her head and sailed off to hang the coats.

"Maybe they just fancied a few fireworks..." she muttered under her breath.

"What was that, Luv?" I asked.

"Nothing, Sweetheart. Their loss – that's all."

We moved into the sitting room and made ourselves comfortable. I wrestled with a bottle of Riesling while Sherry handed around a couple of bowls of crisps and Bombay mix.

"Mmmm – something smells delicious," remarked Andy, wrinkling his nose. "What do we eat in this dimension?"

"Well – you're just going to have to wait and see," teased Sherry, "but I promise you this – it *will* be spicy. I was determined to lob the odd firecracker in somewhere."

I clapped him on the shoulder and filled his glass and then moved over to where Morag sat. I was just about to fill her glass when she placed her hand over it.

"Oh, no thanks. Still on the wagon, I'm afraid. Do you have any sparking water or coke?" she asked.

I raised an eyebrow and joked that this must indeed be a different dimension. Morag raised her own brows even higher. She glanced over at Sherry.

"I can't eat soft cheese or shellfish either."

Sherry met these words with a blank face.

"But we weren't going to offer you any. You don't like shellfish – I know that."

"Good grief, woman, can't you take a hint? I can't drink alcohol or eat shell fish or soft cheese because I'm going to have a baby. You remember, I told you I had a doctor's appointment, a few weeks back…?"

Sherry stared in confusion. Morag began to turn pink. I rushed in to save the situation.

"Congratulations, Morag, Andy. That's wonderful, isn't it Shez?"

Sherry neither nodded nor smiled but apparently managed to find her tongue.

"Is Andy the father then?"

"Jeez, Sherry. What do *you* think?" Morag's tone was tight. She was beginning to sound scarily displeased.

"Now, Shez. Not sure that was very funny." I added in a low voice.

"Well, I certainly thought, I was…" chimed in Andy with a chuckle. "But maybe I should've double-checked."

"Well, it's just that you two haven't been together very long and I thought that Andeep's family were insisting on an arranged…"

"Not now, Shez," I hissed.

But it was too late. Morag was spluttering now.

"You're all bloody mad. Really? I announce that I'm going to have a baby and all I get is the third degree. Is this all the support I can expect from the lot of you?"

The three of us exchanged a tense look. We might have been in a dimension in which gunpowder had never been invented, but Morag seemed in imminent danger of exploding right in the middle of the living room.

"I think it's amazing, truly, I do." I said hoping to diffuse the situation but Morag just ignored me.

"And you, Sherry? I thought you were supposed to be my best friend."

"I'm sorry," said Sherry. "To be honest – I don't think I like babies very much…"

"Shez! You can't say that…" I clapped my hands to my face. But this time it was Morag who leapt to her friend's defence. She broke into a grin.

"Bravo, Sherry. Good for you. Most women are brainwashed into going gaga over babies. I don't think I'm all that keen on them, for that matter, but they assure me that it's quite different when it's your own. I wouldn't have said I had a maternal bone in my body but like it or not, these wretched female hormones kick in and you just find yourself feeling broody, or something, despite all that. D'you know what I mean?"

Sherry remained silent. I doubted she did.

"I do…" I piped up. "That is, I don't think it's only women who get that kind of longing. I mean, isn't it just the old biological imperative to procreate? In our own way, we males must feel it almost as keenly as females, otherwise wouldn't the human race just have died out?"

I stopped and suddenly wanted to kick myself. A flash of something suspiciously like pain contorted Sherry's pretty features, though fortunately, I seemed to be the only one to notice. Andy groaned. *He sincerely hoped that this was not going to be another one of those discussions about men and how they are all driven by their dicks.* I laughed and tried to keep the joke going but it was not enough.

"Are you going to get married, now?" asked Sherry in a quiet voice.

"I'm having a baby – not a lobotomy," sighed Morag. "Besides which, I can't see Andy's parents ever agreeing to such an idea. You were right. They *are* still banking on arranging a good marriage for him. However, I think we might have to compromise and move in together. I'm not doing all the work myself and this one is great with babies. For real. I've seen him in action."

Andy held up a hand.

"What can I say? I come from a big family. And Sikh men are surprisingly hands-on."

With that, he blinked away what looked like a tear and pulled Morag to him, kissing her. He was beaming with pride. I might never have had a real father myself, but I knew enough to guess that he would be brilliant at it.

After they had gone Sherry slumped next to me on the sofa and sighed;

"Honest, Jonno. I was beginning to think they'd never leave…"

"But they seemed so happy. Didn't you think? And Morag. It's true what they say. She was positively glowing…"

"Well, they *weren't* arguing all night, I'll give you that, but I don't really want to talk about them anymore, if that's okay with you. Besides, I've been dying to show you something. Just wait there and give me a moment."

She left the room and I heard her feet on the stairs. I had a feeling that I should have quizzed her about her reaction to Morag's news but she clearly wanted to drop the subject and I knew better than to push it.

A minute later she returned, carrying her handbag and a pair of extra heavy padded cotton gloves, which she pulled on. Her face shone with excitement.

"Now, you know you said I should look for a primer or some kind of a key, well, you might think this is crazy, but I think I found it - just bear with me."

She reached into her bag and pulled out a bundle of leather cloth. I squinted as she unrolled it and then held up a solid metallic object, about the same size and shape as the cardboard centre of a toilet roll. I looked at it more closely. It bore no markings and its surface seemed unbroken by any seam or opening. I glanced at her and scratched my head.

"I know. Not exactly what I was looking for, but listen…"
Sherry talked on in a hushed voice.

As anticipated, she had finally discovered the object up in the attic wrapped in the leather rag. It was powerful, more powerful than she could have imagined. She had been wearing gloves, as she always did, but even that precaution had not fully shielded her from its effects. She had experienced something strange before she even touched it and, when she did make contact with it, had received a jolt almost as powerful as an electric shock.

The next thing she knew, it was as though she found herself in mental and physical freefall. Her mind seemed full of words, whispers at first, but growing clearer the more she focused. And finally, the image of the book appeared. This was the key to the book. It had to be. She had re-wrapped the object and made her way down to the kitchen. Then holding it in one hand, she had taken out the book, opened it to the middle and then placed her free hand on the page before her. The effect had been as immediate as it was unexpected.

Ancient thoughts flooded into her mind, some so strange, they made no sense. She moved her fingers. The letters and symbols seemed to rise up to meet her cells, sucking her back into a torrent of consciousness that she did not recognise as her own. At first, she had broken away, terrified that she would lose her mind in the maelstrom of ideas and images that swept her along. And then she simply surrendered herself to the current. There were no words to describe what happened next and it had lasted only seconds. But she knew what the book was now. It was the secret lore of the Shapeshifters, an ancient account of their race and way of being.

I moved closer.

"Can I see?"

Sherry hesitated and then handed it to me.

"I don't see why not."

I took the object and weighed it in my hand. It was unexpectedly heavy but otherwise, I felt nothing amiss. I shook it and held it to my ear. Something about the way the weight shifted in my palm suggested a sense of sand or some loose material inside. I shrugged and passed it back to Sherry who bit her lip and whispered;

"You know what this means, don't you? That I should be able to read it now. The book, I mean."

I twisted my mouth.

"Perhaps. But look, just promise me you'll be careful. We, neither of us have the slightest idea what we're dealing with here."

Sherry nodded. But I could see the excitement in her eyes and knew what that meant. I might as well have been telling Marie Curie to take it easy with the radium.

In the beginning, Sherry's enthusiasm for the task of uncovering the secrets contained in the old writings fairly bubbled over and she would delight in sharing random bites of information with me. A lot of it, she said, was merely tedious descriptions, much like looking back at any historical records, but she still found it fascinating.

"Did you know," she beamed one evening, "that many centuries ago, my kind could transform into multiple organisms all at the same time, like a flock of birds or a nest of rats…"

"Oooh, lovely," I teased.

"No, but really, imagine being able to bleedin' fly. The writings suggest that our capacity to maintain cohesion in such states began to decline for some unknown reason and the act became too hazardous."

"Well, what does that mean?"

"I dunno. Maybe some of the birds flew off and got lost. Maybe they just all went off in different directions and couldn't reintegrate. Wild, huh?"

"Does The Book say anything about your origins, at all? You know, where your race came from or how you all came to have these remarkable powers."

Sherry shook her head.

"Not so far. Though I'd love to know. I rather think it's more a kind of handbook than a history. There's a whole load of stuff about the social organisation and the functions of each group within it. It does sound a lot like a hive in many respects. Those like me serve the purpose of enabling access to stored memories and seem akin to worker bees. We have a certain amount of autonomy but seem naturally subservient to those above us. Julian, on the other hand, appears to be one of the members the records refer to as *a director,* one of a select number of beings who sit at the top of the hierarchy. I haven't come across any reference to what we might think of as a supreme leader, however. In fact, I get the impression that directors do, at times, function as a united consciousness, as it were. At least, that is how it is supposed to go…"

"Do you think it still works like that?"

"I don't know. But I don't believe so. The book warns of the dangers posed by agitators within the system – mavericks who threaten the social cohesion. Sound like anyone we know?"

I nodded. It certainly did.

The next time she mentioned her progress with translating The Book, however, the discussion did not go quite so smoothly. It was a Friday evening and it was already growing dark out in the street when I heard her come in. I looked up as she entered the sitting room and thought that she looked particularly tired.

"You're late, Luv. Been hard at it?"

She nodded and flopped into an armchair. I got up, kissed her on the top of the head and then poured her a vodka. I handed it to her with a smile.

"Have you learned much new?"

Sherry shook her head.

"Not a lot. It's such slow going. But I get the impression that it all used to be so much easier…"

"How do you mean?"

"Shifting shape. It takes such an effort for me to do it now and I feel this – this *reticence* about it. Ambivalence, maybe. I get the impression it used to be like changing your clothes. I had begun to think it was just me. That, because my identity as Sherry is so important to me, I find it distressing to drop it despite the occasional physical urge to shift shape. But perhaps it isn't just me. Perhaps the longer we have stayed in human form, the more human we have become. Look at Julian. I didn't get the impression he changed very often even though it had been years since he had been with your Mum."

"Well, it's an interesting idea. After all, I rarely think of you as anything *but* human. I know that's probably because I virtually grew up with you, but still."

Sherry stared at me.

"Gee, thanks. That's good to know." She drained the glass of vodka and then looked away.

"You're not angry now, are you? But, Shez, I meant it in a good way. I certainly didn't mean to piss you off. I just meant..."

Sherry shook her head.

"It's okay, Jonno. I'm not human and I can never give you what a human woman could. I know that. But you don't have to rub it in."

I threw up my hands in exasperation. I had not meant that at all and yet I did not know what to say to make her believe me. So, instead, I said nothing. At length, she sighed and, much to my relief, changed the subject. She never could stay mad at me for long.

A week or two later, however, Sherry once again returned home in an odd mood. She seemed restless and preoccupied. I had rather gotten the impression that she had decided to avoid the subject of shapeshifting altogether since our last little misunderstanding and was loath to bring it up myself. I'd never liked arguing and I couldn't bear it when she seemed angry with me. Yet, on this particular evening, I could see she was itching to say something so took a chance.

"Anything new going on for you, Shez? Only you seem a bit – er, a bit distracted.

"Really? I'm fine. It's all fine."

"Oh, well, good then, I guess. I'll put the oven on then, shall I? You put your feet up..."

Sherry broke in.

"Only, I'll tell you something else I discovered. Julian was wrong when he said that shapeshifters cannot procreate with humans. They can under very particular circumstances, though little good will the knowledge do *us*."

I blinked.

"Really? That certainly is quite a discovery." I hesitated. It was a delicate subject. But then she had thrown it out there. "Well, do you want to tell me a bit more about it, anyway?"

It turned out, she did. And what she told me was quite fascinating.

Shapeshifters in human female form could not conceive. The biological processes involved were far too complex and prolonged. In male form, however, there were conditions under which a shapeshifter had been known to impregnate a human woman. It was exceedingly rare but not impossible.

"It's all in the DNA," explained Sherry. "You recall that when I changed into the panther in Epping, I used a cat's genetic material as a pattern and literally copied parts of the animal's genetic code. I did the same with the seal's fur. Well, over time the accuracy of the copies degrades. In fact, it happens pretty quickly. It is no problem for us, our new form adapts and drops functions that it does not require. My digestive system is a great example. We don't derive nutrition from food as you do, so eventually the copy becomes more of a sketch, if you like. My digestive tract might look like any other human's at a glance, but I doubt it would stand up to closer scrutiny. But you know that already."

I grimaced. I could certainly attest to the oddness of Sherry's bathroom habits.

"Of course, I no longer need the physical DNA of anyone to become Sherry or Shalto or even Sherton Myam, because they are so familiar to me."

My curiosity got the better of me at this point.

"Hang on. Does that mean there was a "real" Sherry once – a human woman, I mean?" I asked instantly cursing myself for my want of sensitivity. "Sorry – that came out wrong but you know what I mean."

Sherry frowned but let it pass.

"I guess it does. Though, who knows, she may have lived a hundred years ago, or even a thousand. I can't remember and, in any case, I may have changed beyond recognition with the passing of time. I'm kind of glad I don't remember her really, if you know what I mean?"

I nodded. The last thing I meant to do was interrogate her but I was struggling to stifle the questions that were forming in my mind.

"So, what about Julian, then? Who was he based upon? And could he actually be my father?"

Sherry shook her head in vexation.

"I don't *know* who he was. From the fleeting memory impressions, I experienced that day in the Spotted Dog, however, I'd be willing to bet that he assumed his current form a very long time ago. But that is precisely the point. There is no way he could have fathered you. Look, the only time it is remotely possible is during the initial hour or so following a novel transformation - whilst the copies of the genetic code remain extremely accurate and we have replicated every last detail of the original."

I shrugged.

"Gee. It kinda makes you wonder what the offspring would be like, doesn't it? But I guess that doesn't help us much, does it?"

"Well, The Book doesn't say much about how such a child would turn out, and it's true that it doesn't change things for us, but I'm not even halfway through it yet, and I'm still discovering so much. But you're not going to start thinking about her, are you? Tell me you won't."

"Who? I don't know what you mean, Luv?"

"The original Sherry. The girl I based myself upon."

I put my arms around her.

"Don't do it to yourself, Shez. Don't even go there. Not even for a nanosecond. As far as I'm concerned there is only *one* original Sherry and *she* sitting here in my arms."

Sherry looked into my eyes and smiled.

From that day on, however, something changed. Sherry regularly returned home, spent and taciturn. Whenever I asked her what she had been doing, it was always the same answer - *translating the book*. And when I asked her how it was going, she would only ever nod and say something non-committal.

She always insisted that everything was fine but I could see that it was taking a toll on her. Eventually, I suggested that she bring the book back to our place, where she might at least study it in comfort, but she would not hear of it. *I didn't understand and never could.*

Her words stung but I resolved to respect her privacy about it. It was the same old tension in a new form. There were aspects of her existence as a shapeshifter about which she would always remain guarded. But I got it. Sherry was first and foremost my wife and best friend. As intrigued as I might be, my love for the flesh-and-blood reality of my wife always overrode my scientific curiosity. We had barely been married for five months and I was still besotted. Sometimes, when we made love, I could not have told you where I ended and she began. Was it her heart I felt beating beneath her ribs, or my own? Anything else seemed irrelevant.

Besides, the workload for PhD was becoming increasingly demanding and I had little mental space for anything besides quantum gates, Bell States and superposition. Talk about quantum entanglement! There were days when the workings of my brain felt like a bowl of spaghetti.

34

The following Spring, on February 15th US time, Richard Feynman passed away. He was only sixty-nine but, given his involvement in the infamous Manhattan Project and his subsequent exposure to the radioactive fallout when he witnessed the detonation of the first atomic bomb, it was probably a miracle he lived that long. That circumstance, however, did little to lessen either the blow of loss to the world of physics, or to the young physicists the world over who had come to idolise him. I, for one, felt temporarily devastated. I'd learned at too young an age how fragile life could be and his loss, though remote to me in many ways, felt deeply personal.

Morag, meanwhile, blossomed with all the gigantic magnificence of a she-whale. The midwives had told her that the baby was of normal size and development yet, by the time Easter had come and gone, I reckon we all secretly suspected that she was about to squeeze out a fully formed three-year-old.

The birth when it finally happened, was mercifully straightforward and astonishingly rapid. Morag had been two weeks overdue, and could barely waddle to the front door by the time her waters broke. Andy had phoned Sherry and told her, they were on the way to the hospital and that she had better get there as fast as she could. Morag had pleaded with her to stay with her during the delivery. Her mother would only fuss and annoy her. Sherry had not been keen but Morag's persistence had finally worn her down.

"I've called a cab to take me over there," she said grabbing her handbag and pulling on her jeans and sweatshirt. "You can come and pick me up at the hospital when it's all over. And don't look at me like that, Jonno. It's not that I don't want to be there for her, and I doubt it's the first time I've seen a human birth in the flesh, as it were – it's just that it all seems so – so unnecessarily violent."

I smiled.

"Perhaps. But I'm not sure there's another way, is there? Barring surgery, that is."

Sherry shrugged mysteriously and kissed my cheek, then finished dressing. The cab driver was honking the horn outside already. She had a birth to get to.

Looking back, I came to see the birth of baby Richard, as the turning point in all our lives. The name had been Morag's one grudging concession to Andeep's role as co-parent. Their son might not have taken his father's family name but at least he could bear tribute to *one* of his heroes, and Everett had seemed a bit too out there, even for Morag.

Morag was dozing by the time I got to the maternity ward and Sherry seemed to have slipped out for a moment but Andy greeted me with a hug. He was grinning from ear to ear and couldn't seem to stop. There could not have been a prouder father on the planet that night. He lifted the newborn baby out of its cot and invited me to meet his son. I peered into the tiny sleeping face and felt my breath catch in my throat. I wanted one of my own. I knew I did. But I hadn't known how much I'd wanted one until I saw those perfect lips and tiny nose. I slapped Andy on the back in congratulations. He showed me how to hold the baby's head and passed his precious bundle into my arms. I cradled it to my chest and marvelled at its tiny fingers and thick black hair.

Just at that moment, Sherry walked in. She looked at me and smiled, but there was tightness around her eyes. I handed the baby back to Andy and embraced my wife. It was time to get her home, we could come back in the morning to see Morag and the baby.

It was an awkward journey home. I felt as though I'd done something wrong but didn't want to bring it up, as I had no wish to upset Sherry, but it was she who finally broke the ice.

"I've never seen such a change in someone, as I saw in Morag this evening. I couldn't imagine her taking to motherhood, yet somehow, the moment she held that baby in her arms, she softened somehow. And do you know what? If only Andy had realised, I reckoned, for all her big words, she would probably have accepted a proposal of marriage from him there and then, if he'd just had the balls to ask her."

I shrugged. I could feel her looking at me.

"Well, we'll see if it lasts, shall we? I'm sure it's an emotional time for any woman."

"And man."

I nodded. There was no arguing with that. And then I said something really stupid.

"You know, as physicists and mathematicians we're always looking for miracles of nature in equations or particle accelerators, or billions of miles away at the edge of the cosmos, but then you see it there – right in front of you. The mystery of life. And we are all a part of it. It makes you think, really."

It had certainty seemed to make Sherry think. I didn't hear a peep out of her for the rest of the night. I knew I'd put my foot in my mouth again but didn't know how to get it out again. I did feel that way and to pretend anything else would have simply been disingenuousness.

Little Richard, through luck or genetic inheritance, turned out to be one of those delightful babies that sleep through the night from day one. We all joked that any baby of Morag's would hardly dare do otherwise but that was a bit unfair. Morag took to motherhood like a duck to water, surprising us all with her patience and capable pragmatism whilst taking it all in her stride. Long before the birth, she had sworn that she was not going to turn into one of those dreadful mothers who can talk of nothing but their precious infant and she had remained true to her word. Before long, she was carrying on with her life as though nothing had happened. She continued to participate in our liveliest debates while the baby slept over her shoulder or in a sling, she wore about her neck. Yet she could still enjoy shocking us.

The first time they came around to our place after Richard was born, she announced that she had, after all, elected to breastfeed him.

It was easier and more convenient at the end of the day, she said, *and whilst she deplored the paternal propaganda that breast was best, it was a great way of shedding baby weight.* Sherry nor I were hardly likely to disagree, yet neither of us had been quite prepared for the immediacy of the demonstration that followed.

"Get over it," she pronounced as she pulled up her shirt and revealed an enormous brown nipple. "What could be more natural?" I looked away as she guided it into her son's mouth but she was not going to let me off that lightly.

"Really, Jonathon? It's precisely that kind of squeamishness that has kept women out of the halls of power, all these years. And I can tell you, I'm going to make a point of demanding the university provides zones for breastfeeding within the college campus, the moment I return. It's about time we came out of the shadows."

It was a good point, but it didn't make me squirm any the less and I can't say that Sherry looked any more comfortable than I.

By the end of that first visit, something else had become clear. Despite being present at the birth and allowing Morag to squeeze her hand in a vicelike grip – Sherry had consistently passed on the opportunity to hold little Richard, citing all manner of implausible excuses.

"Oh, come on, Shez - the baby won't bite you," I finally blurted out once we were alone again. "Morag is beginning to get suspicious and will wind up taking it personally. Do you honestly want to fall out with her over this?"

"You don't understand, Jonno. They don't like me. It's like bleedin' dogs. You know full well, they always bark at me. They can smell that I'm not one of your lot. Believe me, a baby's olfactory sensitivity is way superior to yours. They know their mother by her smell, long before they're able to recognise her by sight. And they can sense something when something isn't right. Take it from me, that kid will howl the place down if it gets one whiff…"

I bit my lip. I could see the logic of her reasoning. A baby crying in distress when someone new picked him up was one thing, but every time? It could be a problem.

"Well look," I said, "I think there might be a solution to this. I can't guarantee it will work, but just hear me out…"

The next time we visited Morag and Andy, Sherry waited until Morag had finished feeding Richard and then offered to hold him. Morag couldn't have looked more pleased Throwing me a nervous smile, Sherry leaned over and scooped up both the child and the towel on which he lay.

"Oops, you don't want that," remarked Morag trying to pull the towel away. "It's got yuk all over it."

"No, no—you're all right. It's fine…" replied Sherry breezily, tucking the towel against her chest and stroking it with her fingers. Richard, reassured by the comforting smell of his mother's milk nestled contentedly against her, cooed and closed his eyes."

"See, there. I knew it. You're a natural," sighed his mother. "And would you look at the soppy grin on this one's face." She nodded towards me.

I winked at Sherry. But she didn't look quite as chuffed as I had hoped. In fact, it struck me that she didn't look very happy at all.

35

"I can't believe he'll be two this weekend," I sighed.
Sherry raised her eyebrows and then looked down at her hands. I tore a few crumbs off the piece of bread I was holding and threw it to the ducks that loitered on the water's edge. Little Richard squealed and strained against his restraints. He loved going for walks in his pushchair but was itching to get his tiny fingers on the beady-eyed creatures who gobbled up the bread and then quacked and honked for more. I gave him some bread to throw then watched his eyes widen in anxiety as a couple of rather large geese got a little too close.

"Shoo," I said waving my hands but the birds just ignored me. "Go on, shoo." I tried again, launching myself off the bench and flapping my arms. Richard shrieked with excitement then broke into chuckles of delight. I looked back at him and let out a loud honk of my own. Then, flapping some more, I skipped along the edge of the wide pond, scattering the ducks and drakes as I went.

"What do you reckon to the ducks then?" I asked as I slumped panting onto the bench.
Richard made a popping sound and then yawned noisily. He had yet to say his first proper words but made himself understood by the tone and frequency of the pops. Morag and Andy both seemed unconcerned by his delayed speech. *He'll say something when he needs to – like Einstein*, Morag had insisted. *I don't hold with the modern mania for conformity in a child's development.*

"What do you reckon that meant?" I asked.
Sherry looked at the toddler, twisted her mouth in thought and then shrugged her shoulders. The idea of babysitting had, as usual, been mine but she never actually objected and we generally ended up enjoying ourselves.

"Well, I reckon it means he's had enough," I returned, tucking the blanket securely around his chest and legs. "We should probably be heading back. It looks like rain. What?"

There was a look on Sherry's face that I had come to recognise. She had something to say and I needed to listen. I met her gaze. She smirked and patted the seat next to her. I looked at Richard. His eyes were already closing. I adjusted his woolly hat and then plumped myself on the bench next to her. Sherry pushed her arm through mine and snuggled up next to me.

"Jonno – I was wrong. I think there may be a way…"

"A way for what, Luv?"

"A way for us to have a child. One of our own. I know how much it means to you - and I know you say it that doesn't matter, but anyone with bleedin' eyes can see that it does. I want to make you happy and I think I've found a way."

I felt the muscles in my neck tense up. The memory of our last painful discussion on the topic flooded back into my mind. That time I had tentatively suggested that we might look into the possibility of adoption. It was the closest I'd ever seen Sherry to distraught.

You don't understand. I'm not like you. I couldn't love it, I know I couldn't. And the child wouldn't love me. It would sense there was something amiss. I'm not enough for you. I knew it. You want me to be human. You say you don't, but you don't mean it and now you'll leave me as I always knew you would.

Her words had filled me with guilt and then, of course, I had just gotten angry in return. I accused her of being melodramatic. *She was perfectly fine with Richard and just seemed determined to make an issue where there wasn't one. Besides I had made no such demands on her and was only thinking about what would make us both happy. I should've known that she'd make it all about her.*

When I finally calmed down, I could see that she had a point. Whilst Richard never reacted *negatively* to Sherry, it was always me he turned to for cuddles or acknowledgement almost as though she was merely part of the furniture rather than someone with whom he could interact. Perhaps this was because Sherry didn't exactly go out of her way to engage him, but what if it was something more fundamental? And perhaps I *was* changing the goalposts. Asking for something she could never give.

I wondered about Julian and my mum. He had tried at least, for nearly five years. But, in the end, he had been unable to sustain the role of parent. He said that he'd loved me but I began to wonder whether I had ever loved him. I couldn't remember – and perhaps that was evidence that Sherry was right.

We hadn't spoken of it since. I looked at Sherry and shook my head, wary of touching a nerve.

"You seemed pretty sure that it would be a mistake to adopt, the last time we spoke…"

"That's just it. We don't have to adopt. I discovered something in that old book. I didn't tell you, at first, because - well, I wasn't sure. But the more I read, the more I realised that there *is* a way. Shapeshifters do not *generally* reproduce - they don't need to. But that doesn't mean they cannot."

"Are you sure about this, Shez?"

"Yes. Completely. We *can* procreate though obviously not – well, not in the ways that humans do. There is no pregnancy as such, so first of all, we would have to pretend that I am expecting. Shove a cushion up my dress, that sort of thing. It shouldn't be so difficult. I could even attend some antenatal classes, you know, go through the motions. Anything to avoid raising suspicions that there is anything unusual about the situation. In fact - I know this sounds crazy, but I think it would be better if we moved, made a fresh start – you know, somewhere where there was nobody who knew us. Nobody who could start asking awkward questions."

"Sorry? Do you mean like Morag and Andy? But they are our best friends. And I thought you adored Morag?"

"I do. But you know what she's like. Nothing gets past her and she wouldn't hold back with the questions. It would just be too risky…"

"I guess. But our little circle, well, that has been our world, really, since Mum died, anyway - and I've still to write up my PhD. I can't just up sticks and abandon it now."

"I'm not suggesting we do anything straight away. There is still a lot I need to work out. Besides, what I said was that I'd found a way of having a child of our own. I didn't say it wouldn't involve sacrifice. I thought it was *you* who desperately wanted to have a child. *I'm* happy for things to go on as they are. But just think. We could at least start planning for it."

I stole a glance at Richard. A little bubble had formed at the corner of his mouth as he dozed. I did want one. I just did. I leaned forward and wiped the baby's face with my handkerchief then wiped a tear from my eye.

"Okay. I see what you mean. What you say makes sense, I guess. Morag and Andy have *their* little family. We can make one of our own. Maybe we can visit again once the danger of Morag noticing anything odd has passed."

Sherry pursed her lips and shrugged a "we'll-see" kind of shrug.

"So how does it work? The baby thing, I mean."

"Well, remember how we met?"

I snorted. I wasn't likely to forget. Though, I suppose, sometimes it did almost feel like a particularly vivid dream.

"Well, we may not be able transform ourselves into a flock of birds anymore, but a shapeshifter can still *literally* be in two places at the same time. We can divide portions of our corporeal substance and inhabit them consciously across considerable distances. Doing it in the case of a finger or an eye was very straightforward. Forming a whole being would of course be a vastly more complex undertaking and may take some managing at first. There are still a few details that I need to make sure of…"
I scratched my head.
"But wouldn't your baby just be an extension of you, then? And how would that work?"
Sherry looked at me and shifted uncomfortably on the bench.
"Not technically - no. It's a whole different process. Look, I'll do my best but it is difficult to explain. According to the book, when we split off substantial parts of ourselves for sustained periods, the new entity eventually evolves a new and separate consciousness with its own memories and hence - a novel and distinct personality."
I blinked and stared at her in astonishment.
"Sorry, Shez. I'm not sure I am getting my head around this very well. Can you explain a bit more?"
"Well, at first, a baby would be an extension of myself, but as it grew it would develop a discrete ego and begin to function independently of me. As far as I can tell, I would need to sleep when it was awake, and vice versa, but eventually - well eventually it would become a completely new being and would grow up into an adult. And that's not all. I may be wrong but there is a passage in the book that seems to point to a way that I can incorporate your DNA into the new entity so that it truly would be part of us both and share some of your characteristics. I'm still a bit vague about that part, but I'll get there…"
I looked at her, not knowing whether to laugh or cry.
"Are you absolutely certain about this, Shez?"
Sherry took my hand and squeezed it.
"Pretty well. Yes. It's all there."
"And would it be painful? This process, I mean."
"I don't believe so, but you would need to care for the infant whilst I was sleeping and it was awake."
"I don't mind. That would be, well, wonderful. I'm sure I can find a research post that allows me to work from home. Lots of people manage it these days."
"Well, there would be no bottles to prepare or nappies to change. Our baby would need vodka, same as her mum…"

We both laughed.

"Better not let social services hear you saying that," I teased.

"That's exactly what I mean about having to be ultra cautious," she replied with a grave face.

"Oh, Shez. We could make it work. I know we could."

"There's one thing I have to ask of you though, Jumbo. Are you 100% sure this is what you want? Because, after a point, there can be no going back. "

My eyes drifted back to Richard's face. He looked like a little sleeping angel.

"Oh, Shez," I breathed. "I'm sorry if I sounded a bit reluctant about things changing. This is more important to me and I want it more than anything else in the world."

I took her face between my hands and kissed her hungrily.

"That's what I thought..." she whispered, returning my embrace.

36

I puffed in annoyance. I'd had no choice but to leave the car two streets back from the tiny terraced house we were renting. We were very pleased with the compact but neat two-up two-down and had quickly come to call it home, but the parking was getting crazy in Didsbury, especially in the afternoons when locals and visitors alike tended to congregate around its trendy little cafés and shops. Then again, it was the village feel of this leafy little suburb of Manchester that had attracted us to it, in the first place, so we only had ourselves to blame. Still, I was itching to get home and tell Sherry my news.

I had spent the morning in the Faculty of Science and Engineering at the university. The work I had put into my PhD dissertation had paid off and, what's more, Quantum algorithms were fast becoming hot stuff. The Dean more-or-less offered me my choice of research positions. I knew that I would have parenting responsibilities soon enough, but the post I finally accepted required only a minimal teaching commitment and, beyond that, the necessity to attend the department physically was extremely flexible. It would be perfect.

I couldn't deny the thrill of excitement I experienced when The Dean took the time to show me around the famous Rutherford Building - the birthplace of particle physics. The block had long since been given over to university administration but still managed to inspire me. I thought of Mum and smiled. She had been so keen for me to attend the same university where the great New Zealander had first split the atom in 1919 and now, just over eighty years later, I had finally arrived.

I looked over my shoulder, hoping I would not forget where I had left our dear old mini. All these backstreets looked the same to me. Still, it was a small fly in a large pot of otherwise perfectly acceptable ointment. Besides, the day had turned out fine and it wouldn't do me any harm to stretch my legs. Sherry and I had both enjoyed strolling around exploring the area when we had first arrived. Perhaps I'd have a stab at enticing her out for some fresh air later on.

As I approached the end of our road, I stepped off the pavement to make room for a tall woman towing a small Sikh child who had stopped and turned to watch a ginger cat that was sleeping in a window box.

"Look, Mummy. Pussy cat," the child shrieked, pointing.

"Yes, Sweetheart. The word is simply *cat*. You don't have to talk like a baby, now. But you are correct. Well observed."

I stopped in my tracks. I would have known that voice anywhere.

"Morag? Richard? What on earth are you two doing here?"

"Good question," replied the woman abruptly. "We certainly made a mistake in believing we might expect any kind of welcome."

"You've been to our house?"

"To the doorstep - at any rate."

I felt a tug on my jacket. I looked down. Little Richard beamed up at me. I squatted down and patted him on the head.

"Hi, mate. How are you doing? Goodness, haven't you grown?"

"They do that," remarked Morag stiffly. "He'll be five in July."

Richard held up four fingers and giggled. I pulled a face of impressed astonishment and then straightened up.

"Morag. How did you find us?"

"Well, you didn't send us your new address so I got Andeep to contact someone in your department at the university. It took a bit of chicanery to get it but you know Andy, he can be very persuasive when he wants to be."

"How is he?"

"He's okay. Misses his mate, though."

"Ouch. Yes, sorry. Still, it must be great now Richard is getting to that age when they are so full of curiosity about the world. And you're bringing him up in the Sikh tradition, after all?" I nodded towards the little topknot. Andy must be pretty chuffed."

"We've agreed not to cut his hair until he is old enough to decide for himself. For the moment he thinks it's pretty cool to wear the kara, like his Dad. But we'll see."

Richard held out his arm and proudly showed me the steel kara on his little wrist.

"Well, that's certainly cool, isn't it, Mate?" I grinned.

But Morag did not seem in the mood for social pleasantries.

"Look. Excuse me for being blunt," she said in a clipped voice, "but we didn't come all the way up to Manchester to stand on the street and discuss cross-cultural child rearing, and *his nibs* here is going to need the toilet soon. You know that Sherry virtually slammed the door in my face?"

I didn't, obviously, so shook my head.

"I'm so sorry. Can I give you a lift to the station? Or maybe we could find a café. Sherry's, um- going through a bit of stuff at the moment..."

"I could see that. She's expecting, isn't she?"

"Yes. And it's taking a bit of a toll…" (I hated lying but was unsure what else to do.)

"And when *were* you going to tell us? Or even let us know where you were. It's been three months since you sold the house, Jonathon. I thought we were all best friends. Sherry was there at this one's birth, for fuck's sake. Richard has missed you - and so have I, for that matter. If you must know, I think you have both behaved very selfishly."

That did it. Typical Morag. Laying down the law as usual. Still, it made the next bit so much easier.

"I don't have anything to tell you, Morag. Things change. We *are* going to have a baby and we *don't need* anyone else. I'm sorry if that does not fit into your little world plan but that's the way it is. I'm sorry you had a wasted journey, but nobody invited you up here - you simply chose to poke your nose where it wasn't wanted. Now, Good Day to you."

I wasn't sure why, but I decided not to mention bumping into Morag to Sherry and she certainly never referred to the visit. From that day on, however, she would change the subject whenever their names came up. It was then that it dawned on me that she had never had any intention of rebuilding the ties of our former friendship. It made me feel a little sad but I put it down to her being ultra-cautious. We had made our bed and now we would have to lie in it.

The day we had set for our child's "birth" was 23rd June. Alan Turing had been born on that day, so it seemed as good as any other.

I could hardly wait, myself, and not just because I longed for the day when I would finally become a father. Sherry was often moody and short with me for no good reason. We had always rubbed along so easily before so I wasn't sure how to handle it and just did my best to wear it. I reminded myself that all women experience emotional ups and downs during pregnancy. Sherry may not have had the hormonal changes to cope with, but doubtless the stress of faking a pregnancy and the build-up to the long-awaited event was taking its own kind of toll. Nevertheless, as the day drew closer, I developed an increasingly strong sense that I was failing her somehow. Once or twice, she even accused me of being immature. It was so unlike her.

It hadn't been easy for either of us. For the last four months, she had worn first a cushion and later a whole pillow stuffed down her clothes, even when we were at home by ourselves. The thing was, I couldn't understand why she didn't simply mimic a pregnant woman. I asked her once and then immediately regretted doing so. Sherry had stared at me with a strange look on her face. *I could*, she had said, *but I have no wish to.*

At the same time, her consumption of vodka increased exponentially. She was, she pointed out, drinking for two. Her body required more energy. I almost wondered if that was the cause of her crankiness, though it had never affected her before and I was not going to be foolish enough to suggest it.

As the summer approached, she emptied the spare room and decorated it with pictures of cute animals and Disney characters. We had hung the Warhol in there but decided to leave it. It hadn't been made for children but was brightly coloured and I liked the idea of my mum guarding over her grandchild.

From there on in, we spent our weekends shopping for cots, blankets, mobiles and most of the things a newborn infant generally requires. Sherry was taking no chances. We would need to have them in the house, no matter how little they were used. It was vital that every last detail appear as normal.

We took particular pains to become on nodding terms with the neighbours and made a point of waving as we hauled child gates and cots in through our front door. Sherry signed up for a local antenatal class and even exchanged names with a couple of the other expectant mothers though otherwise kept herself to herself.

"I feel sorry for them," she told me one evening. "I expect my 'labour' will be taxing but I can't imagine what it must be like waiting to go through the torture that awaits those women. I saw enough of it with Morag."

I raised an eyebrow. It was the first time she had voluntarily mentioned her old friend in months.

"Well, even Morag said it was all worthwhile in the end, which is pretty amazing when you think about it."

I had expected Sherry to laugh but she had merely sighed and muttered.

"Well, perhaps it *is* extraordinary what we will do for love…"

During the final couple of weeks, Sherry assumed the telltale pregnancy-waddle common to the final stages of gestation and took to spending increasingly long periods upstairs, poring over the ancient book. She seemed more relaxed in herself but I became increasingly troubled by an uneasiness I could not quite put into words. Finally, it slipped out in a cry of protest.

"I know I shouldn't complain, Shez, but nothing has been quite the same since you found that book. We never seem to have fun or just hang out anymore."

"I know, Luv. It's just that I have to get this right..." Sherry murmured stroking my hair. "And then everything will be fine."

When the "due-date" at last arrived, Sherry went to shut herself in the bedroom and expressly prohibited me from entering.

"Not under any circumstances. Promise me, Jonno. You know how I feel about this. It may take half an hour or so but I'll call you the moment I'm ready. Oh, and one more thing..."

She reached up and plucked a strand of hair from my head and then smiled with raised eyebrows.

"Now, tell me, do you want *our* child to be a boy or a girl? We've never really talked about it..."

My head began to spin.

"I don't know - a little girl, if I'm honest. I suppose I always dreamed of having a daughter but..." I stopped and seized her wrist. I could hear my voice trembling. "But Sherry, are you absolutely certain about this? That no harm will come to you, I mean."

Sherry closed her eyes and squeezed my hands.

"Don't worry. It's all going to work out exactly as I've planned, I promise. I love you, Jonno. I always have and I'm going to give you all you ever wanted."

I watched helplessly as she closed the door behind and then made my way downstairs, wondering why she had not looked me in the eyes.

37

The following thirty minutes were the longest of my life. I paced around the kitchen and living room reeling off the prime numbers as I had once done as a kid when practising in the park with my football. It was the only thing I could think of to keep my mind off whatever was happening in the bedroom upstairs and was oddly comforting. I knew more than I had known back then by heart but still needed every ounce of concentration once I hit 5003.

I had just reached 7001 when I finally heard Sherry call my name. I raced up the stairs and peered around the door. Sherry lay on the bed and there, bundled in her arms lay a tiny baby. I tiptoed over to the bed, half deafened by the throbbing of blood through my ears and wondered if hearts really could burst with happiness.

"Jonathon, meet our daughter," she smiled.

I peered down into the little face that slumbered peacefully in the crook of Sherry's elbow. Our baby could not have been more beautiful had we plucked her straight out of a Raphael painting.

"You can hold her, Jonno She won't break."

I sat on the edge of the bed and Sherry placed her gently in my arms. She was so tiny but felt reassuringly heavy against my chest. I folded back the edges of the baby blanket and squinted at the tiny fingers in amazement. I held her face to my cheek. Her skin was as smooth and soft as sugar-dusted marshmallows and her hair was as fine as dandelion down. Everything seemed perfectly normal. Except for one thing. I frowned despite myself.

"What is it?" Sherry's voice was tense with concern.

"Nothing. Nothing at all. She is perfect. In fact, she is completely wonderful. Thank you."

"But?"

I had never been able to fool Sherry.

"There is no *but*. Honestly. It was just - just that baby smell. You remember. That distinctive smell their skin gives off. Stephen had it and..." I stopped, wanting to kick myself.

Sherry looked at me and twisted her mouth.

"Well, you might be grateful when she fails to emit a few other baby smells that are not so palatable."

I chuckled, relieved that my tactlessness had not done more damage.

"I love her already," I gushed. "But what are we going to call her?"

"You choose, Jonno. I gave her *her* shape, now you must give her *her* name."

"Okay. Well, I've always liked the name Lucy and well – she will be the light of our lives. Do you like it?"

"Like it? It's just perfect. Lucy. Lucy Cooper. It fits her exactly."

She looked away and then, closing her eyes, stretched out a hand.

"I'm very tired, Jonno. I'm going to sleep a while and leave you to get to know your daughter. Is that okay?"

"More than okay. I can never thank you enough, Sherry. Honest to God, I think I must be the luckiest man on the planet, right now."

I kissed her on the forehead and watched as she dozed off.

A moment later the baby's eyelids fluttered and opened. Two enormous blue eyes stared up at me, seeming almost to twinkle. Was it recognition? I couldn't be sure. My daughter cooed and gurgled, writhing contentedly in my arms.

"Sherry?" I whispered hesitantly, but there was no obvious reaction. Lucy looked back with the same unfixed gaze I'd seen in Richard when he was a newborn. But then I grinned and she chuckled. I pulled a face and a frown of concern creased her little face. She seemed a little more responsive than I remembered Richard being, but a baby non-the-less.

"Well, I never..." I breathed. I was a father. I guess I hadn't believed it until that moment. But there I was holding a tiny being that was totally dependent on us. Suddenly, it all made sense. The transformation that had overtaken Morag and Andy. The sacrifices my mother had made. I touched my daughter's fleshy little button of a nose with my finger. It was exquisite. So perfect. Suddenly and quite uninvited, Julian flashed into my mind. He'd said that he had loved me, but he couldn't have felt what I was feeling now. Because if he had, then he could never have left. I shook my head. I had spent a lifetime shutting him out of my heart, but now that same heart was so full that I just felt sorry for him.

While Richard had been a "good" baby, Lucy turned out to be uniquely accommodating. She would sleep through an entire day while I was at the University and only wake on my return when Sherry would retire to the bedroom for a nap. She required no messy diaper changing and I didn't even have to worry about sterilising bottles or making-up formula. Once Sherry had told me how much vodka to feed her, I was perfectly able to satisfy her whimper of hunger. After that, I would sit and cuddle her as I watched the evening news or tell her about my day. Sometimes I wished that Sherry could be there to share in the magical moments, like the times she would blow a bubble and then burble in pleasure, but I would recount it all in careful detail once Sherry woke up again. Then, we would spend hours just holding hands on the sofa and gazing at our sleeping child.

It was an unusual routine, but then so is that of any new parents. Sherry appeared exhausted by the effort of the birth and slept a great deal longer than usual at first. After a couple of weeks had passed, however, she took to staying up half the night, so that I could catch a few hours of uninterrupted sleep. I had protested at first. It was only right that I should do my fair share and I could survive – just about. Sherry had shaken her head. *She could see the dark circles beneath my eyes. All babies spend a great deal of their time sleeping. Lucy would be no different.* Besides, Sherry had never been one to sleep for particularly long stretches at any time. I couldn't argue with that. Ever since we had been together, I had regularly awoken in the small hours to find her reading or just sitting gazing out of the window. Indeed, I had become so used to it that I had long since ceased to think of it as in any way unusual.

They say that becoming a parent changes you, and something was certainly changing in me.
"You know, Shez," I began one evening, as Lucy lay snoring gently on my lap. "I hadn't thought it possible to feel more affection for my unconventional wife than I already did yet seeing you cradle our daughter in your arms has been something else. Something I could never have anticipated. And I'm just starting to wonder how I could have taken somebody so wonderful for granted for all these years. I know it's because, in a way, I kind of grew up with you. But since Mum left, you've become my whole world and now you've made my life complete. And suddenly I realise I've never once asked myself what I'd done to deserve such singular and unexpected luck."

Sherry looked at me. I could see that she looked tired and was just beginning to drift off to sleep. I looked at Lucy, the moment when those tiny eyelids would blink open. The moment my heart would always skip a beat in anticipation.

"Why me Shez?"

"Why you, what?" asked Sherry dreamily.

"Why would the remarkable Sher-Ton My-Am choose to share their life with a socially challenged kid from the East End?" Sherry smiled and murmured.

"I can't think what's come over you, Jonno. It's not like you to dwell on things – it's one of the things I've always loved about you..."

"I know – Mum always said I had a knack for editing out the noise - but being a dad, well, it *has* changed me. So, why me, Shez? Why me?"

"Because you always needed me..."

The summer months sped by so fast, I could hardly keep track of time. Lucy grew rapidly and seemed more responsive with every passing day. The slightly dazed look in her eyes turned to concentrated curiosity and the delight of recognition when she saw my face.

By the time the shadows began to lengthen, I had adopted the habit of strapping Lucy into her stroller and taking her out for an afternoon walk, while Sherry napped. Sometimes we would visit the park where I would point out the ducks and birds and try to name the flowers and trees. Often, I would explain the roadblocks I had encountered with my research project, nutting out the issues in extensive detail while Lucy gurgled and chuckled. I doubt that she understood a word I said but didn't seem to mind and it often helped me to see the problem from a fresh angle.

One afternoon, however, Lucy had seemed particularly interested in a group of tiny ducklings on the water's edge, following them intently with her eyes.

"Ducklings! Little lucky-duckies!" I announced gleefully, glad for once, to change the subject from qubits to quackers.

Lucy looked at me and I could have sworn she almost rolled her eyes. Was that Sherry I saw? I wondered about the whole shared consciousness thing and how exactly it worked. Knowing that Sherry was uncomfortable with questions, I had, as ever, kept them to myself. But suddenly I was itching to understand.

That evening as we snuggled together on the couch, I gave in.

"I wondered, did you see the ducklings this afternoon, when we down by the pond?"

Sherry turned to me with an expression on her face I couldn't read but said nothing. I realised that I should probably let it drop, but the scientist in me would not be silenced this time.

"Only I was just trying to get my head around, you know, this shared consciousness thing…"

Sherry closed her eyes and then opened them again.

"I think I *did* dream about ducks if that is what you mean. But the dream seemed very far away and I'm not sure whether was truly mine. Like when some objects trigger memories and I cannot tell whether they belong to me or were someone else's experiences. I'm not sure, this is all bleedin' new to me, as well, remember, but I believe that Lucy's discrete essence is developing already. I had not thought it would be so soon…"

She looked away.

"But that is good, isn't it? What we were aiming for?" I asked.

Sherry smiled, but her tone was flat, preoccupied almost.

"Yes - yes. Exactly. I really should record the process in The Book. It will be a valuable addition to our understanding of this phenomenon."

I blinked. I'd all but forgotten about The Book, yet something in the way she spoke sent an odd chill down my spine. I swallowed hard.

Sherry picked up on my discomfort at once. She patted my arm.

"Sorry, Luv. Didn't mean to sound so clinical. But you know how important all that stuff is to me…"

"Of course. I didn't mean to be such a chump about it. It had just slipped my mind, that's all."

As the nights closed in and the shops around us began to fill up with all manner of Christmas goodies, it suddenly struck me that Sherry was looking unusually tired. I had been watching her, one particular evening, as she moved around the kitchen preparing our supper. Perhaps it was the harsh light from the overhead fluorescent strip, but I suddenly noticed how dull her usually glowing skin seemed and how her hair too seemed to have lost its lustre. I looked at her carefully. She seemed smaller somehow. Shrunken almost. I knew that she had lost a lot of weight but she had assured me that this was only normal. The idea that any part of this could be considered remotely normal eluded me but then, what did I know? I knew that she would not welcome any fussing but I could at least test the water.

"Are you okay, Shez? You're not overdoing it are you, you look worn out?"

Sherry met my concerns with a smile of derision. *She was fine. And in any case, everyone expects a new mother to look knackered. To look otherwise would draw suspicion and that was the last thing we needed.*

I was about to ask her, who on earth there was to suspect anything was amiss but stopped myself. There were our neighbours, I supposed, and then of course the local shopkeepers. I was forgetting. Sherry did lead some kind of a life when I was at work. Perhaps she was right. I nodded and changed the subject. If things had indeed been normal, I would have insisted she visit the G.P to ask about a tonic or have her iron levels checked, but this was out of the question. I did my best to quash my misgivings and resolved to be more attentive. She was doing such a brilliant job and the last thing she needed was for me to mither her with my foolish worries.

That Christmas, I respectfully turned down an invitation to spend the festive season with my uncles and we spent our first Christmas together at home as a proper little family. We even go to see a bit of snow. We bought a tree and some lights and a truckload of presents for Lucy. She was a bit too young to understand what all the fuss was about but the day couldn't have been more perfect.

Curiously enough the slippers and dressing gown I had bought for Sherry were all miles too big, but Marks and Spencer's were always happy to change things, so she was perfectly happy anyway.

"I prefer you to be bigger and stronger than me," she teased when I remarked on it. "It makes me feel safe, somehow."

It was an explanation, but not one that completely satisfied me. Still, I was used to Sherry knowing best. She had, after all, been around a great deal longer than I had.

Almost twelve months had passed since Lucy had arrived in our lives. Excited as I was, by the idea of my daughter's first birthday, I couldn't help feeling a little sad that the three of us would still be unable to share it, together, for Lucy's consciousness was still to fully individuate from Sherry's. Yet the signs were unmissable. My daughter's curiosity about the world was developing exponentially, at this point, and with it emerged a personality that was all her own. She would laugh riotously when I pulled a silly face and put her tiny hand to my cheek when I was engrossed with thought. She still loved our afternoon walks and would gaze around her with a scientist's eye for detail. Her concentration exceeded Stephen's, at that age, by a mile as did her comprehension. She hadn't as yet tried to speak but easily understood my meaning. Sometimes I wondered if this was just Sherry that I saw. But it was more than that, I could feel it. My infant daughter was growing into a remarkable little girl.

And soon she would be one year old. I decided to buy a birthday cake for the occasion even if I was the only one who would eat it. Besides she would adore the candles and pretty icing and perhaps I could have it made in the shape of a unicorn or one of those little pink Clangers she loved to watch on TV.

The food issue did worry me, though. Lucy seemed to thrive well enough on a diet of vodka but I still remembered the difficulties Sherry had experienced before she had learned to tolerate food in her system. Communal eating was and always had been such a big part of what it was to be a member of the human race. I took a deep breath and broached the subject with Sherry the week before the birthday.

"I'm sorry but it's been playing on my mind a lot, recently, Shez. How's she going to manage among her peers when she starts school – at lunchtime and all? I can't bear to think of her being the odd one out. I had enough of that as a kid. I know we can think of some cover story, but all the same…"

"Don't worry, Jonno. We can start her on solids soon. Just like any other baby. If you bring her up to chew and swallow food and tolerate the whole unpleasant business of holding it inside her until she can unload it, she'll easily pass as completely normal. I found a section about it in The Book. I don't know why it was such a problem for me. Maybe I just forgot how when I forgot everything else, or maybe it was just something I always struggled with."

"Maybe, Shez. Julian suggested as much, now I come to think of it."

"Hmph. Not sure I'd rely on anything *he* said, but you're right. He did make it sound that way. Anyway, you can try Lucy with a biscuit or something soon and see how she gets on. It'll be easier once she understands, but the sooner she gets used to the foreignness of the food inside, the better. She won't have to miss out on a key social activity, I promise you."

Her words were music to my ears.

"Sherry - you're the best. I honestly don't know what I'd do without you."

"Well, it's all in The Book and The Book will be Lucy's birthright once…" Her words trailed off.

"Once what?" I felt my chest constrict. "Once what, Shez?"

"Once she's old enough to understand. That's all I meant."

I breathed again. But the little alarm bell just behind my sternum continued to sound. Sherry was smiling but she was holding something back. There was something she wasn't telling me. I looked at her and frowned. She seemed so frail lately. She had always worn baggy jeans and sweatshirts but now the clothes seemed to hang off her. At first, we had joked about her new supermodel figure but lately, I was beginning to worry about where it would all end. This wasn't skinny, it was stick thin. And she'd become even shorter. I'd noticed just the other day when she stood next to me in her bare feet. The tip of her nose was barely level with my shoulder now. I recalled what she had said about enjoying the feeling that she was smaller than me, but we had started off pretty much equal in height. It didn't seem normal somehow. But then again, normal had little meaning here. I understood that my wife and daughter shared their body mass in this early phase but Sherry had seemed very vague about when exactly Lucy would assume some kind of autonomous physical development. Perhaps the proposed transition to solid foods was a good sign.

"It is all going to be all right, isn't it Sherry?"

"Listen, Jonno. We have a beautiful daughter who turns one next week. Pretty soon she'll be walking and talking and no doubt wrapping you around her little finger. I'd say that was pretty bleedin' marvellous, wouldn't you?"

I nodded and *wrapped* my arms around *her*. It was. And I would never be able to thank her enough.

38

Lucy took to solid food with the enthusiasm of a naturalist set down on the shore of a pristine island wilderness. Every bite was a new adventure and every novel flavour a cause for excitement. Turning the baby rusks around in her little fists, she would jam them into her mouth and then giggle at the sensation of the crumbs as they melted on her tongue. And she never once cried from discomfort once the food began to make its way through her system. If her mother had had issues with food, she was not going to follow suit.

She was also growing rapidly and it wasn't long before she pulled herself up onto her tiny feet and took her first faltering steps. I held my arms out to her and beamed with pure happiness as she wobbled into them. It was a moment I would never forget. Sherry, meanwhile, was missing it all. It seemed so unfair. All I could do was describe our daughter's milestones to her- and I had never been great with words. And then it hit me. Why was I telling her about it when I could show her? I cursed myself for being such an idiot and rushed out and bought a video camera that very afternoon. After that, I filmed as many of her waking moments as I could, sharing them with Sherry once our daughter was tucked up for the night. It wasn't the same as being there but it was way better than my feeble attempts at narration.

I watched Sherry's expression as she saw her daughter's waking moments for the first time. Her face was crinkled in concentration and reminded me of someone trying to remember who the person they saw in the picture in front of them was.

"It's unbearable that you are missing out on so much..." I said, squeezing her fingers.

"It won't be forever," she replied with a little smile.

"Thank goodness, because you look as though you're wasting away as it is."

It was no joke. Lately, Sherry had become so weak that she had begun to struggle to get up from the bed. Her sunken cheeks put me in mind of one the students in our department who was rumoured to be suffering from anorexia even though I knew full well that she was consuming as much vodka as ever. Yet she would only ever brush off my concerns, telling me not to be such an old fusspot. I put my arm around her shoulders and tried once more.

"Seriously though, Shez. I wish you'd take better care of yourself. I know you keep telling me that everything is going to plan but you're beginning to worry me."

She turned her head away from the flickering video images and fixed me with an earnest stare.

"It's worth it, isn't it? Lucy, I mean."

"Well, of course, it is. And look, don't get me wrong, I don't mean to sound ungrateful, not at all, but the truth is, I miss you. I miss *us*. Does The book give any indication how much longer it will take for Lucy to exist independently - of you, I mean."

Sherry shook her head and looked back at the screen.

"Show me the bit where she stands up and toddles towards the camera again, I want to see the look on your face as you watch it, and did she really say Dada?"

"I think so. It's a bit difficult to tell…"

Happily, watching our daughter together every evening seemed to do Sherry a world of good. She looked brighter and, to my relief, the easy closeness I thought we had lost, seemed to return. I only wished that the idea of getting the video camera had occurred to me earlier.

A couple of weeks later Sherry sat me down and asked me for a favour. *She had been worrying about The Mausoleum, oh it was secure enough she knew, but she would just like to check up on it. And she missed it. She knew it was a bit of a risk but if we stayed close to the house, we were extremely unlikely to bump into anyone we knew - and besides we had been away long enough to avoid raising any eyebrows about the presence of a baby.*

Nothing easier, I had replied. *The term break was coming up. We could set off on a Sunday morning to avoid the traffic and be there by early afternoon. We could pack the car and take everything we might need with us. That way we wouldn't need to venture out, once we got there.*

Sherry threw her arms around my neck and thanked me. *She knew that she'd been a bit run down lately but she had a feeling that seeing the old house again would be the perfect tonic. She had put so much work into cataloguing its memories that it had become a part of her. A part she was eager to share with our daughter.*

I couldn't help raising an eyebrow at this last comment. I wondered what Lucy would make of it, and how she would react to the touch and feel of those objects to which Sherry was so intimately connected.

"Do you know? How Lucy will react, I mean," I asked.

Sherry had shaken her head.

"I assume that she shares the same capacity but I can't be sure. She's not that mobile yet, so it shouldn't present too great a problem. But if it puts your mind at rest, we can take the playpen with us, just in case."

I nodded in agreement although I did not feel altogether relaxed about the idea. The prospect of my eighteen-month-old daughter having to cope with an avalanche of confusing images and sensations every time she touched something was rather alarming.

"And you are really up to the journey. Honestly Sherry - I know you've been looking better lately but you still seem as weak as a kitten to me. You never said that this whole having a baby business would take so much out of you. I don't like to sound like a nag but - this shrinking business, is it normal?"

I grimaced. *Normal?* There I went again. The words sounded absurd, even to me.

"Sorry," I added, "I just feel so in the dark about it all."

"Trust me. Jonathon. It will all work out in the end. Being back in the house will help, I just know it. Lucy will be fine and besides I may not be – that is, there may not be another suitable opportunity for quite a while."

As ever I capitulated to Sherry's logic. She had got us this far and seemed to know what she was doing. Most of all, I just wanted her to be happy.

The journey from Manchester was uneventful but long and tedious. Sherry did her best not to fall asleep so that Lucy would not awaken and distract me from the road ahead, but I could see she was struggling to keep her eyes open. I pictured the time when we could finally all be awake together. Meanwhile, I was obliged to open a window to let some fresh air in and nudge Sherry gently in the side every time I sensed that she was nodding off. By the time we reached Luton, I had resorted to turning up the volume on the radio in the hope that the sounds of Kylie Minogue, UB40 and MC Hammer on Radio 1 would chase away her drowsiness. It must have helped because she only nodded off once or twice and then only long enough for Lucy to whimper and yawn before closing her eyes again.

"Well, here we are, at last," I exclaimed as I swung the car into the driveway. Sherry sighed with relief.

The Mausoleum looked exactly as it always did, except for the metal security gratings we'd had installed on the ground floor windows and doors. It had cost an arm and a leg, but we could hardly have left the place uninhabited for so long. It would have been tantamount to issuing an open invitation to every burglar and would-be squatter in the post-code. It didn't look very pretty but then The Mausoleum was never going to score a spread in Home and Garden magazine. For all that, I was surprised at how glad I felt to see it again.

Sherry searched for her keys while I got out and walked around the front of the car to open her door for her. She stumbled stiffly out of her seat and set to work on the heavy security locks whilst I lifted Lucy from the back seat and placed her against my shoulder. She had been sleeping for hours and I already missed her smile. "Not long now," I whispered, kissing her cheek as I picked up the shopping bag that had lain on the floor below her.

Inside, the hallway smelt a little musty. The old place needed a good airing. Sherry began to open doors but I waved her onwards. I handed her a bottle of vodka.

"Never mind that now. We can put the central heating on and that should help. You head on down to the kitchen and have a drink. I'll fetch the stuff from the boot presently and then you can have a good long sleep while I take care of her nibs."

Sherry kissed me gratefully and patted the baby on the back. She flicked on the hallway lights and made her way along the passage, putting one hand out to steady herself as she went. The warm glow of the electric light bulbs transformed the space, igniting the old house back into life. I stood in the hallway for a moment and looked at her old gloves hanging on the wall near the door. I shook my head and cuddled Lucy then followed after her.

Down in the kitchen, I noticed the old phone on the wall. I lifted the receiver up and held it to my ear.

"Well, what do you know?" I grinned. "Still connected. Good old Sykes and Skynner, huh? Still paying the bills."

Sherry didn't reply but stumbled slightly as she made her way to the chair, grabbing onto the counter for balance. Shifting Lucy up onto one shoulder, I replaced the phone and guided Sherry safely onto the seat. I poured her a vodka and handed it to her. She accepted it wordlessly and tipped it wearily to her lips. She was going to need a hand getting up the stairs. Hell, I might even have to carry her. Meanwhile, the first thing I needed to do was grab the playpen from the car. I looked at Lucy's sleeping face and smiled.

"There's no way I'm letting you loose in here," I whispered. "Not for thirty seconds."

A couple of days passed and Sherry did indeed seem to rally a little, especially in the evenings when she would drift from room to room like someone in a dream, seeming almost to draw energy from the objects she had once done her best to avoid. Left alone she would study The Book and revisit the entries in the inventories she had left concealed behind the dresser. Mornings remained a bit of a struggle though and I encouraged her to stay in bed for as long as she liked whilst I enjoyed time with Lucy, who seemed strangely oblivious to her change in surroundings. If she was affected by anything in the house, then she didn't show it. Nevertheless, I did my best to steer her away from anywhere except the kitchen and our bedroom and was not beyond popping her into the playpen if I had to leave her alone for even a moment. We had meanwhile, decided that the risk of running into anyone on the common who might know me was extremely low, so opting to take Lucy out for a daily stroll in her pushchair was a no-brainer.

Early on the fourth morning of our stay, however, I woke up to the sound of Lucy crying out. I looked around in panic and saw a surprised-looking Lucy sitting next to Sherry, who was lying on the bedroom floor. I rushed over and shook her gently but had a job to wake her. I felt my pulse race as I shook harder until she finally opened her eyes. I looked at Lucy, ready to catch her as she keeled over, but she just went on staring at me too. But the next minute her head drooped and she was gone.

"Did you see that, Shez? Did you? It was just a few seconds but you were both conscious at the same time. But what happened to you? You had me worried sick there. I – oh never mind what I thought. Are you okay?"

Sherry managed a brittle smile.

"Now don't nag me, Jonno. I'm fine. Or, at least I will be after a good long bleedin' kip. As for Lucy - it's wonderful. Don't you see, we're nearly there. Lucy is beginning to individuate. I *am* feeling pretty spent, but that's partly due to the change in our routine and the fact that Lucy is so much more active, now, both physically and mentally."

I listened to her and it dawned on me, for the first time, that since Lucy was awake whilst Sherry slept then, technically, Sherry had no real rest of any kind. When I looked at it that way, it was a wonder she was functioning at all. I helped her into bed and volunteered to take Lucy out for a walk in the pushchair so that we did not disturb her. I realised that this was no real solution, but I could at least see to it that Lucy did not overexert herself physically.

It was a lovely day outside. The sun was shining but not so fiercely that we needed to stick to the shelter of the trees. Normally, I would have crossed over the road to the Common and made for the pond but that morning, I found myself wandering down the side roads towards Manor Park Cemetery, where Mum had been cremated. It was such a peaceful place and Lucy would not get overexcited by the sight of ducks and geese. At the same time, it seemed strange to be back there again.

The only time I had returned since that difficult day had been with Mrs Worth to plant a small rosebush in the garden of remembrance. It had seemed a bit of a half-arsed way to mark the passing of an entire life to me, back then, but then again neither Mum nor I subscribed to the notion of an afterlife and she had always loved roses. It had been Mrs Worth's idea in any case and, in retrospect, I suspect it was more for her sake than my own. Still, that morning, I felt pleased that we had left some abiding memorial of her and I was genuinely curious to see how the rosebush had fared. I remembered that it had been an apricot cream, a colour my Mum would have loved.

I smiled down at Lucy and guided the pushchair through the towering wrought iron gate and along the gravel path to the chapel and the little garden of remembrance. Lucy was a little too young for explanations but loved the statues of angels and cherubs and pointed in glee whenever we passed one. I didn't however have much luck finding my mum's rosebush. I didn't see any reason why it shouldn't be there, but there were just so many clustered together in the cramped garden bed and I couldn't see her name on any of the little metal plaques. Then again, I wasn't sure that we'd had one made. I knelt next to Lucy and pointed out the pretty flowers with a heavy sigh. My mum's name on a silly little plaque hadn't felt important at the time but, suddenly, all these years later, I wished I'd thought to do it, after all.

I shook my head and wiped my eyes. I needed to sit down and find somewhere to give Lucy a drink. I looked around for a bench. The cemetery was all but deserted at this time of the day so we would have our pick. I headed for a spot in the shade of a towering larch tree. It was the kind of tree that begged to be climbed. I smiled and told Lucy that I would teach her to climb trees when she was a bit bigger. She chuckled and I teased her that she would turn out to be a bit of a tom-boy like her mother. I took her bottle out of the buggy pocket and handed it to her. Just then a grey squirrel lolloped into view. Lucy squealed but it seemed in no hurry to move on. "Squirrel," I said slowly and distinctly. "Schwiffal," echoed Lucy and everything seemed all right.

The schwiffal put on quite a show gambolling around between the graves and running up and down the tree and I would have been happy to sit there just following his antics for hours. However, we had only been watching him for a few minutes when I suddenly experienced an unsettling feeling that we, ourselves, were being observed. I reached for Lucy and undid her safety strap. I hoisted her out of the stroller and pulled her onto my lap. She smacked her lips in delight but then, all at once, her smile froze and she began to wail. I hugged her close to me and tried to soothe her but she just held her little hands over her ears and wailed some more. I looked around in alarm. There, a little behind us stood a tall elegantly dressed man. I had not seen him for years but there was no mistaking my father.

"Dad...?" I breathed. "What on earth are you doing here?"
Julian raised an eyebrow.

"Hullo, Jonathon. It's a fair question. I sometimes come here to – well, you can believe it or not, but I miss her – still. I do. And don't ask me how, but I somehow sensed that you were back and were close by. You – not Sherry. It doesn't make sense and I can't explain it, but there it is. It's certainly good to see you, Jonathon. Not exactly the reunion I was hoping for, but ..." he shrugged sadly.

I frowned. Lucy's wailing had subsided into a hoarse whimper. I hugged her to me. I had to admit that he seemed sincere. After all, there didn't seem any other explanation for his presence. And it was then that I realised that I felt a sense of relief. He was the one person in the world who might have an understanding of what I was going through.

"I suppose I should introduce you to your granddaughter..."
I looked down at my daughter and kissed the top of her head. Julian too fixed his eyes upon her for the first time but his reaction could not have taken me more aback. He blanched and physically staggered a little. I could see that he was lost for words which seemed in itself entirely unprecedented, but I could make no sense of it. I rose from the bench and started towards him but halted in my tracks. Lucy had begun to wriggle uncomfortably in my arms. Julian raised a hand.

"No, stop. Do not bring her any closer, I beg you. If it's true, though I can hardly believe what I am seeing – Jumbo, tell me I'm wrong. Tell me she didn't do it?"

"I'm sorry? Who didn't do what?"

"Tell me that Sher-Ton, I mean - your wife did not..." He seemed unable to continue, passing his hands over his face. Something close to a groan escaped his lips.

"It was The Book, wasn't it? She found the book. I assumed she would never be able to decipher its meaning without access to our memories, but she's found a way, hasn't she?"

I nodded wordlessly. Lucy began crying softly. I stroked her hair and looked away.

"And does she - do *you*, understand the implications?"

I looked back at his face and swallowed hard. My mouth felt suddenly dry.

"You're frightening me, now Julian. Sherry did find something in an old book. She told me it was your way of reproducing; that you don't generally feel the need to reproduce because you are in effect immortal, but that it *is* possible."

"Renewal - not reproduction," corrected Julian. "When a shapeshifter wishes to complete a cycle of consciousness..."

"What are you talking about? What do you mean -"complete a cycle of consciousness"? Why on earth would Sherry want to do such a thing? She's happy - *we* are happy. You're not making any sense..."

Julian raised his hand to hush me.

"Let me finish, son. You wouldn't believe how insanely dull a thousand years of life can become. After a while, we crave excitement, something different. Anything to relieve the monotony of going on being and shifting shape is no longer enough. Why do you think I got myself involved with gangsters and the East End underworld? The buzz we get from the danger is like taking speed, for us. Occasionally, we happen upon more pleasant distractions like falling in love with a mortal, as I did with your mother – but that is rare and look how I screwed that one up. Besides, love with a mortal cannot last and ends only in loss and further desolation. Eventually, we succumb to melancholia altogether and actively seek the peace of oblivion, but our ending is only the completion of a cycle. Even as we unburden ourselves from one stale state of consciousness, we can create a fresh one."

"What are you saying?" I cried, growing a little wild. "Sherry hasn't grown tired of life. She is still here, back in our house. You must have it wrong…"

Julian shook his head.

"There can be no mistake. The process involves dividing off our physical cells until there is a critical mass that is capable of developing a new and discrete consciousness. Generally, the transition is quickly completed and is both painless and peaceful. The new self emerges and then absorbs what remains of the original corporeal entity. This child, here, is still mostly an extension of your wife, separate in space though not in substance. I can feel her."

"Action at a distance…" I breathed.

"Sorry?"

"On, nothing. It's a thing in quantum physics – just one of the wacky bits. It had quite a bit to do with my area of research as it happens. But listen to me. I know about the new consciousness thing. Sherry and Lucy, here, were both fleetingly awake and aware earlier today. They will both continue to exist once Lucy completes the transition."

Julian shook his head again and this time I saw a thousand years' worth of sadness in his face.

"I can feel that the process is at a critical stage. This new entity is teetering on the cusp of true sentience. It is a transition that generally takes a day or two at most yet your wife has found a way to manipulate the process beyond recognition. I cannot fully explain it and I can sense the pain that Sherry has endured to bring this about but, trust me, there is no way that both can survive once it is complete."

I looked into his eyes, praying to see deceit there, but there was none.

"Look, son. Sherry may have found a way to extend the transition and the will to endure it somehow but, mark my words, once the transition of her consciousness is complete, physically, she will wither and dwindle before your eyes until almost nothing viable remains. If this child is to grow physically at anything like a normal human rate, you will have to endure witnessing your wife's protracted and irreversible demise."

I looked down at Lucy, who clung fiercely to my neck. She seemed so solid, so full of life, just as Sherry had always been. And then I thought of the Sherry, sleeping back at The Mausoleum. The sunken cheeks; the loss of height and mass. The recent weakness and confusion. I wondered how I could have been so oblivious to the catastrophe my wife had set in motion. And then I wondered what could have driven her to do it. I felt my eyes fill with tears. I knew the answer to that well enough. We had been happy but I had wanted more. I pressed my head against Lucy's and felt something break inside me. I looked up at Julian.

"We have to stop her. Do you hear me? Help me, Julian, you've got to help me…"

Julian stared down at his feet and sighed.

"It's not that easy. Even if there was a way to halt the process now, your child would never grow, never develop her full faculties and Sherry would be unable to sustain the terrible strain of maintaining two consciousnesses. I'm sorry but it *is* already too late. The transition may just about be reversible but they cannot both survive this. You must choose between them."

I squeezed my eyes shut and pressed my face into Lucy's hair. Julian's voice became soft, gentle almost.

"I'm sorry, my son. I never intended to fail you as a father but I have done so twice, now. Firstly, by deserting you, though at the time I thought I was doing the right thing. And secondly, by failing to tell you both the truth about Sherry."

I opened my eyes.

"What truth? What are you talking about? And what does it have to do with Sherry and what she has done?"

"Everything. I was not entirely honest when I said that I broke contact with Sher-Ton My-Am to teach them a lesson. There was an element of truth in that, but it was more for their protection than anything else. Sher-Ton was an invaluable assistant to me back in the day. She ran one of my clubs, sometimes as a manager, sometimes as a croupier. She was very popular with the punters and they trusted her. They weren't all east-end lowlifes, we had a very mixed clientele as you will already know. Sher-Ton kept her ears open and her wits about her and made sure our celebrity clientele did not run afoul of our, shall we say, less salubrious patrons. She was very fond of Bobby Moore who was a regular in both my establishments…"

I rolled my eyes. That name. It seemed to have haunted me my entire life.

"Everybody loved him," continued Julian. "He was one of nature's true gentlemen and - well, in any case, the East End was changing rapidly at that time. In 1969 The Krays were jailed, opening up a power vacuum. All kinds of vermin crept out of the sewers to fill it. In August 1970 Moore received an anonymous letter demanding ten thousand knicker or they would kidnap his kids. He was devastated. He withdrew from playing football and for a while there, the whole family became virtual prisoners in their own home. About that time Sher-Ton got wind that some small-time cock-roach, Teddy Rogers, had been boasting about his involvement. She grassed on him to The Met. It was a big mistake. Rogers had cobbled the letter together but was acting for The Krays while they were inside. The twins were not happy about it. I knew it would not take them long to trace the grass back to the club, the Krays may have been banged up but they still had plenty of bent coppers on their payroll, so I pulled her out.

I banished her to the old house in her male form and took her memories. No one was looking for a middle-aged man, so I judged she would be safe enough. I also thought it might teach her not to meddle. There was, of course, a good chance that I might fall under suspicion. Ronnie and Reggie had never had a problem with me but were notoriously paranoid. I wasn't taking any chances. It wasn't myself I worried about, though, it was you and your mother.

I lost no time in disassociating myself from you both. It wasn't so difficult. Margot the glamourous socialite was barely recognisable as the plain single mother, especially when I moved you both into that little house near the park. I had always made it my business to keep particulars about my life closely guarded and knew that I could rely on Messers Sykes Skynner and Sykes for their complete discretion in managing my affairs. Margot had had a part-time job there, since before you were born, which made it perfect, as it meant that they could keep me in the loop as to how she was doing. I'm pretty sure she cherished a hope of returning to complete her legal studies one day, but I guess she never got the chance.

In any case, leaving you and your mother was the hardest thing I ever had to do. I won't deny that I struggled to adapt to the everyday responsibilities of fatherhood, but I loved you both and sincerely wanted to give it a go. At first, I made a point of visiting whenever I could, though I took extreme precautions to ensure no one was watching. But then Margot told me that you were finding the situations too unsettling and asked me to stay away for a while, just until things settled down. I was gutted, of course, but she insisted that we put your well-being first..."

At this point I interrupted.

"I'm sorry but I don't remember being particularly upset and I certainly don't remember her telling me anything of the sort..." Julian eyed me and chewed his lip.

"I have no right to expect you to believe me, but it is the truth, I promise you. I wasn't there for your birth – you came earlier than we had expected and I was away. Men were not exactly welcome in the labour wards in those days, in any case. But the first time I saw you, it was as though something between us just clicked. And believe it or not, you doted on me. From the moment you first began to toddle you would follow me around and used to get very mopey when I was not at home. Margot used to joke that the two of us seemed joined at the hip. Of course, that made it very difficult once I'd moved out. Margot told me that you used to scream the place down after my visits. Had a few terrific tantrums, by all accounts. She wasn't trying to make me feel guilty, either. It got so bad, she became quite worried, especially because you found it difficult to catch your breath. And that's when she told me that it would be better if I stayed away for a while.

I didn't want to – but I agreed. She wouldn't have suggested it unless things had been very difficult. At first, I thought it would just be for a few weeks, but when the weeks turned into months, I realised that she no longer wanted me in your lives. I couldn't fathom it. I knew how much she loved me yet something had changed and it was as though she simply closed the door in my face. Perhaps she thought the risk was too high or that it was simply all too complicated. I don't know because she never explained. When I asked about you, she simply told me that you seemed to have pushed me out of your mind."

I looked away. I didn't recall any of this father-son closeness so perhaps it was the truth. Mum had always said it was my default way of dealing with things – and then there was that dent in the kitchen cabinet door.

"So that was it, was it?" I demanded curtly.

Julian seemed prepared for my anger.

"Looking back, I should have questioned it - fought harder for you both, but I was so utterly crushed that I simply slunk back into the shadows and missed out on all those years of seeing a new life develop and grow. Of course, I made financial provision for you and I suppose I pinned my hopes on the idea that your mother would tell you all about me on your eighteenth birthday when she told you about the Trust Fund, I had set up for you. But I guess she never got the chance and now I'll never know if she even intended to talk to you about me."

I recalled the picture of the two of them together, she had left in the file. She had been going to say something about him, but what that was I, too, would never know.

"But you're not even my *real* father..." I protested.

"You are wrong. I may not have been your biological father, but you are my son and always have been. I feel it, viscerally, even now. Can you honestly tell me that this little one here is any less your daughter because she is not technically your flesh and blood?"

I bowed my head and felt Lucy's cheek against mine. I felt my heart contract within my chest.

"You're right. But we were talking about what Sherry has done and I don't see what the history between you and I has to do with that."

"Well, there was another motive behind my decision to strand Sher-Ton My-Am in the house alone. It was an attempt to escape my past and rewrite my destiny. An increasing number of us had grown tired of our way of life, our interconnection with each other, and the total reliance on another being for one's memories. I told you years ago that many of us left for the USA decades earlier. That was true. Yet the migration did not change anything. I was over there visiting when you were born. We talked of finding more radical ways to break free yet none of us knew if it was even possible to function without access to our memory keepers.

Sher-Ton My-Am had been my memory keeper and my conduit to all the memories stored in that old house. Abandoning them there for a few months seemed the best way to ensure both their and my family's safety but I began to wonder what it would be like to cut them off completely?

I couldn't imagine what it would mean for me and I wasn't entirely sure that Sher-Ton My-Am would even survive it, but when the opportunity arose, it seemed worth the risk. It worked. I lost any access to my historic memories but found I could manage without them. I was free. That same freedom cast Sher-Ton My-Am adrift and memoryless, but it seemed a small cost for independence.

Of course, I did not bargain for Sher-Ton My-Am taking a fancy to you. Perhaps it was the resemblance to Bobby Moore. Perhaps it was some faint imprint of me that I left on you from childhood. Who can tell? It most certainly arose from their sudden and enforced individuation. Our kind craves connectedness and a sense of belonging and tends not to thrive outside the collective mind and this is especially true for those in the lower orders. I failed to factor in the probability that they would seek to fill so fundamental a need and it was careless of me. I can also see that I made a grave error in leaving that damned book within their grasp, though none of our kind has been able to penetrate its meaning in millennia.

As for this relationship that has developed between you, I can't say it didn't shock me when I saw the two of you at Margot's funeral. I thought of intervening then, but it also made for an interesting study into inter-species relations. A study that I have, I now realise, let go too far."

I flinched and stepped back at this last part. If his words had seemed supremely human a few moments earlier, the coldness in this last statement appalled me. Not to mention his treatment of Sherry whom he seemed to regard as entirely dispensable in his schemes.

Furthermore, the nerve he'd touched when he had mentioned my resemblance to Moore was jangling again. The image of Julian dangling those car keys flashed back into my mind. He had categorically denied that Moore had played any part in my conception, but I was beginning to wonder how he could be so certain. Moore's treatment for testicular cancer may have compromised his fertility, but sometimes life will defy medical certainties. If my parents had had the open marriage, I suspected them to have had, then I didn't see how he could be so sure of anything. The questions whirled around my mind, surprising me by how much I still longed to know the answer. I turned away from him. The idea of confronting my father about my suspicions that he'd been a wife-swapper was totally beyond me. Besides, there were more important issues at hand. I turned back. I may not have liked it, but he was the only person in the world who had any comprehension of the choices that faced me.

Julian, meanwhile, drew his own conclusions about my hesitancy.

"Forgive me," he continued, "Perhaps you will think of us as heartless but I assure you that it is the opposite. We love as passionately as humans and those we love become a part of us. I loved your mother; so much so that I thought I could free myself from the need for all others but, in the end, I could not give her what she most needed and I paid the price. Sher-Ton My-Am seems to have found a way but will pay with their very being. Perhaps it is our need to be everything to you that is our true weakness."

I looked at him without speaking. I saw the logic in his words yet still did not want to believe them. He reached inside his coat and took out a card.

"Take my contact details. I know I gave them to you before and you chose not to use them. I promise that I will not intervene without your invitation and I don't know what you will decide, but if you or Sher-Ton My-Am ever need me, if I can ever be of service, you can always reach me at this number and I won't let you down. You have my promise."

I took the card with a nod and placed it in my pocket. Then, thanking the man I still thought of as my father in a tone that came out more formally than I had perhaps intended, I turned on my heel and returned to the bench where I had left Lucy's buggy. She had remained unusually quiet throughout the exchange and was still resting her face against my collar. I slid her back into her seat and peered enquiringly into her eyes. She returned my gaze with a look of unquestioning trust. I looked away and then straightened up, aware that Julian had already moved off. I stole a parting glance over my shoulder and then steered the stroller back to the main gate without another backward glance.

Back at The Mausoleum, I let myself in and headed to the kitchen where I unstrapped Lucy and laid her down in her carry cot. I stroked her face and told her to take a nap then kissed her on her plump little cheek. Her eyes sparkled with pleasure. Next, I raced up to the bedroom where my wife lay sleeping in bed. Her body was so slight now that it hardly disturbed the covers. I wondered what it would be like in another month's time – another year's, another three years. The mental image almost made me want to vomit.

All of a sudden, I was seized by an impulse to run or scream, or weep or just do *something*, but Sherry's eyes were already flickering open.

"You saw him? You saw Julian, didn't you? He was in my dream."

"Never mind Julian. Why didn't you tell me?"

Sherry recoiled at my words but gathered herself and spoke with a coolness that chilled my blood.

"And what if I had? You wanted a child more than anything in the world and I wanted to make you happy because your happiness is more important to me than anything else on the planet. Isn't that what it means to love someone?"

"But I love you - and I love Lucy, but how can I love her when it is at your expense?"

Sherry shook her head sadly. She reached out her hand to me. It seemed so small, already. I clasped it and then hung my head and let it go.

"Sherry, I need to know. What would happen if I chose you?"

"I would re-absorb our child back into myself. But I don't know how I would stand the grief. Do you?"

I avoided the question.

"And if not? If I choose Lucy?"

"Soon now, Lucy's consciousness will take dominance and this one will complete. I'll slip into something like a coma and she can continue to absorb parts of my physical remains until she is fully grown. Eventually, anything left of Sherry will cease to exist, much in the way all humans eventually do. It's always been the price you have been prepared to pay for the gift of having children, hasn't it? Tell me. Doesn't every human woman take precisely the same risk each time she bears a child?"

"To some extent, perhaps. But no, Sherry -no. Your logic is flawed. It may be a *risk*, but it is by no means a certainty. Besides, humans do not generally have it in their power to make such a choice - and it is not fair of you to ask this of me."

"But Jonno, *I* have not asked *you* to do any such thing. It is *I* who made the choice. Oh Jonno, I saw, first hand, the way your mother loved you and realised that there is no stronger and more enduring bond than that which lies between a parent and their child. Lovers come and go but a child is forever. This way, I know that you will always keep me in your life."

I looked at her aghast and then hid my face in my hands.

"I'm sorry. I can't talk about this now…"

I rose from the bed and headed back down the stairs. The last thing I saw, as I turned to close the door, was Sherry staring silently up at the ceiling.

Down in the kitchen I poured myself a large glass of vodka and swallowed a large gulp. I spluttered as it hid the back of my throat. "Fuck!" I pushed the glass to one side and paced around the kitchen. The situation had become like an equation that I couldn't balance. Yet there had to be a solution if I could only see it.

I reached for the notepad and biro I had left lying on the dresser. I started with Julian, jotting down all that I knew or could remember. First and foremost - he was a shapeshifter, not exactly a minor detail. Powerful and perhaps a little ruthless. Certainly, more than a little reckless. He had wanted to be a father yet did not seem to have the first clue what that really meant. He had done what he could to make his wife happy and had then given up on both of us at the first hurdle.

I tapped the pen against my forehead. I'd always wondered how he could have done it - walked away from the woman he seemed to have loved so deeply - and now I found myself obliged to entertain the possibility that it had, after all, been out of love.

For the first time in years, I thought about the events that had unfolded on the day of my eighteenth birthday. Mum had been about to tell me something - something very important about my father and then Julian had turned up at the funeral only days later.

I had always been convinced that she had been about to reveal the truth about my father but perhaps there had been more – much more. For the first time since I'd lost her, I wondered whether my mum had harboured hopes that we could be reunited as a family, once I was old enough to understand the truth about my unusual origins. It wasn't wholly ridiculous. I knew how sorely she missed him. I suddenly recalled how I had overheard her talking out loud to him, the evening before. Perhaps she truly was hoping for a reconciliation. It would go a long way to explaining her Mum's disorganisation that day. She had forgotten to collect my special cake before the bakery closed. Not such a big deal in itself but it was very unlike her to overlook such an important detail, unless perhaps she had been preoccupied by something very much more important.

I thought back to our conversation earlier. Julian had sworn that he loved us both. I found myself wondering whether he had somehow pinned his hopes on a reconciliation, too. Back at the time of Mum's death Julian had simply struck me as being an obnoxious git yet today, for the most part, he had been altogether different. Thinking about it, it was possible that, back then, he had simply been trying to mask his disappointment and vulnerability. Perhaps I had been mistaken about him.

At the same time, I had to admit that, only that morning, he had shown unforgivable indifference regarding Sherry's fate. I felt myself bristle with resentment. Still, it would be foolhardy to allow my anger about that to negate the other positives completely. And he had at least tried to protect her.

I chewed the end of my pen. The guy was complex, that was for sure. Still, the empathy he had expressed was genuine. I couldn't have doubted it if I'd wanted to. Not if I was being fair. And it was not so much what he had said as *how* he had been with me. I had felt a connection with him, I couldn't explain. A connection that was still resonating within me, if I was honest. Surely, the Julian, to whom I had spoken today was the Julian, my mum had known and loved. It had to be, otherwise her attachment to him seemed wholly inexplicable.

I looked back through my notes. When I added it all up, it led to one conclusion. For years, I had written my father off as vain and incapable of any real feelings. Perhaps I had misjudged him, after all.

I refilled my glass and sat at the kitchen table. Lucy was sleeping soundly so Sherry must still be awake. I stared into my drink and did a mental recap of my arguments. They seemed sound enough but were only the first half of the equation.

My thoughts returned to Sherry upstairs on the bed. I took up my pad and pen and started afresh on a blank page. I wrote her name and scrawled a question next to it but then hesitated. I wanted to stick to the facts but doubted if I could be completely objective, right then. I was still reeling from the discovery that she too had been planning to abandon me all along. She, who had been my whole world for years. My best friend, my lover, my wife and my family. I couldn't begin to imagine myself without her and the realisation that she had been planning to opt out of our life together had stunned me like the shock of a physical blow. Yet, the numbness in my heart must already have been wearing off. I looked at the question again. *Is she as capable of love as a real human?* I shook my head. I already knew the answer.

There could be no doubt that shapeshifters felt love as deeply as any human, I had seen it in my father's face when he had spoken of my mum and every day in Sherry's unflagging devotion. I could even see it there at the centre of her misguided but undeniable logic. Sherry had borne Lucy out of love and her desire to make me happy and her actions had created still more love. I had never imagined that I could care for something the way I cared for Lucy and her arrival in our lives had only made me love Sherry more.

Nonetheless, that love was tearing me in two now and yet there she lay upstairs, expecting me to stand helplessly by as she simply dwindled away into nothingness. I shuddered. The image pulsated in my brain like a scene out of a horror movie. Still, the alternative seemed no less awful. The equation could not be balanced, no matter what I did - in which case, there could only be one solution. I drained my second glass of vodka and slammed it down on the table.

The noise must have roused Lucy as she woke suddenly with a little hiccup. I leaned over the bassinet and gazed down at her, wondering if that meant her mother had fallen asleep. She gurgled sleepily and smiled up at me with eyes the size of grapes. She seemed for all the world like a perfectly normal baby but I suddenly found myself wondering just how much she truly understood. I picked her up and she reached eagerly for my cheek. I nibbled her fingers and then laid her gently against my shoulder, not sure I could look her in the face. I glanced around the kitchen with a sigh and carried her out into the hallway and up the stairs.

I tiptoed along the landing and peered around the door of our old bedroom. Sherry lay asleep in the bed. I thought back to the first time we had spent the night there and almost sobbed out loud. I clutched the frame of the door, not sure that I could see it through, but then the nightmarish image of my wife withering slowly away came to my rescue. I exhaled sharply and slipped noiselessly inside.

Lucy had started to fidget as I crossed the room, but as I placed her on the bed next to Sherry, she immediately became very calm. She placed her thumb in her mouth and snuggled closer to her sleeping mother, who instinctively shifted and folded her body around her. I noticed that two of them appeared to be breathing in perfect synchronicity. For a second, I wondered if they might both be asleep, but as I bent closer, I saw that Lucy's eyes were wide open and that she was watching me closely. I swallowed hard and turned away.

I grabbed my hold-all from a chair in the corner of the room and hastily stuffed a few things into it. Then, leaning over the bed, I kissed the two beings I loved most in the world.

"Forgive me," I whispered, "but I can't do this and I won't be part of it anymore."

If Lucy understood she gave no sign and continued to observe me steadily as I stepped softly out of the room and closed the door behind me.

Back in the kitchen, I looked around in a kind of daze. Talking myself through the next steps, I placed the rest of my belongings in my bag and then reached into my pocket for the little card that Julian had given me. I stared at the printed letters and numbers and then placed it in the middle of the kitchen table. I looked at the phone but shook my head. Not yet. Not without some kind of closure. Words seem so inadequate yet they were all I had. I hunted around for a pen and then picked up the card and scrawled words, I had never thought I would say, on the back.

"Sherry, I'm truly sorry. I'm leaving you In Julian's hands. You must trust him, now."

I couldn't even bring myself to sign it. Turning to the phone I picked up the receiver and then dialled the numbers on the front of the card. The phone on the other end rang out twice and then there was a click.

"Hullo?"

"Dad – it's me. I'm leaving. Sherry and Lucy need you – as soon as you can."

There was no big discussion, no explanations or apologies

"I'm on my way, Jonno. Go now and leave the door unlocked for me. And, son, take good care of yourself."

I couldn't thank him. I couldn't even say Goodbye. I hung up the phone and placed the card back on the table. Then, collecting up my holdall and car keys, I made my way along the hallway as quietly as I could.

I opened the front door and peered out. The street appeared as empty as my future. I shook my head and stepped into it.

39

It was a damp and miserable Friday evening. Four long, lonely weeks had passed since I had returned to Manchester without my wife and daughter. I was sitting in the front room watching the early evening news on TV. I had no interest in what the newsreader was saying but anything seemed better than the numbing silence that had filled the little two-up two-down of late. I'd already drained my first can of Tenants Super for the night and was just nodding off when I was startled by a ring on the doorbell. I froze and then belched as my stomach turned a somersault. It might be Sherry. *Oh, let it be Sherry*, I breathed. But this was the lager talking. I refused to regret my decision - it had been the only logical course of action open to me. At least, that was what I told myself every evening when the price began to feel too high.

It didn't stop me from hoping though. I stared at the front door in confusion. The chimes rang out again. I switched the TV off and hurried to the door, shaking my head as I went. Empty bottles and takeaway containers lay scattered around the living room along with discarded socks and shoes. The place was a tip. But there was no one to care except myself, and *I* did not. It was enough that I managed to get myself along to the university each day, although even that was a struggle on my bad days.

I opened the front door and stepped back in astonishment. A woman in a raincoat stood hunched beneath the shelter of the little porch.

"Joan? What on earth brings you here?"

"Can I come in Jonathon? I need to speak to you." Joan shook some droplets off her umbrella and propped it up against the lintel of the door.

"Me? Why on earth would you need to speak to me and what could bring you – no, wait. It isn't Sherry, is it?"

My head was spinning. I could hear my voice rise almost an octave. Joan reached out a hand.

"No, Jonno. Isn't Sherry here with you?"

I screwed up my eyes and then looked away.

"Sherry's gone," I muttered. "Lucy too."

Joan's face fell.

"I'm so sorry Jonathon. I didn't know." She paused as though deliberating. "I'm here on quite a different matter, as it happens. And I don't want to bother you, but I *have* come rather a long way to tell you. But, look, would you mind if we went inside? It's a bit delicate."

I nodded and ushered her in. I noticed her eyes sweep the room but she made no comment.

"Make yourself at home. I'm sorry if it's a bit messy. Can I get you a cup of tea or something – though I'm not sure we have any milk. I'm sorry."

"Maybe later, then. I could pop out and get a few things if that would help," she replied removing her damp coat and looking around for a coat peg. Her voice was kind and calm and I remembered how helpful she had been at Mum's wake. I pointed to the row of hooks next to the front door and hurriedly cleared the debris from last night's supper off the armchair.

"Well, sit down at least. You must be exhausted. Have you really come all the way here from London? Can I offer you anything at all?"

She loosened the chiffon scarf around her throat and sat down.

"A glass of water would be nice, thanks."

I rushed into the kitchen to find a clean glass and filled it from the tap. When I returned, she was sitting where I had left her but was tugging at a handkerchief she must have taken from her handbag. She thanked me for the water and sat cradling the tumbler in her hands.

"Are you okay, Joan? You look very serious."

"Do I? Perhaps you're right. I have something to tell you, Jonathon and it's not going to be easy for you to hear. I had thought that there might be a slight chance that Margot – but I can tell from your reaction to me being here that she never got around to telling you herself. I hadn't wanted to bring it up before, what with losing her so unexpectedly and everything, but there's a never a good time for these things, is there? Anyway, I've thought about it long and hard but I believe that you are entitled to know the truth..." She took a long sip from the glass.

"The truth about what?"

"About your origins."

My thoughts began to race. The idea that she knew about Julian and even Sherry would not so farfetched. She worked in the solicitor's office that dealt with my father's business and she had known my mum for years. It had never really occurred to me until now, but there must have been other people who were in on the secret of the shapeshifter's existence, besides me and Mum.

"Julian, you mean?"

"Well, indirectly, I suppose. But I was thinking more about your mum – Margot."

My head began to spin afresh. I had not seen that coming and couldn't begin to imagine where she was heading with it. I went to protest but she reached out a hand and shushed me.

"I'm going to tell you a story, Jonno and I want you to hear me out before you say anything, okay? You can ask me any questions once I'm done, but I just need to get it straight. Can you do that? This isn't easy for me and that would be really helpful."

I nodded and waited. She took a deep breath and started her story.

"You wouldn't think it but your mum and I are – I should say, were –pretty much the same age. I know that I must have looked pretty dowdy next to her, even after she had stopped making an effort, but I was not unattractive in my twenties. Anyway, when I first started working for Skynner, Sykes and Skynner, your mum was already working there part-time and immediately took me under her wing. She was incredibly glamorous and was married to this man who seemed almost as glamourous himself. I knew that they had a big house and loads of money and I couldn't understand why she would bother with a job at all, but Margot insisted that she had worked hard for her education and was not going to squander it altogether. I looked up to her and even tried to model myself on her, copying the way she wore her make-up and hair and so forth. I think she found it touching in a way. She certainly never made fun of me or teased me for it.

To be honest, despite the fact that she and Julian seemed to frequent an awful lot of cocktail and dinner parties, I got the impression that she never had many female friends. Indeed, I soon discovered that beneath the social façade she remained a deeply private person.

In any case, our relationship developed from work colleagues to friends. She would keep me amused by relating anecdotes about the sophisticated circles in which she moved, the VIPs and the toffs and those she referred to as the *nouveau riche* and social climbers. As often as not, she would poke fun at the arrogance and hypocrisy of many of those with whom they rubbed shoulders, but I just found the sound of it all increasingly alluring.

I began to beg her to take me along to one of the parties. At first, she simply refused but I guess that I eventually succeeded in wearing her down. She invited me along to a house party she was attending one weekend. It was at the house of a popular TV personality who lived out Essex way. She told me that there would be some high-profile sporting personalities there, as well as a bunch of fashion models and the odd pop star and offered to take me along with her. She said that I would be doing her a favour as she didn't want to turn up alone. Julian was obliged to take care of some business at one of his casinos first and had arranged to meet her there later. I didn't much care about that. I had never met him in person and was far more interested in the prospect of mixing with a bunch of celebrities.

Margot was not so easily impressed – or enthusiastic. She warned me in no uncertain terms that these occasions could get pretty wild. I knew what she meant. It was the sixties. But I was no prude and it just all sounded so exciting. The irony was, that even as I did my best to be like Margot, deep down I knew that all she really wanted was to settle down and have a proper family life. She had told me as much in her quiet moments. She loved her husband and was desperate to have his child but, apparently, there had been complications."

Joan paused at this point and glanced at me. I nodded. *That much I knew*. She cleared her throat and continued on.

"Well, the night of the party arrived and it turned out to be everything I'd imagined. The clothes, the jewellery, the house. It all seemed fabulous. There was even a swimming pool. I felt as though I'd walked onto the set of a Martini advertisement or something. It all seemed so incredibly sophisticated, yet I somehow felt right at home. Margot had lent me one of her cocktail frocks and some jewellery and had done my make-up and hair for me. You wouldn't have recognised me, Jonathon. Nobody would have.

The booze was flowing like water and the air in some rooms the air was thick with the smell of pot. Several of the male guests flirted openly with me and made no bones about their intentions. And some of them were men I recognised from the papers or had seen on the TV. I lapped it up. It was as if I'd become a different person for the night. Honestly, I felt like Cinderella, I really did. Of course, I'd drunk rather more than I should have but I knew what I was doing, right enough, and declined any number of propositions. I found all the attention intoxicating and that seemed enough for me right then.

Anyway, it was getting really late when this rather striking blonde guy walked in. He glanced around the room and made a beeline for me and then began to chat me up. To be frank, the numbers were beginning to thin out and an awful lot of couples seemed to have disappeared into other parts of the house, but I was nevertheless flattered that he had singled me out. I couldn't see Margot anywhere and was beginning to regret that I resisted one or two of the invitations I had received. I flirted right back and you'll never guess who the guy was. Bobby Moore. The man of the moment himself. Our national hero."

I gasped out loud. That name again. I went to speak but Joan held up a finger, reminding me of my promise to save my questions until she had finished. She took another sip of the water and continued.

"Except that it wasn't him. Moore, I mean. Believe me, I knew. We had grown up as neighbours, attended the same school and even played football in the street together. His mum and dad were practically family. Well, I know I looked a little different, but he didn't even recognize my name. I can't explain it. Perhaps he was one of those celebrity doubles you can hire for big events – *celebrity lookalikes*, I think they call them. Although, if he was, he wasn't letting on. And to be honest I didn't care so I didn't challenge him. I'd always had a little crush on Bobby but the real Bobby Moore was happily married. I knew I was just giving in to some weird alcohol-fuelled fantasy, but to be honest, I didn't care. I'll spare you the details and myself the blushes, but suffice it to say we found an unoccupied guest bedroom and the rest, as they say, is history.

I woke up early the next morning alone and wondering if it had really happened. People always talk about the cold light of day but there is nothing more sobering than the spectacle of a house the morning after a party like that. I'd had my taste of the so-called good life and just wanted to get home. I didn't even try to find Margot but hitched a lift with some other partygoers who were heading back to town. I won't say that I was ashamed of myself, because I wasn't. But I wasn't exactly proud either. The following Monday at work, Margot asked why I hadn't waited for her the next morning – she had been worried. I apologised and just told her that I'd had things to do and left it at that.

Six weeks later however I was forced to face the fact that I had fallen pregnant. It was the last thing I needed. With no one else to turn to, I confided in Margot who was sympathetic and did her best to be helpful. She gave me the number of a doctor who was always willing to help unmarried women but apart from the fact that abortion was still illegal at that time, I had been brought up Catholic and it was out of the question for me. All I could do was try to conceal it for as long as possible, have the child adopted at birth and hope I did not lose my position with the law firm.

I know it sounds heartless, Jonathon, but they were different times, truly. My family would never have supported me and an unmarried mother faced dismissal from their employment and a life of poverty and shame. It was no life to offer a child and it would not have been fair to try. People still referred to such children as 'bastards' for pity's sake. I know that things are changing now, but things really did look very bleak, back then.

Fortunately, your mum was just wonderful. She continued to support me and even went with me to an agency, she knew of, to arrange the adoption. Such things were hardly uncommon. It was a well-oiled machine. They would arrange for me to leave London and stay in a private maternity home for two months prior to the birth. I was to take time off work and then tell them that I had been taken ill and was recuperating in a convalescent home in Kent. It would not come cheap, of course. But once again, Margot stepped in to help and insisted that she must bear some of the responsibility. After all, if she had not taken me to the party, it never would have happened. Even then, I never told her what had actually taken place. I suppose I felt a bit of a fool and, to her credit, she never asked.

Are you okay, Jonathon? You looked terribly perplexed. I hope I haven't shocked you. I'm not proud of myself, believe me..."
Joan had paused and was looking at me in concern.

I rubbed my brows. I had been trying to follow her story but could not see where on earth it was leading. And the puzzle about the guy who looked like Bobby Moore was beginning to seriously bug me. It sounded like Julian, up to his tricks to me, but I could hardly say as much and besides where did Joan's pregnancy fit in?

"It's nothing. Please, continue. I'm just trying to make sense of it all."
Joan shook her hands.

"I'm sorry for being so longwinded, but I think you deserve the whole picture. Well, the point is, a couple of weeks later your mum confided in me that she too was expecting. Only *she* was over the moon about it. Couldn't have been happier. Turns out she and Julian had been trying for a couple of years but she had experienced a number of very early miscarriages. She had already managed to carry this baby for a couple of months, so they were delighted. I was happy for her. I could see how excited she was and now we could support each other. You know, swap tips about morning sickness and swollen ankles. We became very close and so, one day, she suggested that she use the same maternity home as I. Her doctor was recommending three months of bedrest prior to the birth as a precaution, so we would be able to keep each other company. It was perfect for me. I hadn't told a soul except for her and, to be honest, the pregnancy hardly showed, certainly not in the first six months, so nobody guessed. That was as I wanted it, I suppose, but I had felt so alone. Now, I knew I wouldn't have to face the labour alone. As for how I would feel giving up the baby - well, I didn't even let myself think about that.

Well, to cut the story a little shorter, it wasn't long before we found ourselves comfortably settled in a very nice maternity home out in the heart of the Kent countryside. We even travelled down together. As it happened, Margot's husband had been called away to the United States on business. There were still three months before their baby was due and he would be back for the birth. It all seemed to have worked out rather well. We had spent a lazy six weeks or so there when the unimaginable happened. Margot had been confined to bed for the duration of her stay and for good reason. One morning she got up from her bed and stood up, just to stretch her limbs, and then doubled over with a cry of agony. The doctors were there at her side immediately, but there was nothing they could do to save the baby. It arrived almost eight weeks early and stillborn. Margot was inconsolable. The nurses asked if she would like them to send a telegram to Julian in the USA, but she insisted that it would be better to wait until he got back home. It wouldn't be fair to tell him while he was so far from home and had so much to think about.

It took her a while to recover physically and mentally and for a while I felt sick with worry about her. The staff at the maternity home were, however, all very kind and insisted she stay until she was ready to face the world again.

Two weeks later my waters broke. Most first babies are late but this one seemed in a hurry to meet the world. I don't know how she did it, but Margot remained at my side throughout the entire labour. It was a little boy, a tad under-weight, but otherwise completely healthy. I hadn't planned to so much as hold him in my arms but when the midwife held him up for me to see, I couldn't resist. I looked into his perfect little face and felt my heart break inside my chest. How could I give him away and never even know what became of him? Then I looked up at Margot. She was smiling but her face was stained with tears. The solution seemed obvious. I offered her my baby knowing that he would be truly loved and would want for nothing."

I leapt to my feet, hardly believing the words my ears were hearing. I shook my finger at my guest.

"Now, let me get this straight. Are you telling me that you, not Mum, were my mother? Is that what you are saying? That's crazy. And how could you possibly conceal something like that?" Joan swallowed.

"Sit down, Jonathon, I beg you. I know this is difficult to hear but I'll try to answer your questions. If you'll just sit down."

I looked at Joan's face and pulled myself up. I realised that I had been towering over her. I hadn't meant to frighten her but she had freaked me out. I closed my eyes and sat down, indicating that she should continue. She thanked me and drained her glass.

"Believe me those private maternity homes were very experienced in arranging these matters. And Margot and I made a pact to keep it a close secret, even from Julian to begin with. That was her idea by the way. Perhaps she feared that he might reject the idea of an adopted child initially and was more likely to accept the idea, once he grew to love it. I'm not sure. In any case, he was still in the USA and so she simply phoned and told him that the baby had arrived prematurely and without warning. He had no cause to doubt her and just caught the next flight home, no doubt relieved that both his wife and baby were well.

We agreed that she could tell you when you reached eighteen if she felt you were ready, but of course, she never got the chance. We also agreed that I would have no direct involvement in your childhood. I could see how you were getting on but nothing more. I had to agree. Any alternative seemed too painful. I couldn't have played the role of honorary aunt or even godmother, not without giving myself away. The only consolation I had, I suppose, was in seeing how much she loved you and how much you loved her in return. In time, I had hoped that I would marry and have a child of my own, but it was not to be. I guess a part of me never believed that I deserved it. Not after giving you up so easily. Can you ever forgive me, Jonathon?"

I wasn't sure how to respond. I didn't quite see what it was she thought I should forgive her for. But I could see that she needed a reply so I tried to think what mum would have said.

"Well, of course. I never had the slightest idea - and I couldn't have felt more wanted by Mum, you know that. Indeed, I rather think it is you who must forgive yourself, Joan. I have no complaints though I suppose I would have liked a better father – but then, perhaps I might not have had one, at all."

At these words, Joan burst into tears. I jerked backwards, rather taken aback. She dabbed at her nose with a handkerchief and drew herself up.

"Your father? Well, that is a whole other complication, I'm afraid."

I asked her what she meant.

"In all the months we had known about the baby, Margot had never asked me about the father. I suppose she felt it was nobody's business but mine, however, once she took you as her own, I suppose it was natural enough that she should be curious. I told her about my encounter with the Bobby Moore lookalike that night. Her reaction was not at all what I had anticipated. She seemed genuinely shocked. Upset even. I tried to get to the bottom of her reaction but with no luck. And that was when she made me swear that I would never reveal the truth to her husband. I mean, I had nothing to do with the guy anyway but I agreed. Actually, though, I don't think it did her marriage any favours in the long term. Secrets have a way of coming between people and she never spoke about it specifically, but I know she felt guilty about keeping him in the dark. And then when things began to unravel – I suppose, it all became too much."

I shook my head.

"What do you mean by unravel? What else was there?"

Joan sighed.

"Look, I know I said that I accepted that I was not part of your life but that was not completely true. I never really knew Julian. I had seen him come into the office from time to time, but he would generally ignore me or be outright dismissive if I had to address him. To be honest, he always struck me as a bit of an arrogant so-and-so at best. I certainly couldn't see what Margot saw in him and wasn't surprised when they parted ways, although she always spoke as though the separation was only temporary.

I must say that his behaviour at her funeral did little to change my impression of him but, Jonathon, he was completely devoted to you and I know that because, after your Mum moved into the house by the park, I became close friends with Gladys Worth."

"Mrs Worth? Our old neighbour?"

"Neighbour and childminder, Jonathon. Look, I know it was wrong, but it was a way of catching a glimpse of you or just hearing about how you were doing. (She never suspected a thing, I promise). Anyway, she was a bit of a gossip and told me all about it. She said that you had been extremely close to your father and was not coping with the separation very well. In fact, you found the visits so unsettling that eventually Margot and Julian had had to put an end to them. Apparently, you suffered from the most terrible tantrums when he had to leave. I wouldn't have believed it from anyone else, but Gladys lived next door and had frequently heard you screaming for hours at a time. She even used to go around to try and help but claimed there was no calming you down at such times. It was as though you found it physically painful to be parted from him."

I buried my face in my hands.

"I'm sorry, Joan. I'm having a hard time processing all of this. I think I've heard enough for one evening, but perhaps we could talk again – another time. I'd ask you stay to tea but I don't think we have anything in. I don't bother much, these days. I'd be happy to give you a lift to the station though. I've only had one…" I nodded to the cans of 'Superbrew'.

"Thanks Luv, a lift would be great – later, perhaps. But look, it's stop raining out, how about I nip out to the shops and cook you something nice for tea. You look like you could do with a proper meal and I don't like to leave you, just yet. It's been a big shock. We don't have to talk about it anymore, I promise. Not if you don't want to."

I looked at her and nodded my head. She had travelled a long way to speak to me and it seemed the least I could do.

"There are a couple of shops on the High Street, just around the back of us," I said reaching for my wallet.

"You're all right, Luv. My treat. Is there anything you particularly fancy? No? Maybe I'll see if I can get a couple of nice steaks then. Nothing like red meat to build you up. Won't be long."

After she had gone, I sat at the little kitchen table and stared at the walls. My mind whirred like a turbine engine. I had so many questions and so few answers. I recalled the dent in the kitchen cabinet but not how it had got there. And, no matter how hard I tried, I could remember nothing of the so-called tantrums. Yet I had no reason to doubt Joan or even Mrs Worth and Julian himself had told me the same story.

Try as I might, the parts of my life did not add up. Julian claimed to have loved me but had been adamant that he could not be my real father despite the strength of this so-called bond between us. On the other hand, I had always been the spit of Bobby Moore and it didn't take a genius to see that Joan's mysterious doppelganger had been Julian. But that just led back to the impossibility of him being my father.

I tugged at a lock of my hair, straining to make the pieces fall into place and - suddenly they did. All at once, I remembered what Sherry had told me that night when she had been so excited about the information she had found in The Book; that Julian had got it wrong and it was possible for a Shapeshifter to father a child with a human in rare and very particular circumstances.

I willed the words of our conversation to return to my mind:

"...*the only time it could be remotely possible is during the initial few hours following a novel transformation whilst the copies of the genetic code remain extremely accurate and we have replicated every last detail of the original.*"

If The book was correct then it was possible that Julian had obtained some genetic material from Moore and transformed into a perfect copy of the footballer right there at the party. Indeed, the copy may have been more perfect than the original. Everyone knew that Bobby had undergone treatment for testicular cancer but Julian's Bobby would have been a cancer-free version – as Moore had been before he had become unwell. Cancer-free and fertile. All at once, a cascade of pieces tumbled into place.

I held up my hand and examined it. It was just a hand. I willed it to change shape but nothing happened. I tried to think back to when I had been sick or injured as a child. That was easy. My childhood asthma aside, I was never ill and apart from the usual grazed knees had never suffered any injury to speak of. Still there was the asthma. But then I remembered the GP who had suggested a different diagnosis. The one that had annoyed my mother, so. The one who had had the temerity to suggest that my breathing difficulties might be emotional in aetiology.

I leapt from my chair and looked around. I saw the breadknife lying on the side and thought of Sherton Myam's finger and then of Sherry following the seal attack. There was only one way to know for sure. I took the knife and drew it across the flesh of my lower arm. Nothing too drastic. Just deep enough to test my hypothesis. A dark line of blood welled up and began to pump out of the wound. I swore softly. I had managed to nick a small blood vessel. Grabbing a tea towel I applied pressure to my arm and raised it above my head.

I looked down at the crimson liquid that had pooled on the worksurface and nodded. That would be sufficient. I counted two minutes in slow seconds and then lowered my arms. I lifted the towel. The bleeding has stopped. I sighed with relief and then offered my arm to the puddle of my blood.

"Come on, then. Do your thing..." I stared transfixed yet couldn't see so much as the faintest ripple. Not so much as a single cell stirred itself. I exhaled sharply and tried again "Come on. Come on..."

Just then, I heard the front door open and Joan bustle in. She called my name. I looked around in panic but the next moment she was standing behind me. I heard a thud as she dropped her shopping bags. I looked around. Her face was so white that I thought she was going to faint.

"It – it was just a silly accident, Joan. Looks worse than it is. Nothing to worry about, really. I think maybe *you* should sit down though - you look a bit on the pale side. I'm sorry to have alarmed you." But even as I spoke, the wound reopened and blood began to seep out again.

Joan might have appeared rattled but she positively flew into action. Rinsing her hands under the tap, she ferreted about in the kitchen drawer for a clean cloth and pressed it firmly to my arm, then got me to lift it above my head again, whilst she maintained her hold. I was surprised by the firmness of her hands.

"I don't think it'll need a stitch. I have some pretty good sticking plasters in my bag. With luck, they'll do the trick. And you needn't look at me like that, Jonathon. I'm a trained first aider. I volunteer with St. John's Ambulance at all kinds of events. You'd be surprised how handy a plaster can be, sometimes."

I couldn't help smiling. It seemed Joan to a T. She let go of my arm but told me to keep it elevated while she mopped up the blood.

"Now – let's have a look," she said gently when she was done. I rested my arm on the counter whilst she inspected it.

"It looks clean enough," she continued, "but I'll just give it a dab with a bit of antiseptic, to be on the safe side."

She reached for her handbag and delved inside. I grinned. Never mind sticking plasters, she seemed to have an entire mini first aid kit in there. She took out a small sachet of anti-septic wipes, unsealed it and then dabbed carefully around the cut. It stung slightly and I winced.

"It'll do that," she smiled, tearing open a plaster and pressing it firmly over the wound. "There – you'll live. Just keep it still for a while – but what worries me more is how you came by such a nasty laceration. I wasn't born yesterday, you know. It's a lot to take in what with everything else going on, I mean. Perhaps I should have waited or at least prepared you before I broke the news. I'm so sorry Jonathon. I hadn't realised about Sherry and – well, I guess I was just all fired up to tell you, so didn't think it through properly."

"Joan – it's okay. Honestly. It was a bit of a shock, I'll admit, but this is not what you think – I swear. It was just a stupid accident."

"All the same – shock can do funny things to people and you might not have been thinking straight. I think it would be better if I stayed – just for the night. I'll be fine on the sofa. I don't want to make a nuisance of myself but it would put my mind at rest."

I shrugged. I could see that she wasn't going to take no for an answer and besides, I didn't relish the prospect of facing the night alone in that empty house, right then.

"Fair enough. It's been a bit of a day and I realise this wasn't easy for you either. But I insist that you take my bed. I can kip down here on the couch. But I just need a bit of space right now, if that would be okay with you?"

"Of course," she said, leading me into the front room. "You put your feet up for an hour and I'll get the tea on. After that, I can change the bed and get us organized. Maybe have a bit of a tidy round, if you'd like." She glanced around the mess that was my home. I smiled weakly, glad that *someone* was happy. Joan asked the way to the bathroom to powder her nose and minutes later I heard the clink of plates and glasses in the kitchen as she embarked on the herculean task of tidying the kitchen and preparing a "proper meal."

It was a bit of an odd evening. Joan knew how to cook a steak, though I couldn't quite do it justice. It made me think about Sherry and how she would have run a thousand miles at the idea of all that meat lying leaden in her insides. Joan did her best to keep the conversation light yet it was heavy going.

We were, after all, pretty well strangers with nothing in common but a bunch of genes and our memories of my mum.

After tea, she stripped my bed and made it up afresh and then set to work on the sitting room. I tried to help but she sent me off to my study, (Lucy's former bedroom), where I stared at Warhol's picture of my mum in tearless wretchedness.

Later, when I had rallied, I went back down to the kitchen and made us both a hot drink. I thanked her for the meal and for tidying up but was glad when she decided on an early night.

The next morning, she asked to take a look at my wound. "Just to make, sure," she said. I offered up my arm and flinched as she peeled back the sticking plaster.

"Goodness me," she exclaimed." It has already closed up. You must be a very fast healer."

I pulled my arm away in alarm.

"Look, stop trying to mother me - you're not my mum and never could be."

The words had hurt her, I could see. She mumbled some kind of apology and went to collect her things. When she returned, I said that I was sorry and offered her a lift to the station, but she declined. *She liked buses. It was,* she claimed, *the best way to see the city.*

"Well, at least stay a bit longer and have coffee with me..." I said sheepishly.

She nodded her head and sniffed back a tear. I filled the kettle and did my best to make small talk but I was thinking about that wound on my arm.

When the time did come for her to leave, she hesitated and then stepped towards me and shyly embraced me. I couldn't return the hug but patted her on the back. She spoke quietly.

"I'm so sorry, Jonathon. I hardly closed my eyes, last night. Did I do the right thing in telling you?"

I nodded.

"It's cool," I said. After all, they say that the truth is always better than a lie. Yet it didn't feel it. She pursed her lips and made her way to the front door but turned around before letting herself out

"You know I will *always* be there for you if you need me and I'll always be glad to see you. I mean it. Whenever you are ready."

I nodded again.

"Goodbye, Joan and thank you - I guess."

I moved to the window and watched as she walked to the end of the road. The moment she was out of view, I let out a torrent of expletives. I wanted so badly to beat my head against the door, but that wouldn't help anyone so I launched a kick at it instead. It hurt like fuck, but at least the pain sharpened my focus. I just needed to sift through the jumble of ideas and memories that were swirling around in my brain.

I limped back to the other end of the room and flopped onto the sofa. So, my mum *wasn't* my mother and there was a distinct possibility that the father who had disowned me would turn out to be my real father, after all. I wondered how it had all become so convoluted.

If it had seemed patent to me that Julian had impersonated Bobby Moore then it must have been glaringly obvious to her. Yet she had kept the knowledge to herself. Joan assumed that Mum had pushed Julian away out of guilt but perhaps it had been anger - anger that he had lied to her when he told her that he was unable to father a child. It made sense, yet, for all my misgivings about Julian, I couldn't believe that he had knowingly misled her.

I cast my mind back to what Sherry had said. She'd suggested that Julian might have been oblivious to the fact that it was indeed possible for a shapeshifter to father a child. Perhaps she had been right. Just because he knew about a bit about The Book didn't necessarily mean that he had read it all, himself. Which was ironic, because if he had done so, then *he* could have given my mother the one thing she so badly wanted.

Given their permissive lifestyle, I was a bit surprised that this had not happened naturally. But, there again, I might have misjudged him. While he had scant regard for the prohibitions of human morality, I could not doubt how much he loved my mum. Perhaps, like Sherry, Julian had only ever wanted to be himself when he made love to his wife.

I yawned. The whirring in my brain was receding to a dull throb. Something about me was different and I had always known it. All through my childhood, I had felt as though I didn't fit in somehow and maybe that had been because I *didn't*. It was time I faced the truth.

I pulled back my sleeve and squinted at the scar again. The fine red line was already fading. I thought about the blood on the kitchen counter and then about the time I had cajoled Shalto into giving up a drop of blood for me to examine under my microscope. What I saw had amazed me, but the sample I had taken from my finger had seemed wholly unremarkable. The blood I had spilt the previous evening might not have scrambled to get back into my veins but something very unusual was going on. That led me to deduce two likely states of affair:

    1) I might not be a shapeshifter but neither was I fully human, after all.

2) Julian, or one of his kind, must indeed be my father.

It would certainly explain the strong sense of connection Julian had experienced towards me and perhaps even Sherry's. Indeed, as subtle as it was, it may still have been the thing that had drawn Sherton Myam to me in the first place.

I stood up and returned to the window, pushing the net curtain to one side. The street outside was empty. I heaved a large sigh. I'd felt alone all my life and that was precisely how I found myself.

All at once, the thought that I could contact Julian jumped into my mind. I hadn't kept his card but I never forgot a number. But then I thought of Sherry and Lucy. Yet there was no *and*, now - only the sickening *or*, I could never face. I hung my head. No matter what Julian was to me, *that* was a door I would have to keep firmly closed at all costs.

40

The refectory was almost deserted when I walked in. I watched a busboy mop a table. The lad looked no more than twenty and was probably a student at Cal Tech himself. Odd to think the guy clearing away the plates might be destined to make the next breakthrough in M-theory.

I glanced around, a little disappointed. The hall seemed blander than I remembered it - more akin to a workplace cafeteria than a student hang-out. Not that I cared that much. I was tired and thirsty and public speaking always gave me an appetite. The faculty staff had of course invited me to join them for supper in the prestigious Hayman Lounge, but I'd made my excuses. I found the small talk and petty point-scoring increasingly unbearable these days. Or maybe that was just the Americans. We British hadn't been raised to blow our own trumpets quite as loudly as our cousins here in the USA liked to and their excess of self-belief never failed to grate on me.

Still, the talk and ensuing debate had gone well. These kids knew their stuff and were like sponges when it came to new ideas. It almost made me want to be twenty-one again. Almost. There was a lot to be said for middle age, even if it was just that the worst seemed to be over.

I approached the cafeteria food bar and weighed up the options. I asked for a coffee and then pointed to a plate of tuna salad in the chilled cabinet. I had to watch my carbs these days. The woman who served me grunted but smiled and winked as she spotted the visitor's card hanging around my neck.

"You know, you don't have to eat this crap, Honey. Your card gives you access to the Athenaeum's dining room. The food up there is a notch up from what you'll find here."

"Thank you. But I like it just fine where I am. It reminds me of my youth."

"I know what you're saying there, Mister. I'm still waiting for one of you geniuses to come up with a time machine. You can keep 2020. It's been a bad year for me and I don't see it getting much better. But I guess I'll be waiting a while, huh?" She handed me my salad with another wink.

I thanked her and made my way to a corner table. A queue was forming now. It must be the time when the seminar rooms and lecture theatres began to empty for the night. Evening lectures were another big thing here. It made sense when I thought about it. Students in US universities routinely took on one or more menial jobs just to keep body and soul together. They seemed imbued with a work ethic entirely unheard of in *my* day.

I poked at my salad and then almost dropped the fork. Out of the blue, my head had begun to throb like a stubbed big toe. I rubbed my temples and reached for the water jug. It was probably dehydration. That or the jet lag. And then just as suddenly, it was gone.

"Mind if I take a seat?"

I looked up. A tall, athletically built young man wearing a baseball jacket and jeans hovered next to my table. He stood with his back to the light and the baseball hat that he wore, even though we were indoors, (an American custom I found particularly irritating), all but obscured his face. I glanced around me and then back at the young man. I was tempted to wave him away but something stopped me. I forced a smile.

"Well, I guess - though...." I made a gesture with my hand in case he hadn't noticed the plethora of vacant tables he could have chosen.

"Oh, I'm sorry. I meant - would you mind if joined you? I just attended your seminar. Dope, man. Just dope."

I stared at him.

"It means great – cool."

"Thank you, then."

"No, really, I mean it. It's right up my street – or alley, as you might say. You're English right?"

"Street is fine," I replied. I am indeed English though I've been in the States for more years than I care to remember."

He set his tray on the table, seated himself opposite me and took an enormous bite from a hamburger. The smell alone made me regret my choice of salad. He chewed for a while. I watched him from below my lashes as I vainly attempted to spear a lettuce leaf with my fork. He still hadn't removed the cap but I could see that his hair was blonde and curly beneath it.

"I wasn't sure it was you, at first," he drawled, still munching. "No shit – weren't you born back in the sixties? You look so young, man. Close up, I mean. What's your secret? I mean – the sixties- far out? You must have known Feynman. Dope, man. What I wouldn't have given..."

"I've never smoked," I replied, hoping to stem the flow of drivel, "and I avoid spending too much time out in the sun so people often say I look young, but that's because all you Yanks, er, sorry - Californians need to get over the suntan thing. Seriously. It's incredibly ageing and gives you cancer. As for Feynman – I'm sorry to say I never got the chance to meet him. He passed away while I was still completing my doctorate in the UK. He was my number-one hero though - after Peter Parker."

My companion paused mid-chew.

"Ah, right. Spider-man. Gotcha. Must have been neat though. Back then, I mean, before the internet and cell phones. I mean – seriously? It was all about to just explode – I mean – wow, Dude."

"Yeah, wow," I echoed, beginning to feel as though I'd been inadvertently sucked into a Bill and Ted movie. "Although, it all happened so gradually in many ways. Just think, there I was working on the foundations for developing quantum computing when we didn't even have PCs, Microsoft or the internet yet. Hard to imagine it now, although I for one reckon, we'd all be better off without the cell phones."

"It's so exciting though, isn't it?" he said wiping his mouth with the back of his hand. "Where we're at now, I mean. The burgeoning field of AI and the quest to get to the bottom of the problem of consciousness. And there you are slap-bang in the middle of it all. I mean, the development of quantum computing has to be the key, don't you think? No kidding, how long d'you reckon it'll be before your lot finally pulls it off?"

"Pulls it off? Sorry?" The kid's enthusiasm did him credit but my head was beginning to throb again.

"The construction of a useful, error-corrected quantum computer..."

"Well, I'd like to think we're getting pretty close to it now though, it's fair to say, we've had a couple of false starts. There are still so many technological challenges..." I sighed, doing my best to stifle a yawn.

"But then, in theory, you could achieve the computational power to mimic human intelligence, right?"

"Well, rudimentary AI is already with us, isn't it? Self-learning systems are growing more sophisticated every day."

"Yes, but – true consciousness. Something that would pass the Turing test. Isn't that the Holy Grail? Or did I get hold of the wrong end of the stick back there?"

I shrugged wearily.

"Maybe, it is. But when we talk about AI we tend to conflate intelligence with consciousness. Of course, that might stand if you accept the *computational* theory of consciousness, but there are convincing arguments that refute that theory. As I explained in my talk, there's a lot to be said for viewing consciousness as an emergent property of the brain's incredibly complex neural networks. Seeing as how the brain is probably the most complex bit of hardware or, for that matter, object in the universe, it's difficult to see how we could ever replicate anything that comes close."

I wondered if I had sounded as irritable as I felt. I emptied a couple of sachets of sugar into my coffee and stirred it, hoping that would help. My tormentor took another bite from his burger and chomped it with an expression of pure pleasure. He swallowed and then continued;

"What about those guys who are trying to map the brain's connections, neuron by neuron, synapse by synapse? Surely the power of a quantum computer is going to be a game-changer for them?"

I smiled.

"That's certainly going to be a big job...."

"But someone's gotta do it, right?"

I smiled again.

"I don't know. Have they? Stephen Hawking warned us that fully realised AI may turn out to be the biggest existential threat to humans...."

"Yeah - you said as much in your talk. Do you really believe that's true?"

I shook my head slowly.

"I don't know. There's certainly little reason to believe that any such entity would be likely to give a toss about us mere mortals. I'm not sure what I think, to be frank."

I pushed my plate to one side. It was getting late and my cerebral cortex was beginning to feel well past its use-by date. I gathered my things together to make a move.

"Just one more thing," he said, placing a hand on the sleeve of my jacket. "Just suppose you could replicate every cell of your brain, one by one, with a manufactured duplicate until you had made a complete facsimile of the entire structure. Wouldn't it think like a human brain and therefore have the same concerns?"

"In theory perhaps, but it would need a human body. You can't divorce the brain from sensations and perceptions, hormones even. This is my whole point."
He nodded.

"Yes, of course. Brains in vats - right? The age-old problem with dualism."
I yawned, no longer caring that it was rude. But nothing was going to deter him.

"That's *my* thing, you see. You lot are trying to harness quantum phenomena to do computation - I'm into nano-engineering. Nanobots, if you will. The idea of making machines so miniscule that they can take over the function of a single cell. Look, the field is still in its infancy but just imagine if we could replace every cell in the human body with a perfectly functioning robot. Didn't you dream of such things as a younger man, when it all lay in front of you…?
I dropped my fork and then reached for my glass and sent it tumbling.

"I'm so sorry," I blurted. "You'll have to excuse me. I'm feeling so very tired. It's been a long day. And, in answer to your question; I don't know that I did dream of such things. I was more into the maths side. If you want to know the truth, it all sounds a bit like science fiction to me…"

"Sure, but yesterday's sci-fi is tomorrow's science, you know that. I'll bet you were bought up on Stark Trek. How many things did Roddenberry predict?"
I shook my head and pushed back my chair.

"I used to think all sorts of things were possible. These days, I'm not even sure that I can trust my own memory. Maybe we believe what we want to believe and confuse dreams with reality. And now, I don't wish to sound rude" I said, rising to my feet, "but I really have had a very long day. Nice to have met you – what did you say your name was?"
The young man grinned and held out his hand.

"I didn't. My name is Lucas. And it was a real buzz to finally meet you, Sir."
I took the hand but couldn't begin to explain what happened next. Every nerve in my body jolted and then jangled as though in response to a static shock. I dropped it hastily and muttered

something incomprehensible, but the grin never left his face. Stunned, I turned and walked away, desperate to escape the building and get back to the privacy of the little bed and breakfast I had booked for the week.

By the time I managed to find my car, my brain was fizzing like potassium in water. I reeled as every memory I had so firmly compartmentalised took turns to burst out and into my mind. That first day in the park. Sherton Myam's peculiarly bland face. Shalto in his parka and Sherry in my mother's dress. Images so vivid it was a wonder I managed to drive at all. By the time I did finally arrive at the guesthouse where I was staying, I was so disorientated that I was obliged almost to crawl up the stairs to my room where I buried my head beneath the pillows on my freshly changed bed. And still, the memories kept on coming, until finally, it appeared before my mind's eye. The little face that pierced straight through the containment field I'd long maintained around my heart. Lucy.

I had never once given into grief in all the long years that had passed, yet when I finally came to myself the pillow case was soaked with tears. I rolled onto my back and peered at the little travel clock perched on the bedside table. 2 am. I drew my fingers through my hair, dragging at my scalp to give me a focus.

Whatever this had been, it was no coincidence. This kid's name had been Lucas, for God's sake. Lucas – Lucy. It didn't require much working out. And all that talk about replacing individual cells to create copies of humans. I wondered how I could have been so dense. Yet I knew full well. That storage room, back in the deepest recesses of my mind. The one into which I stuffed all the things, I did not wish to remember. It had worked a little too efficiently. If I thought about the past at all, it had always been as a confusion of dreams and make-believe so I tended not to. It had just seemed simpler that way.

I lay awake for the rest of the night turning things over in my mind. Maybe, years ago, when I had first moved to The States it was in an unacknowledged hope that I would pick up the trail of the other shapeshifters, but the US was where the work was and so I hadn't needed to admit it to myself. Either way, I never caught so much as a whiff and the demands of the research project I was offered soon consumed my every waking moment. It was a welcome relief. The work left me no time for the messy business of personal relationships. I had work colleagues who shared my passion for quantum processing and the odd game of chess, and I kept in touch with Joan. Well, mainly a letter at Christmas and later an occasional

Skype session. I knew she would've liked to see more of me, but that was the best I could offer.

I'd been content to live in the present and leave the past where it belonged – firmly behind me. Back there in a student cafeteria, however, the past finally appeared to have caught up with me.

But why now, after all these years? I seriously doubted that Lucas had simply stumbled into me by chance and it was not as though I kept a particularly low profile. I was widely published in physics journals and had become a prominent name in my field - the shapeshifters could have sought me out at any time.

Perhaps it was simply time. I had joked about my youthful looks, but the mismatch between my appearance and my biological age was starting to become an issue. Even here in the Mecca of facelifts and Botox. It wasn't so much that I hadn't aged at all. Just that the normal changes were occurring very slowly. I could still pass for thirty-five now which I could just about dismiss by bullshitting about exercise and the latest fad diet, but things would get trickier in my sixties. Eventually, I supposed, I might even become something of a liability. That notion was not, however, a train of thought I cared to pursue.

At the end of the day, I had no way of knowing why he had left it so long or quite what he, or they, wanted of me and there was only one way to find out. I had to find Lucas again. Yet something else was bugging me. All that crap about nanobots. Surely, he'd been pulling my leg. The technology was still at a woefully rudimentary level yet he had spoken of it the way I might speak of microprocessing.

I wrestled with the implications for over an hour and could only draw one chilling conclusion; that Lucas had purposefully revealed something about the true nature of shapeshifters. I had always assumed that shapeshifters were just some other race – exotic, maybe, but living organisms just like me. I recalled briefly toying with the idea that they may have once been an alien race, but Lucas was right, I had watched a little too much Star Trek, back then. Whatever the case it hadn't seemed that important, back then. Not as important as my friendship, in any case.

I groaned. I might have suppressed the scientist in me out of love and loyalty, but I had never in my wildest dreams thought that they might be the product of a technology that was lightyears beyond anything we could even imagine. It made sense in many ways, and if that *was* the case, then they could not have originated from this planet. So, what was I to make of that? And what in Hell's name would that make me? I had accepted that I might not be quite like other people, but part cybernetic-alien? That was altogether too freaky.

I struggled to get into all back into perspective. The nighttime does funny things to our cognitive functions and giving reign to my imagination was not helpful. Maybe there was an obvious and more prosaic account for his bit of theatre – maybe the kid had just been yanking my chain. It *was* another explanation – and according to Occam's razor –the simpler of two competing explanations for a phenomenon is the more likely. I almost laughed out loud in relief. That would be it. He'd been having a bit of fun at my expense. Revenge teasing for my desertion of him/her and Sherry, even. I'd never had a great sense of humour and *he* might know that. I smiled to myself. Sherry had always said that I was a sucker. And then I thought of Sherry. Her lovely face, the gentleness of her hands. If Lucas was Lucy, then Sherry was no more. The thought lay like a lump of lead in my chest and I doubted I would ever sleep again.

As the Californian morning dawned, I rose and showered and then made my way back to the university. I asked all over campus if anyone knew of a Lucas fitting his description, but no one had seen or heard of him. I even chatted up a particularly obliging faculty administrator and persuaded her to allow me a quick scan through the student records – with no luck. Seeing the look of disappointment on my face she suggested that he might simply have been visiting from another university. It was not unusual when a visiting lecturer gave a talk on such a specialized field of research. I smiled and thanked her for her patience and stepped outside into the courtyard to get some fresh air.

The quad was full of students enjoying the early afternoon sunshine, though most were either sitting cross-legged in small but animated discussion groups or lying stretched out on the freshly mown grass. I strolled over to a vacant bench and took a seat. I needed to examine the facts.

Lucas, or whoever he might be, could have shifted his shape and be sitting right there on the neighbouring bench, for all I knew. Although, on reflection, that throbbing I'd experienced in my head when he was close to me, might prove to be a useful proximity alert. Either way, it was evident that he did not wish to be found right now.

But he had made an opening gambit. The next move was down to me. I remembered how it had been when I was a child. Sherton had found me again in his own time and Lucas would do the same. All I had to do was exercise a little patience and bide my time. And, sitting there, feeling the sun on my face, I suddenly realised the perfect place to wait it out. *The Mausoleum*. I would return to London and the run-down old house on Wanstead Flats.

About the Author

Judith S Glover lives in Tasmania with her husband and cats. She studied Fine Art and Philosophy and worked for many years in the U.K as a psychotherapist.

Other books by Judith S Glover published on Amazon

A Little Book of Short Tall Stories

Butter and Whiskey: The ballad of Maggie Doyle

What Cannot be Cured: The Continuing Ballad of Maggie Doyle

The Light of Tomorrow

Visit Judith S Glover at quirky-stories.com

Printed in Great Britain
by Amazon